T
H
E

BEAUTY™

VOLUME FIVE

CAUTION ☣ BIOHAZARD ☣ CAUTION ☣ BIOHAZARD

IMAGE COMICS, INC.

ROBERT KIRKMAN Chief Operating Officer • ERIK LARSEN Chief Financial Officer • TODD MCFARLANE President
MARC SILVESTRI Chief Executive Officer • JIM VALENTINO Vice President • ERIC STEPHENSON Publisher & Chief Creative Officer
COREY HART Director of Sales • JEFF BOISON Director of Publishing Planning & Book Trade Sales • CHRIS ROSS Director of Digital Sales
JEFF STANG Director of Specialty Sales • KAT SALAZAR Director of PR & Marketing • DREW GILL Art Director
HEATHER DOORNINK Production Director • NICOLE LAPALME Controller

www.imagecomics.com

THE BEAUTY, VOL. 5
ISBN: 978-1-5343-1043-8
First Printing. February 2019.

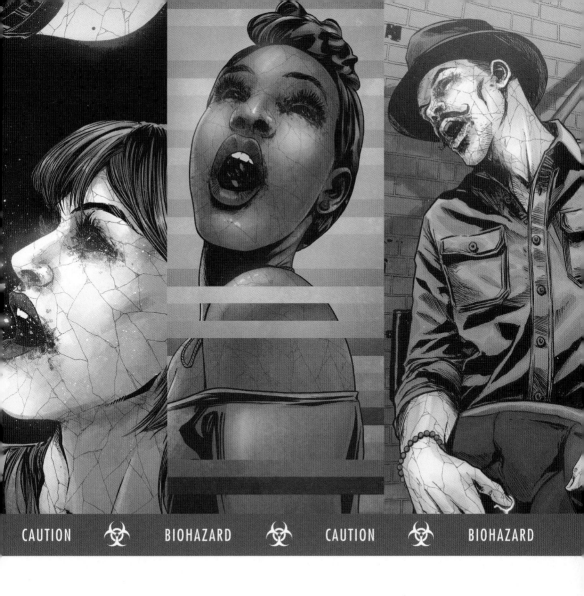

CAUTION · BIOHAZARD · CAUTION · BIOHAZARD

JEREMY HAUN & JASON A. HURLEY
story

THOMAS NACHLIK
art

NAYOUNG KIM
color

THOMAS MAUER
lettering & design

JOEL ENOS
editor

CAREY HALL
production artist

CHAPTER

22

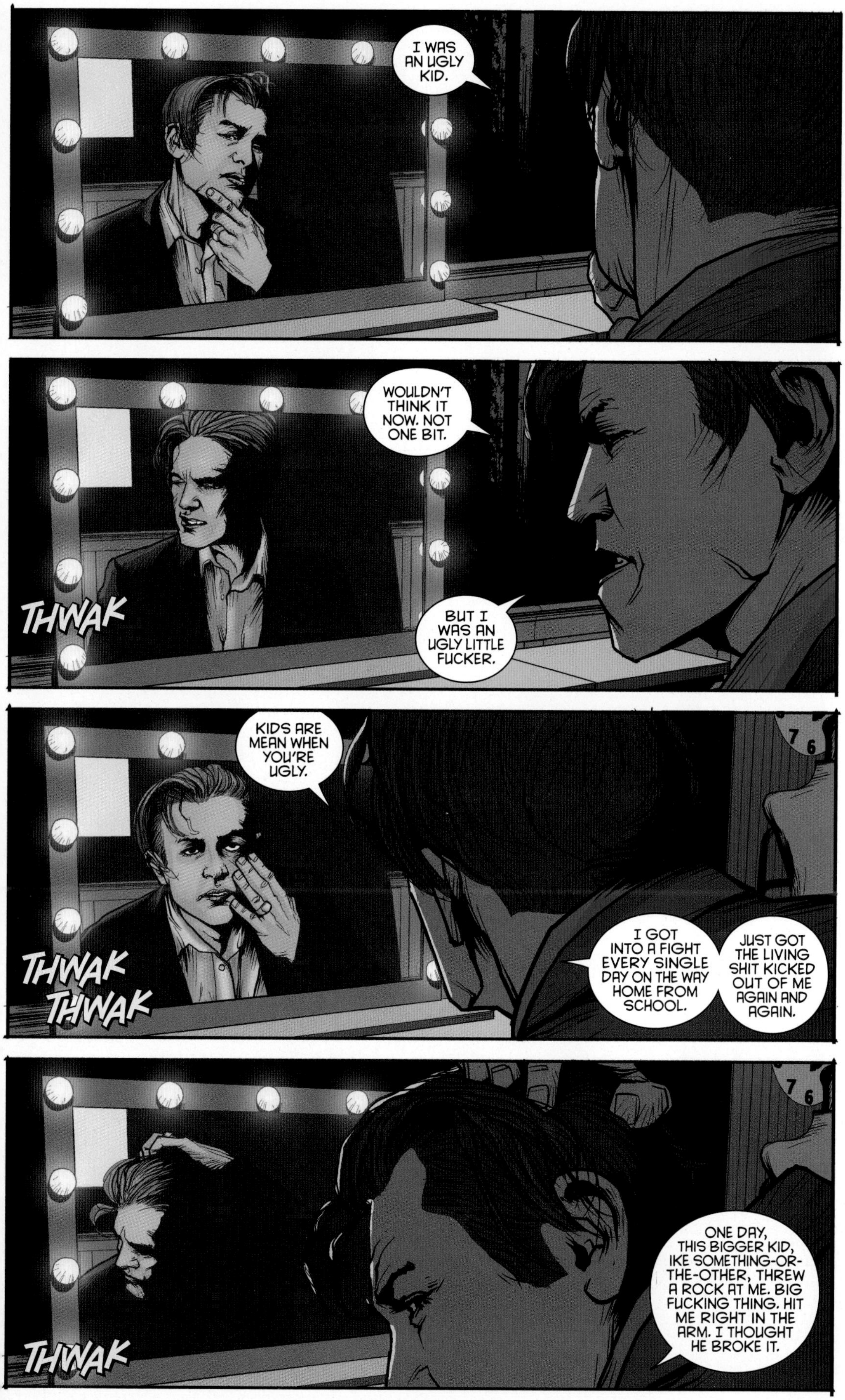
I WAS AN UGLY KID.
WOULDN'T THINK IT NOW. NOT ONE BIT.
THWAK
BUT I WAS AN UGLY LITTLE FUCKER.
KIDS ARE MEAN WHEN YOU'RE UGLY.
THWAK
THWAK
I GOT INTO A FIGHT EVERY SINGLE DAY ON THE WAY HOME FROM SCHOOL.
JUST GOT THE LIVING SHIT KICKED OUT OF ME AGAIN AND AGAIN.
ONE DAY, THIS BIGGER KID, IKE SOMETHING-OR-THE-OTHER, THREW A ROCK AT ME. BIG FUCKING THING. HIT ME RIGHT IN THE ARM. I THOUGHT HE BROKE IT.
THWAK

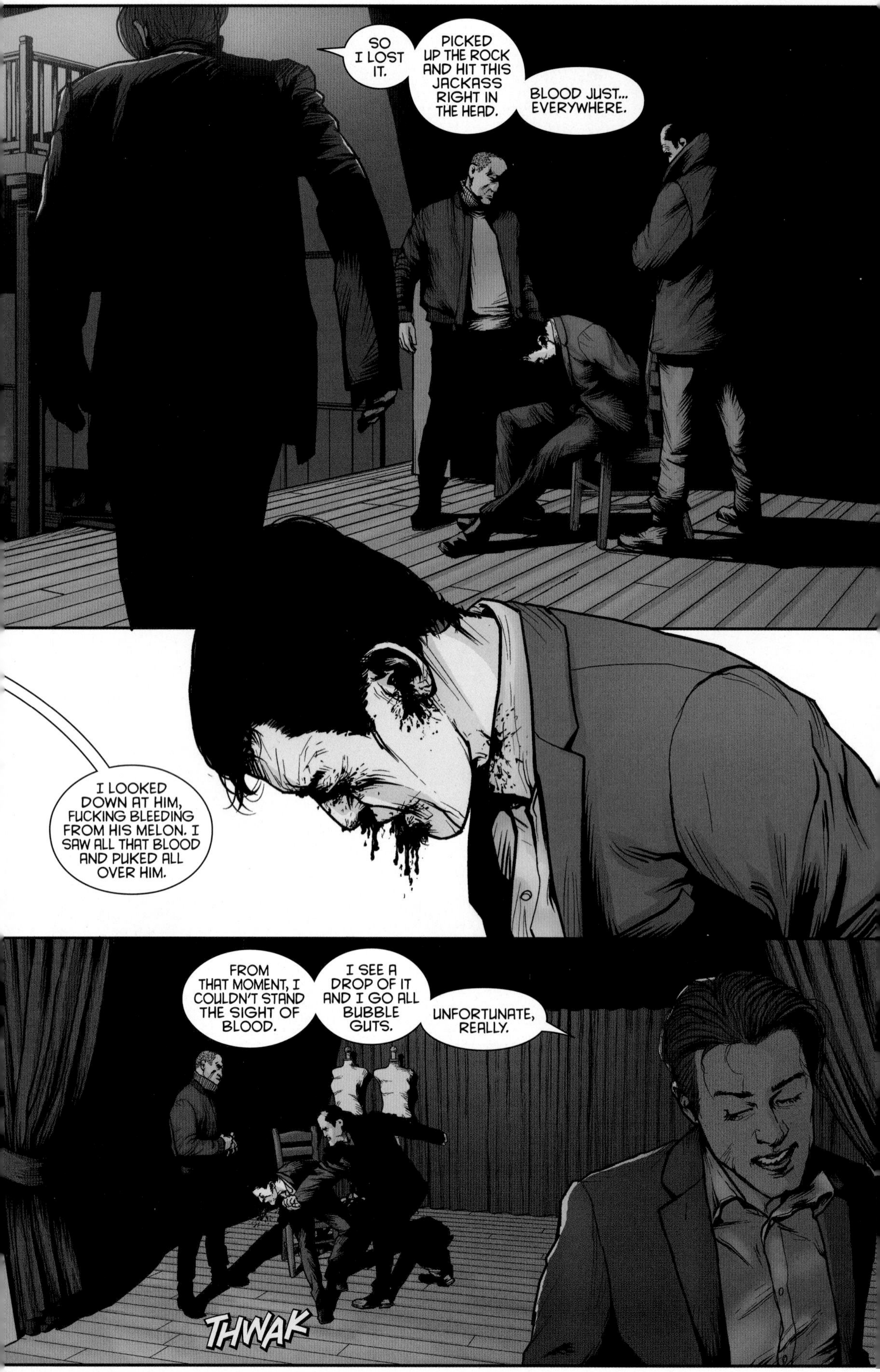

SO I LOST IT.
PICKED UP THE ROCK AND HIT THIS JACKASS RIGHT IN THE HEAD.
BLOOD JUST... EVERYWHERE.
I LOOKED DOWN AT HIM, FUCKING BLEEDING FROM HIS MELON. I SAW ALL THAT BLOOD AND PUKED ALL OVER HIM.
FROM THAT MOMENT, I COULDN'T STAND THE SIGHT OF BLOOD.
I SEE A DROP OF IT AND I GO ALL BUBBLE GUTS.
UNFORTUNATE, REALLY.
THWAK

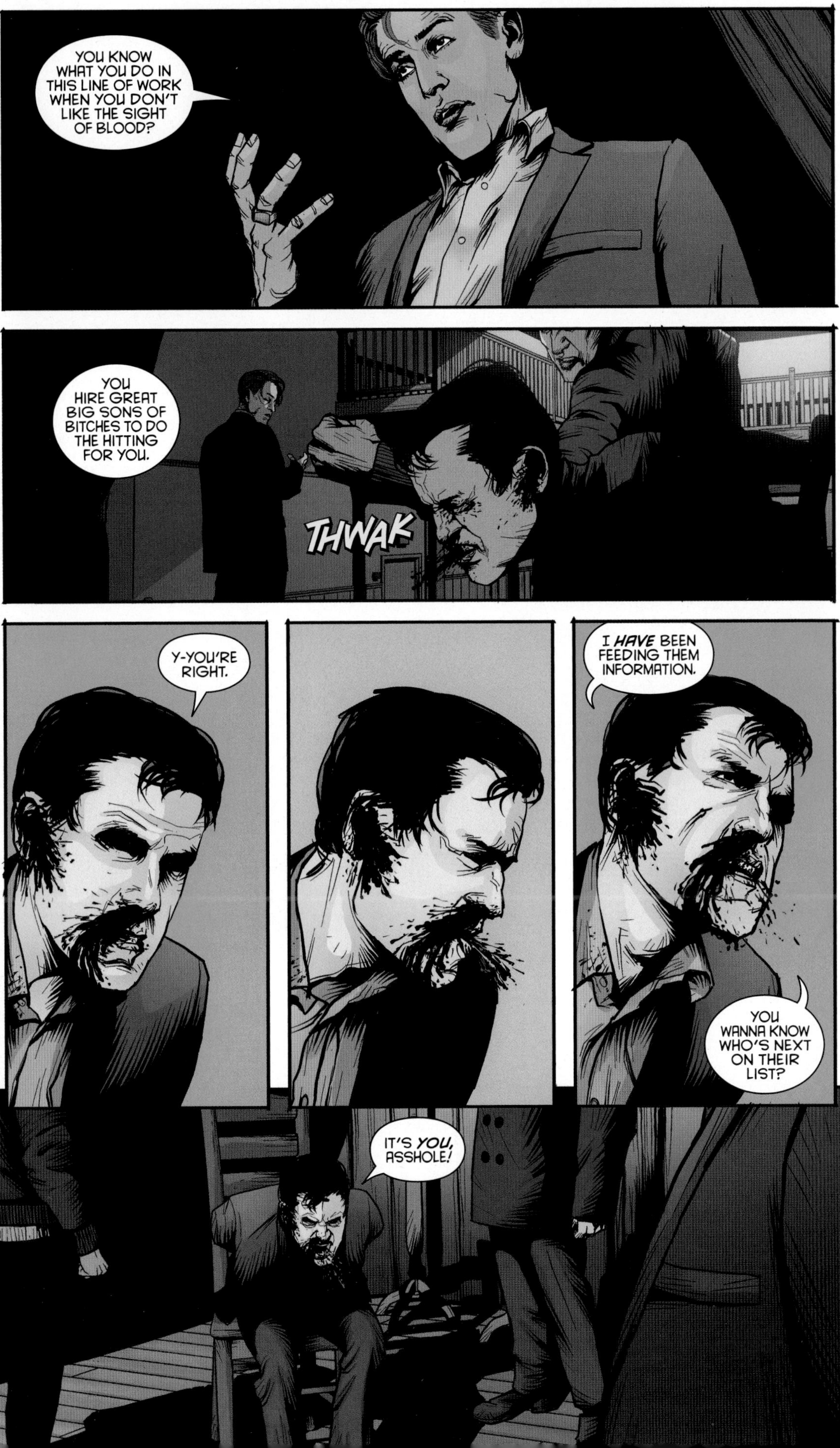
YOU KNOW WHAT YOU DO IN THIS LINE OF WORK WHEN YOU DON'T LIKE THE SIGHT OF BLOOD?
YOU HIRE GREAT BIG SONS OF BITCHES TO DO THE HITTING FOR YOU.
THWAK
Y-YOU'RE RIGHT.
I *HAVE* BEEN FEEDING THEM INFORMATION.
YOU WANNA KNOW WHO'S NEXT ON THEIR LIST?
IT'S *YOU,* ASSHOLE!

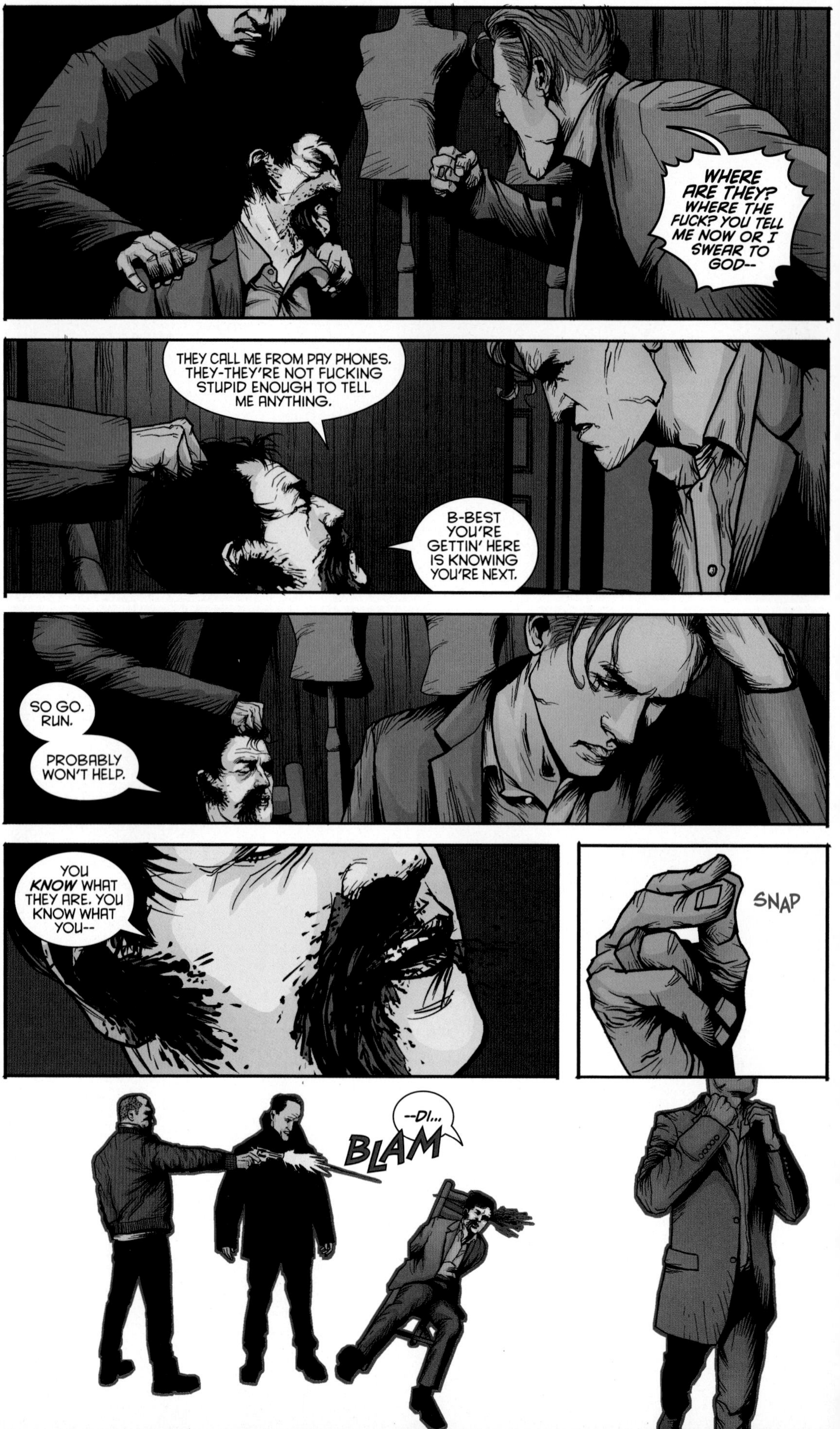
WHERE ARE THEY? WHERE THE FUCK? YOU TELL ME NOW OR I SWEAR TO GOD--
THEY CALL ME FROM PAY PHONES. THEY-THEY'RE NOT FUCKING STUPID ENOUGH TO TELL ME ANYTHING.
B-BEST YOU'RE GETTIN' HERE IS KNOWING YOU'RE NEXT.
SO GO. RUN.
PROBABLY WON'T HELP.
YOU KNOW WHAT THEY ARE. YOU KNOW WHAT YOU--
SNAP
--DI...
BLAM

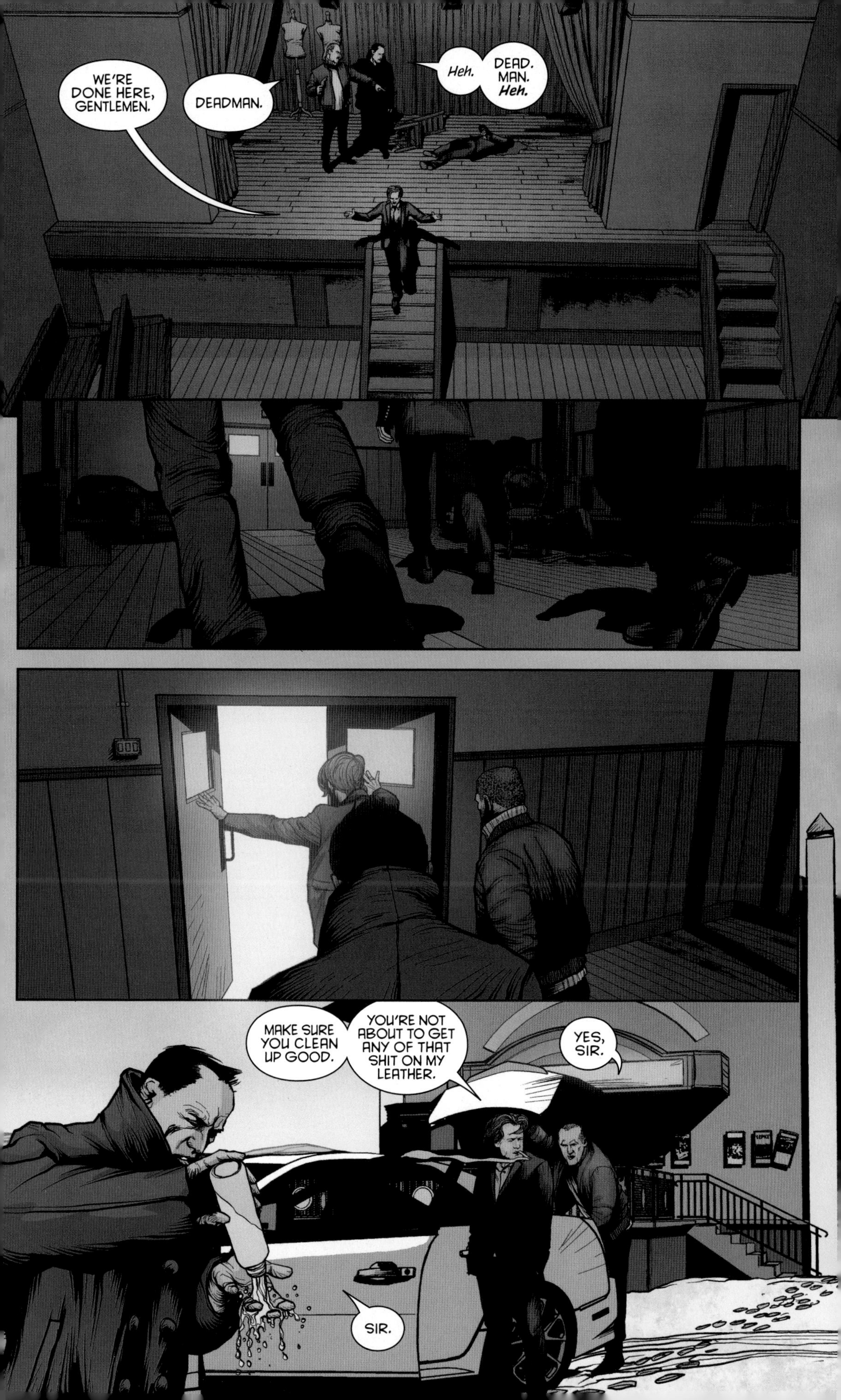
WE'RE DONE HERE, GENTLEMEN.
DEADMAN.
Heh.
DEAD. MAN. Heh.
MAKE SURE YOU CLEAN UP GOOD.
YOU'RE NOT ABOUT TO GET ANY OF THAT SHIT ON MY LEATHER.
YES, SIR.
SIR.

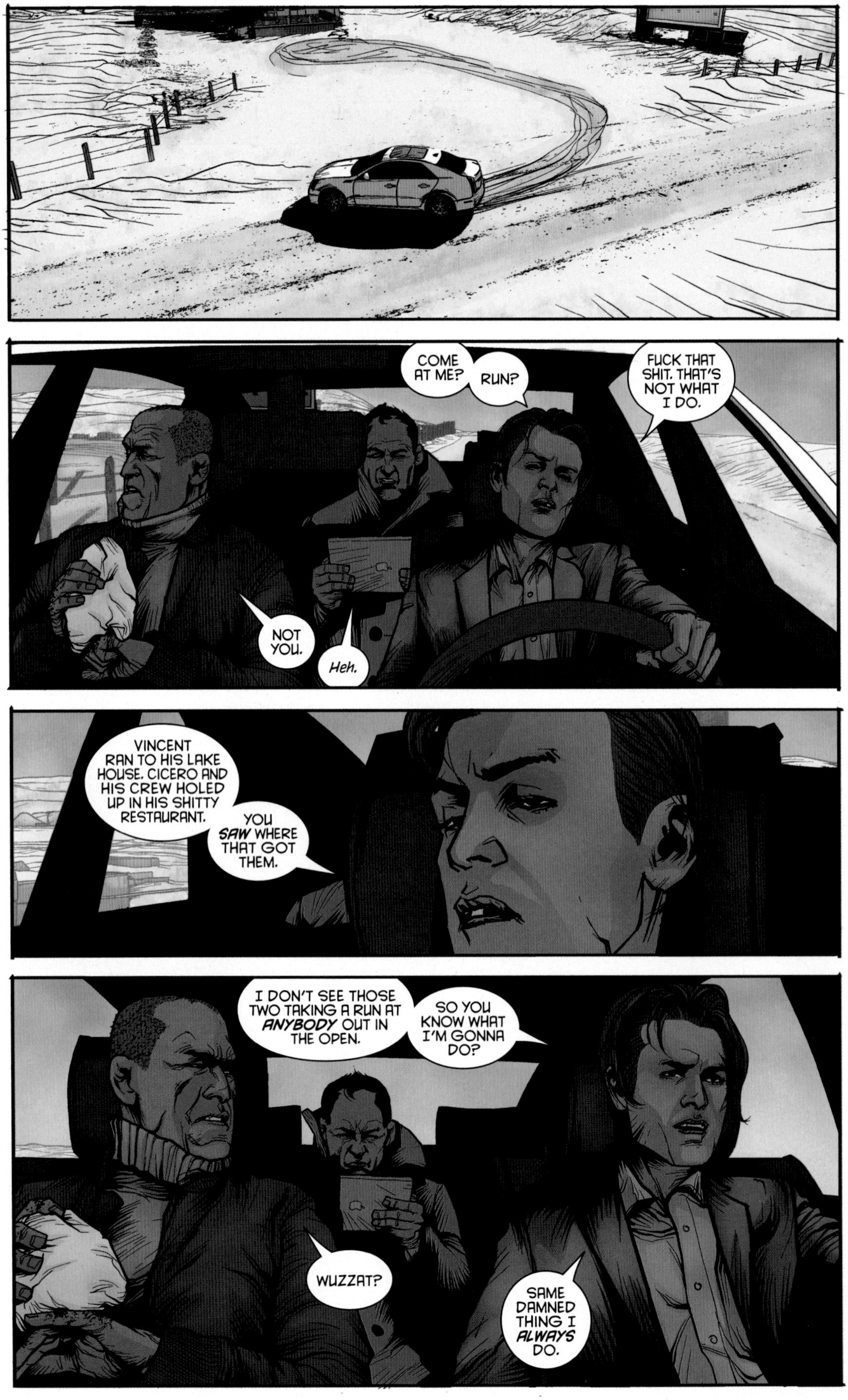
COME AT ME?
RUN?
FUCK THAT SHIT. THAT'S NOT WHAT I DO.
NOT YOU.
Heh.
VINCENT RAN TO HIS LAKE HOUSE. CICERO AND HIS CREW HOLED UP IN HIS SHITTY RESTAURANT.
YOU SAW WHERE THAT GOT THEM.
I DON'T SEE THOSE TWO TAKING A RUN AT ANYBODY OUT IN THE OPEN.
SO YOU KNOW WHAT I'M GONNA DO?
WUZZAT?
SAME DAMNED THING I ALWAYS DO.

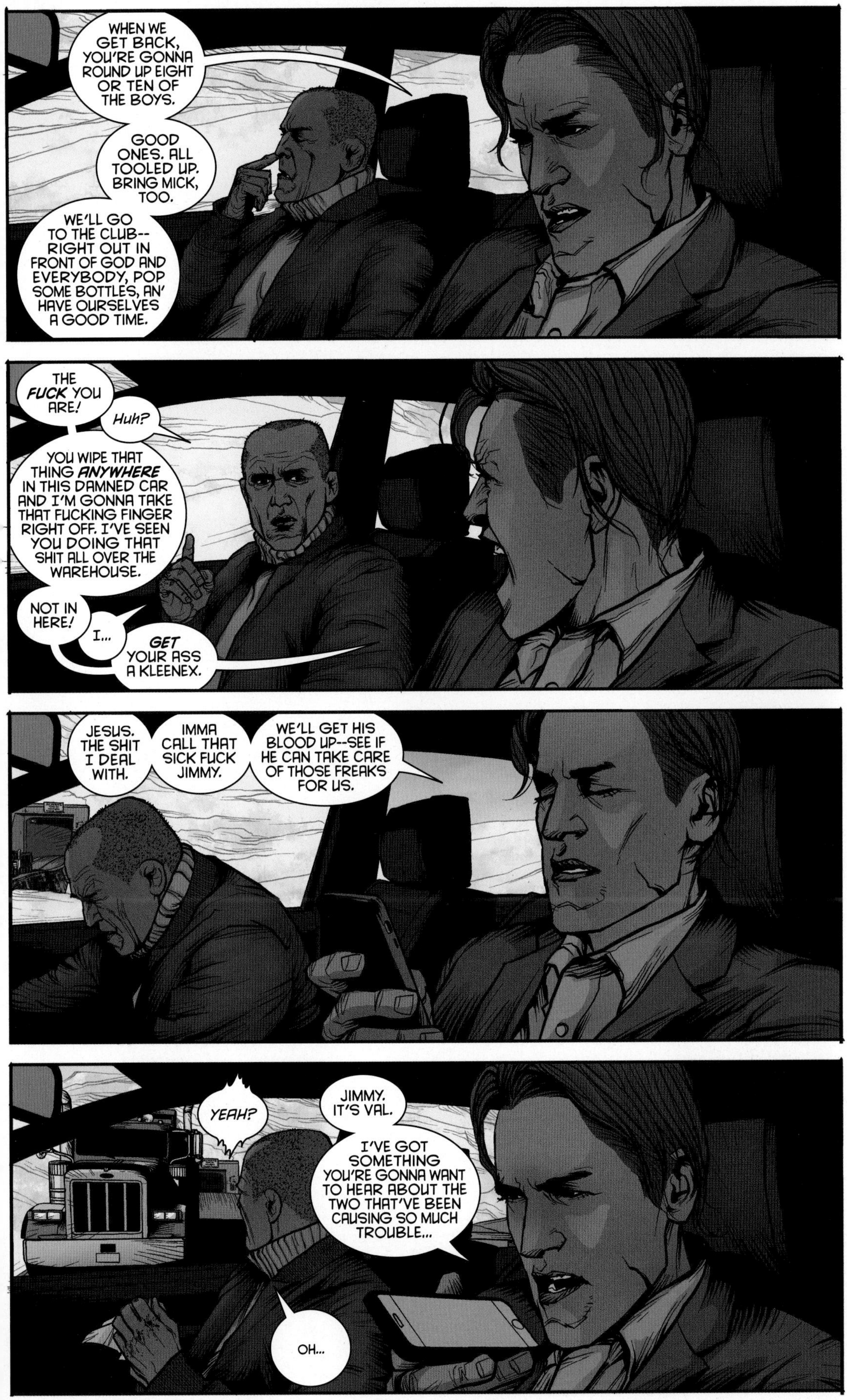

WHEN WE GET BACK, YOU'RE GONNA ROUND UP EIGHT OR TEN OF THE BOYS.
GOOD ONES. ALL TOOLED UP. BRING MICK, TOO.
WE'LL GO TO THE CLUB-- RIGHT OUT IN FRONT OF GOD AND EVERYBODY, POP SOME BOTTLES, AN' HAVE OURSELVES A GOOD TIME.
THE *FUCK* YOU ARE!
Huh?
YOU WIPE THAT THING *ANYWHERE* IN THIS DAMNED CAR AND I'M GONNA TAKE THAT FUCKING FINGER RIGHT OFF. I'VE SEEN YOU DOING THAT SHIT ALL OVER THE WAREHOUSE.
NOT IN HERE!
I...
GET YOUR ASS A KLEENEX.
JESUS. THE SHIT I DEAL WITH.
IMMA CALL THAT SICK FUCK JIMMY.
WE'LL GET HIS BLOOD UP--SEE IF HE CAN TAKE CARE OF THOSE FREAKS FOR US.
YEAH?
JIMMY. IT'S VAL.
I'VE GOT SOMETHING YOU'RE GONNA WANT TO HEAR ABOUT THE TWO THAT'VE BEEN CAUSING SO MUCH TROUBLE...
OH...

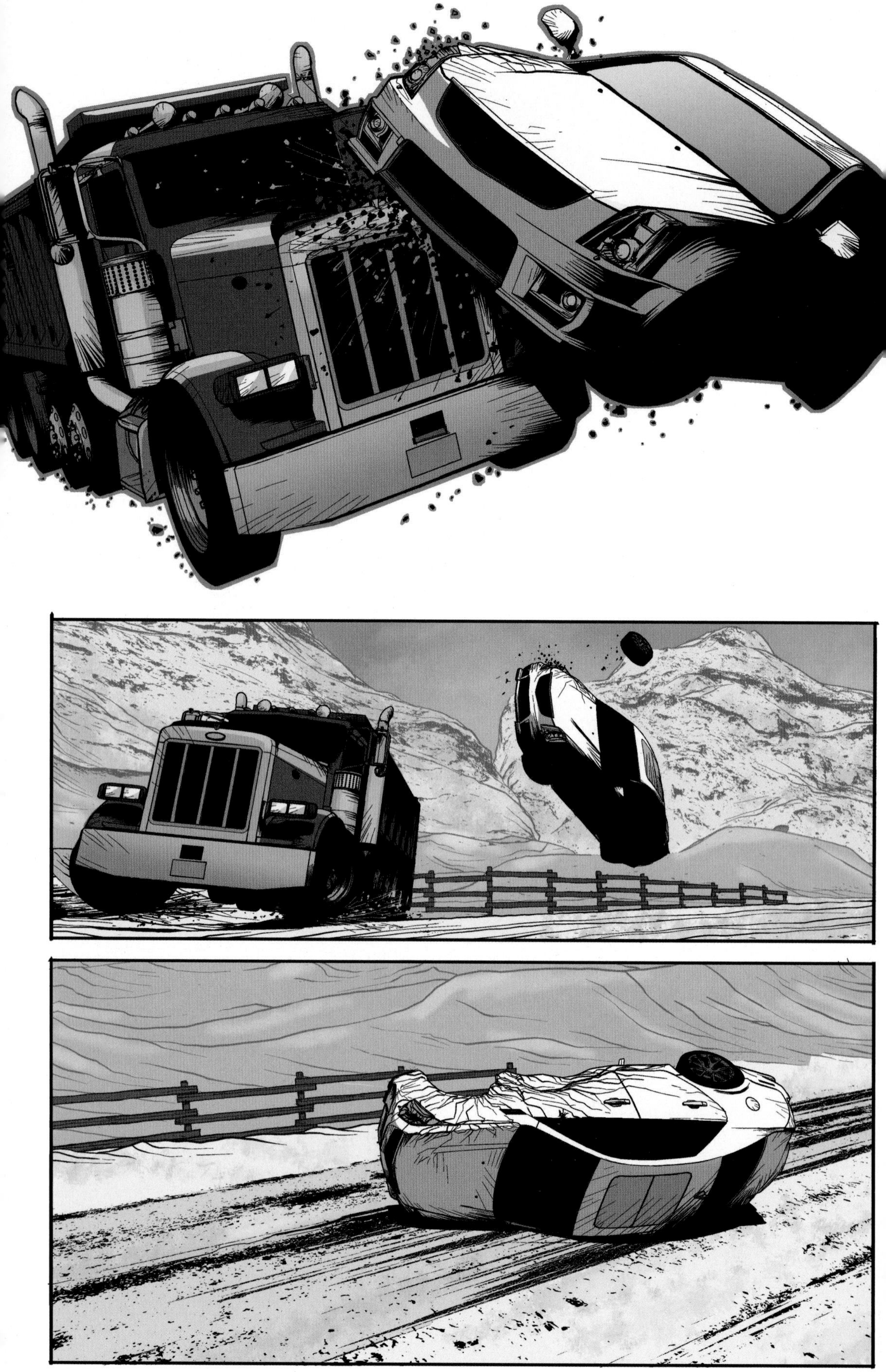

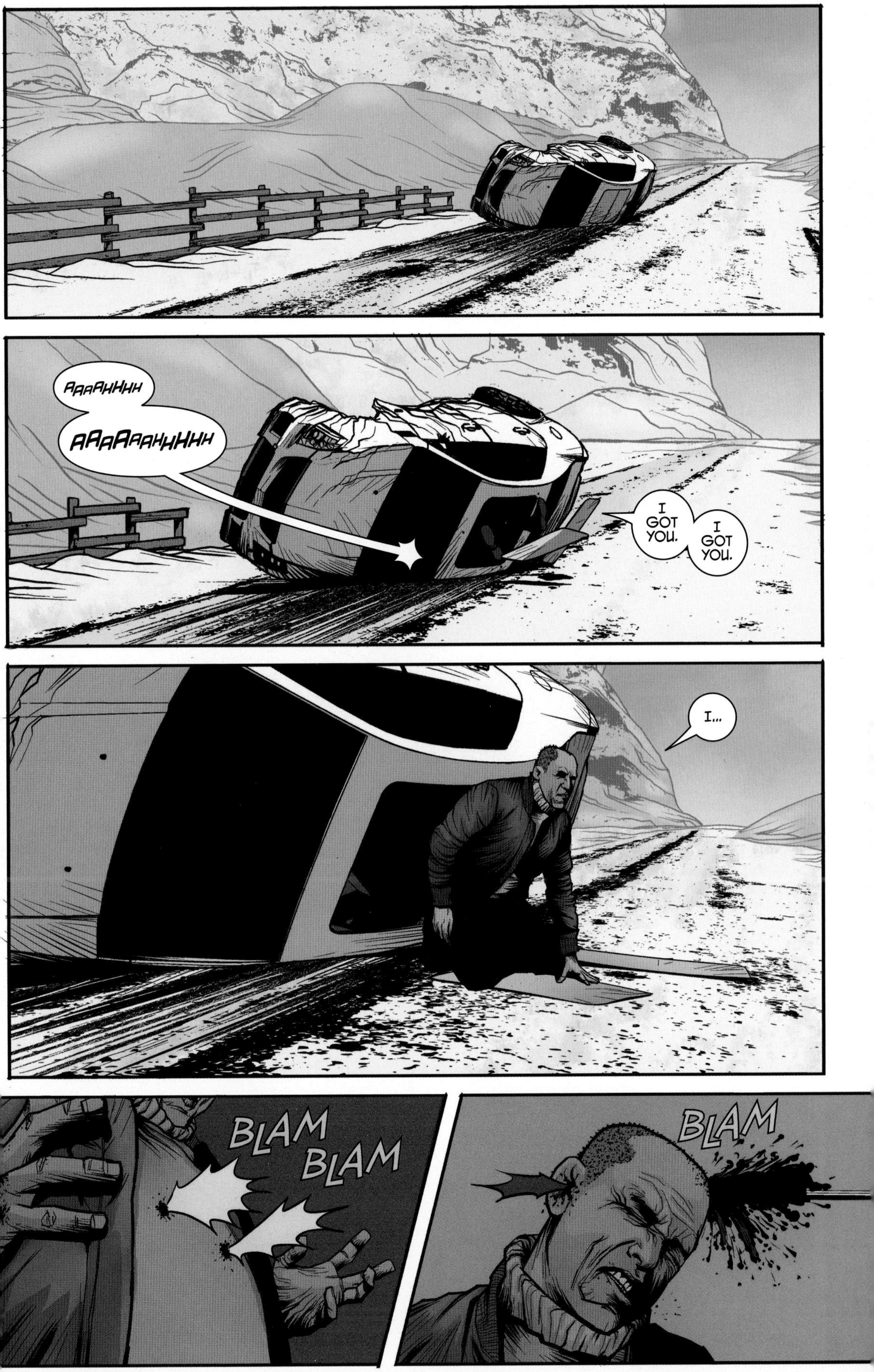

AAAAHHHH
AAAAAAAHHHHH
I GOT YOU.
I GOT YOU.
I...
BLAM
BLAM
BLAM

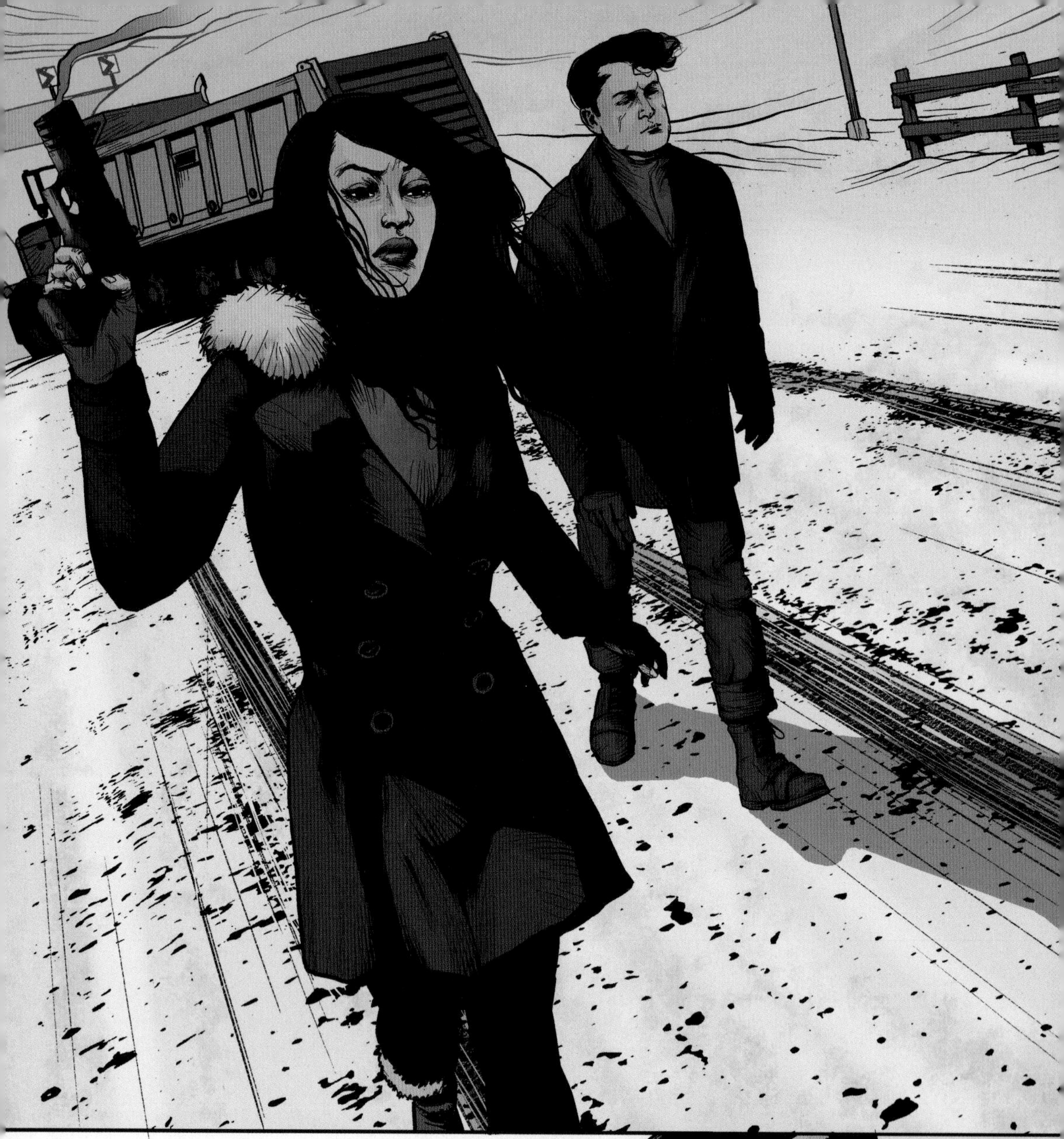

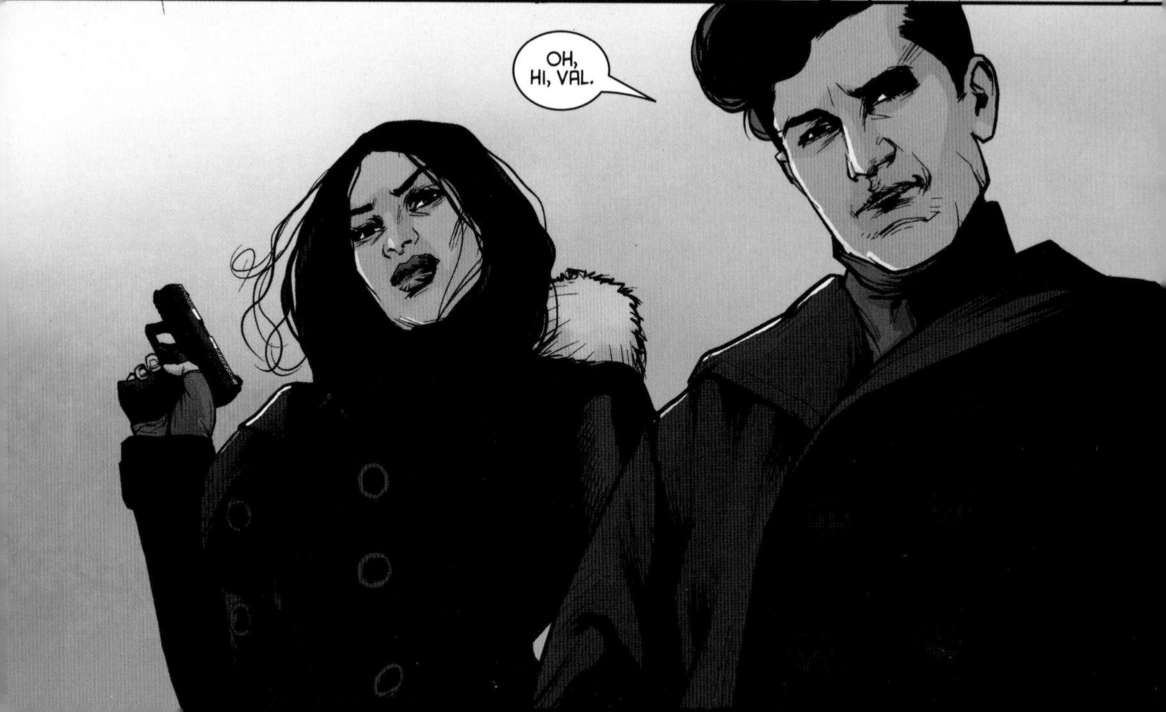
OH, HI, VAL.

WOW, VAL. MICK IS AN ABSOLUTE MESS BACK THERE, ISN'T HE?
POOR STUPID BASTARD.
AHHHHHH
OH, GIVE ME THAT.
FUCK YOU!
AAAAHHHH
THERE YOU GO.
AAAAHHHH
MY FUUUUCKING LEG!
YOU READY FOR THIS, VAL?

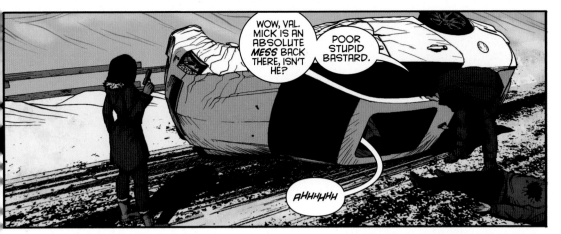

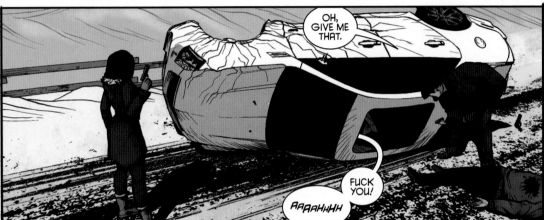

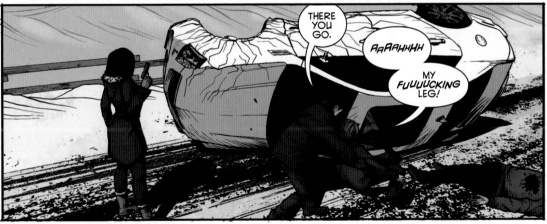

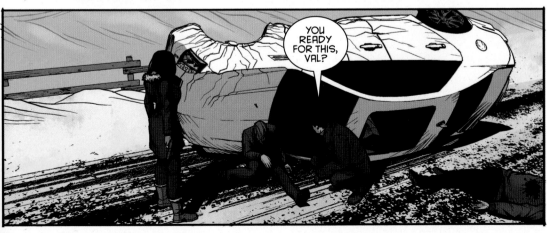

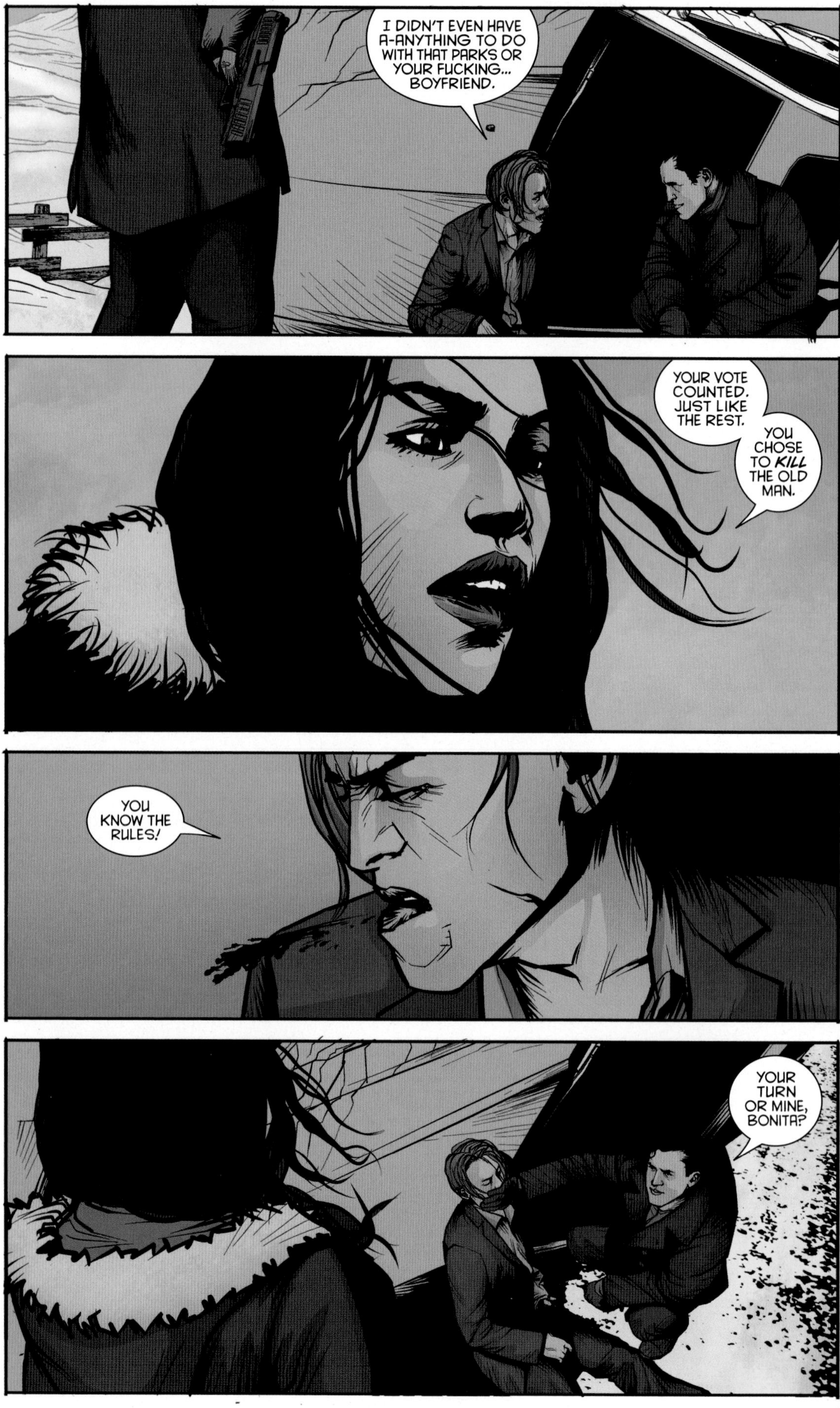
I DIDN'T EVEN HAVE A-ANYTHING TO DO WITH THAT PARKS OR YOUR FUCKING... BOYFRIEND.
YOUR VOTE COUNTED. JUST LIKE THE REST.
YOU CHOSE TO KILL THE OLD MAN.
YOU KNOW THE RULES!
YOUR TURN OR MINE, BONITA?

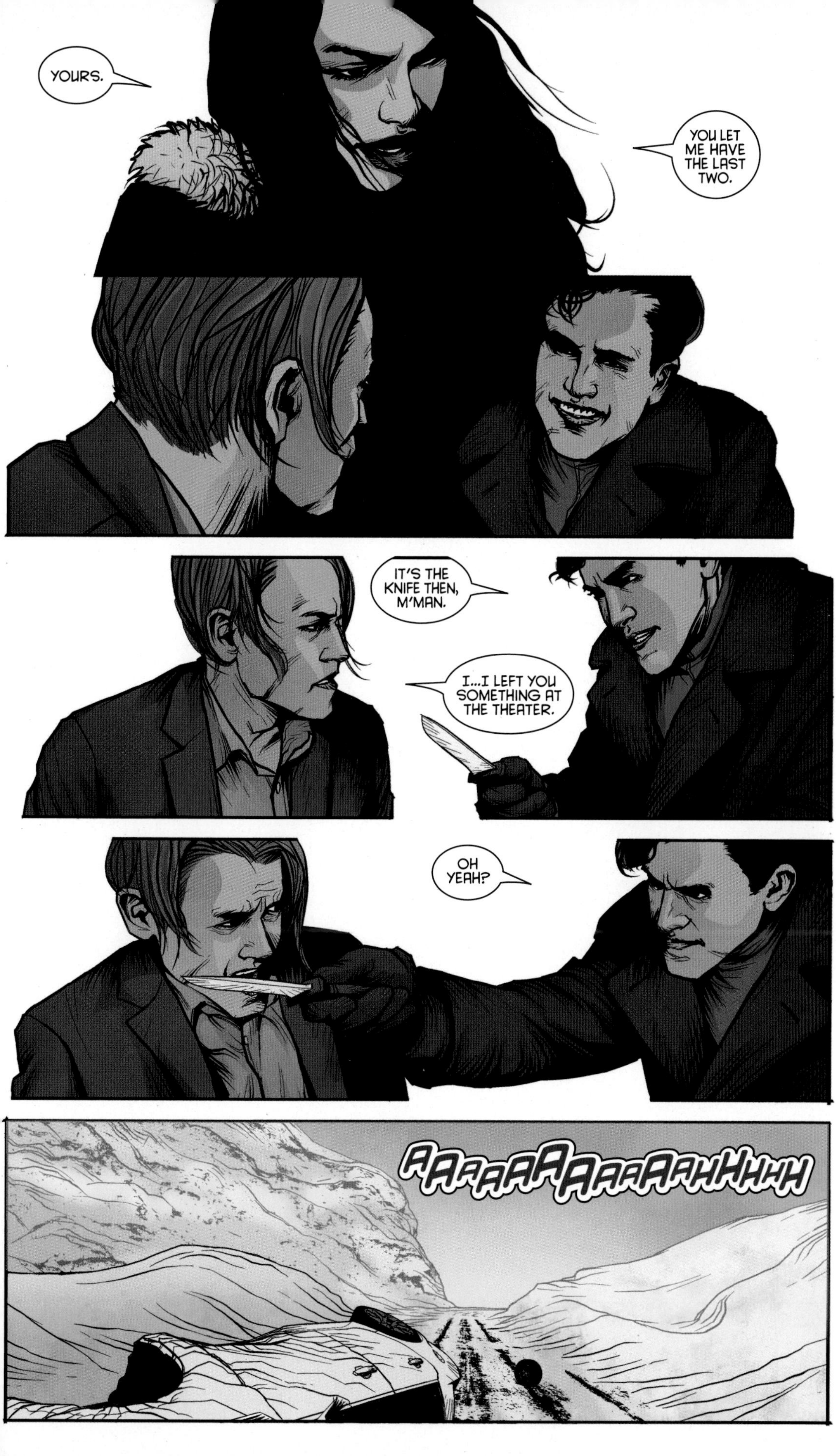
YOURS.
YOU LET ME HAVE THE LAST TWO.
IT'S THE KNIFE THEN, M'MAN.
I...I LEFT YOU SOMETHING AT THE THEATER.
OH YEAH?
AAAAAAAAAAAAAHHHHH

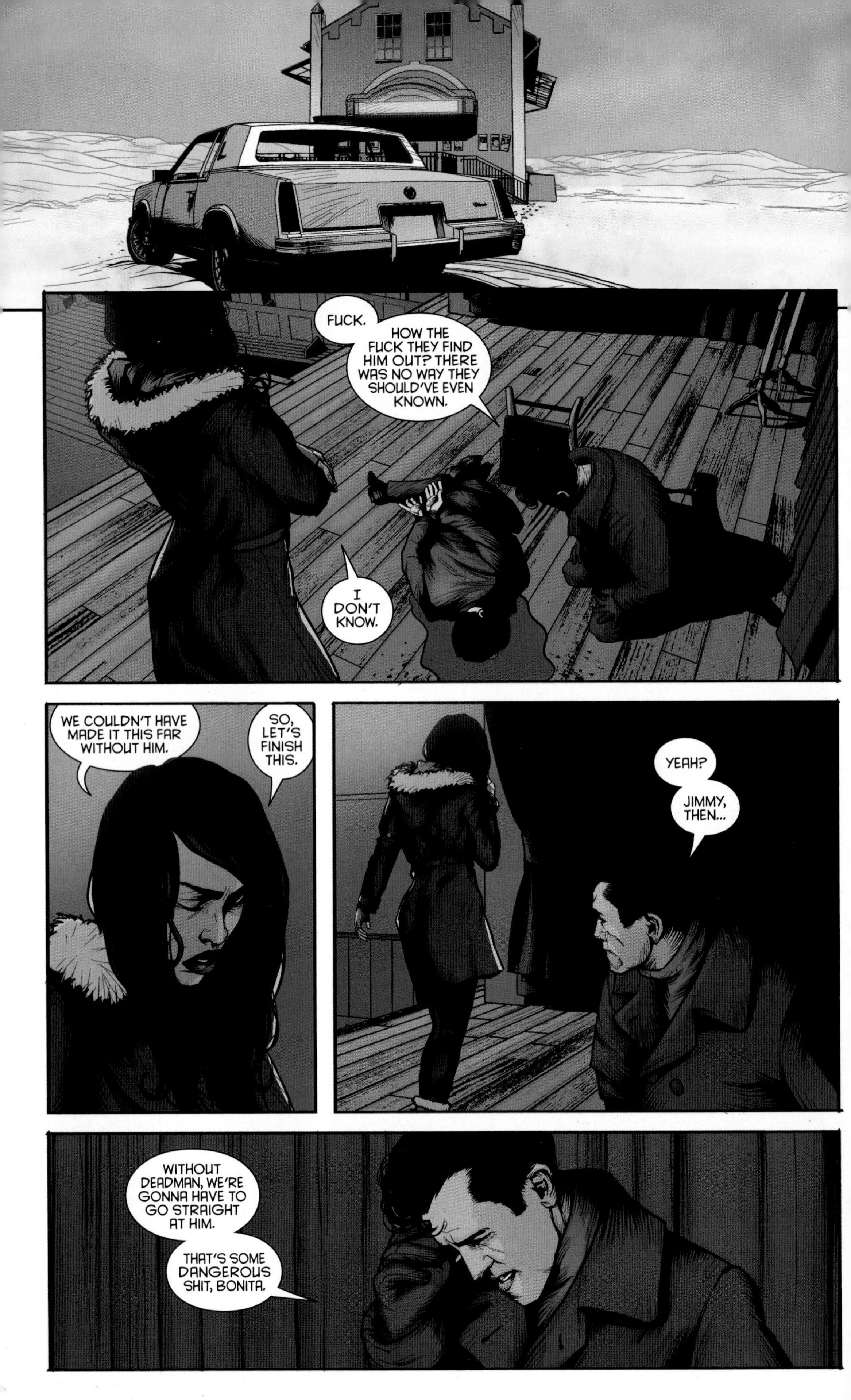
FUCK.
HOW THE FUCK THEY FIND HIM OUT? THERE WAS NO WAY THEY SHOULD'VE EVEN KNOWN.
I DON'T KNOW.
WE COULDN'T HAVE MADE IT THIS FAR WITHOUT HIM.
SO, LET'S FINISH THIS.
YEAH?
JIMMY, THEN...
WITHOUT DEADMAN, WE'RE GONNA HAVE TO GO STRAIGHT AT HIM.
THAT'S SOME DANGEROUS SHIT, BONITA.

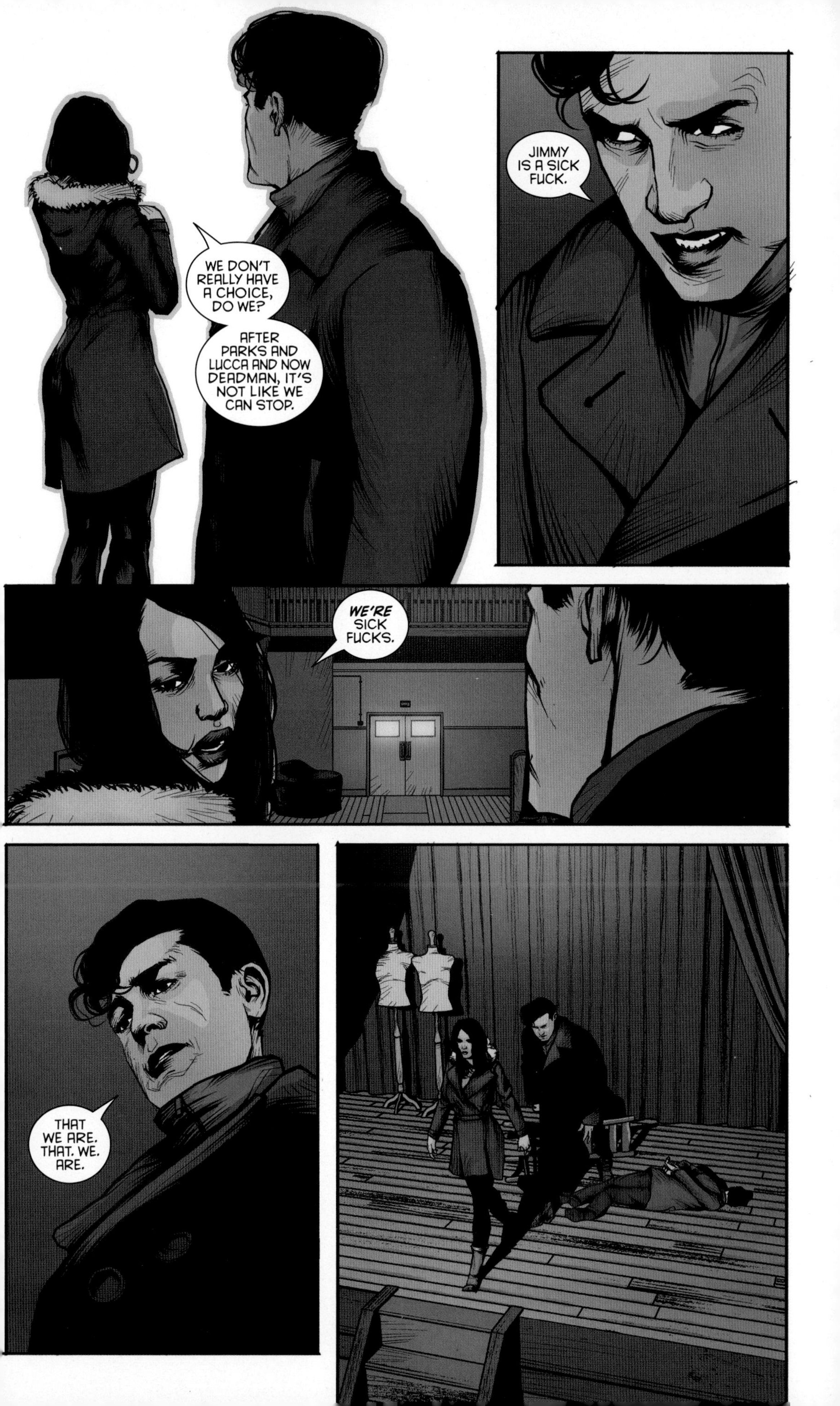

WE DON'T REALLY HAVE A CHOICE, DO WE?
AFTER PARKS AND LUCCA AND NOW DEADMAN, IT'S NOT LIKE WE CAN STOP.
JIMMY IS A SICK FUCK.
WE'RE SICK FUCKS.
THAT WE ARE. THAT. WE. ARE.

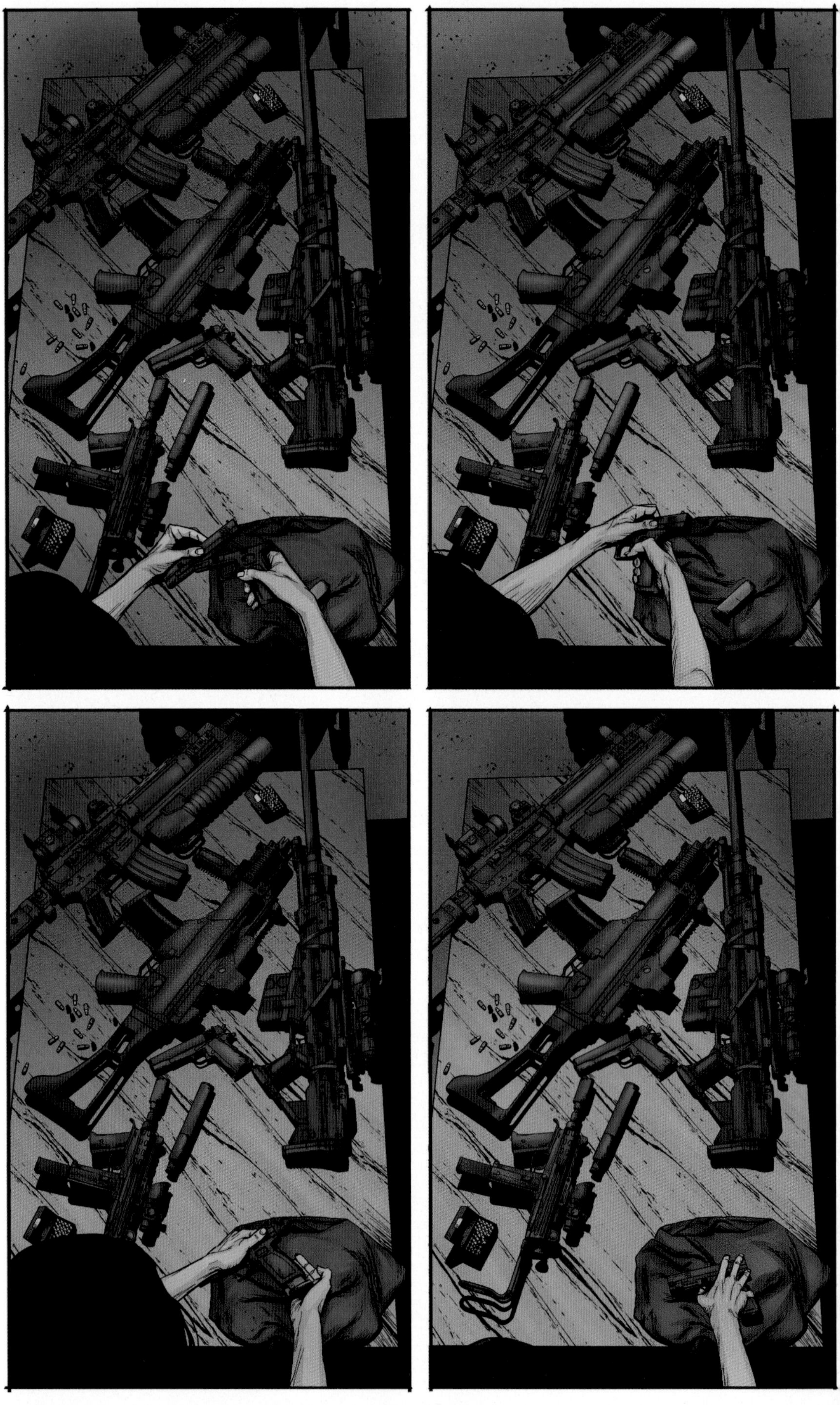

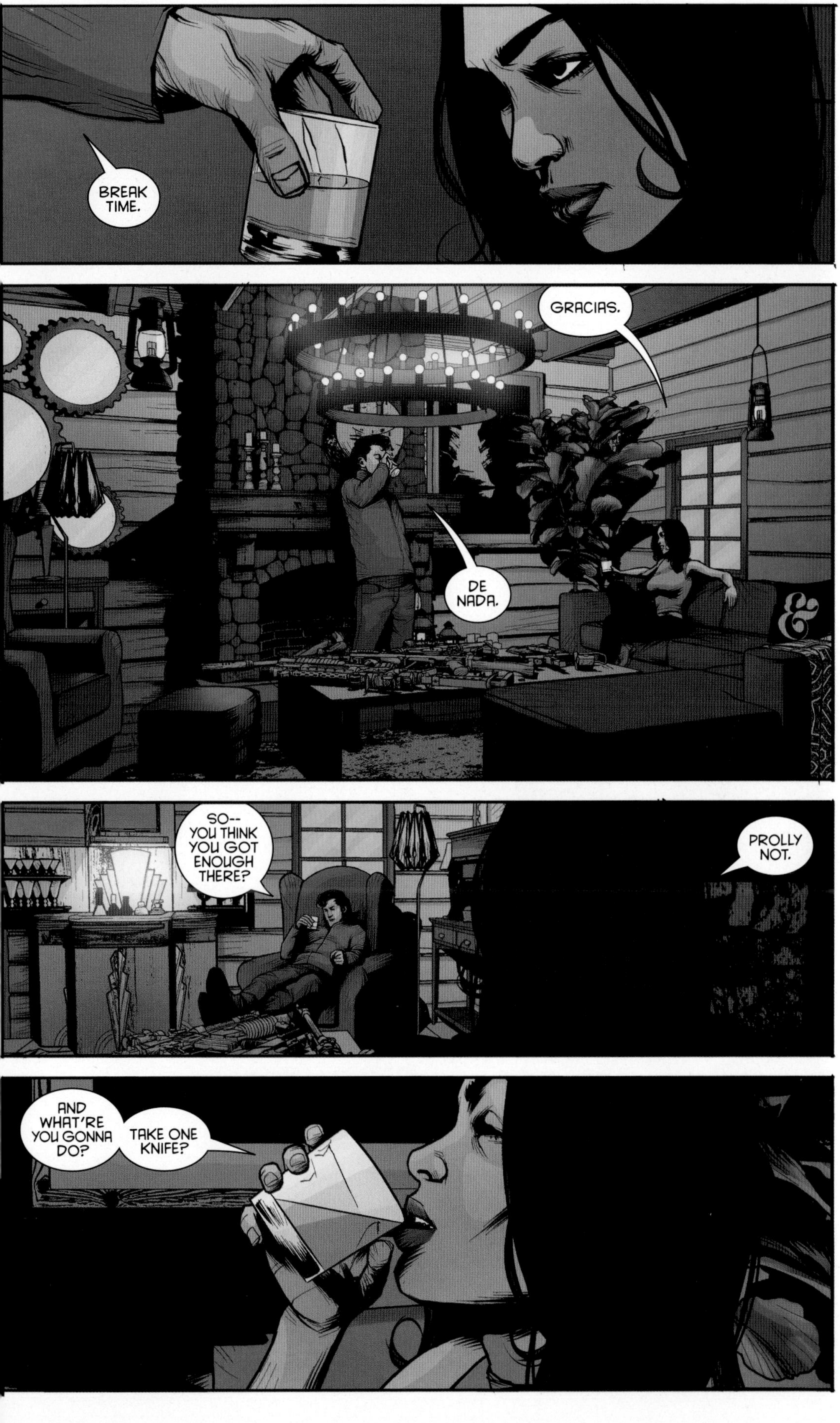
BREAK TIME.
GRACIAS.
DE NADA.
SO-- YOU THINK YOU GOT ENOUGH THERE?
PROLLY NOT.
AND WHAT'RE YOU GONNA DO?
TAKE ONE KNIFE?

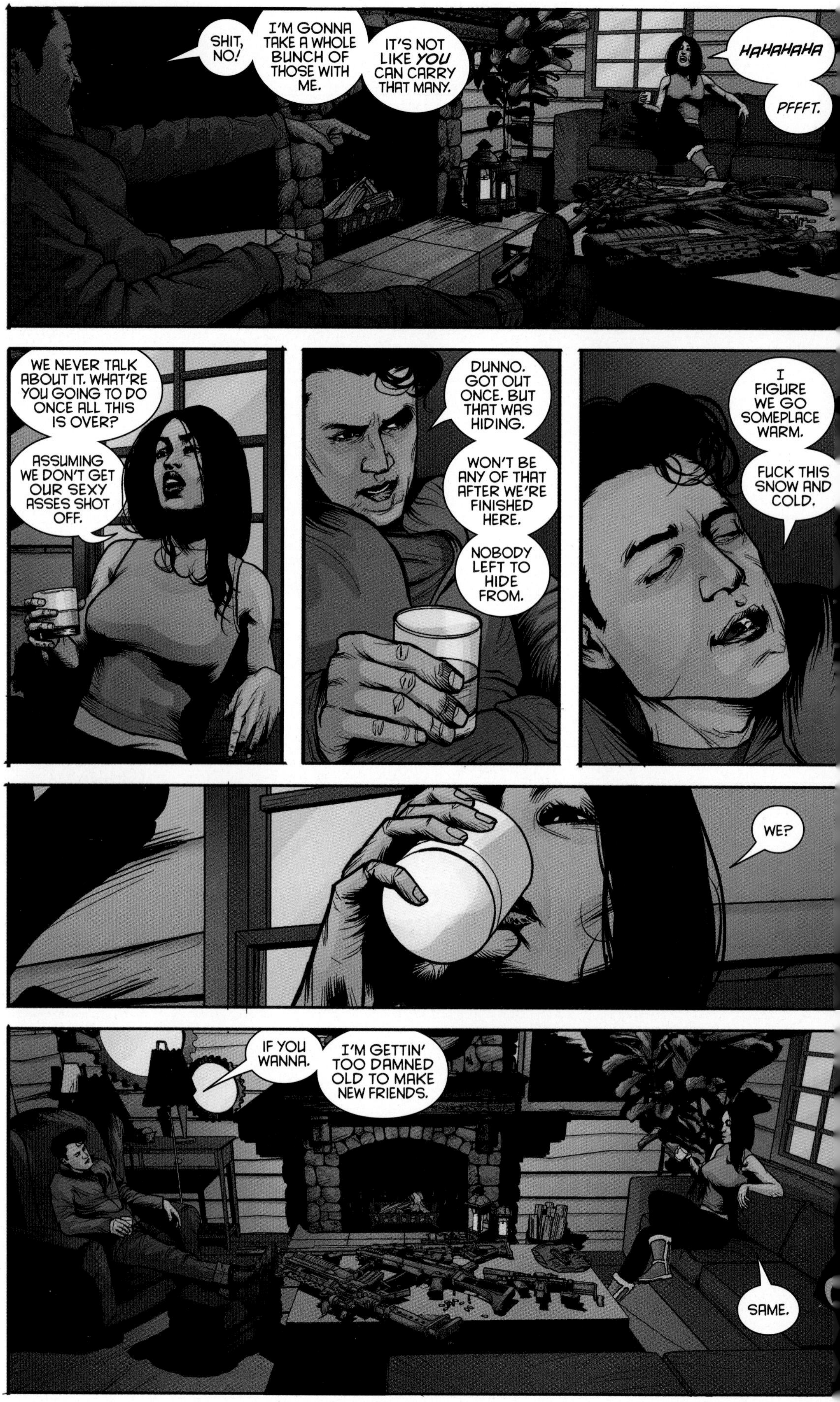
SHIT, NO!
I'M GONNA TAKE A WHOLE BUNCH OF THOSE WITH ME.
IT'S NOT LIKE *YOU* CAN CARRY THAT MANY.
HAHAHAHA
PFFFT.
WE NEVER TALK ABOUT IT. WHAT'RE YOU GOING TO DO ONCE ALL THIS IS OVER?
ASSUMING WE DON'T GET OUR SEXY ASSES SHOT OFF.
DUNNO. GOT OUT ONCE. BUT THAT WAS HIDING.
WON'T BE ANY OF THAT AFTER WE'RE FINISHED HERE.
NOBODY LEFT TO HIDE FROM.
I FIGURE WE GO SOMEPLACE WARM.
FUCK THIS SNOW AND COLD.
WE?
IF YOU WANNA.
I'M GETTIN' TOO DAMNED OLD TO MAKE NEW FRIENDS.
SAME.

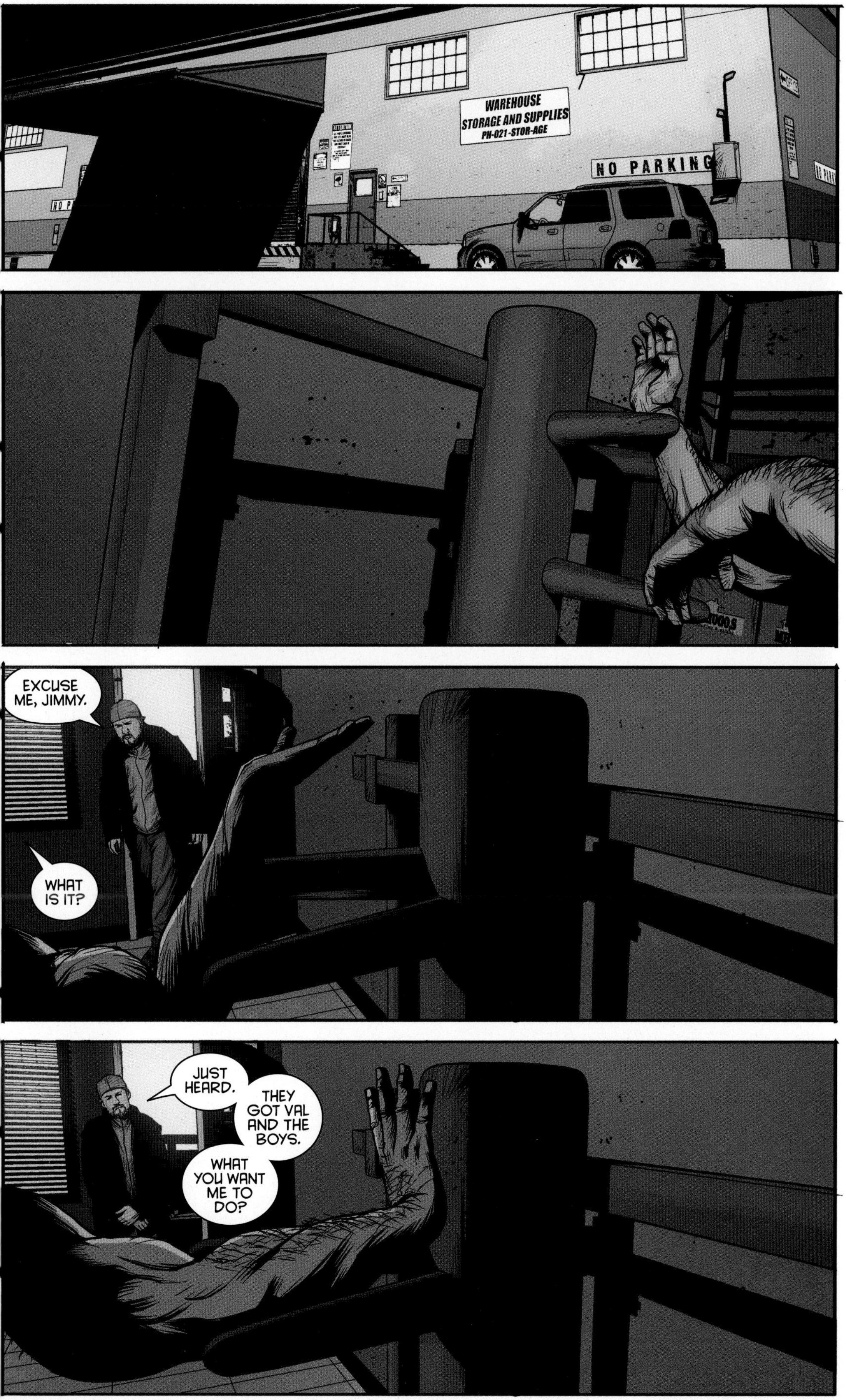
WAREHOUSE
STORAGE AND SUPPLIES
PH-021-STOR-AGE
NO PARKING
EXCUSE ME, JIMMY.
WHAT IS IT?
JUST HEARD.
THEY GOT VAL AND THE BOYS.
WHAT YOU WANT ME TO DO?

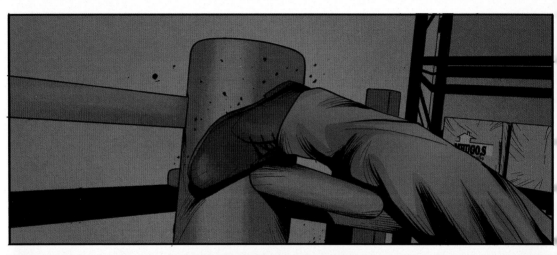

CALL UP BIANCHI.

TELL HIM I'M GOING TO TAKE CARE OF THIS. PERSONALLY.

THIS IS *DONE.*

CHAPTER

23

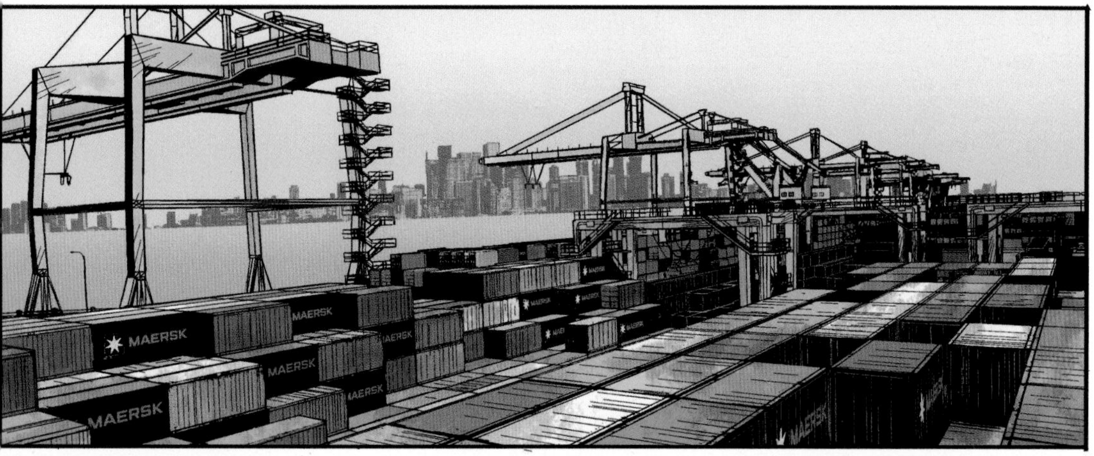

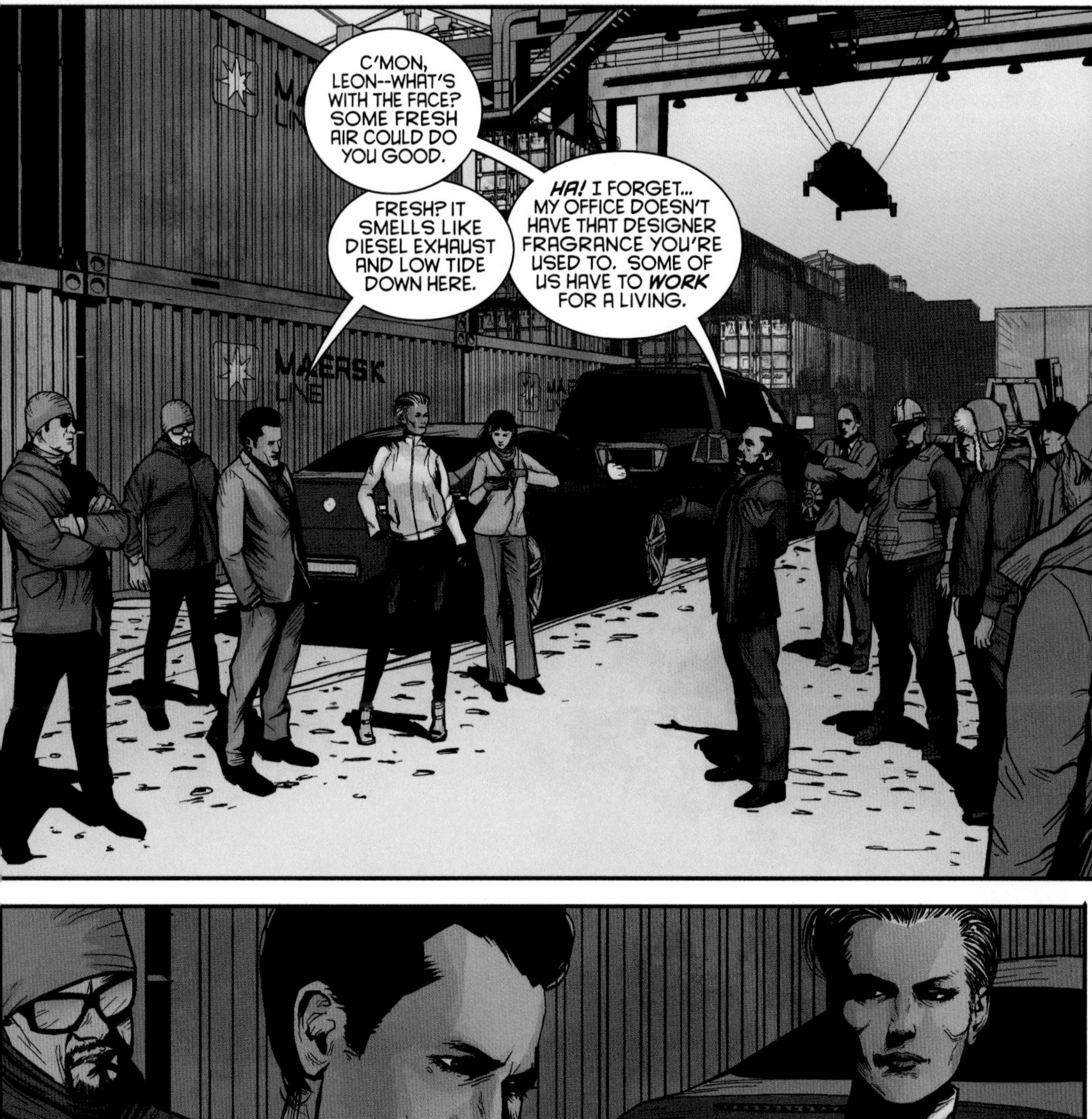
C'MON, LEON--WHAT'S WITH THE FACE? SOME FRESH AIR COULD DO YOU GOOD.
FRESH? IT SMELLS LIKE DIESEL EXHAUST AND LOW TIDE DOWN HERE.
HA! I FORGET... MY OFFICE DOESN'T HAVE THAT DESIGNER FRAGRANCE YOU'RE USED TO. SOME OF US HAVE TO WORK FOR A LIVING.

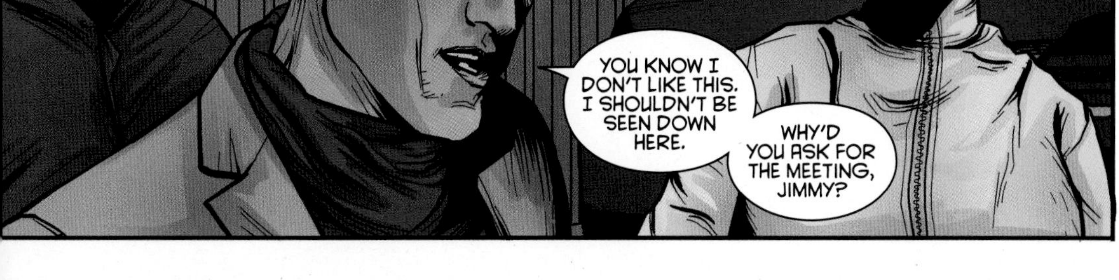
YOU KNOW I DON'T LIKE THIS. I SHOULDN'T BE SEEN DOWN HERE.
WHY'D YOU ASK FOR THE MEETING, JIMMY?

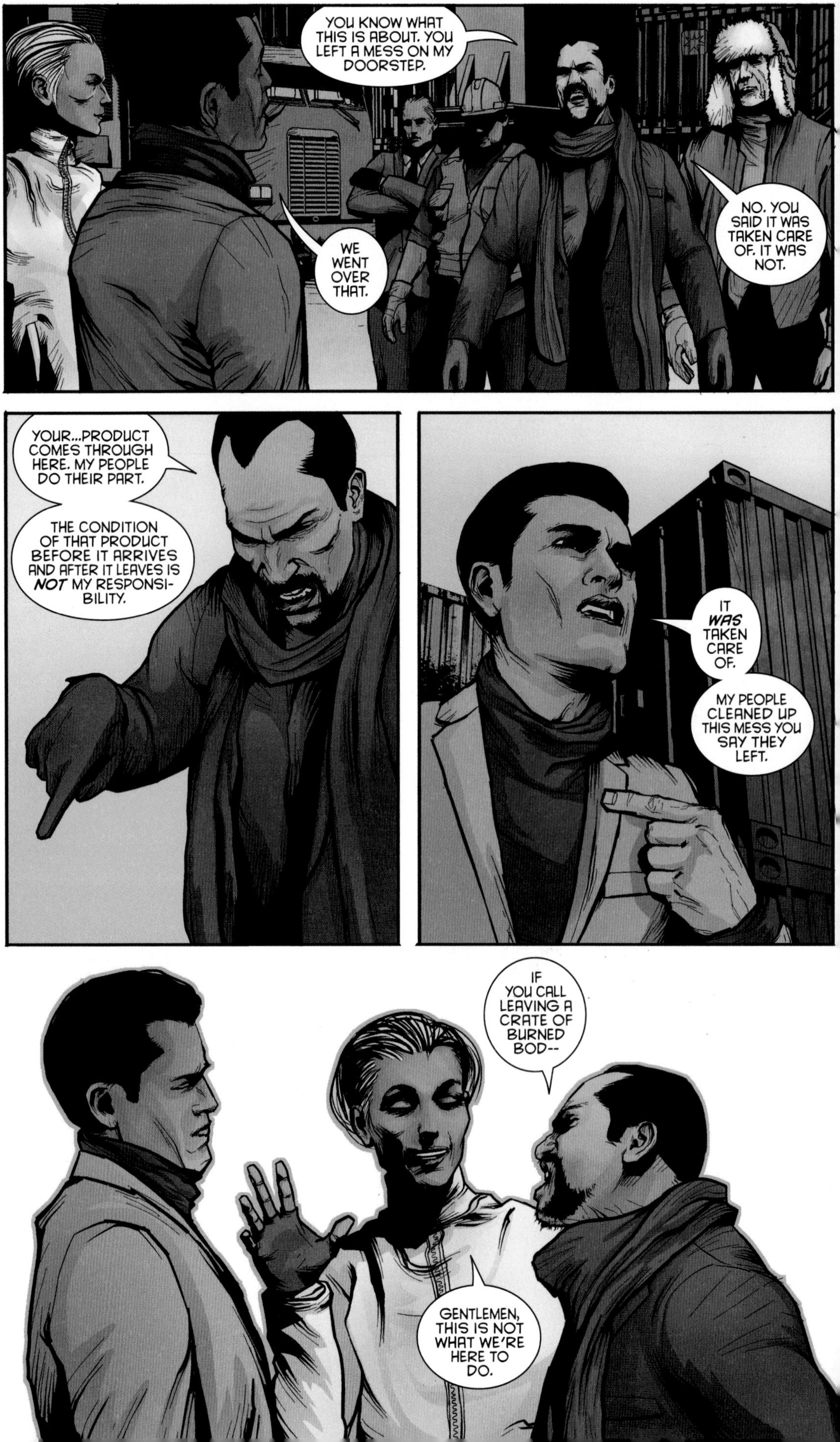

YOU KNOW WHAT THIS IS ABOUT. YOU LEFT A MESS ON MY DOORSTEP.
WE WENT OVER THAT.
NO. YOU SAID IT WAS TAKEN CARE OF. IT WAS NOT.
YOUR...PRODUCT COMES THROUGH HERE. MY PEOPLE DO THEIR PART.
THE CONDITION OF THAT PRODUCT BEFORE IT ARRIVES AND AFTER IT LEAVES IS *NOT* MY RESPONSI-BILITY.
IT *WAS* TAKEN CARE OF.
MY PEOPLE CLEANED UP THIS MESS YOU SAY THEY LEFT.
IF YOU CALL LEAVING A CRATE OF BURNED BOD--
GENTLEMEN, THIS IS NOT WHAT WE'RE HERE TO DO.

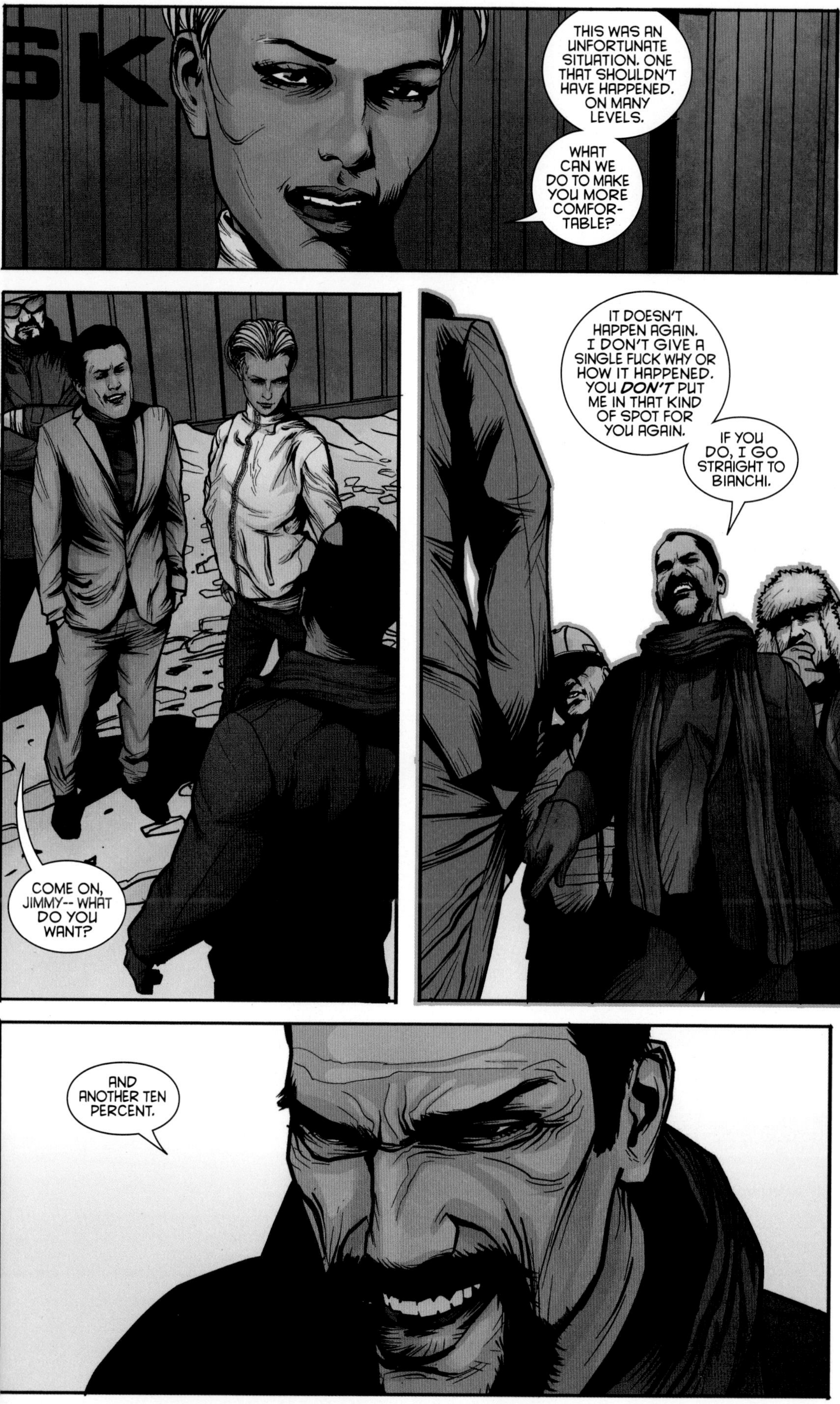
THIS WAS AN UNFORTUNATE SITUATION. ONE THAT SHOULDN'T HAVE HAPPENED. ON MANY LEVELS.
WHAT CAN WE DO TO MAKE YOU MORE COMFOR-TABLE?
COME ON, JIMMY-- WHAT DO YOU WANT?
IT DOESN'T HAPPEN AGAIN. I DON'T GIVE A SINGLE FUCK WHY OR HOW IT HAPPENED. YOU ***DON'T*** PUT ME IN THAT KIND OF SPOT FOR YOU AGAIN.
IF YOU DO, I GO STRAIGHT TO BIANCHI.
AND ANOTHER TEN PERCENT.

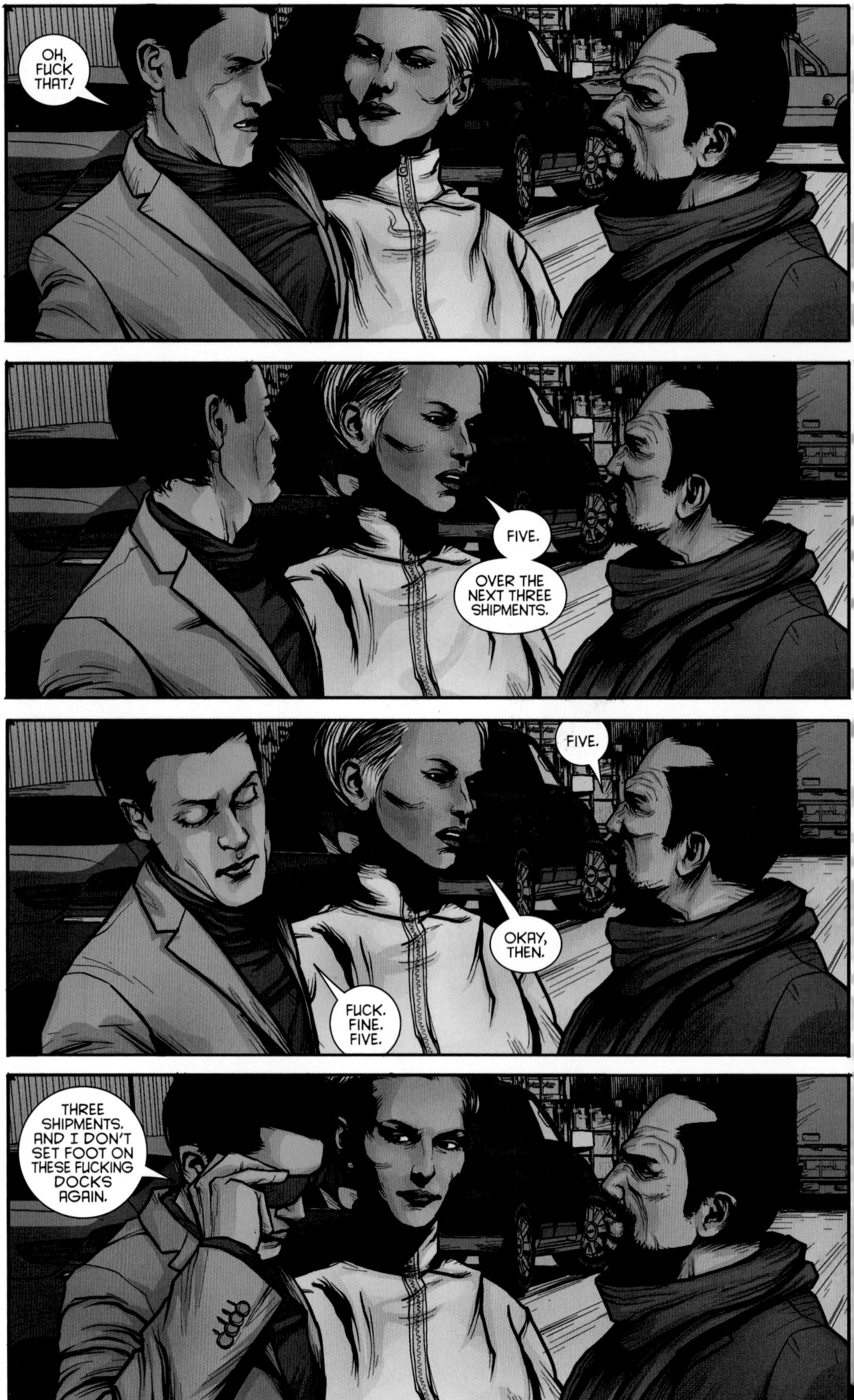

OH, FUCK THAT!
FIVE.
OVER THE NEXT THREE SHIPMENTS.
FIVE.
OKAY, THEN.
FUCK. FINE. FIVE.
THREE SHIPMENTS. AND I DON'T SET FOOT ON THESE FUCKING DOCKS AGAIN.

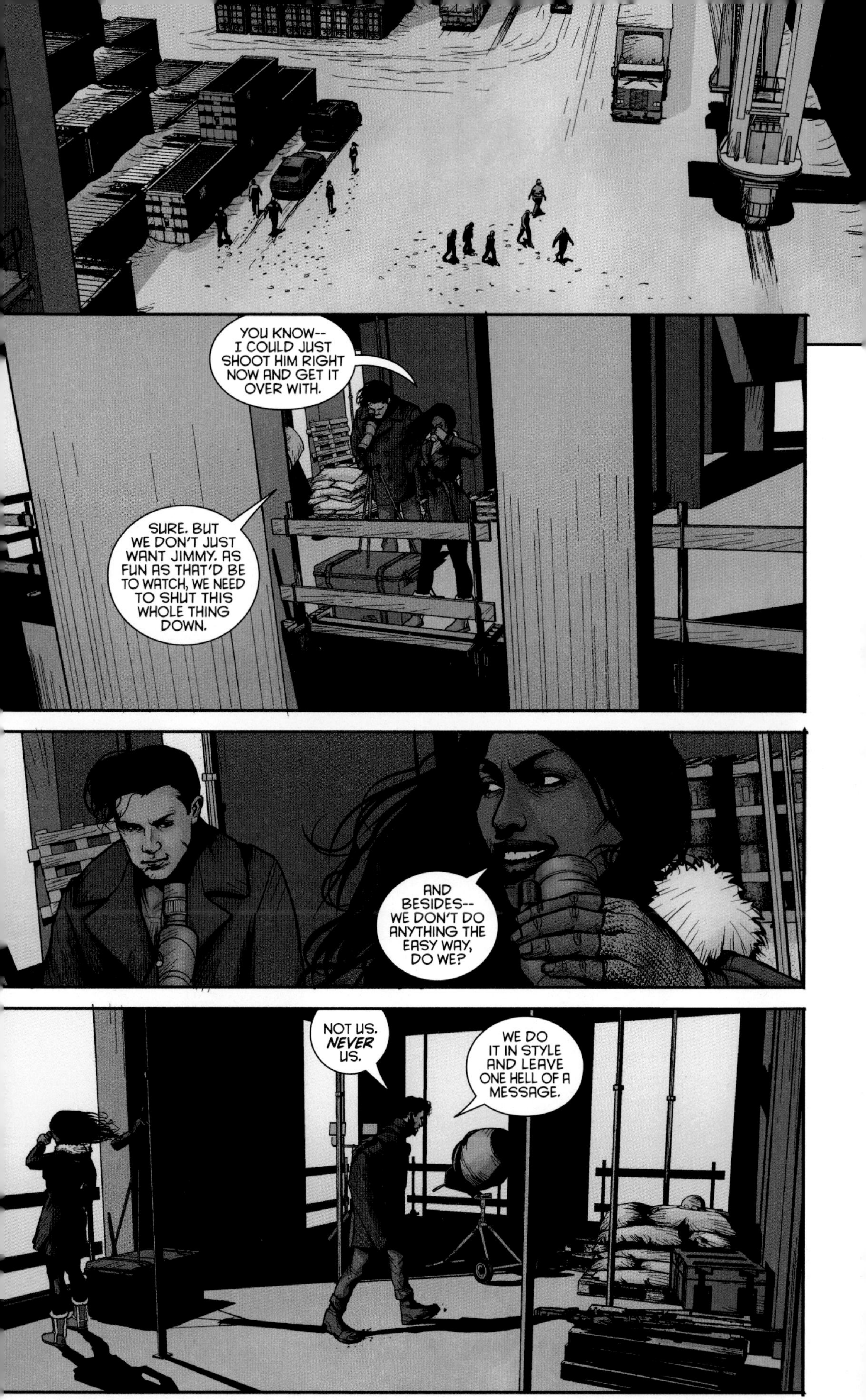
YOU KNOW--
I COULD JUST SHOOT HIM RIGHT NOW AND GET IT OVER WITH.
SURE. BUT WE DON'T JUST WANT JIMMY. AS FUN AS THAT'D BE TO WATCH, WE NEED TO SHUT THIS WHOLE THING DOWN.
AND BESIDES-- WE DON'T DO ANYTHING THE EASY WAY, DO WE?
NOT US. *NEVER* US.
WE DO IT IN STYLE AND LEAVE ONE HELL OF A MESSAGE.

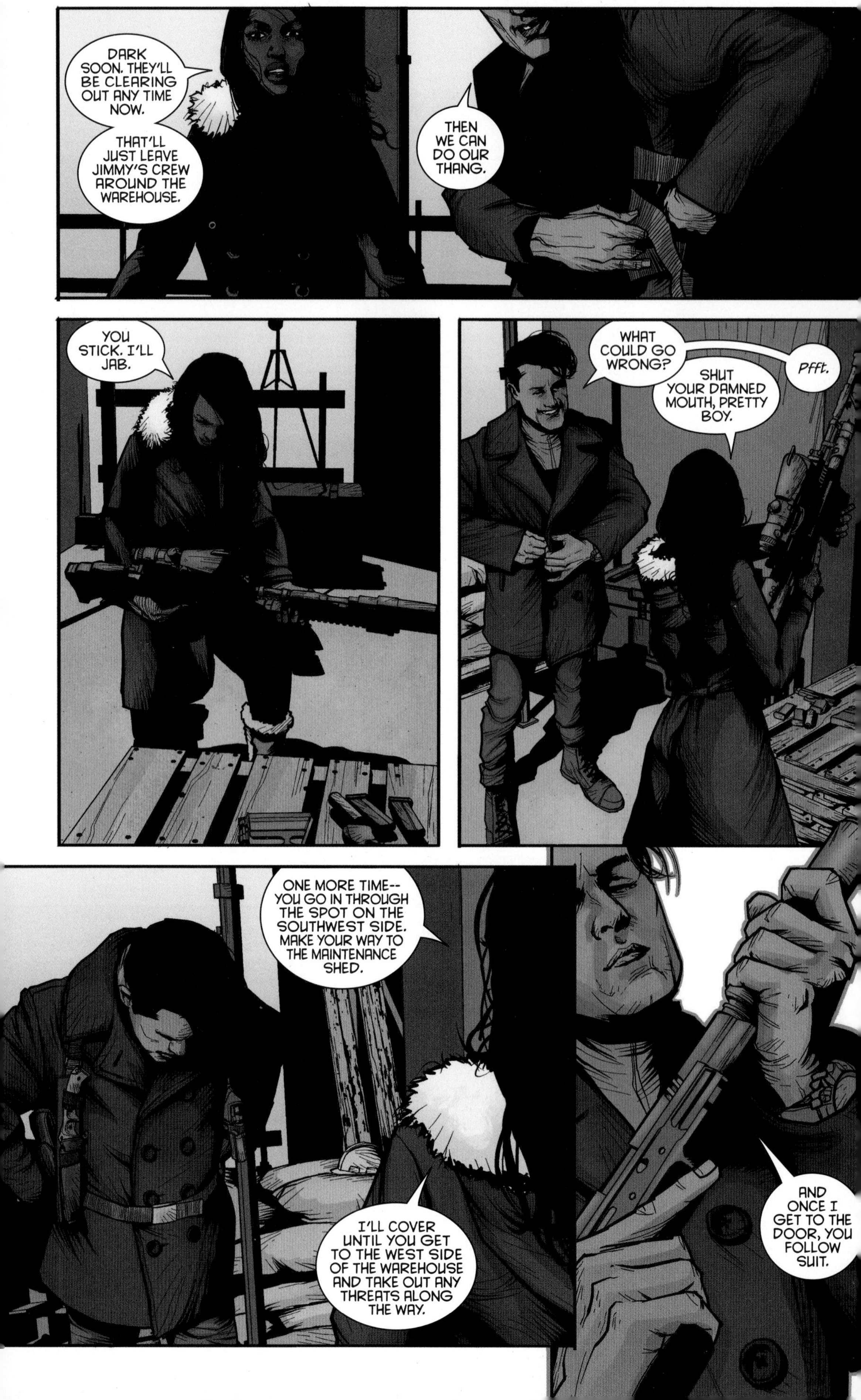
DARK SOON. THEY'LL BE CLEARING OUT ANY TIME NOW.
THAT'LL JUST LEAVE JIMMY'S CREW AROUND THE WAREHOUSE.
THEN WE CAN DO OUR THANG.
YOU STICK. I'LL JAB.
WHAT COULD GO WRONG?
Pfft.
SHUT YOUR DAMNED MOUTH, PRETTY BOY.
ONE MORE TIME-- YOU GO IN THROUGH THE SPOT ON THE SOUTHWEST SIDE. MAKE YOUR WAY TO THE MAINTENANCE SHED.
I'LL COVER UNTIL YOU GET TO THE WEST SIDE OF THE WAREHOUSE AND TAKE OUT ANY THREATS ALONG THE WAY.
AND ONCE I GET TO THE DOOR, YOU FOLLOW SUIT.

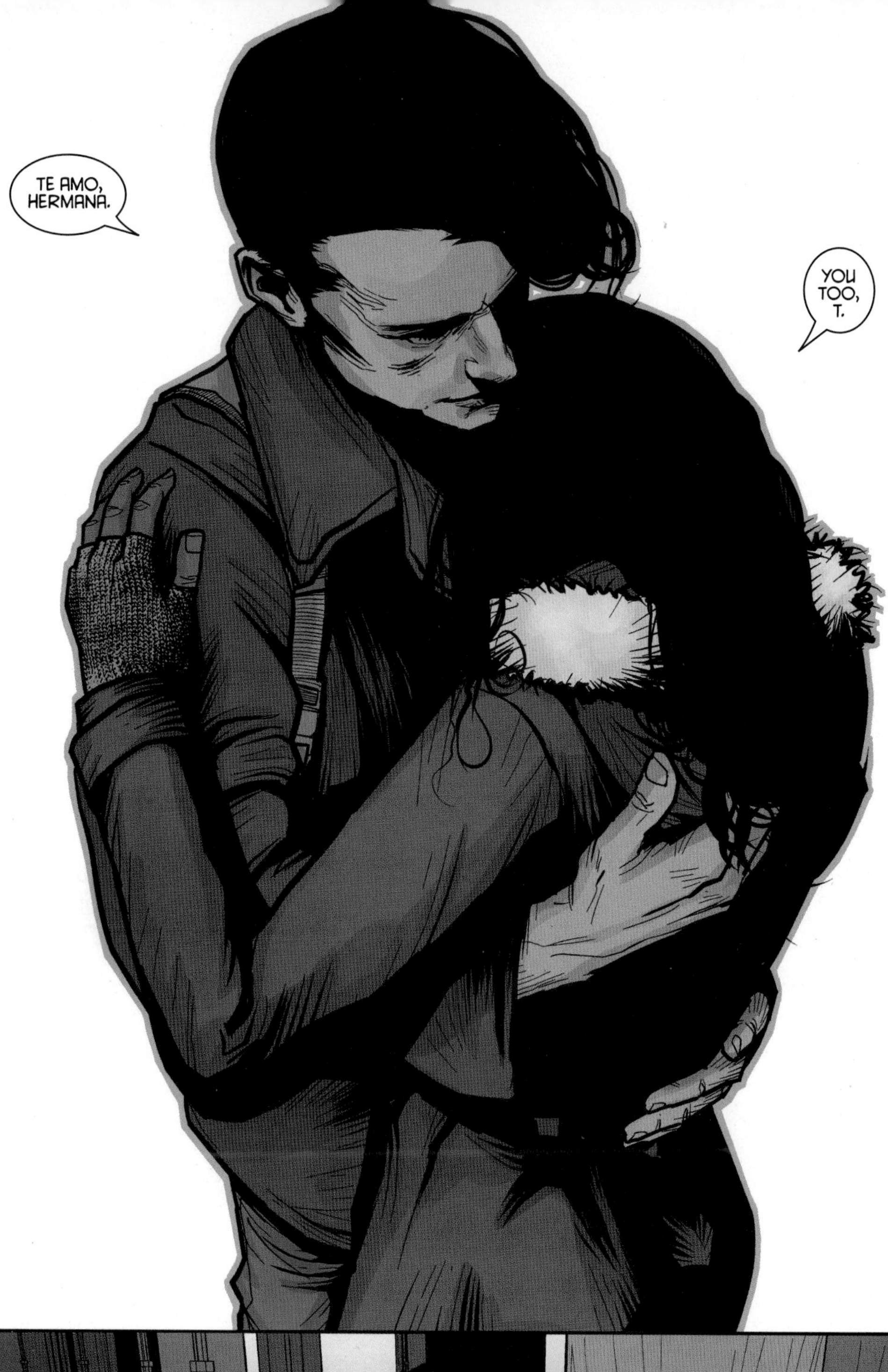
TE AMO, HERMANA.
YOU TOO, T.

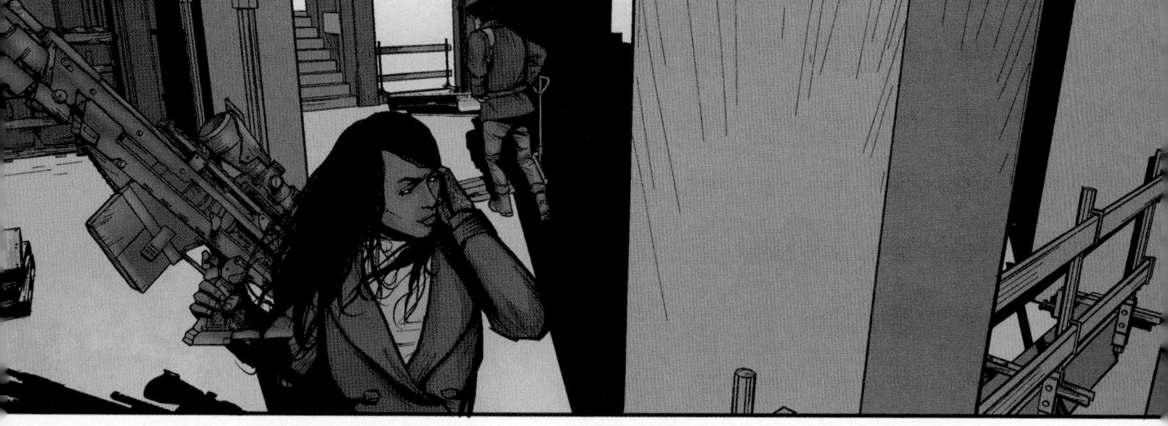

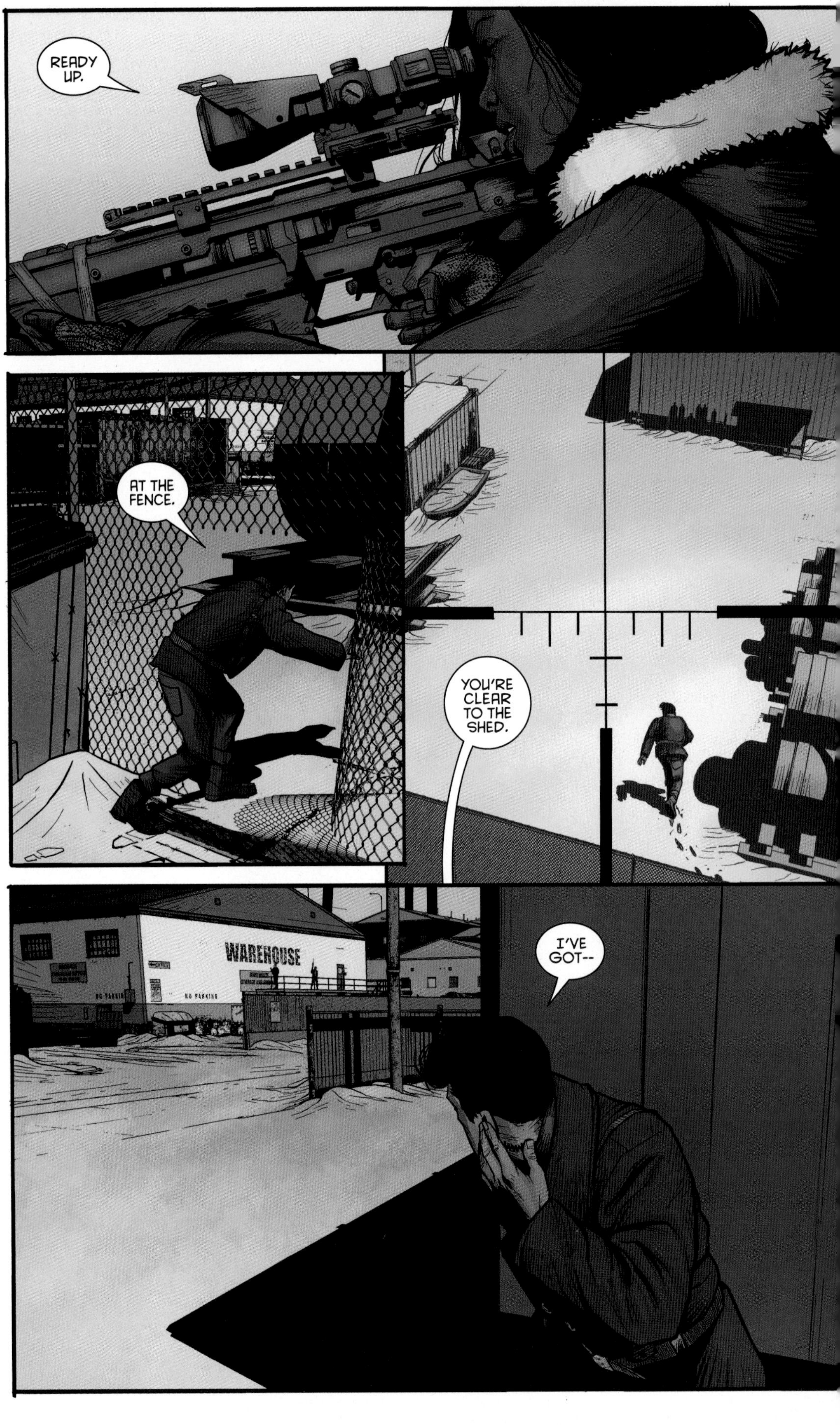
READY UP.
AT THE FENCE.
YOU'RE CLEAR TO THE SHED.
WAREHOUSE
NO PARKING
NO PARKING
I'VE GOT--

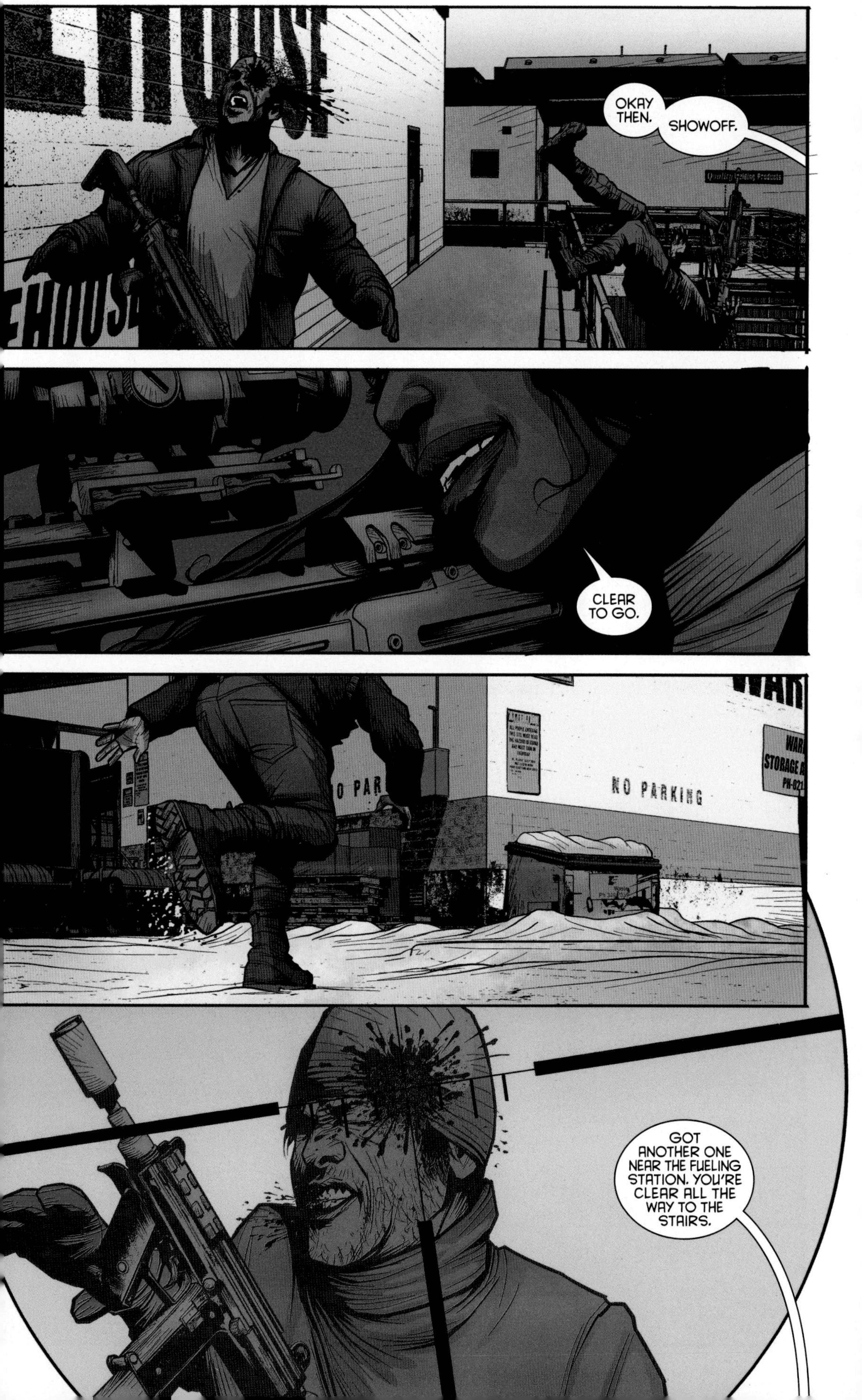
OKAY THEN.
SHOWOFF.
CLEAR TO GO.
NO PARKING
GOT ANOTHER ONE NEAR THE FUELING STATION. YOU'RE CLEAR ALL THE WAY TO THE STAIRS.

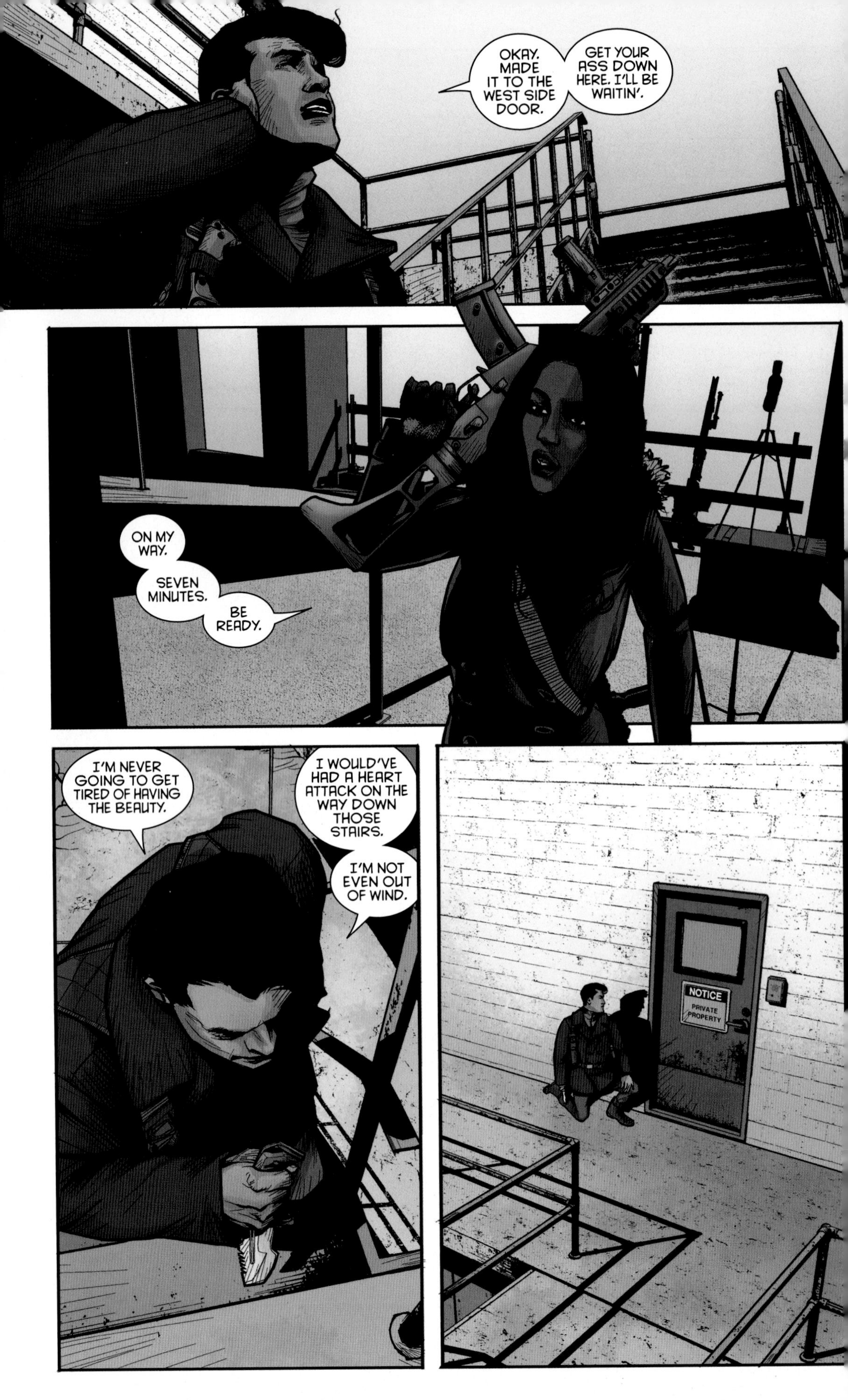

OKAY. MADE IT TO THE WEST SIDE DOOR.
GET YOUR ASS DOWN HERE. I'LL BE WAITIN'.
ON MY WAY.
SEVEN MINUTES.
BE READY.
I'M NEVER GOING TO GET TIRED OF HAVING THE BEAUTY.
I WOULD'VE HAD A HEART ATTACK ON THE WAY DOWN THOSE STAIRS.
I'M NOT EVEN OUT OF WIND.
NOTICE
PRIVATE PROPERTY

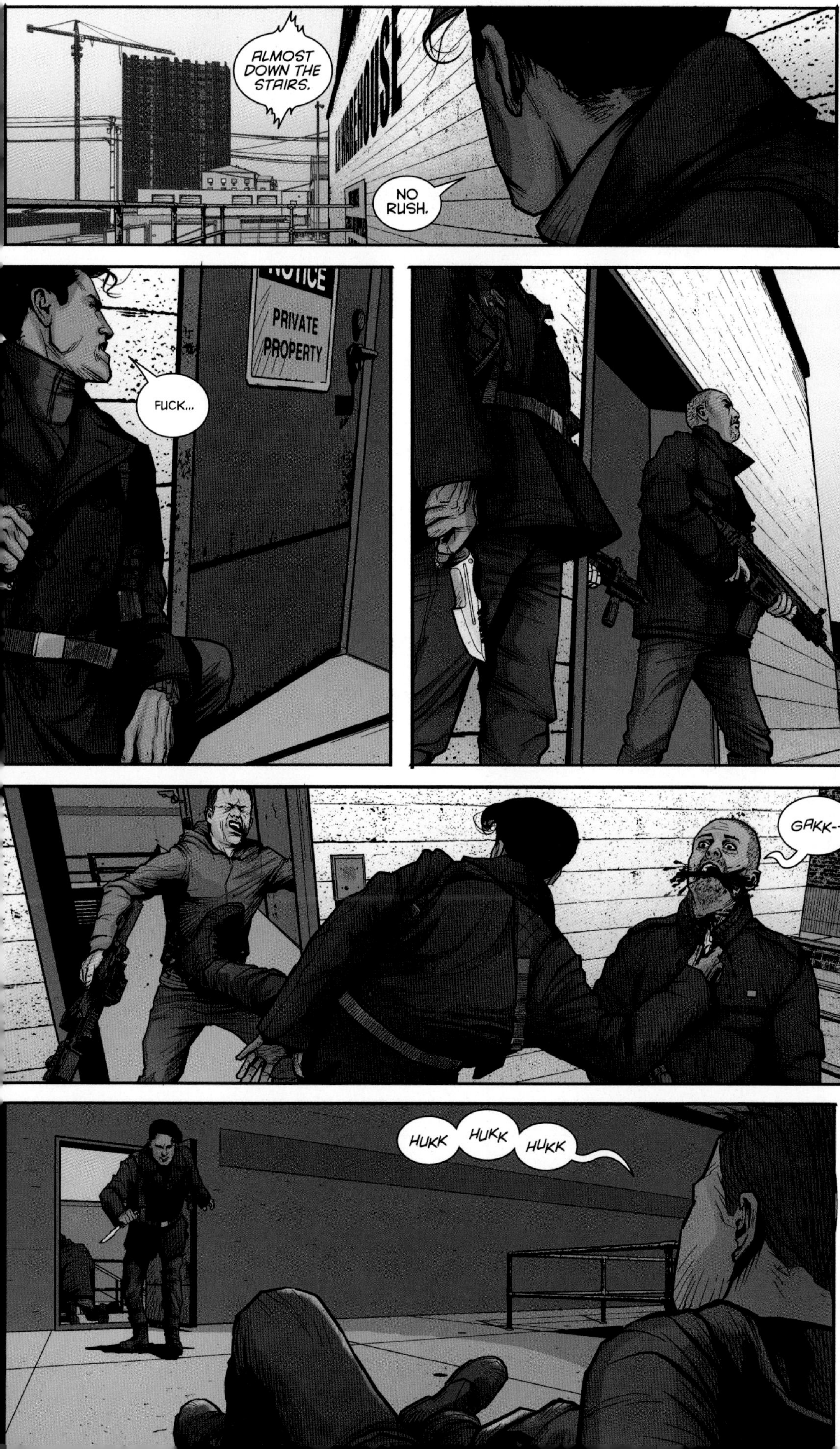
ALMOST DOWN THE STAIRS.
NO RUSH.
NOTICE
PRIVATE PROPERTY
FUCK...
GAKK--
HUKK
HUKK
HUKK

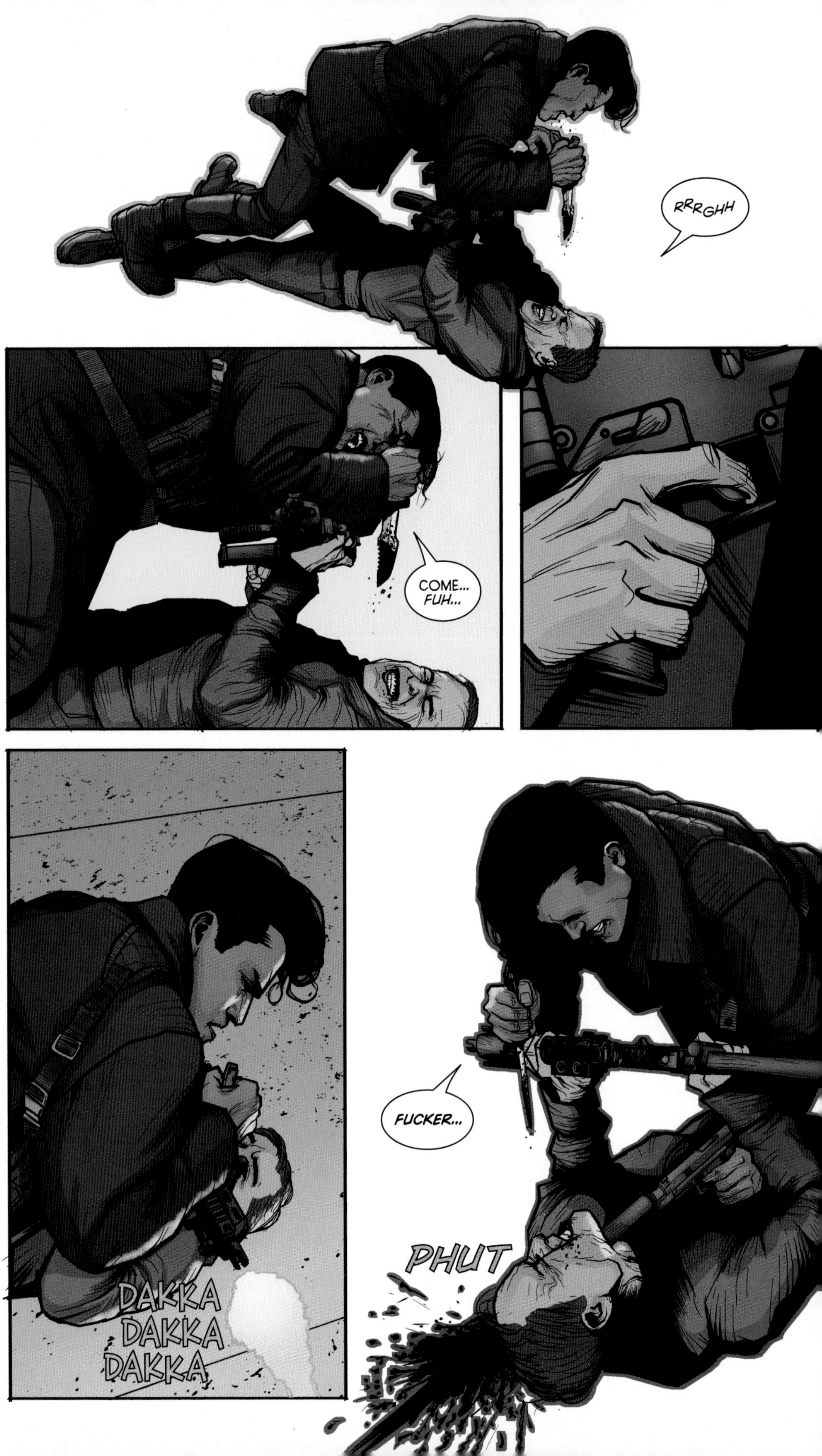
RRRGHH
COME... FUH...
FUCKER...
PHUT
DAKKA
DAKKA
DAKKA

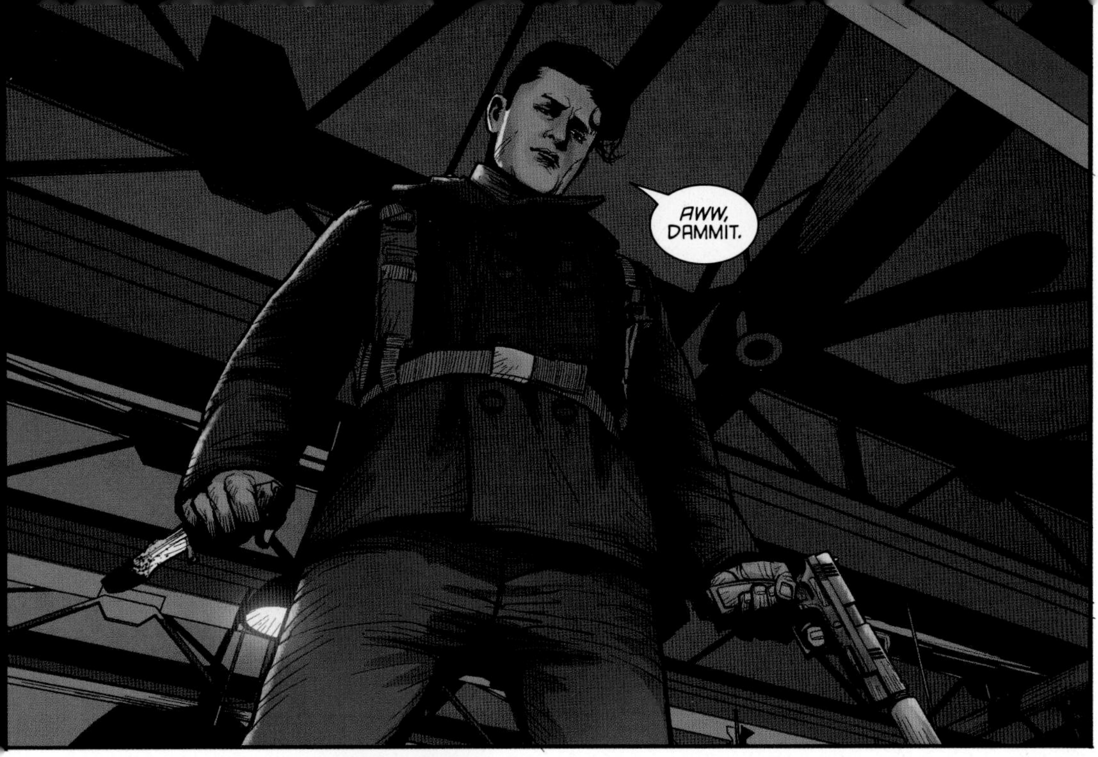
AWW, DAMMIT.

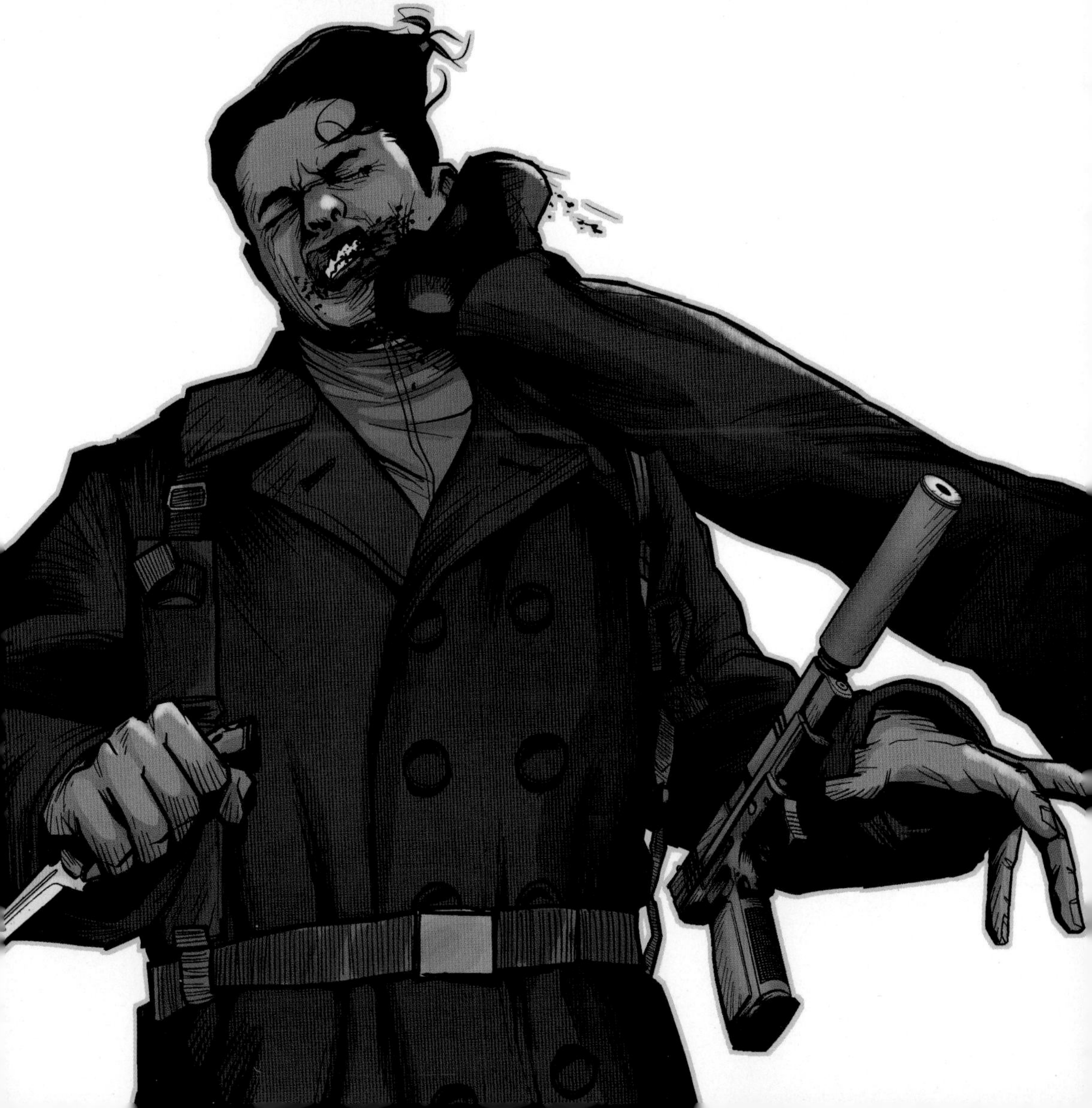

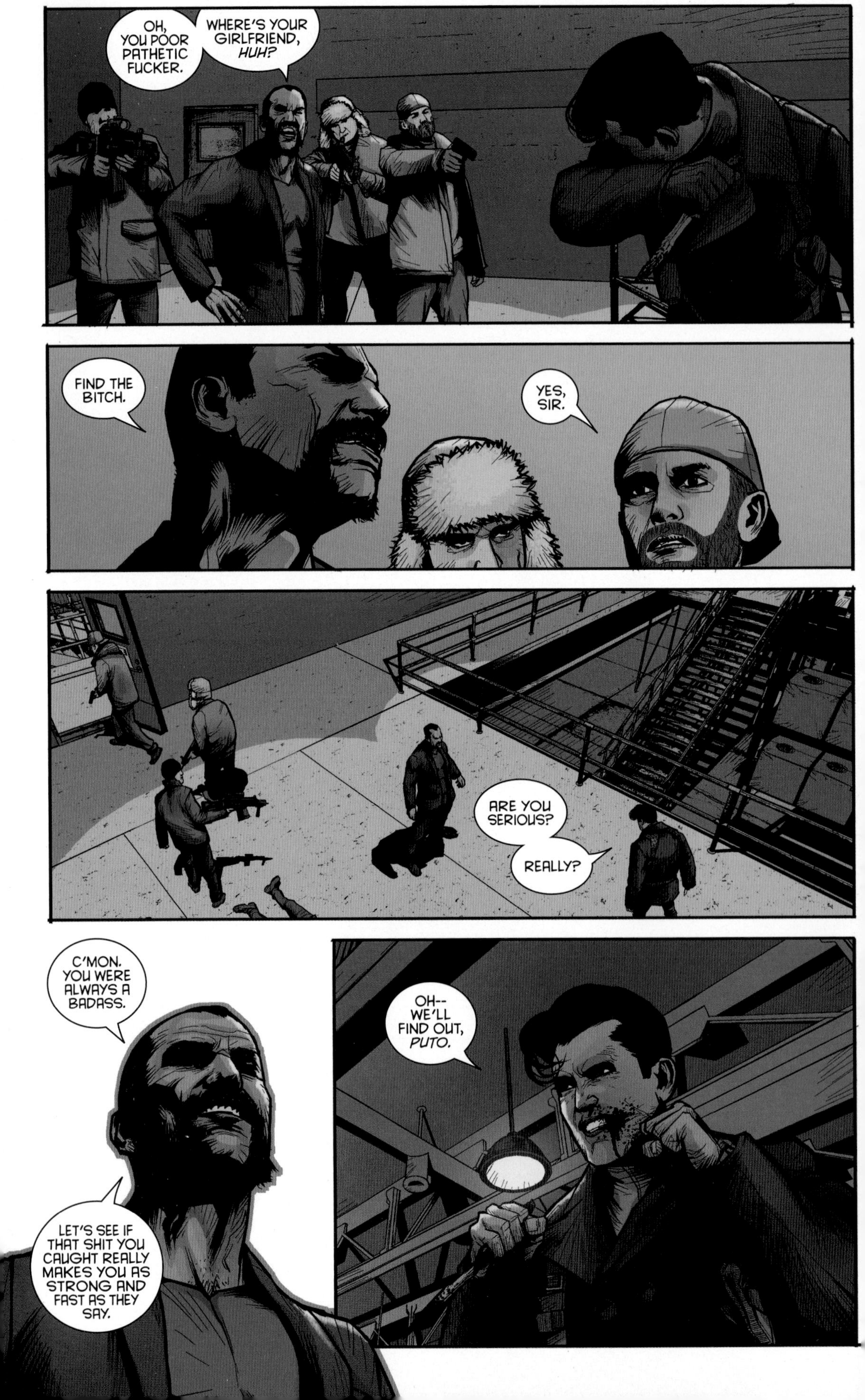

OH, YOU POOR PATHETIC FUCKER.
WHERE'S YOUR GIRLFRIEND, *HUH?*
FIND THE BITCH.
YES, SIR.
ARE YOU SERIOUS?
REALLY?
C'MON. YOU WERE ALWAYS A BADASS.
LET'S SEE IF THAT SHIT YOU CAUGHT REALLY MAKES YOU AS STRONG AND FAST AS THEY SAY.
OH-- WE'LL FIND OUT, *PUTO.*

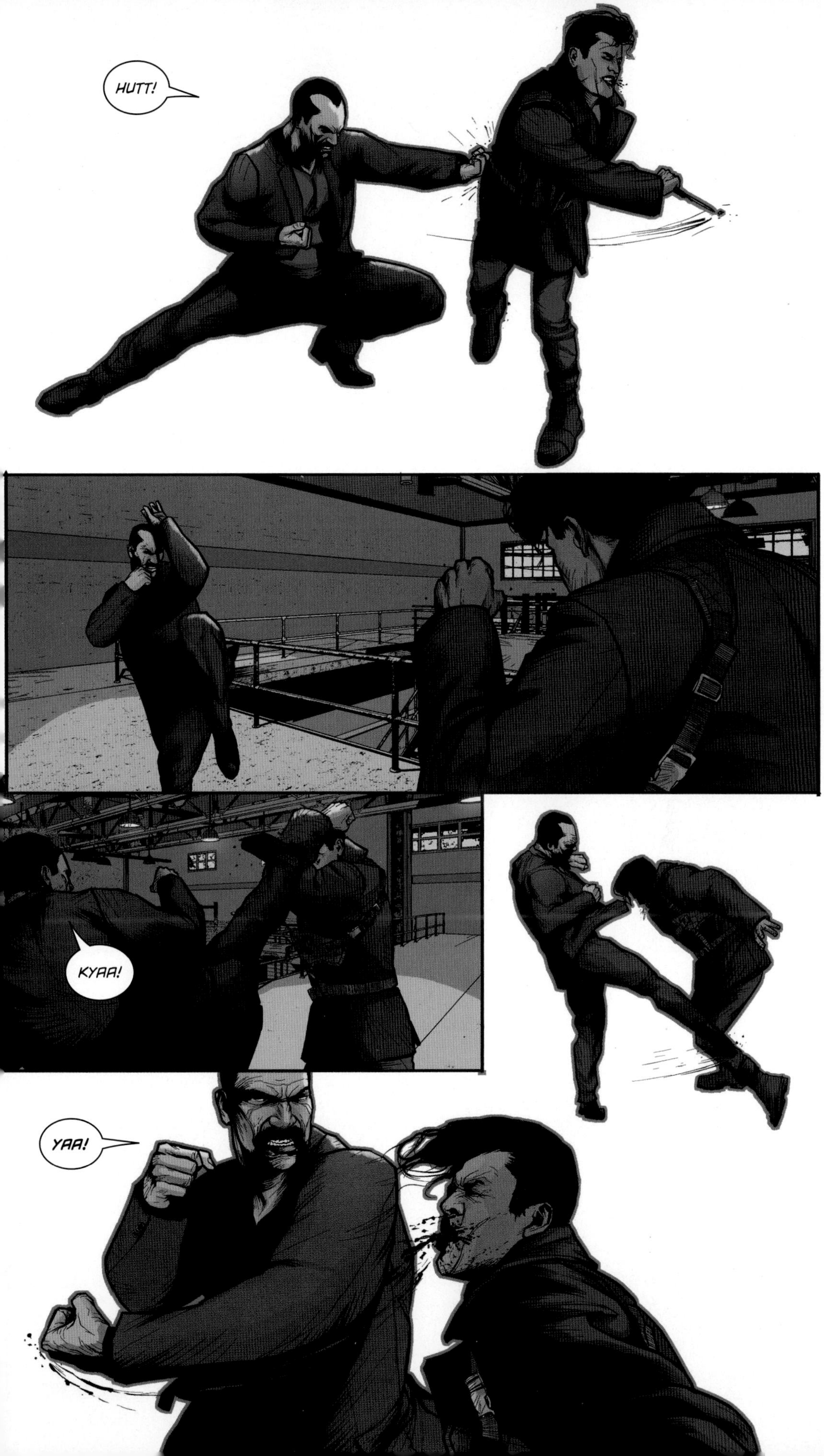
HUTT!
KYAA!
YAA!

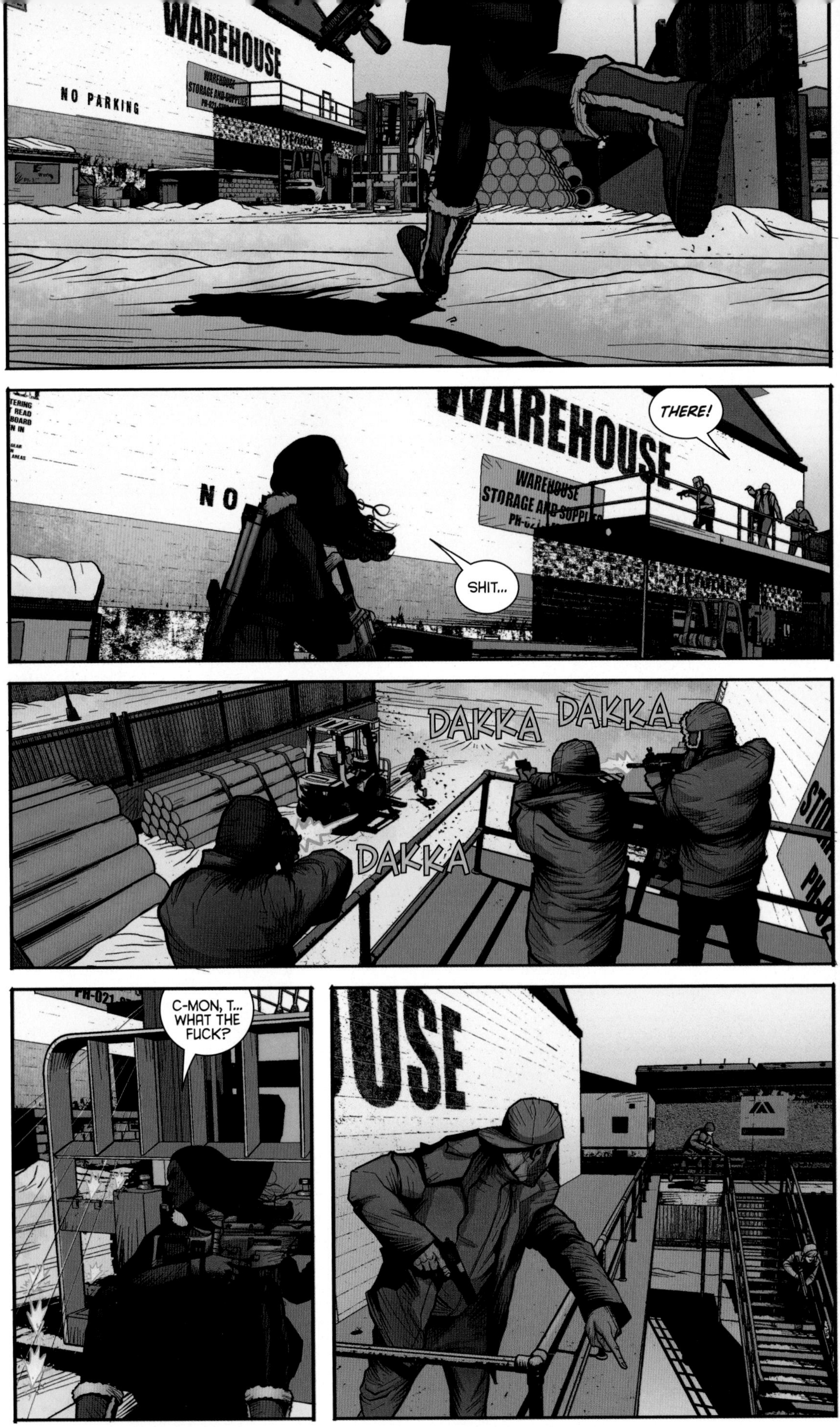
WAREHOUSE
WAREHOUSE
STORAGE AND SUPPLIES
NO PARKING
THERE!
SHIT...
DAKKA
DAKKA
DAKKA
C-MON, T... WHAT THE FUCK?

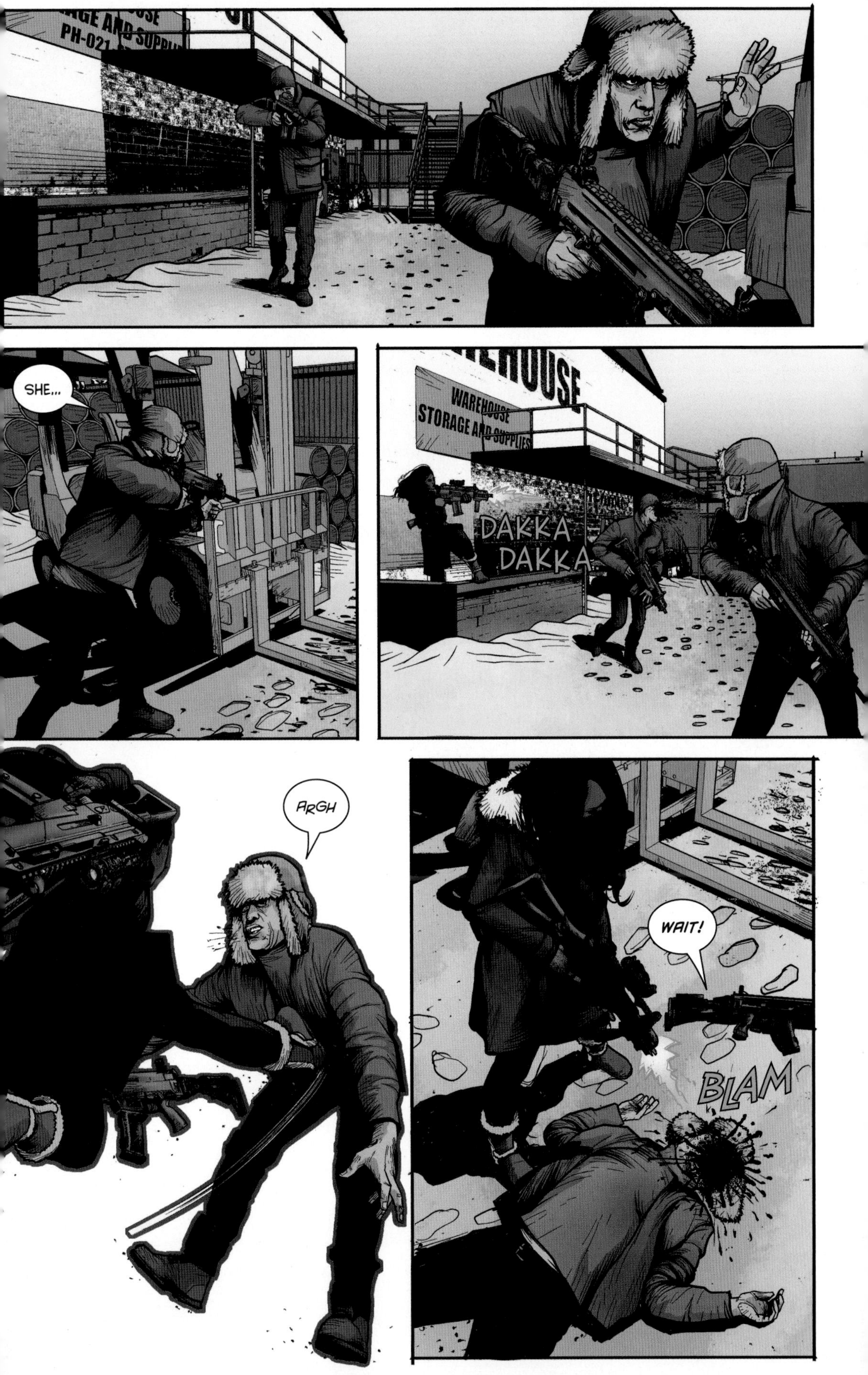

WAREHOUSE
STORAGE AND SUPPLIES
PH-021
SHE...
WAREHOUSE
STORAGE AND SUPPLIES
DAKKA
DAKKA
ARGH
WAIT!
BLAM

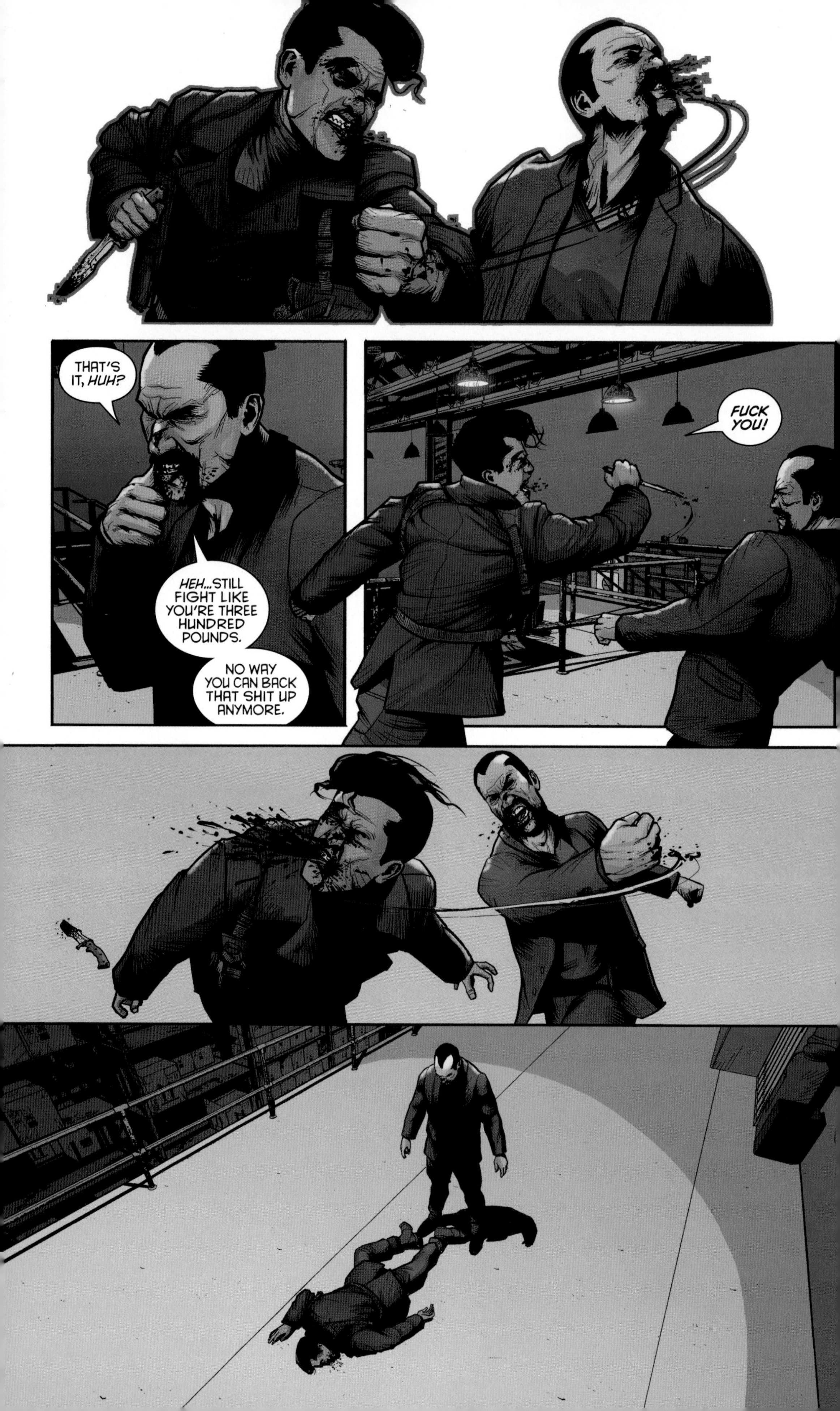
THAT'S IT, HUH?
FUCK YOU!
HEH...STILL FIGHT LIKE YOU'RE THREE HUNDRED POUNDS.
NO WAY YOU CAN BACK THAT SHIT UP ANYMORE.

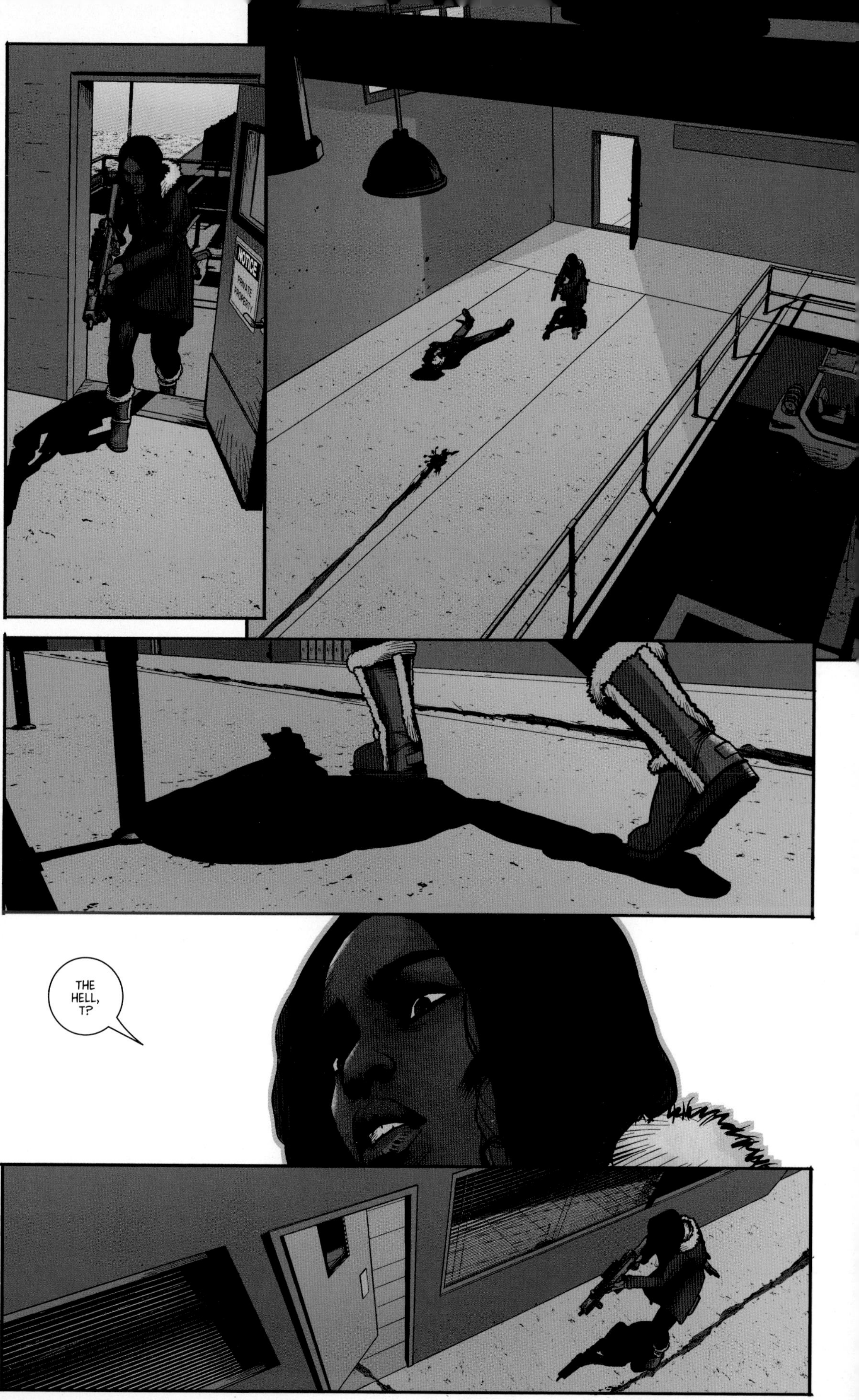
NOTICE
PRIVATE PROPERTY
THE HELL, T?

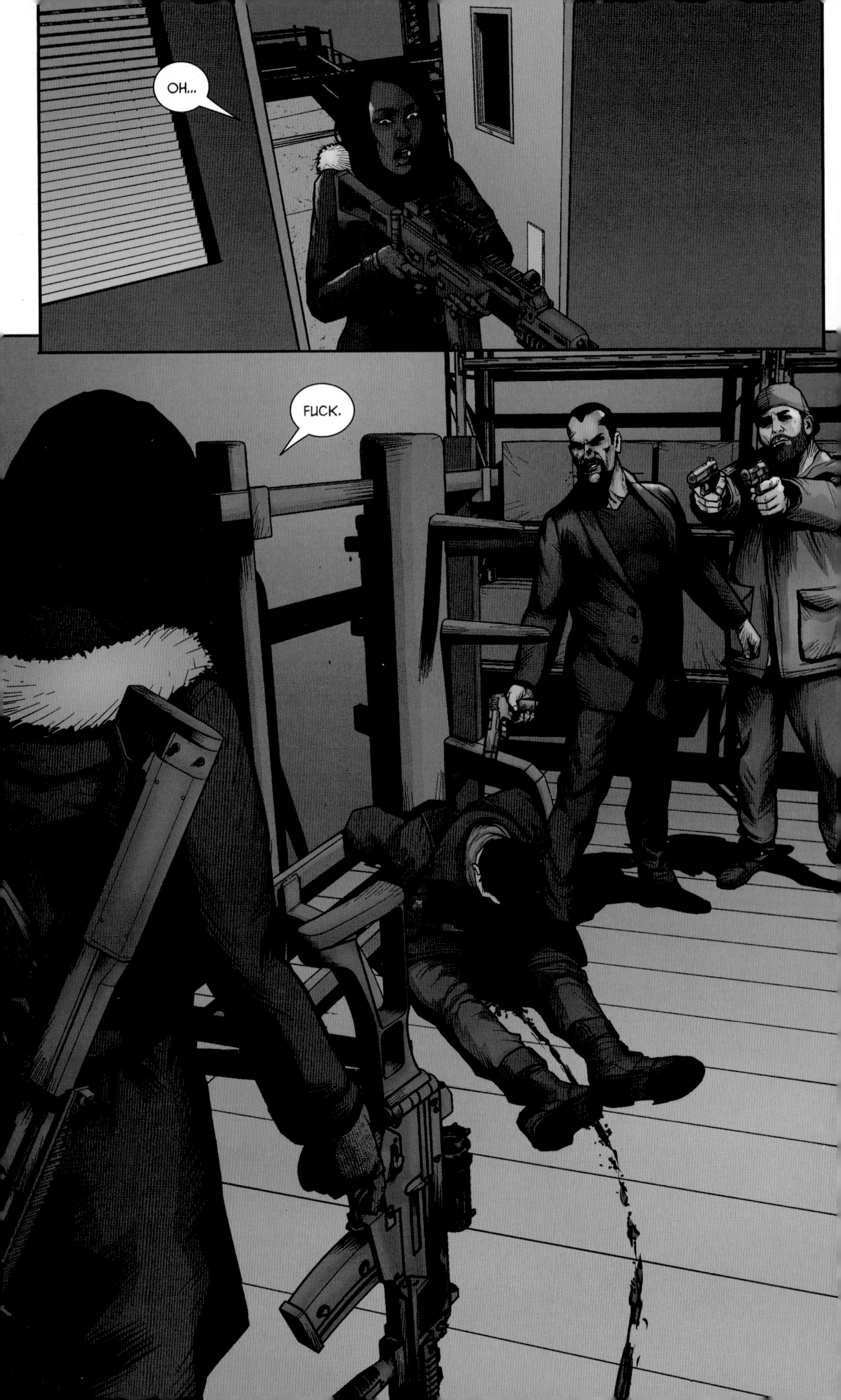
OH...
FUCK.

CHAPTER

24

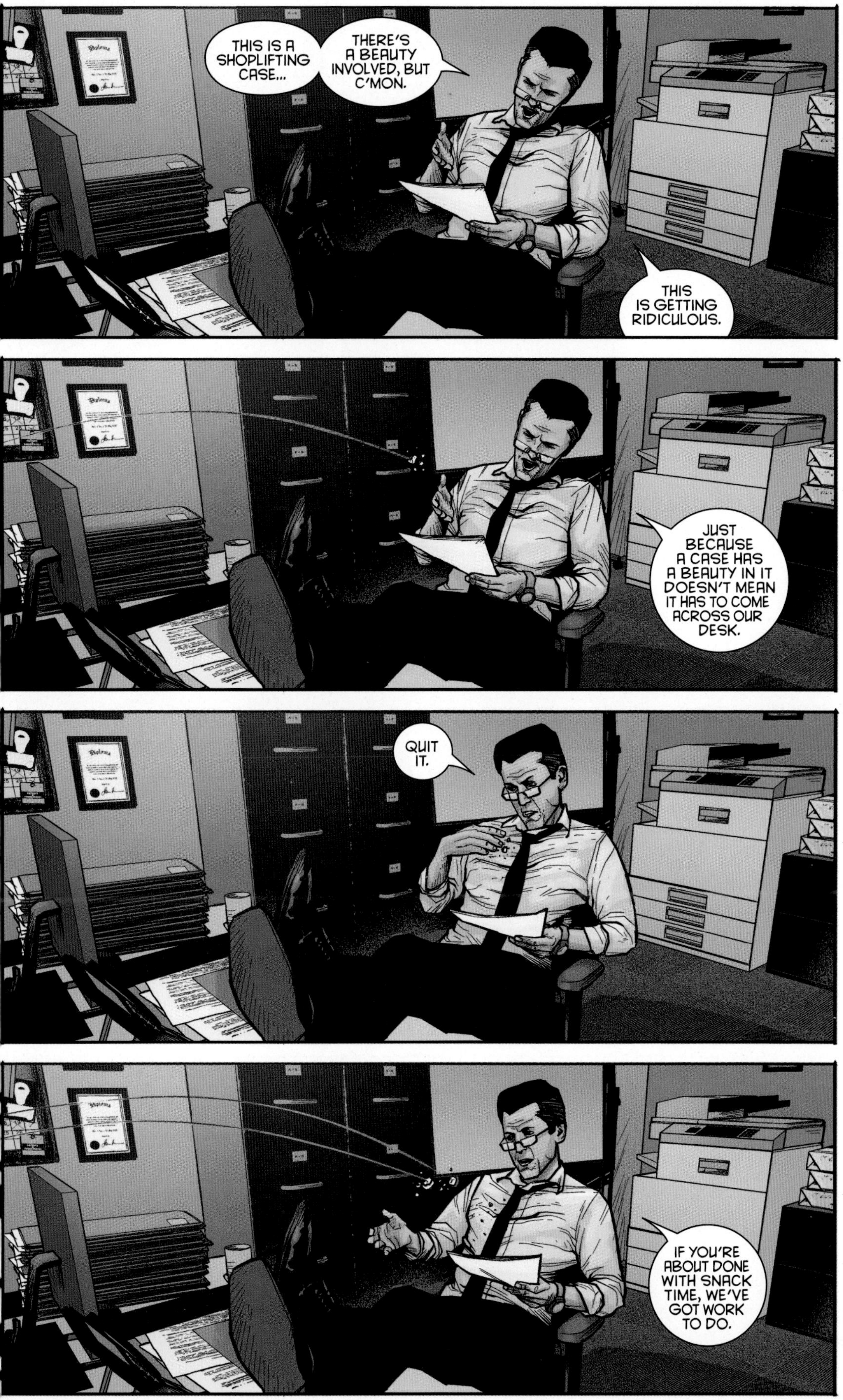
THIS IS A SHOPLIFTING CASE...
THERE'S A BEAUTY INVOLVED, BUT C'MON.
THIS IS GETTING RIDICULOUS.
JUST BECAUSE A CASE HAS A BEAUTY IN IT DOESN'T MEAN IT HAS TO COME ACROSS OUR DESK.
QUIT IT.
IF YOU'RE ABOUT DONE WITH SNACK TIME, WE'VE GOT WORK TO DO.

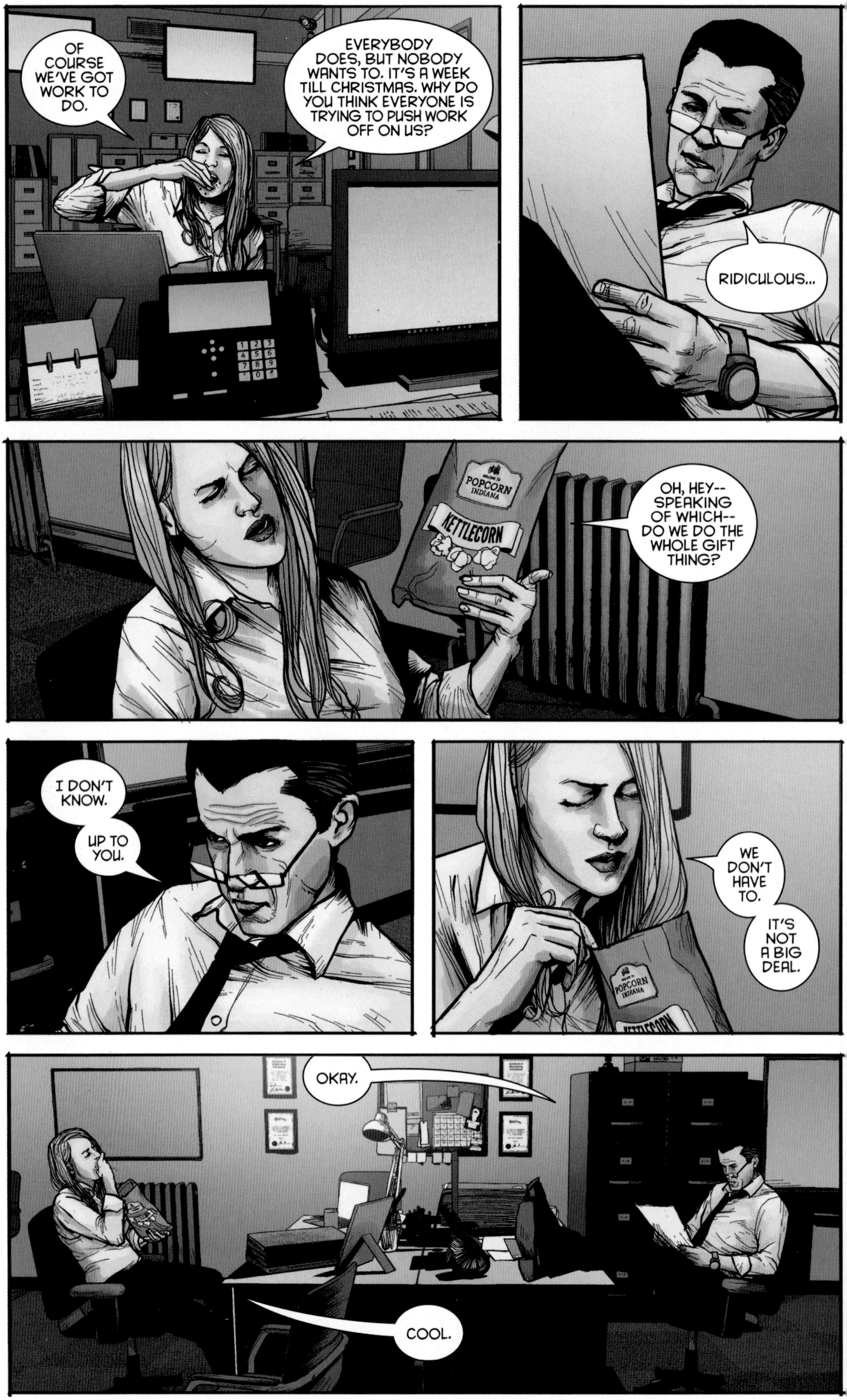

OF COURSE WE'VE GOT WORK TO DO.
EVERYBODY DOES, BUT NOBODY WANTS TO. IT'S A WEEK TILL CHRISTMAS. WHY DO YOU THINK EVERYONE IS TRYING TO PUSH WORK OFF ON US?
RIDICULOUS...
POPCORN INDIANA
KETTLECORN
OH, HEY-- SPEAKING OF WHICH-- DO WE DO THE WHOLE GIFT THING?
I DON'T KNOW.
UP TO YOU.
WE DON'T HAVE TO.
IT'S NOT A BIG DEAL.
POPCORN INDIANA
OKAY.
COOL.

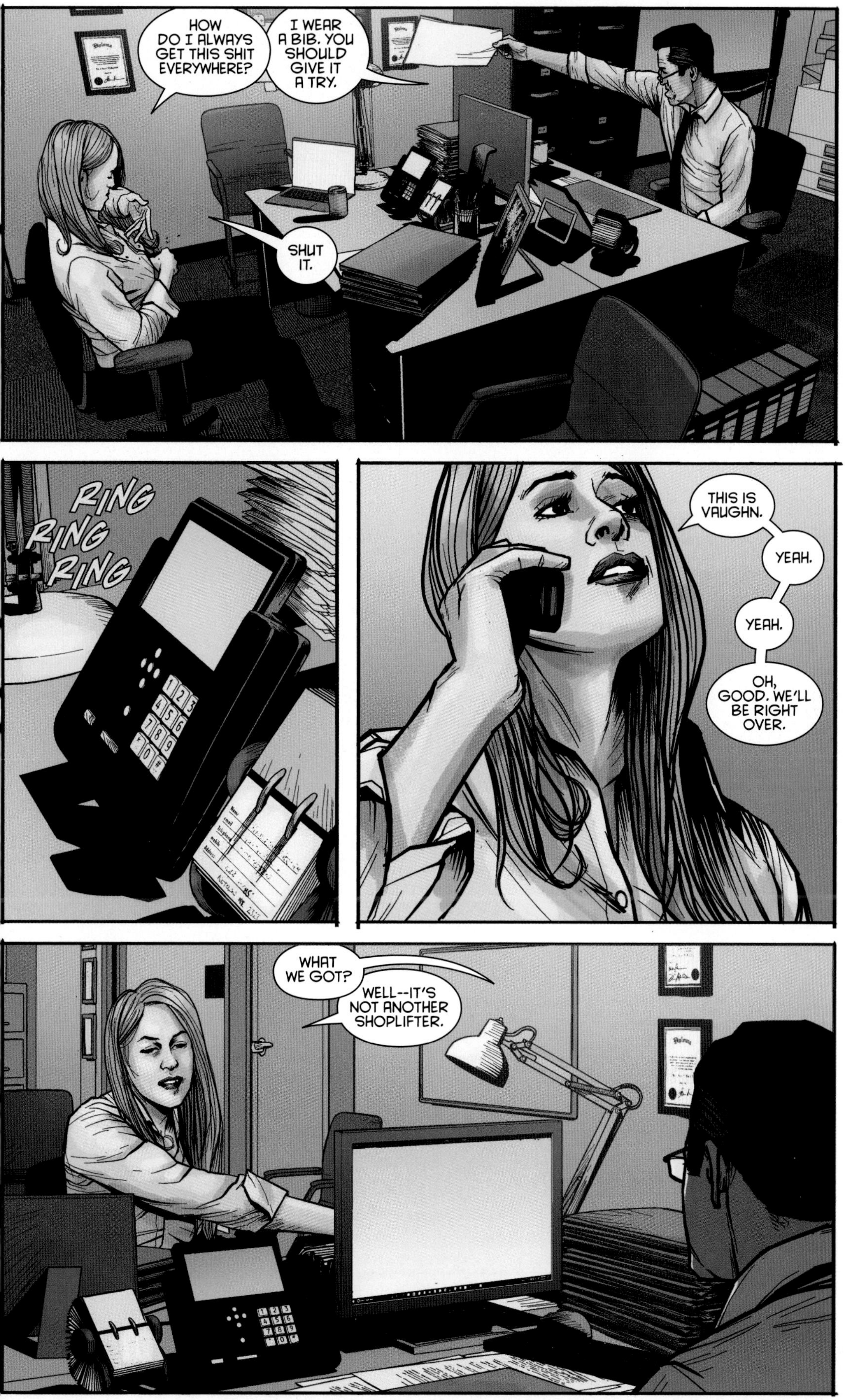
HOW DO I ALWAYS GET THIS SHIT EVERYWHERE?
I WEAR A BIB. YOU SHOULD GIVE IT A TRY.
SHUT IT.
RING RING RING
THIS IS VAUGHN.
YEAH.
YEAH.
OH, GOOD. WE'LL BE RIGHT OVER.
WHAT WE GOT?
WELL--IT'S NOT ANOTHER SHOPLIFTER.

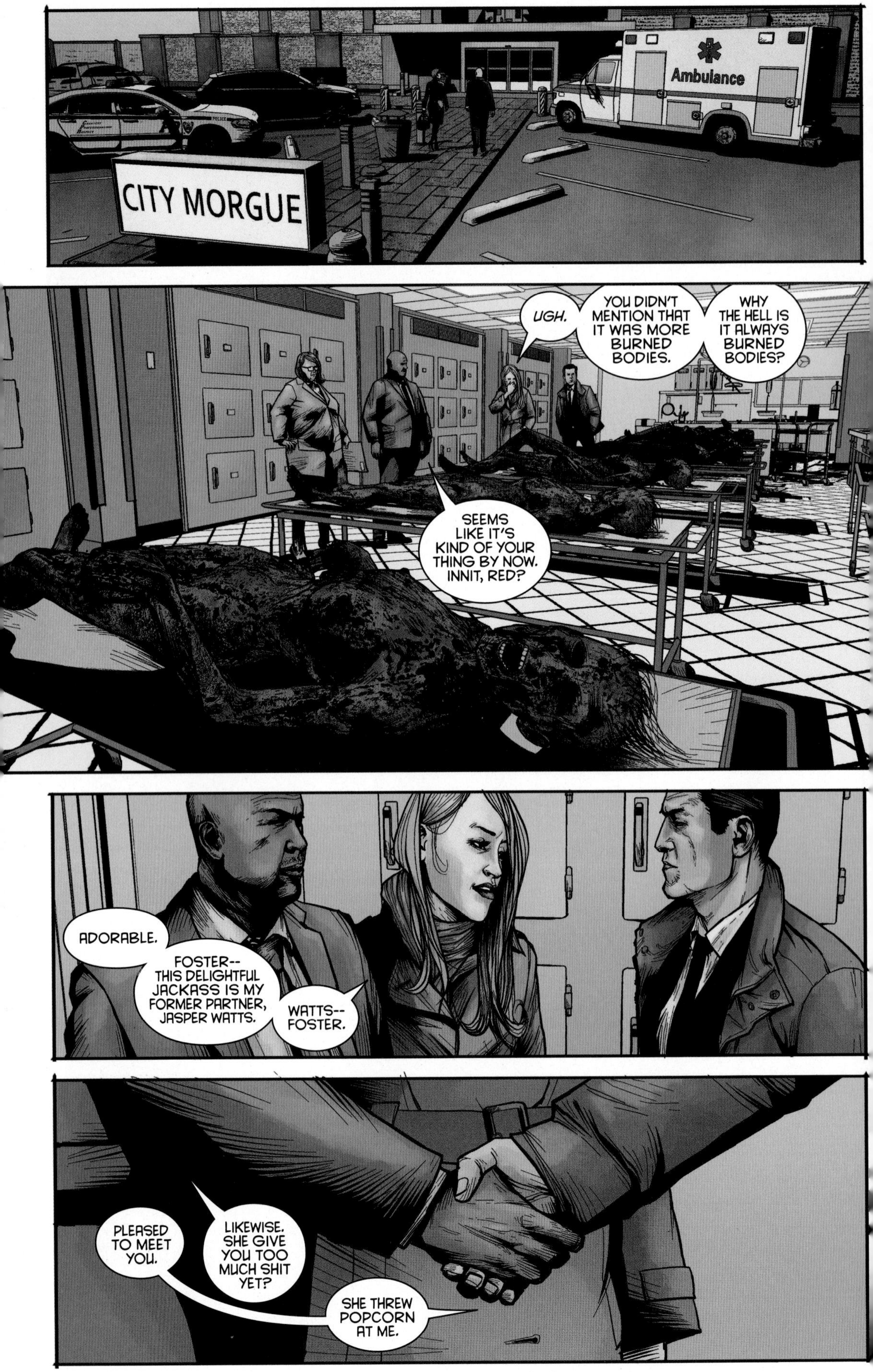

CITY MORGUE
Ambulance
UGH.
YOU DIDN'T MENTION THAT IT WAS MORE BURNED BODIES.
WHY THE HELL IS IT ALWAYS BURNED BODIES?
SEEMS LIKE IT'S KIND OF YOUR THING BY NOW. INNIT, RED?
ADORABLE.
FOSTER-- THIS DELIGHTFUL JACKASS IS MY FORMER PARTNER, JASPER WATTS.
WATTS-- FOSTER.
PLEASED TO MEET YOU.
LIKEWISE. SHE GIVE YOU TOO MUCH SHIT YET?
SHE THREW POPCORN AT ME.

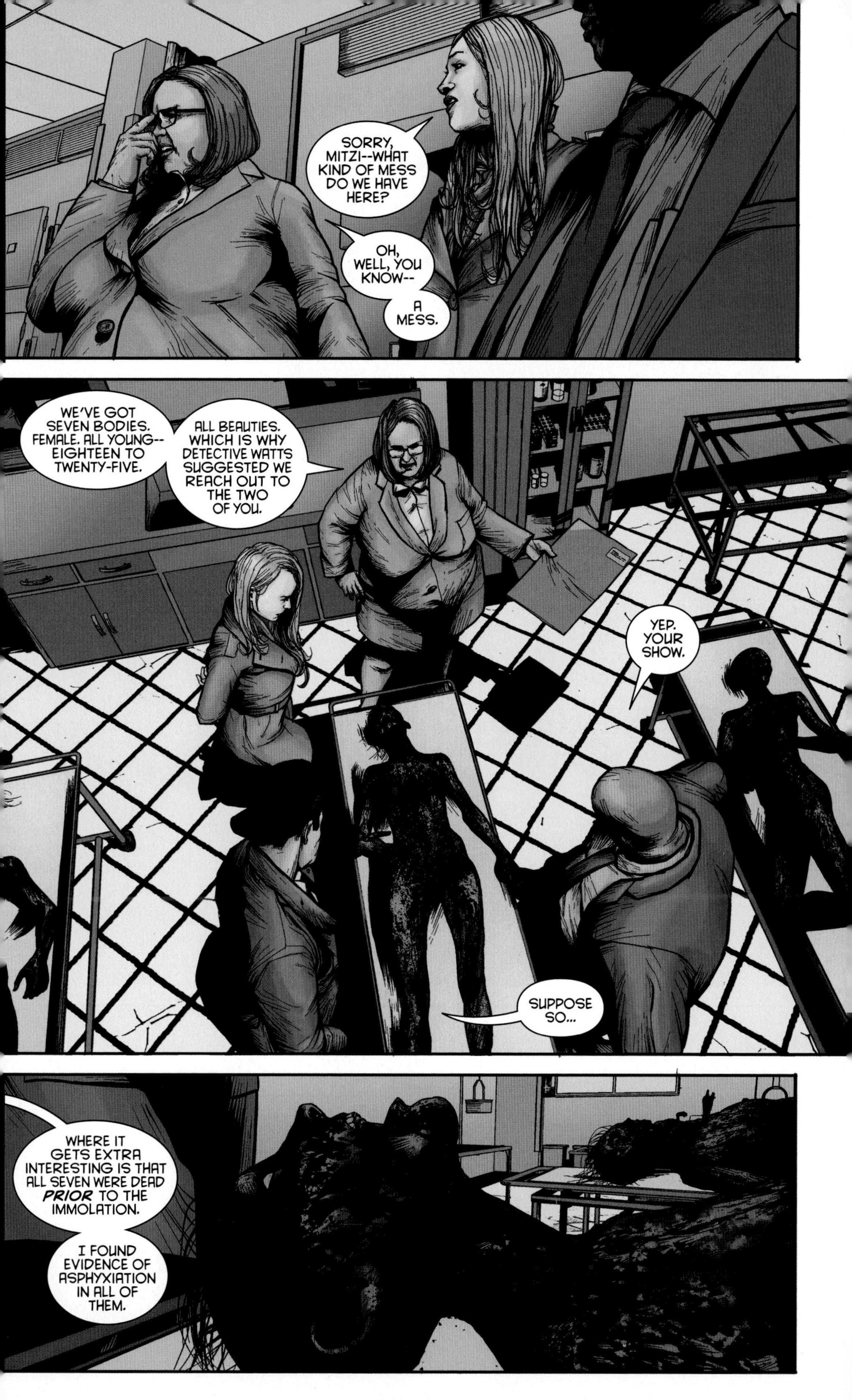
SORRY, MITZI--WHAT KIND OF MESS DO WE HAVE HERE?
OH, WELL, YOU KNOW--
A MESS.
WE'VE GOT SEVEN BODIES. FEMALE. ALL YOUNG-- EIGHTEEN TO TWENTY-FIVE.
ALL BEAUTIES. WHICH IS WHY DETECTIVE WATTS SUGGESTED WE REACH OUT TO THE TWO OF YOU.
YEP. YOUR SHOW.
SUPPOSE SO...
WHERE IT GETS EXTRA INTERESTING IS THAT ALL SEVEN WERE DEAD *PRIOR* TO THE IMMOLATION.
I FOUND EVIDENCE OF ASPHYXIATION IN ALL OF THEM.

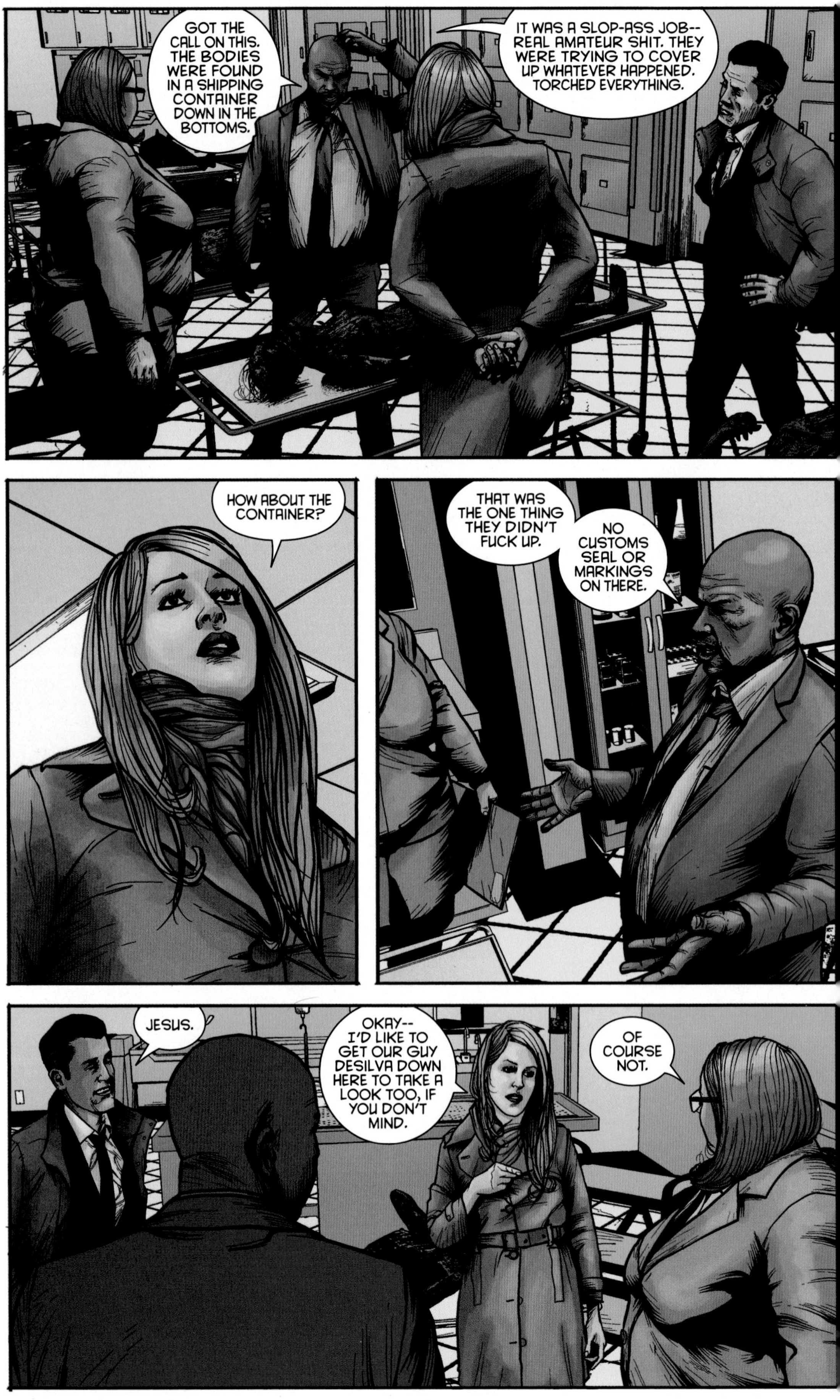
GOT THE CALL ON THIS. THE BODIES WERE FOUND IN A SHIPPING CONTAINER DOWN IN THE BOTTOMS.
IT WAS A SLOP-ASS JOB-- REAL AMATEUR SHIT. THEY WERE TRYING TO COVER UP WHATEVER HAPPENED. TORCHED EVERYTHING.
HOW ABOUT THE CONTAINER?
THAT WAS THE ONE THING THEY DIDN'T FUCK UP.
NO CUSTOMS SEAL OR MARKINGS ON THERE.
JESUS.
OKAY-- I'D LIKE TO GET OUR GUY DESILVA DOWN HERE TO TAKE A LOOK TOO, IF YOU DON'T MIND.
OF COURSE NOT.

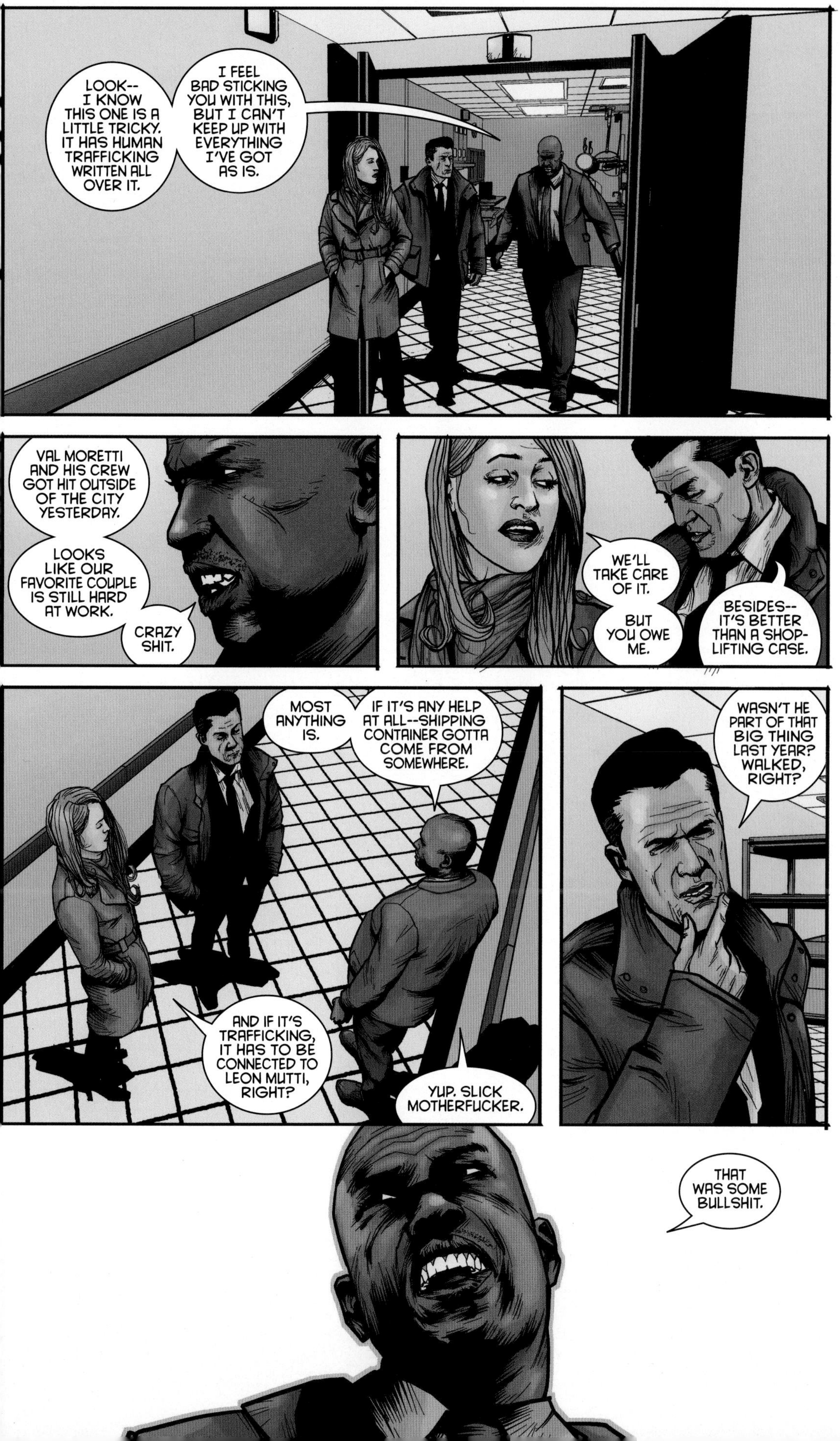
LOOK-- I KNOW THIS ONE IS A LITTLE TRICKY. IT HAS HUMAN TRAFFICKING WRITTEN ALL OVER IT.
I FEEL BAD STICKING YOU WITH THIS, BUT I CAN'T KEEP UP WITH EVERYTHING I'VE GOT AS IS.
VAL MORETTI AND HIS CREW GOT HIT OUTSIDE OF THE CITY YESTERDAY.
LOOKS LIKE OUR FAVORITE COUPLE IS STILL HARD AT WORK.
CRAZY SHIT.
WE'LL TAKE CARE OF IT.
BUT YOU OWE ME.
BESIDES-- IT'S BETTER THAN A SHOP-LIFTING CASE.
MOST ANYTHING IS.
IF IT'S ANY HELP AT ALL--SHIPPING CONTAINER GOTTA COME FROM SOMEWHERE.
AND IF IT'S TRAFFICKING, IT HAS TO BE CONNECTED TO LEON MUTTI, RIGHT?
YUP. SLICK MOTHERFUCKER.
WASN'T HE PART OF THAT BIG THING LAST YEAR? WALKED, RIGHT?
THAT WAS SOME BULLSHIT.

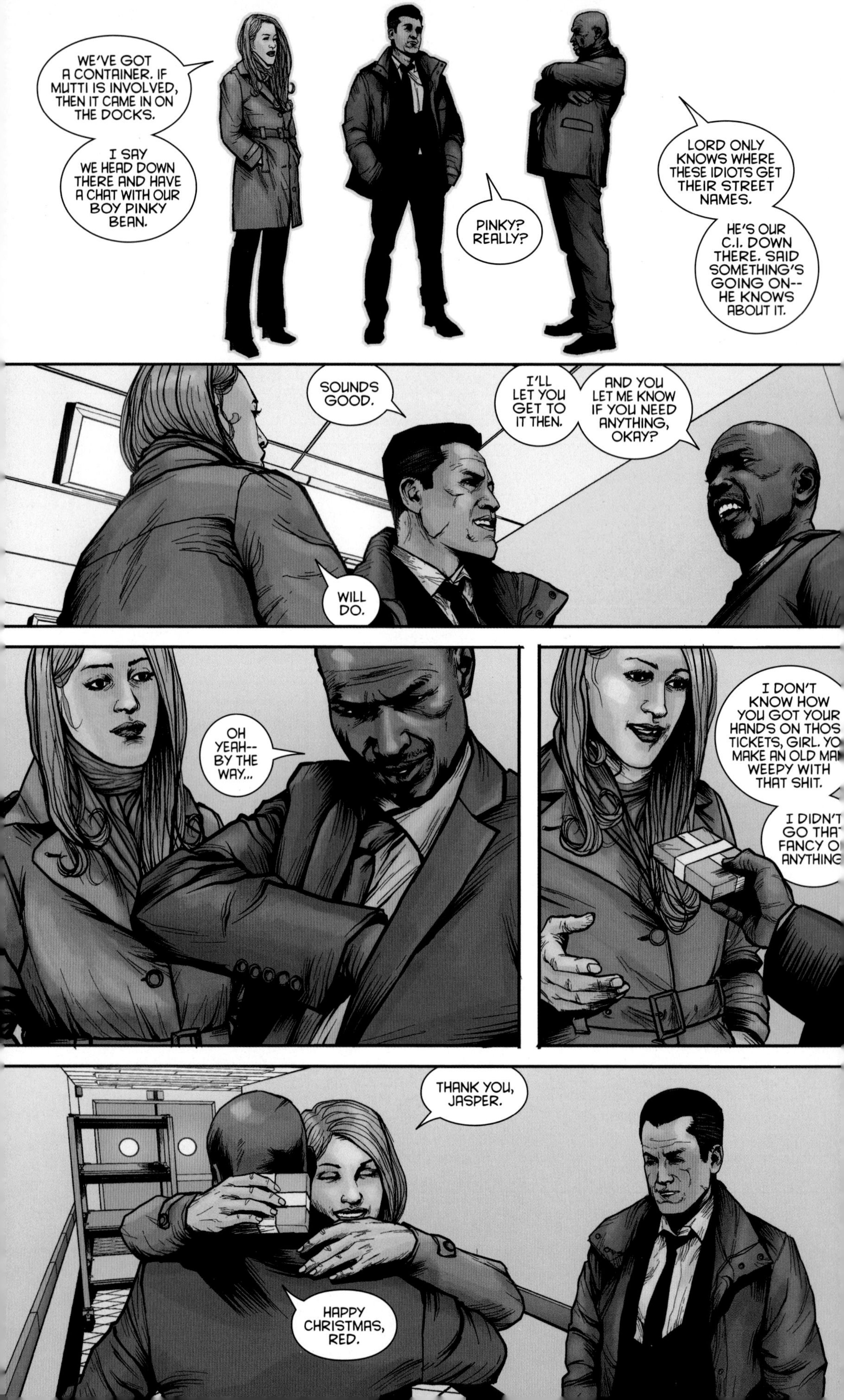

WE'VE GOT A CONTAINER. IF MUTTI IS INVOLVED, THEN IT CAME IN ON THE DOCKS.
I SAY WE HEAD DOWN THERE AND HAVE A CHAT WITH OUR BOY PINKY BEAN.
PINKY? REALLY?
LORD ONLY KNOWS WHERE THESE IDIOTS GET THEIR STREET NAMES.
HE'S OUR C.I. DOWN THERE. SAID SOMETHING'S GOING ON-- HE KNOWS ABOUT IT.
SOUNDS GOOD.
I'LL LET YOU GET TO IT THEN.
AND YOU LET ME KNOW IF YOU NEED ANYTHING, OKAY?
WILL DO.
OH YEAH-- BY THE WAY...
I DON'T KNOW HOW YOU GOT YOUR HANDS ON THOS TICKETS, GIRL. YO MAKE AN OLD MA WEEPY WITH THAT SHIT.
I DIDN'T GO THA FANCY O ANYTHING
THANK YOU, JASPER.
HAPPY CHRISTMAS, RED.

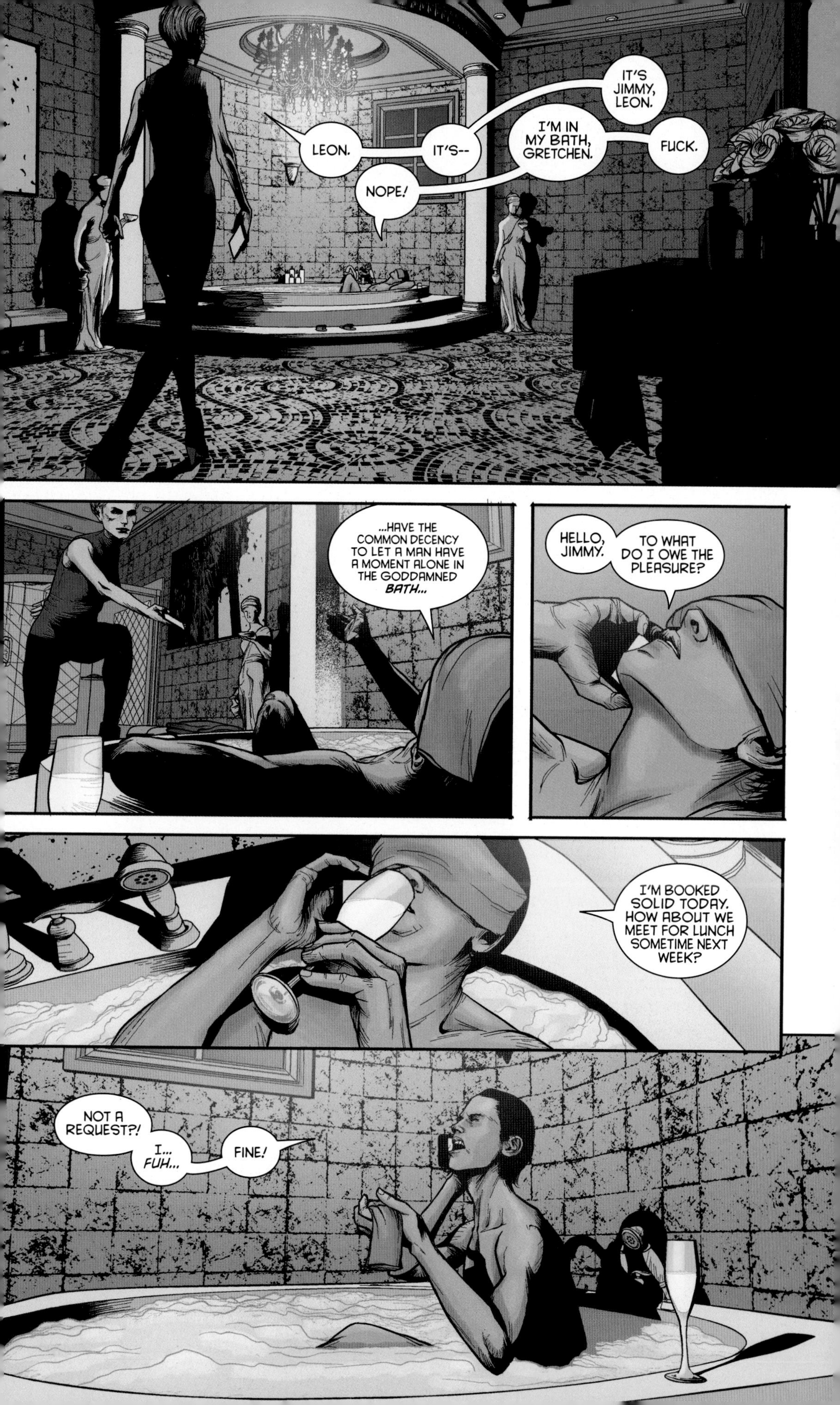
LEON.
IT'S--
IT'S JIMMY, LEON.
I'M IN MY BATH, GRETCHEN.
FUCK.
NOPE!
...HAVE THE COMMON DECENCY TO LET A MAN HAVE A MOMENT ALONE IN THE GODDAMNED *BATH*...
HELLO, JIMMY.
TO WHAT DO I OWE THE PLEASURE?
I'M BOOKED SOLID TODAY. HOW ABOUT WE MEET FOR LUNCH SOMETIME NEXT WEEK?
NOT A REQUEST?!
I... *FUH*...
FINE!

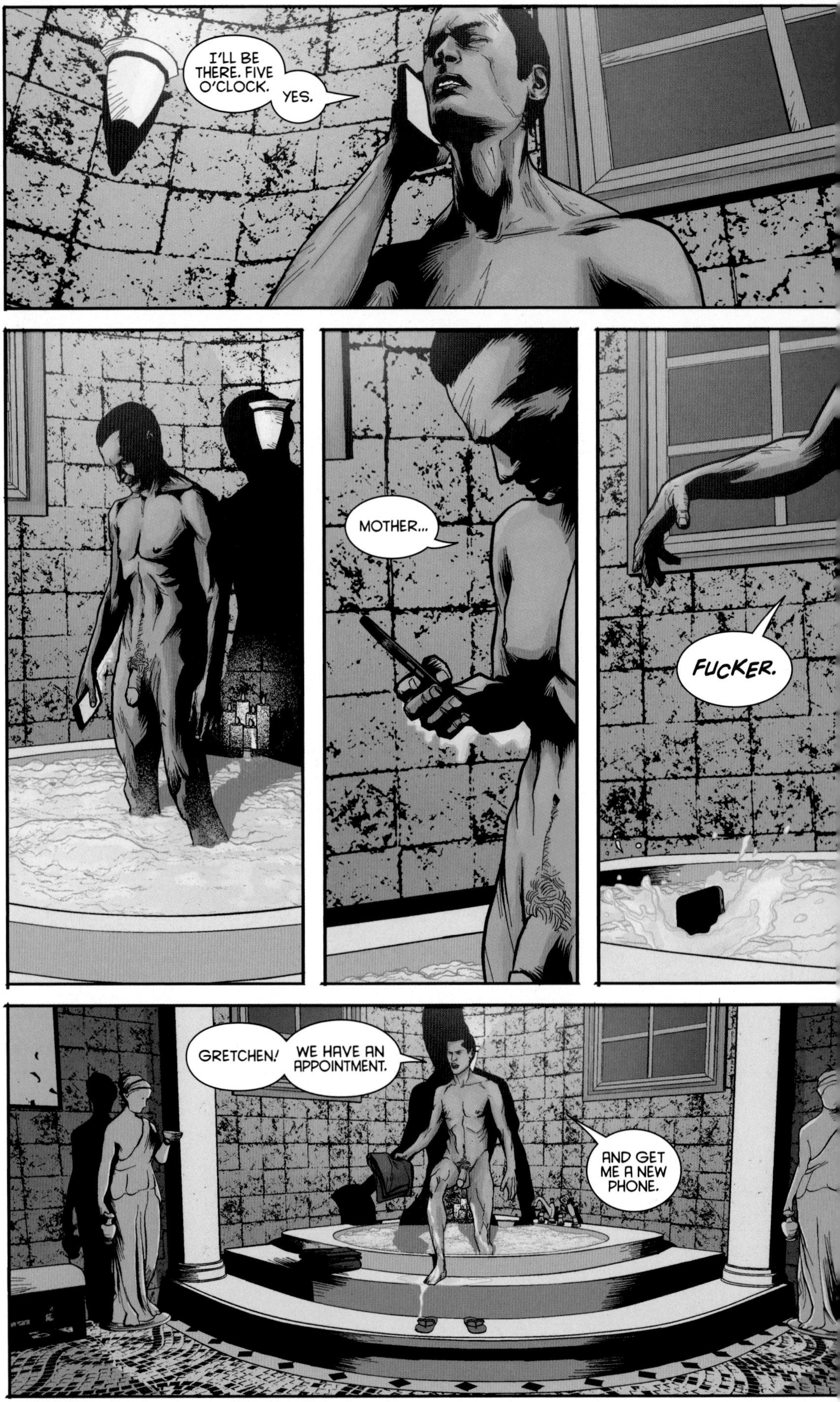
I'LL BE THERE. FIVE O'CLOCK.
YES.
MOTHER...
FUCKER.
GRETCHEN!
WE HAVE AN APPOINTMENT.
AND GET ME A NEW PHONE.

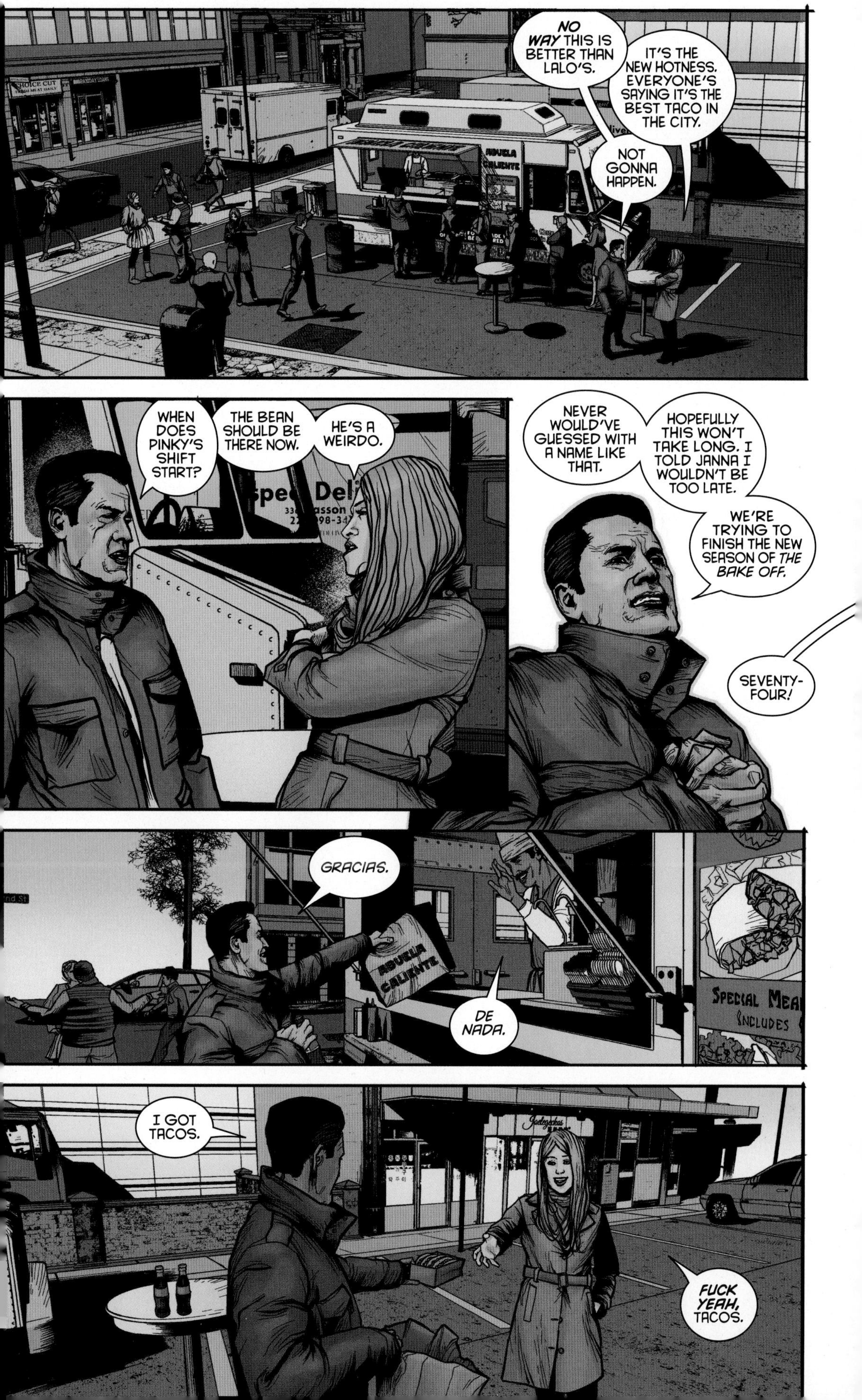
NO WAY THIS IS BETTER THAN LALO'S.
IT'S THE NEW HOTNESS. EVERYONE'S SAYING IT'S THE BEST TACO IN THE CITY.
NOT GONNA HAPPEN.
ABUELA CALIENTE
WHEN DOES PINKY'S SHIFT START?
THE BEAN SHOULD BE THERE NOW.
HE'S A WEIRDO.
NEVER WOULD'VE GUESSED WITH A NAME LIKE THAT.
HOPEFULLY THIS WON'T TAKE LONG. I TOLD JANNA I WOULDN'T BE TOO LATE.
WE'RE TRYING TO FINISH THE NEW SEASON OF THE BAKE OFF.
SEVENTY-FOUR!
GRACIAS.
ABUELA CALIENTE
DE NADA.
SPECIAL MEA
INCLUDES
I GOT TACOS.
FUCK YEAH, TACOS.

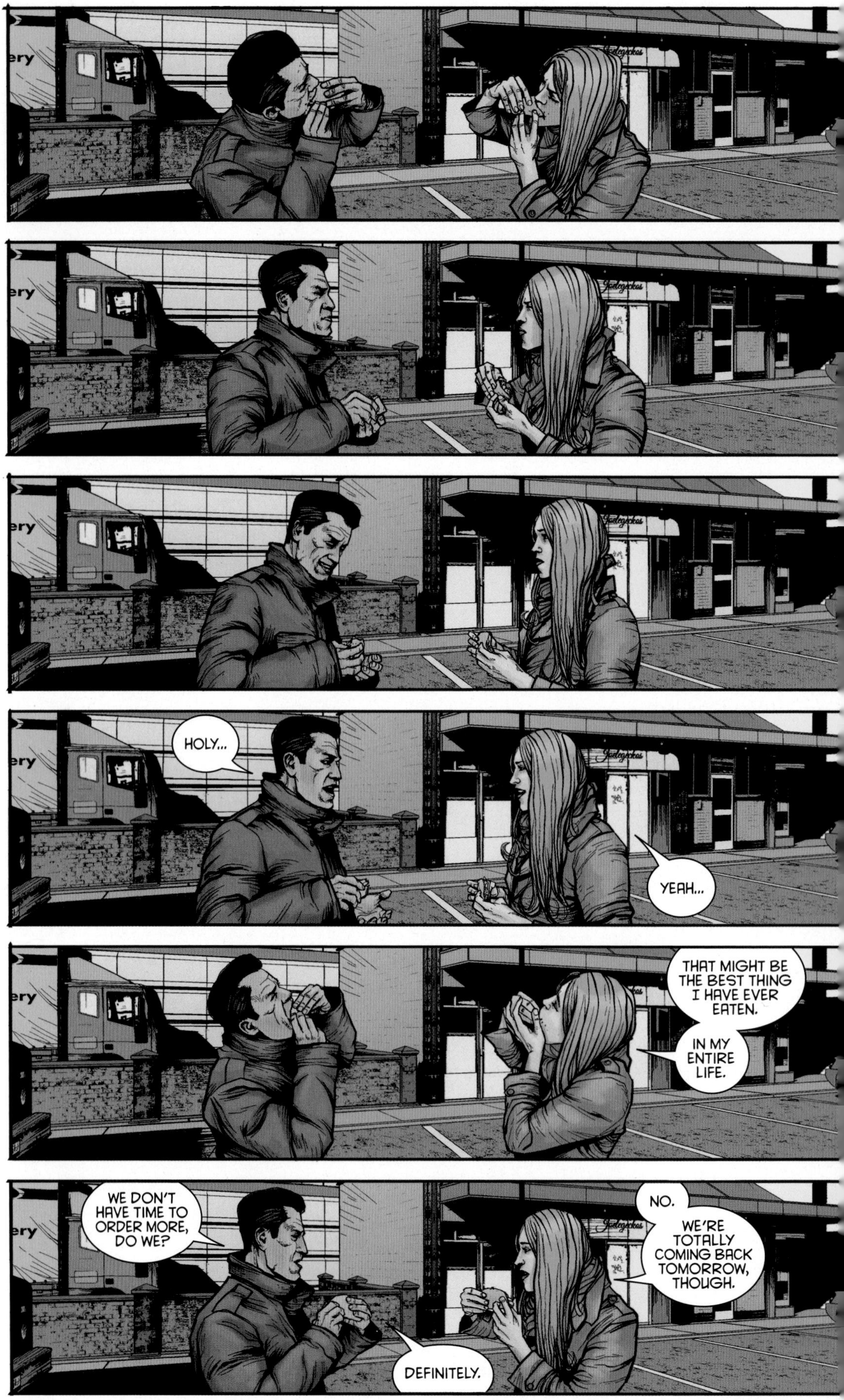

HOLY...
YEAH...
THAT MIGHT BE THE BEST THING I HAVE EVER EATEN.
IN MY ENTIRE LIFE.
WE DON'T HAVE TIME TO ORDER MORE, DO WE?
NO.
WE'RE TOTALLY COMING BACK TOMORROW, THOUGH.
DEFINITELY.

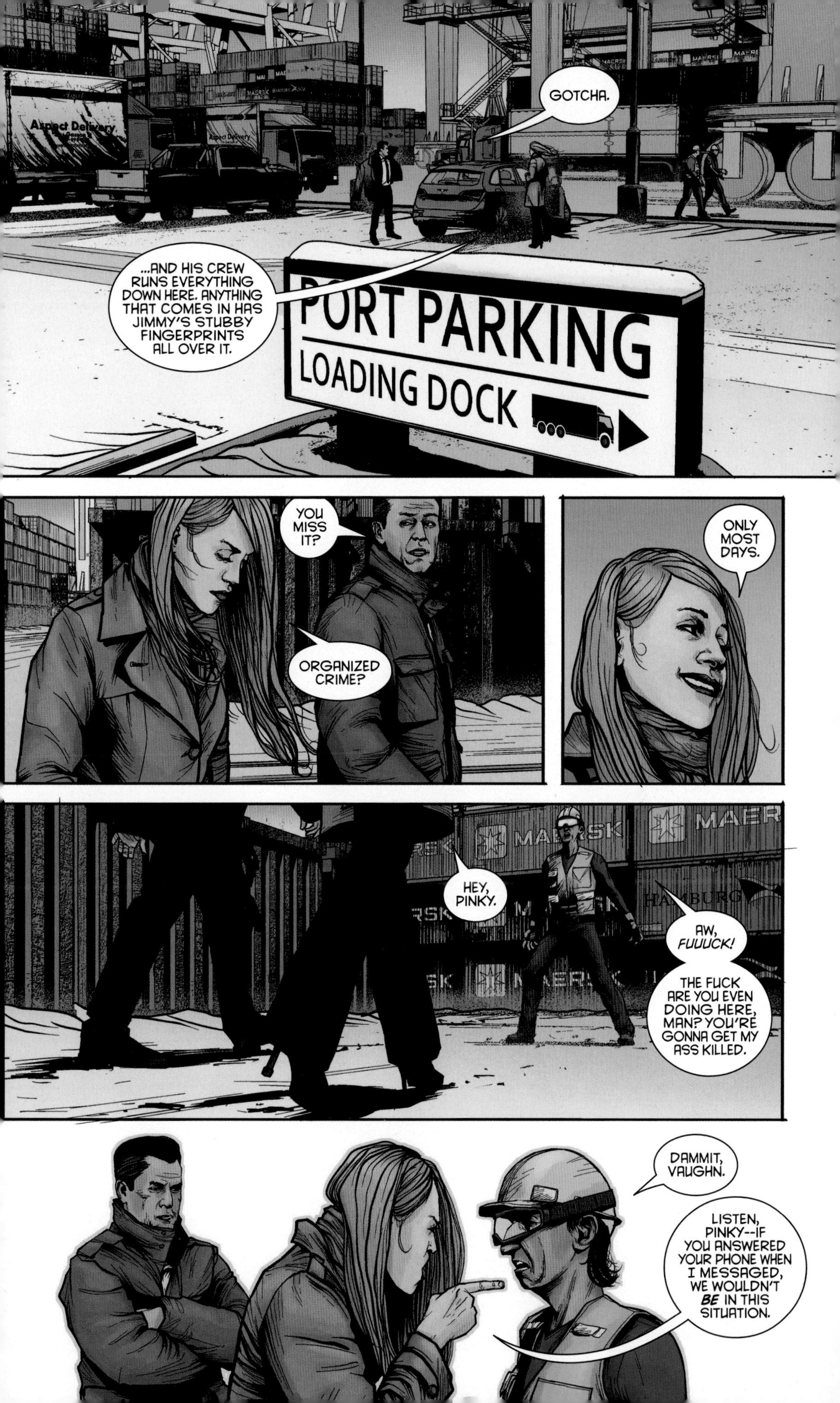
GOTCHA.
...AND HIS CREW RUNS EVERYTHING DOWN HERE. ANYTHING THAT COMES IN HAS JIMMY'S STUBBY FINGERPRINTS ALL OVER IT.
PORT PARKING
LOADING DOCK
YOU MISS IT?
ORGANIZED CRIME?
ONLY MOST DAYS.
HEY, PINKY.
AW, *FUUUCK!*
THE FUCK ARE YOU EVEN DOING HERE, MAN? YOU'RE GONNA GET MY ASS KILLED.
DAMMIT, VAUGHN.
LISTEN, PINKY--IF YOU ANSWERED YOUR PHONE WHEN I MESSAGED, WE WOULDN'T ***BE*** IN THIS SITUATION.

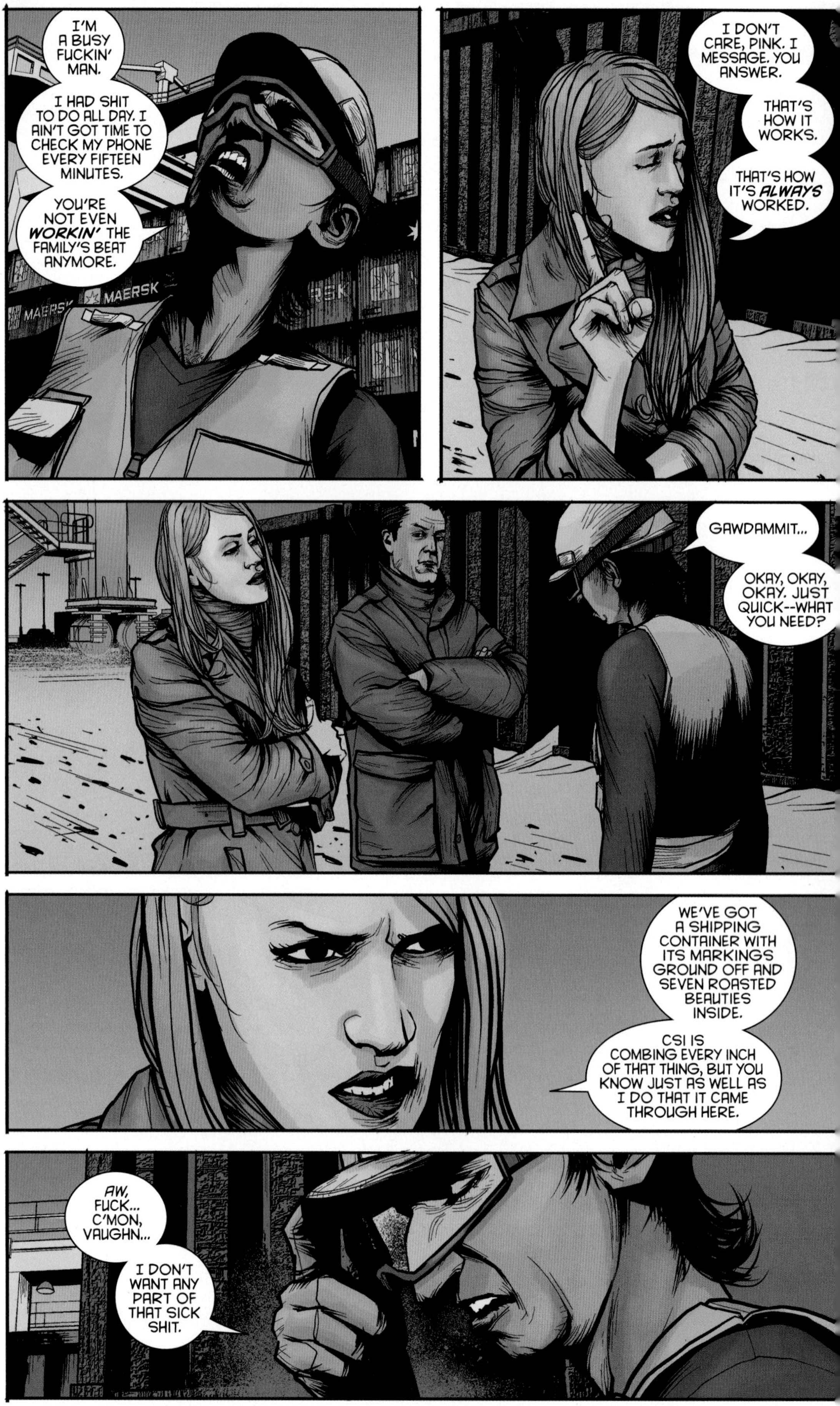
I'M A BUSY FUCKIN' MAN.
I HAD SHIT TO DO ALL DAY. I AIN'T GOT TIME TO CHECK MY PHONE EVERY FIFTEEN MINUTES.
YOU'RE NOT EVEN ***WORKIN'*** THE FAMILY'S BEAT ANYMORE.
MAERSK
MAERSK
I DON'T CARE, PINK. I MESSAGE. YOU ANSWER.
THAT'S HOW IT WORKS.
THAT'S HOW IT'S ***ALWAYS*** WORKED.
GAWDAMMIT...
OKAY, OKAY, OKAY. JUST QUICK--WHAT YOU NEED?
WE'VE GOT A SHIPPING CONTAINER WITH ITS MARKINGS GROUND OFF AND SEVEN ROASTED BEAUTIES INSIDE.
CSI IS COMBING EVERY INCH OF THAT THING, BUT YOU KNOW JUST AS WELL AS I DO THAT IT CAME THROUGH HERE.
AW, FUCK... C'MON, VAUGHN...
I DON'T WANT ANY PART OF THAT SICK SHIT.

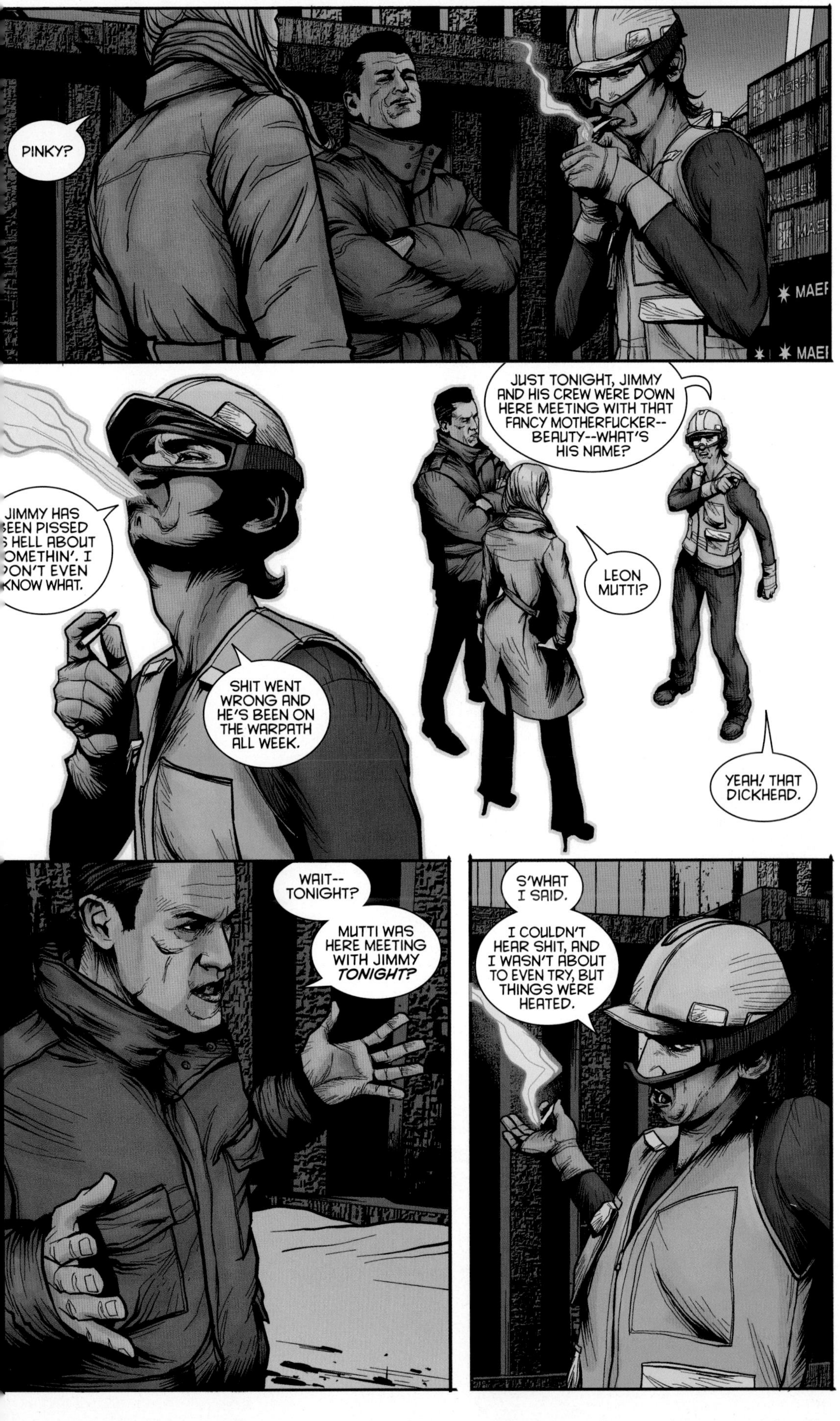
PINKY?
JIMMY HAS
BEEN PISSED
AS HELL ABOUT
SOMETHIN'. I
DON'T EVEN
KNOW WHAT.
SHIT WENT WRONG AND HE'S BEEN ON THE WARPATH ALL WEEK.
JUST TONIGHT, JIMMY AND HIS CREW WERE DOWN HERE MEETING WITH THAT FANCY MOTHERFUCKER-- BEAUTY--WHAT'S HIS NAME?
LEON MUTTI?
YEAH! THAT DICKHEAD.
WAIT-- TONIGHT?
MUTTI WAS HERE MEETING WITH JIMMY *TONIGHT?*
S'WHAT I SAID.
I COULDN'T HEAR SHIT, AND I WASN'T ABOUT TO EVEN TRY, BUT THINGS WERE HEATED.

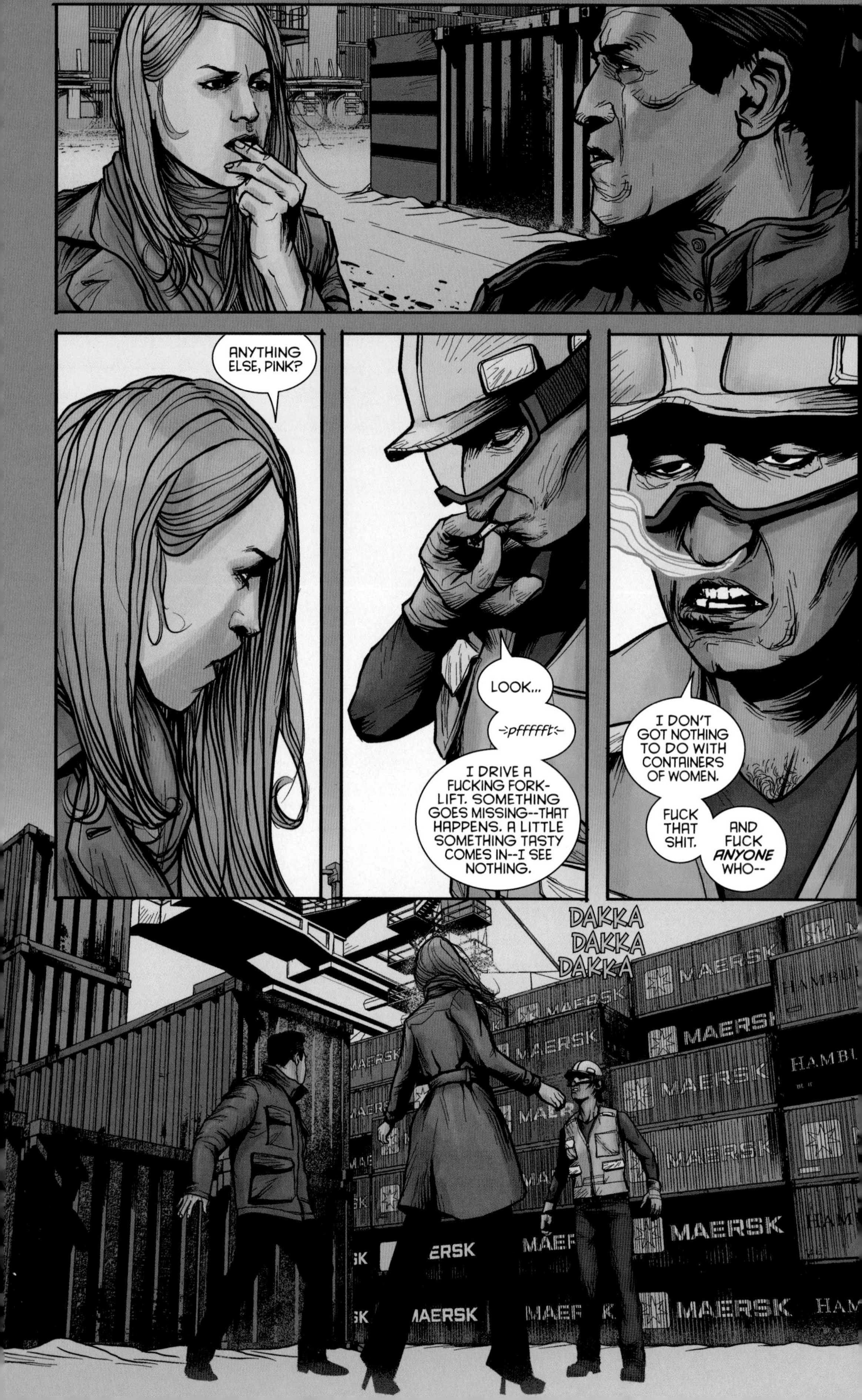

ANYTHING ELSE, PINK?
LOOK...
~pffffft~
I DRIVE A FUCKING FORK-LIFT. SOMETHING GOES MISSING--THAT HAPPENS. A LITTLE SOMETHING TASTY COMES IN--I SEE NOTHING.
I DON'T GOT NOTHING TO DO WITH CONTAINERS OF WOMEN.
FUCK THAT SHIT.
AND FUCK ANYONE WHO--
DAKKA DAKKA DAKKA
MAERSK
HAMB

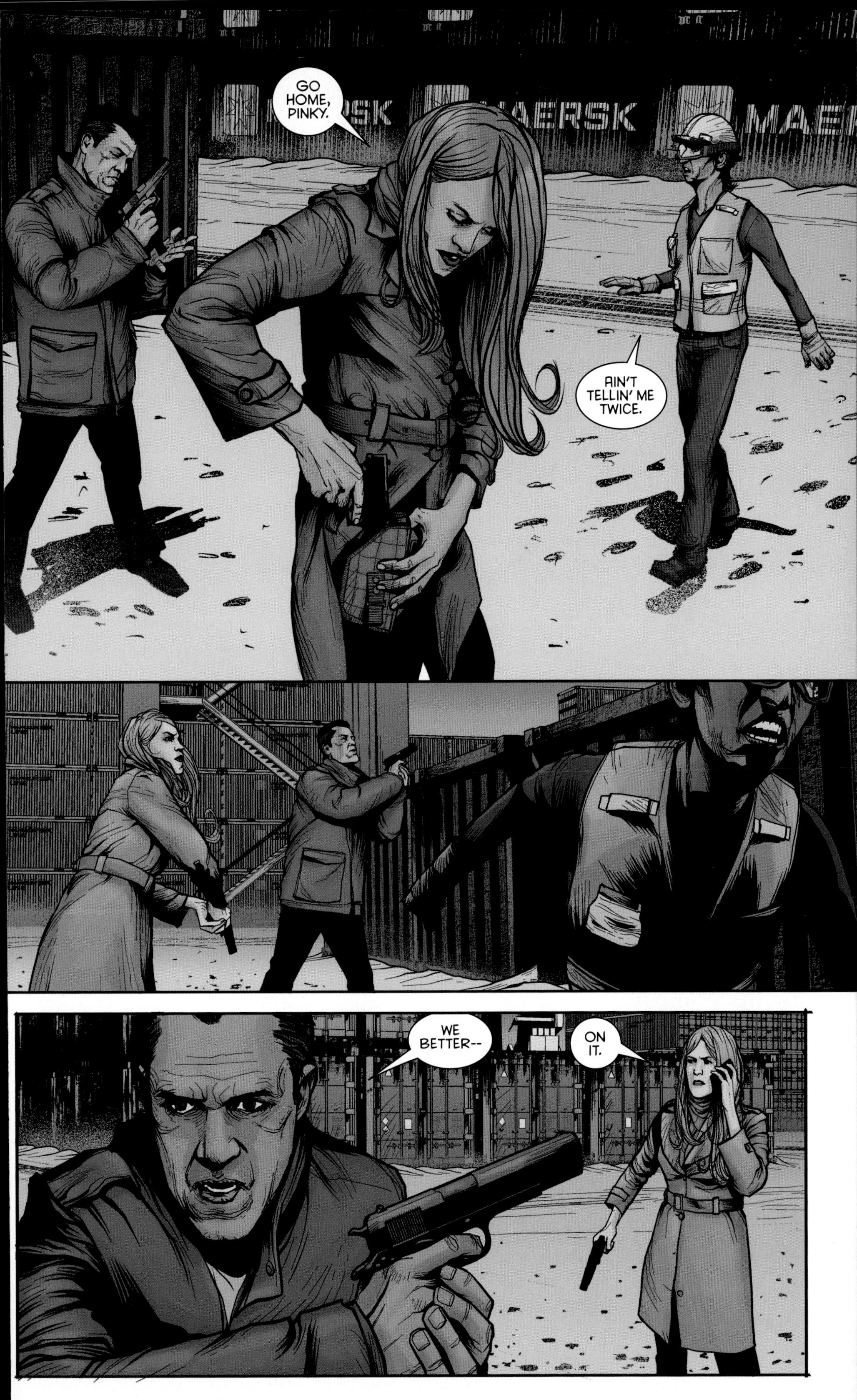
GO HOME, PINKY.
AIN'T TELLIN' ME TWICE.
WE BETTER--
ON IT.

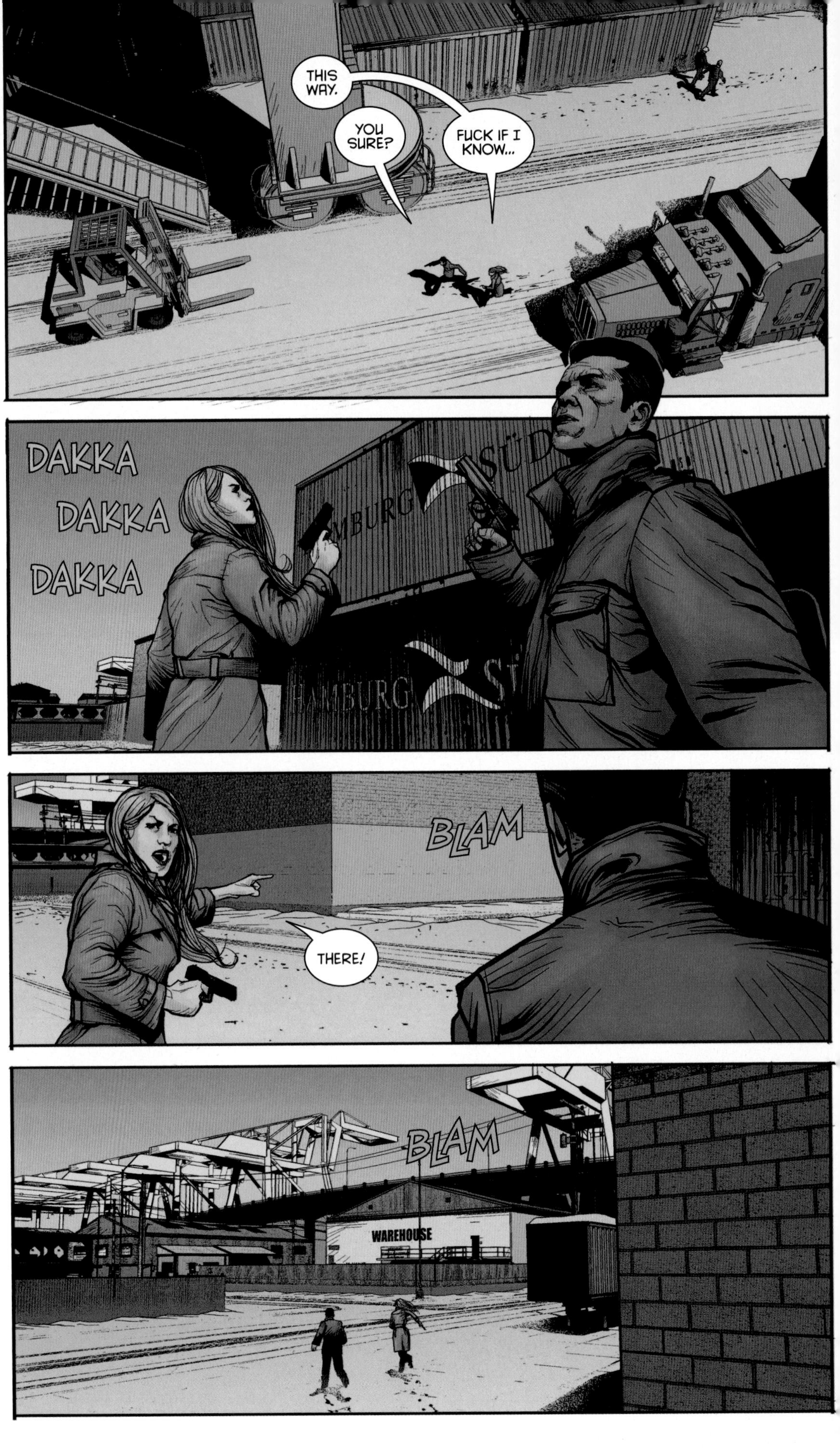
THIS WAY.
YOU SURE?
FUCK IF I KNOW...
DAKKA
DAKKA
DAKKA
BLAM
THERE!
BLAM
WAREHOUSE

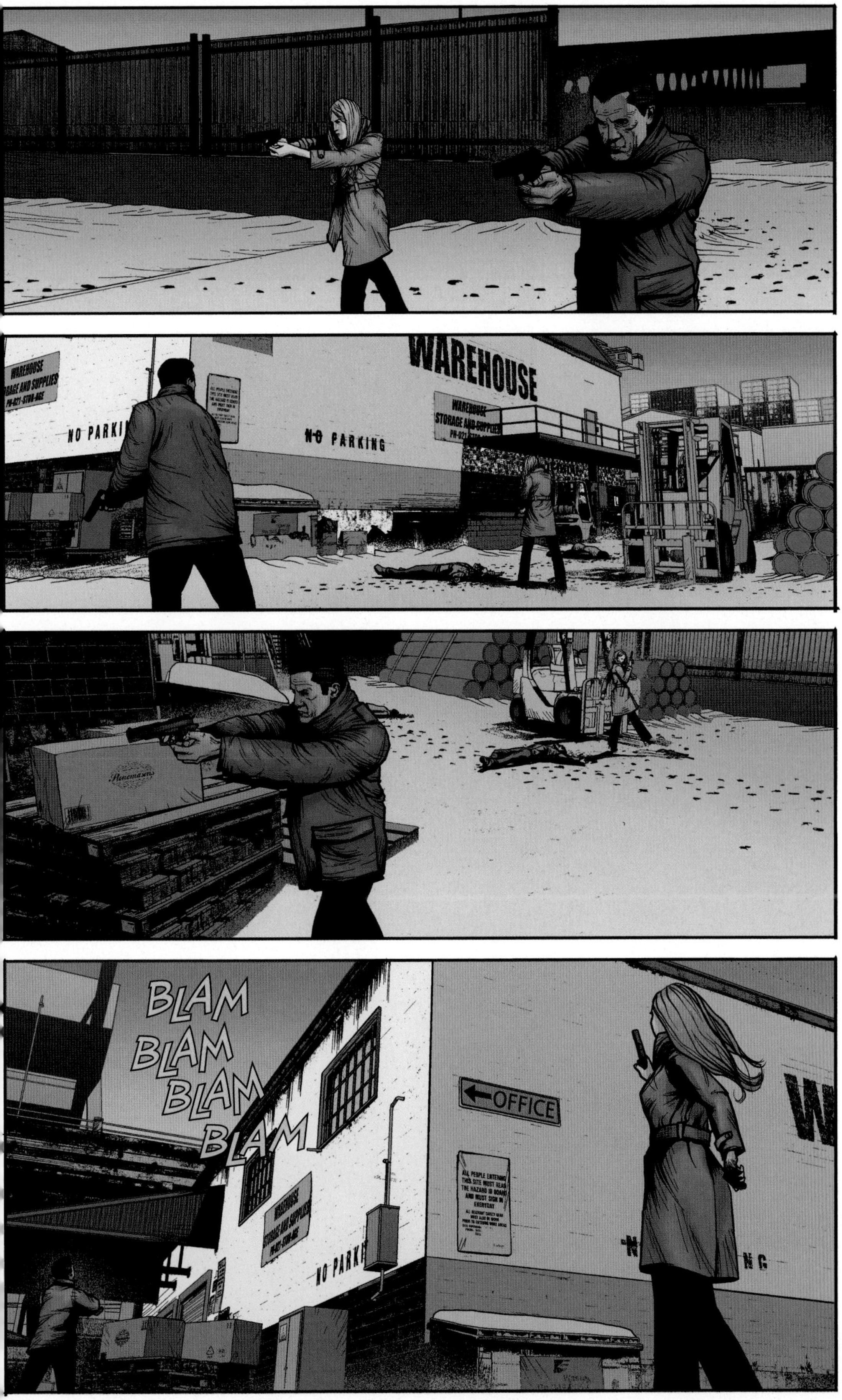

WAREHOUSE
STORAGE AND SUPPLIES
NO PARKI
WAREHOUSE
NO PARKING
WAREHOUSE
STORAGE AND SUPPLIES
BLAM
BLAM
BLAM
BLAM
OFFICE
WAREHOUSE
STORAGE AND SUPPLIES
NO PARKI

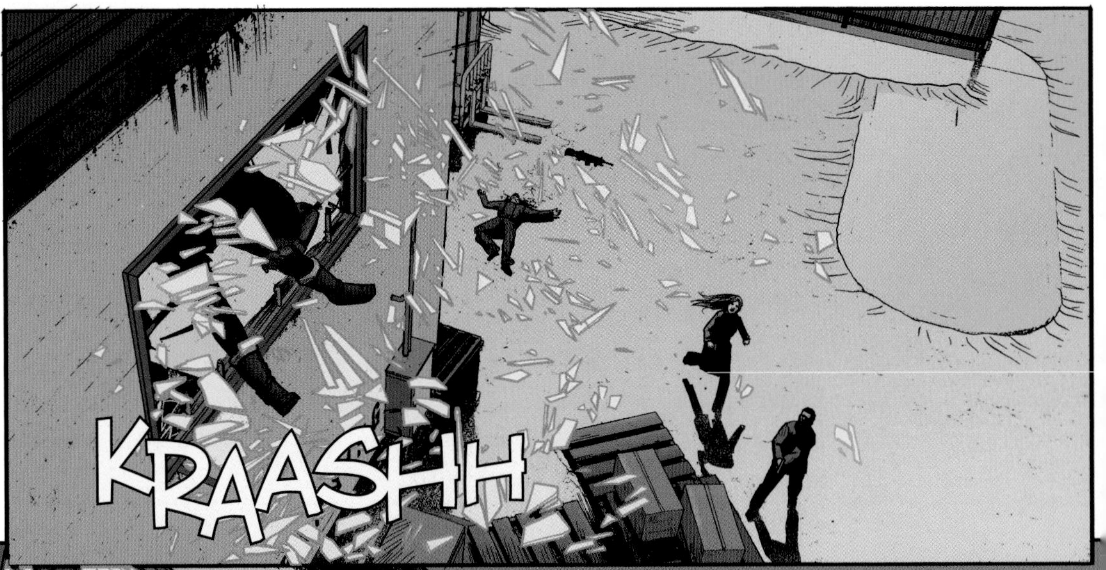
KRAASHH

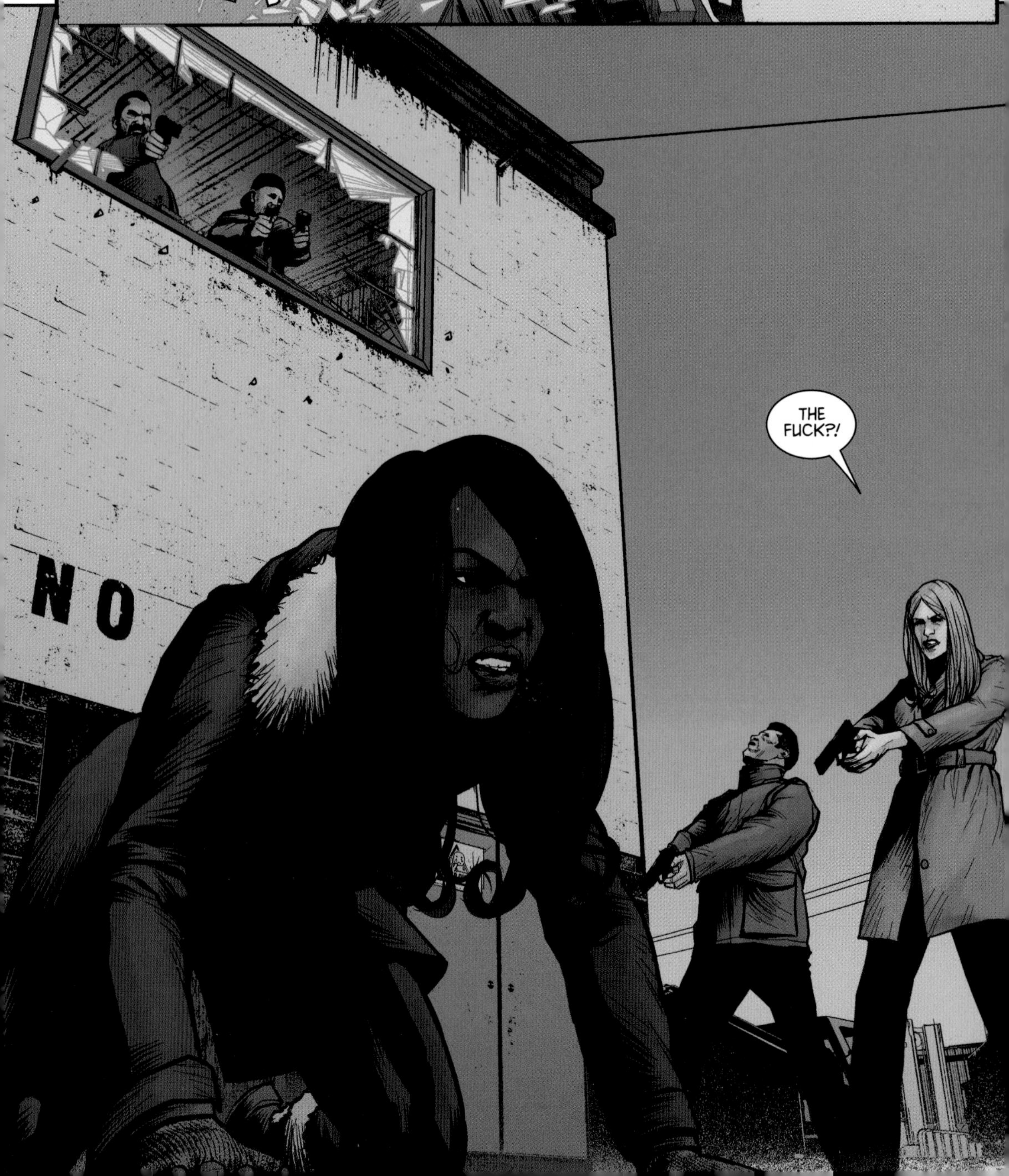
THE FUCK?!
NO

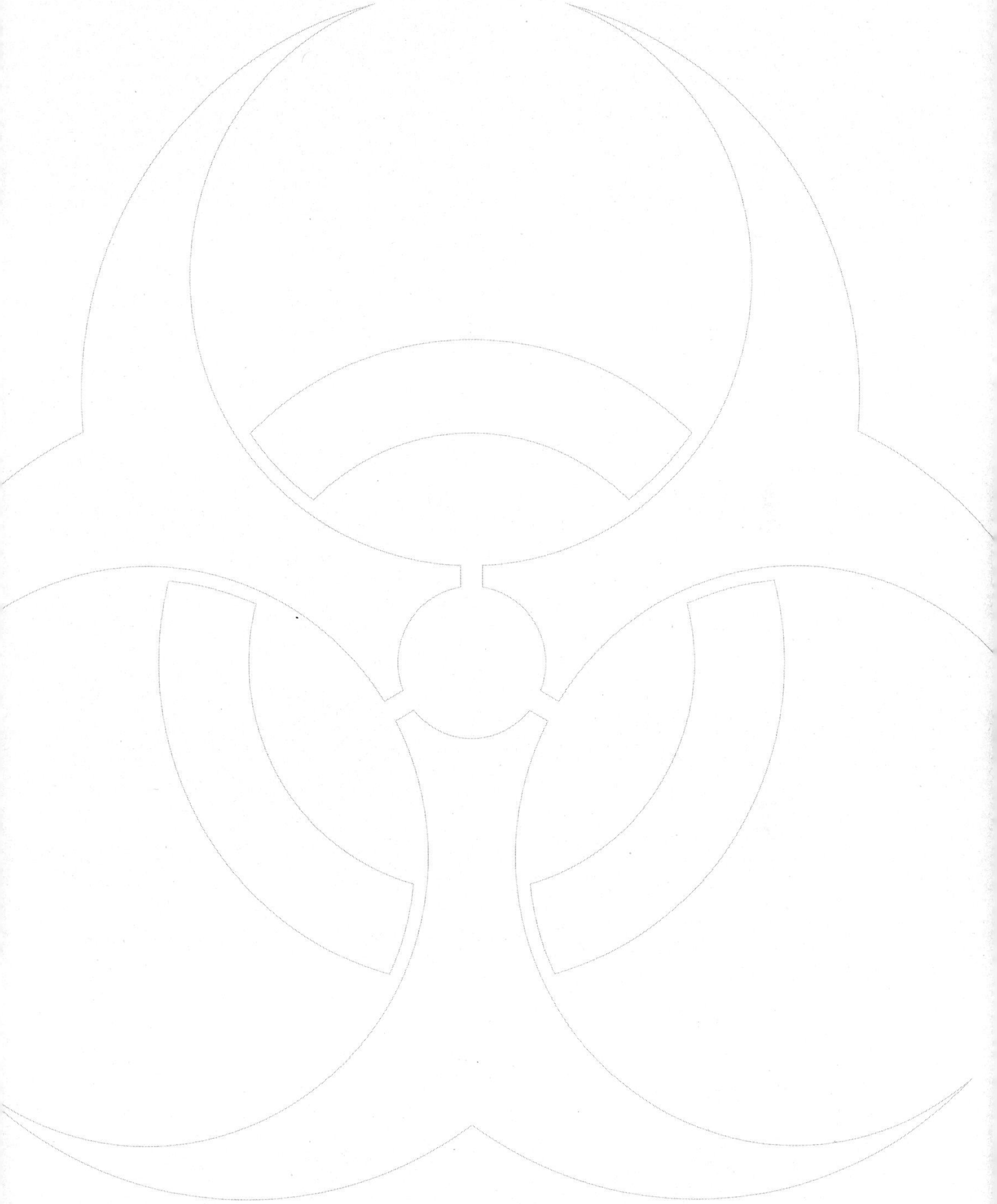

CHAPTER

25

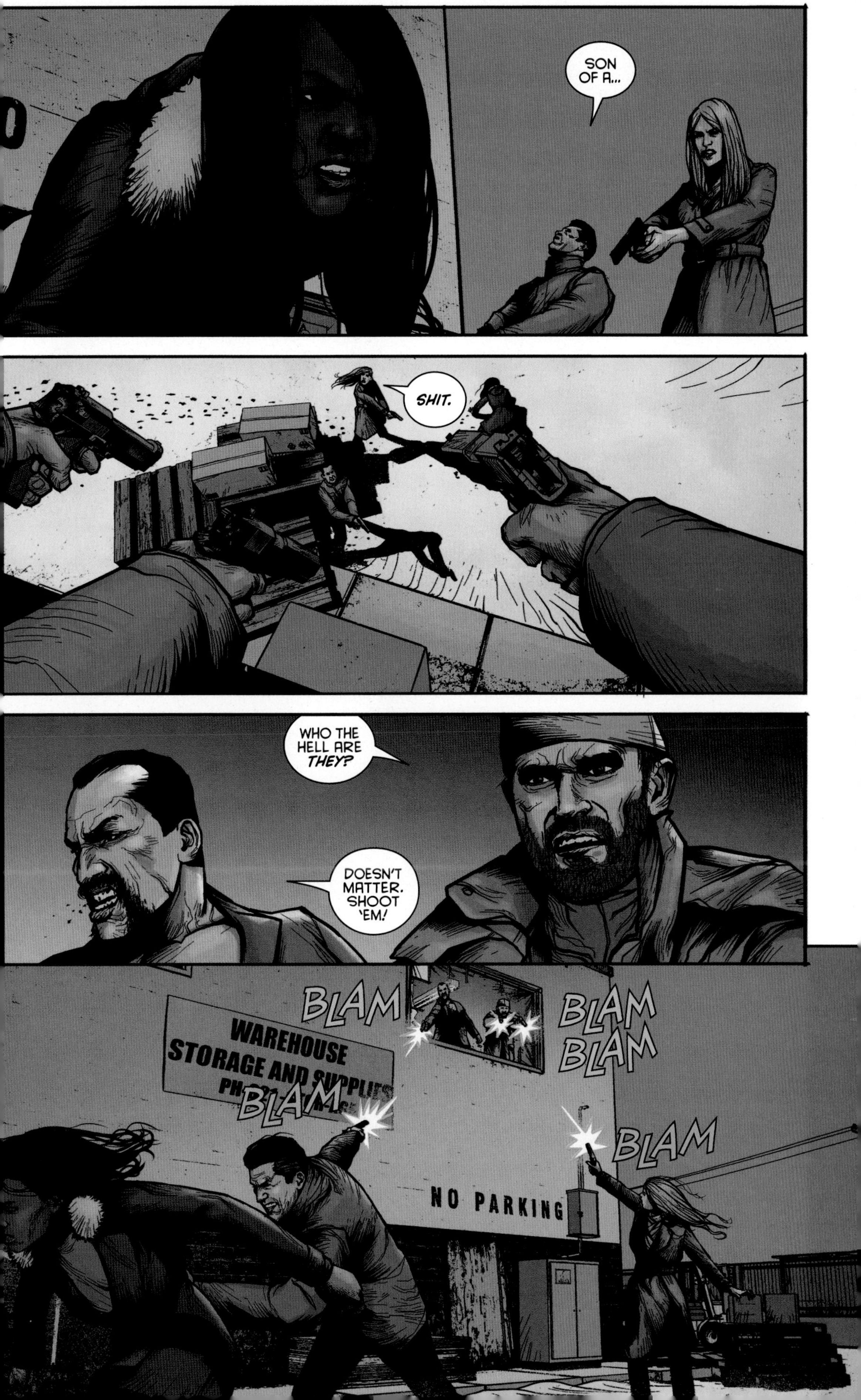
SON OF A...
SHIT.
WHO THE HELL ARE *THEY?*
DOESN'T MATTER. SHOOT 'EM!
BLAM
BLAM
BLAM
WAREHOUSE
STORAGE AND SUPPLIES
BLAM
BLAM
NO PARKING

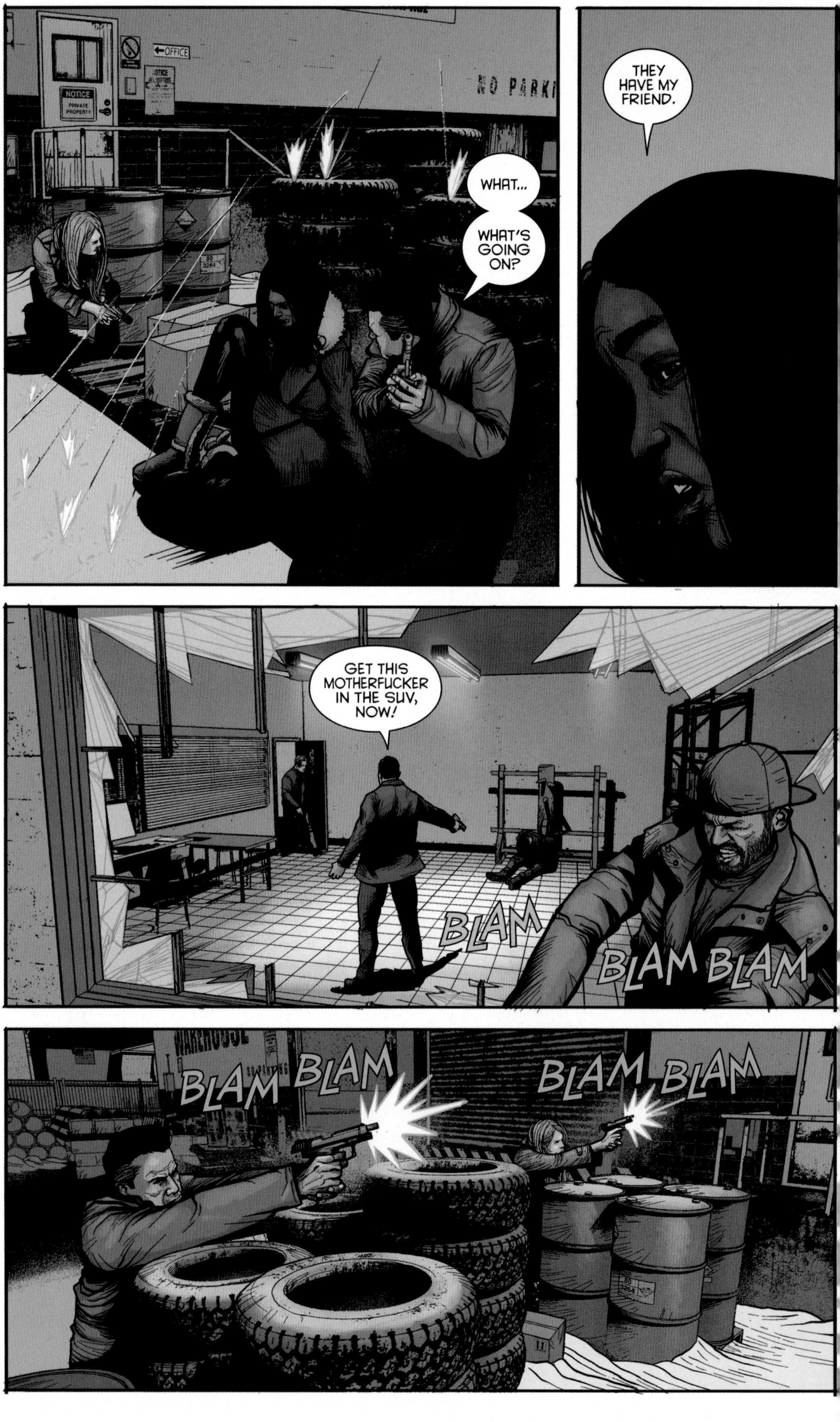
NOTICE
PRIVATE PROPERTY
OFFICE
NO PARKI
WHAT...
WHAT'S GOING ON?
THEY HAVE MY FRIEND.
GET THIS MOTHERFUCKER IN THE SUV, NOW!
BLAM
BLAM BLAM
WAREHOUSE
BLAM BLAM
BLAM BLAM

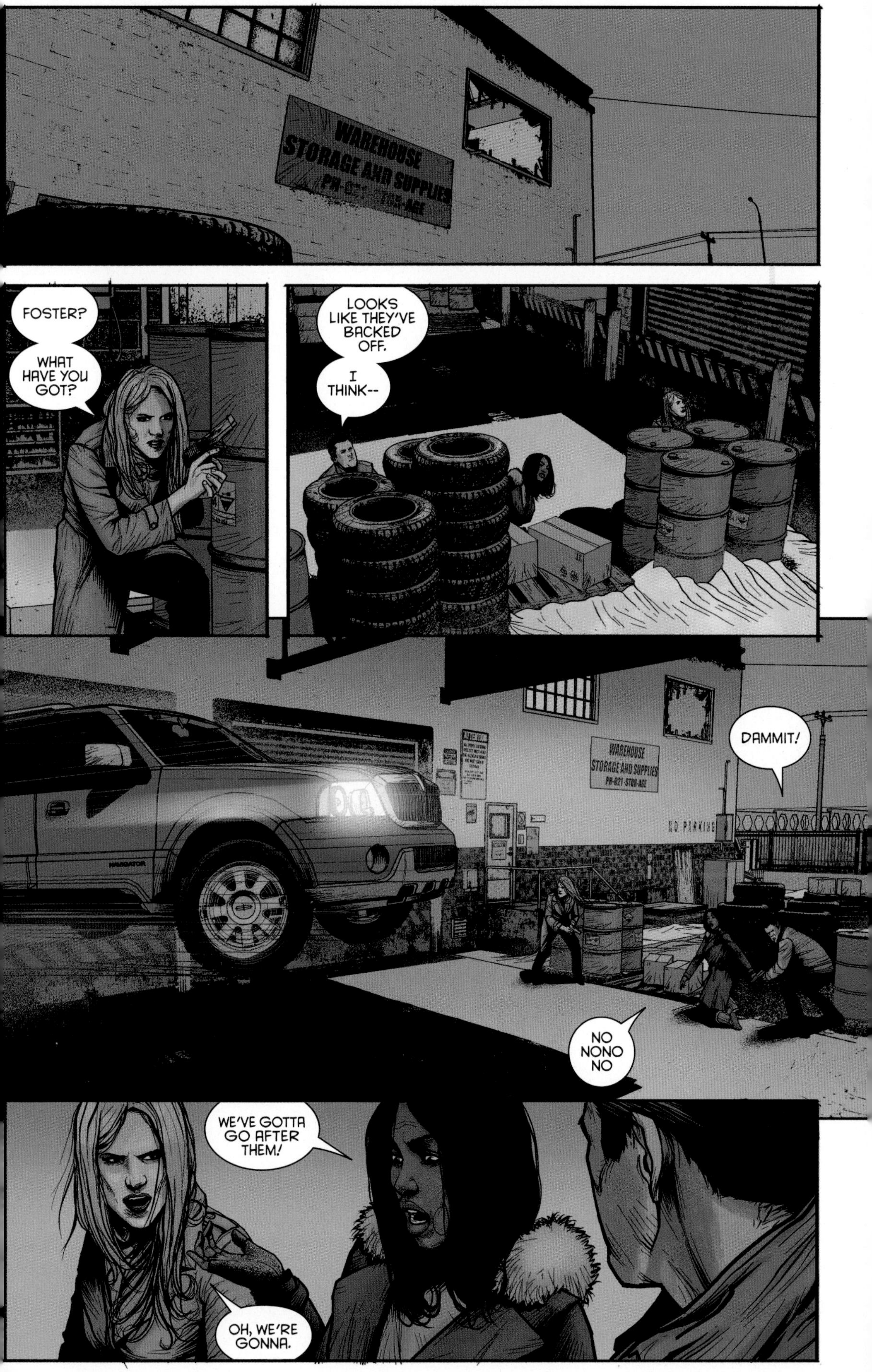
WAREHOUSE
STORAGE AND SUPPLIES
FOSTER?
WHAT HAVE YOU GOT?
LOOKS LIKE THEY'VE BACKED OFF.
I THINK--
WAREHOUSE
STORAGE AND SUPPLIES
PH-021-STOR-AGE
NO PARKING
DAMMIT!
NO NONO NO
WE'VE GOTTA GO AFTER THEM!
OH, WE'RE GONNA.

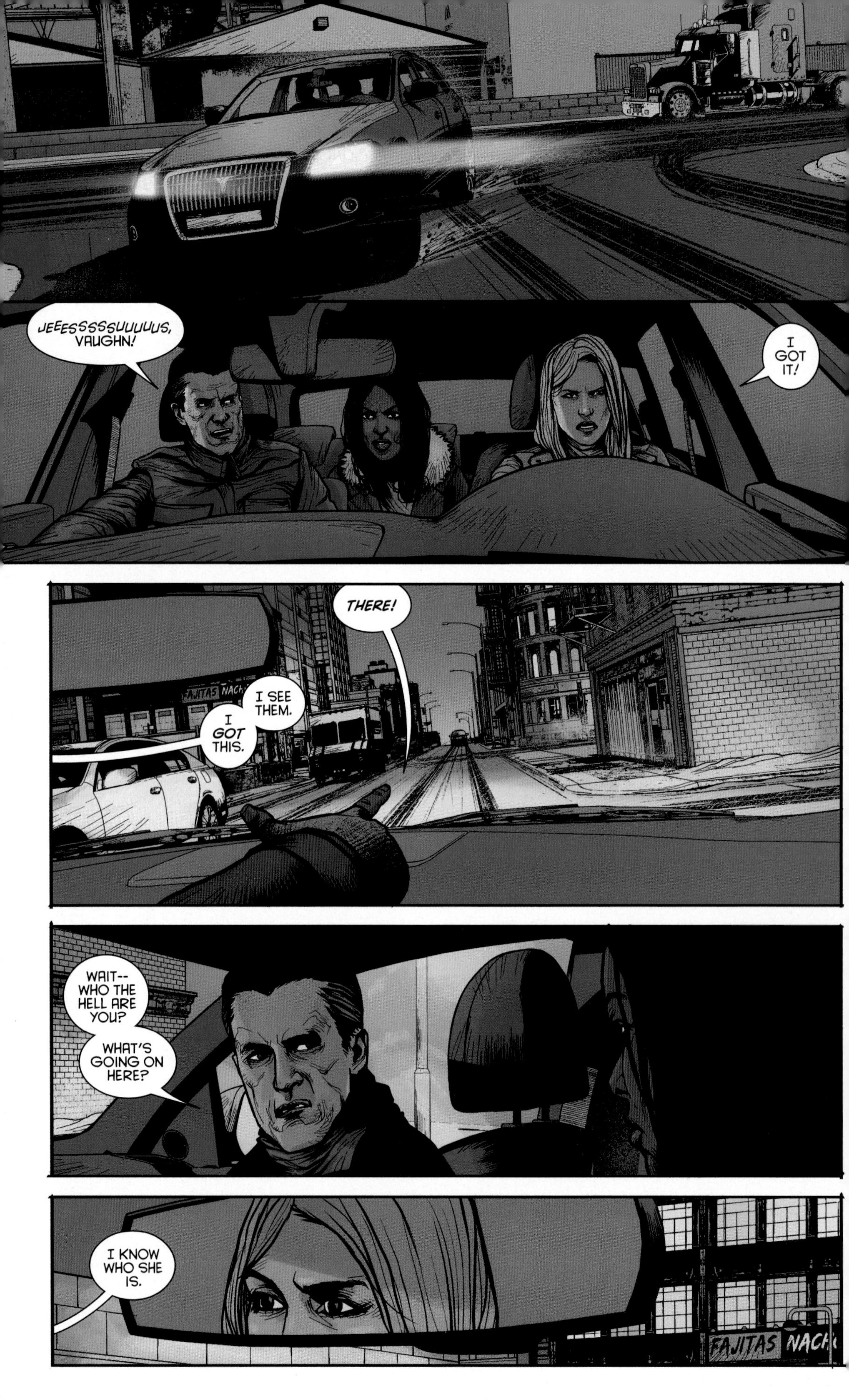
JEEESSSSSUUUUUS, VAUGHN!
I GOT IT!
THERE!
I SEE THEM.
I GOT THIS.
FAJITAS NACH
WAIT-- WHO THE HELL ARE YOU?
WHAT'S GOING ON HERE?
I KNOW WHO SHE IS.
FAJITAS NACH

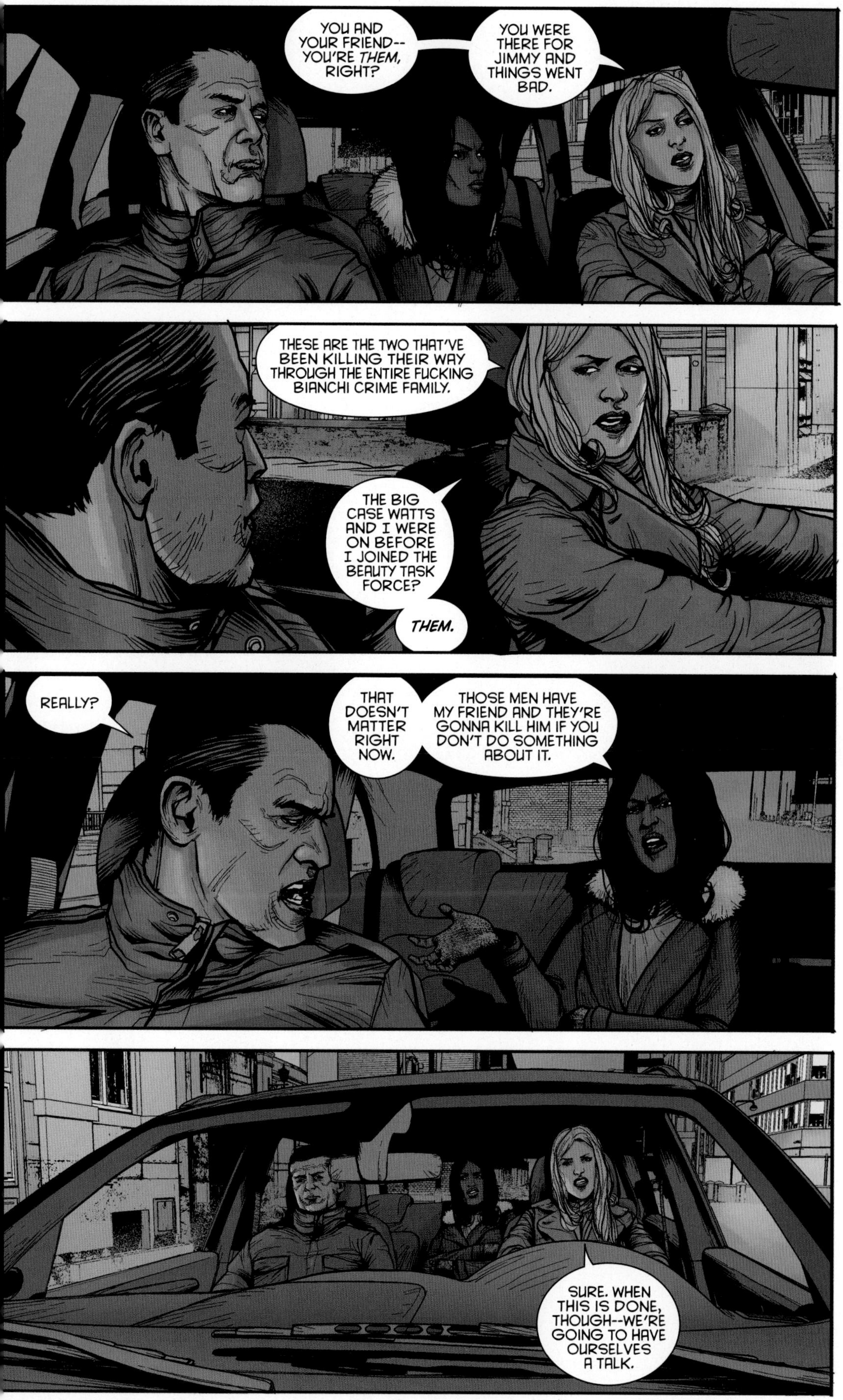
YOU AND YOUR FRIEND-- YOU'RE *THEM*, RIGHT?
YOU WERE THERE FOR JIMMY AND THINGS WENT BAD.
THESE ARE THE TWO THAT'VE BEEN KILLING THEIR WAY THROUGH THE ENTIRE FUCKING BIANCHI CRIME FAMILY.
THE BIG CASE WATTS AND I WERE ON BEFORE I JOINED THE BEAUTY TASK FORCE?
THEM.
REALLY?
THAT DOESN'T MATTER RIGHT NOW.
THOSE MEN HAVE MY FRIEND AND THEY'RE GONNA KILL HIM IF YOU DON'T DO SOMETHING ABOUT IT.
SURE. WHEN THIS IS DONE, THOUGH--WE'RE GOING TO HAVE OURSELVES A TALK.

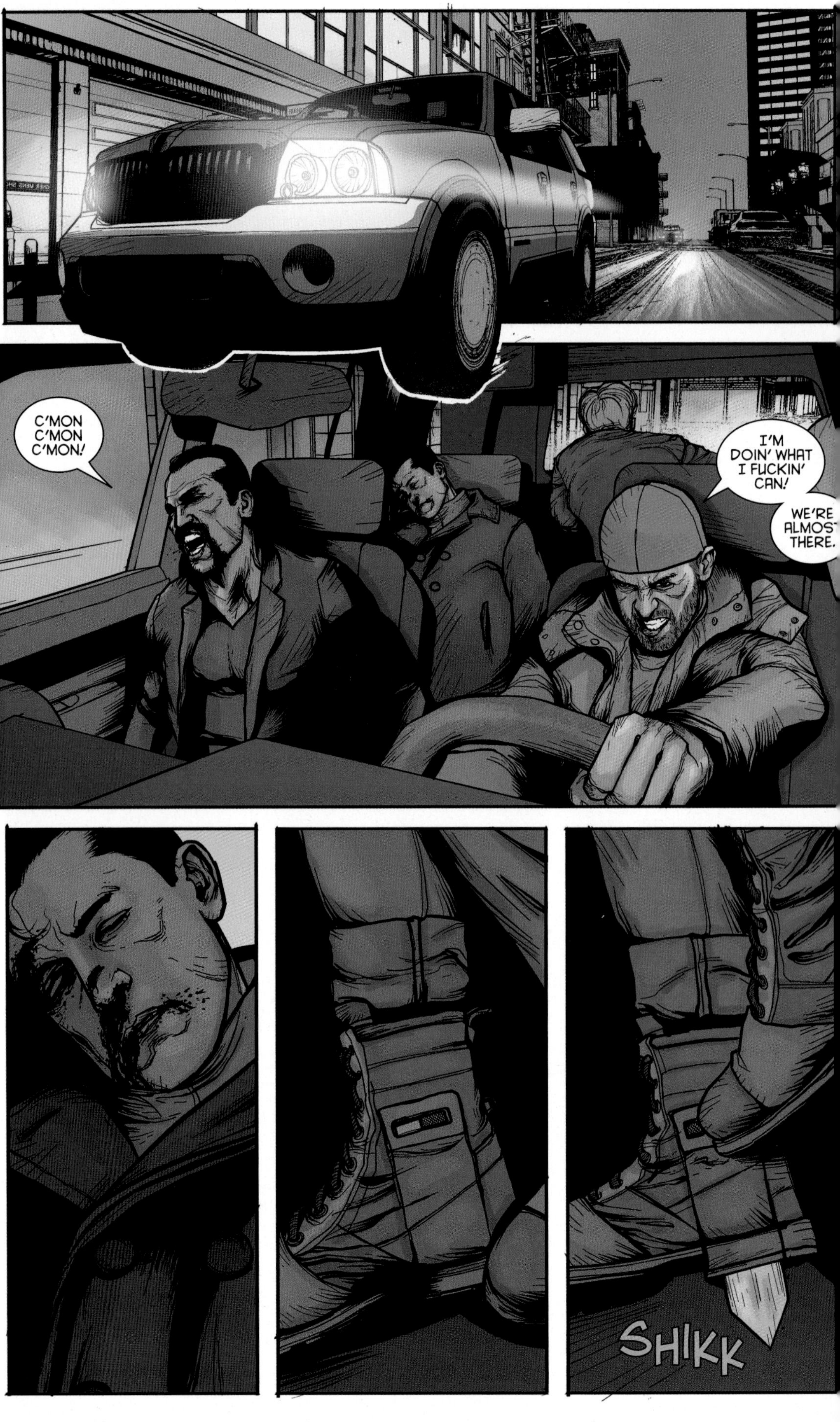

C'MON C'MON C'MON!
I'M DOIN' WHAT I FUCKIN' CAN!
WE'RE ALMOST THERE.
SHIKK

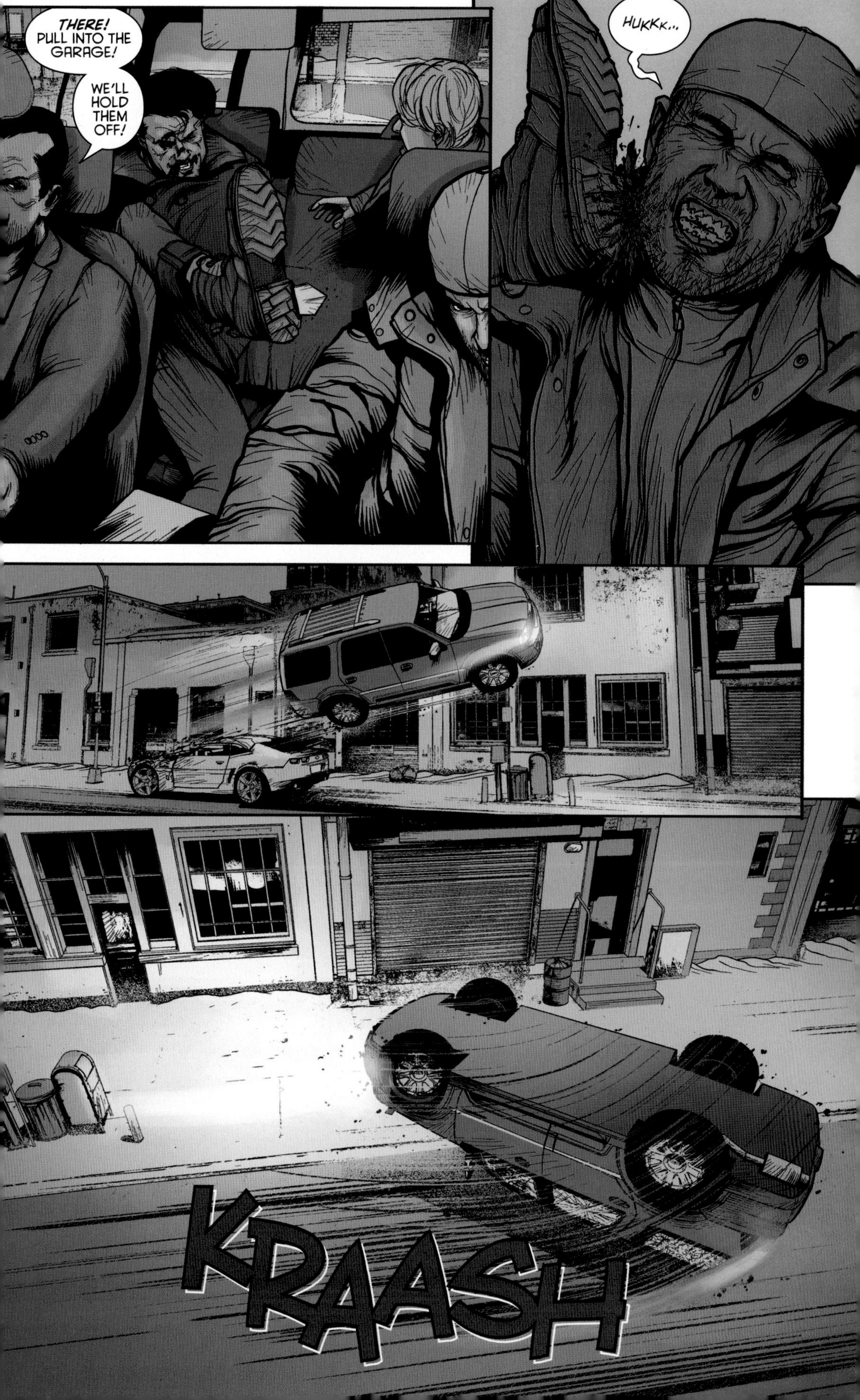
THERE! PULL INTO THE GARAGE!
WE'LL HOLD THEM OFF!
HUKKK...
KRAASH

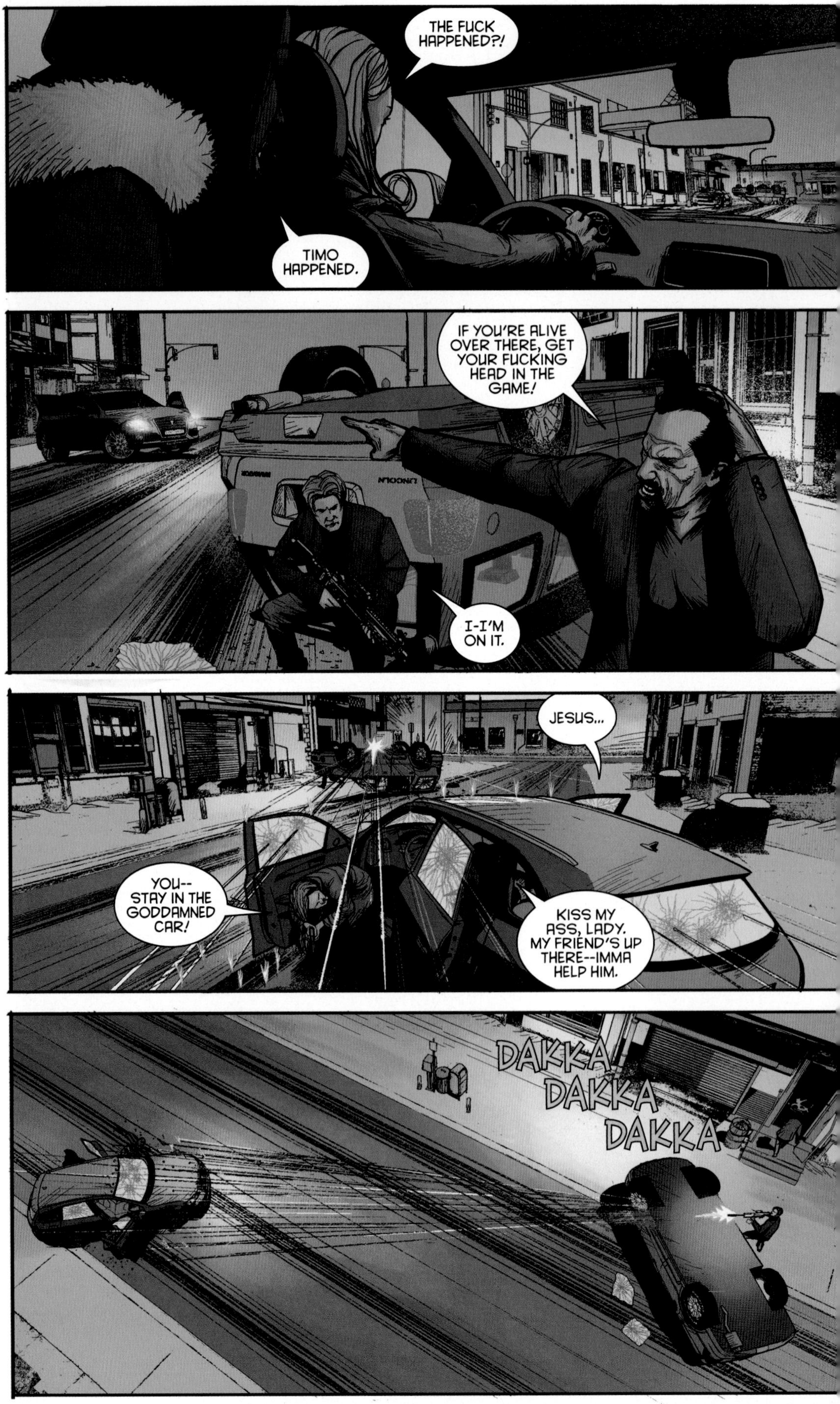
THE FUCK HAPPENED?!
TIMO HAPPENED.
IF YOU'RE ALIVE OVER THERE, GET YOUR FUCKING HEAD IN THE GAME!
I-I'M ON IT.
JESUS...
YOU-- STAY IN THE GODDAMNED CAR!
KISS MY ASS, LADY. MY FRIEND'S UP THERE--IMMA HELP HIM.
DAKKA DAKKA DAKKA

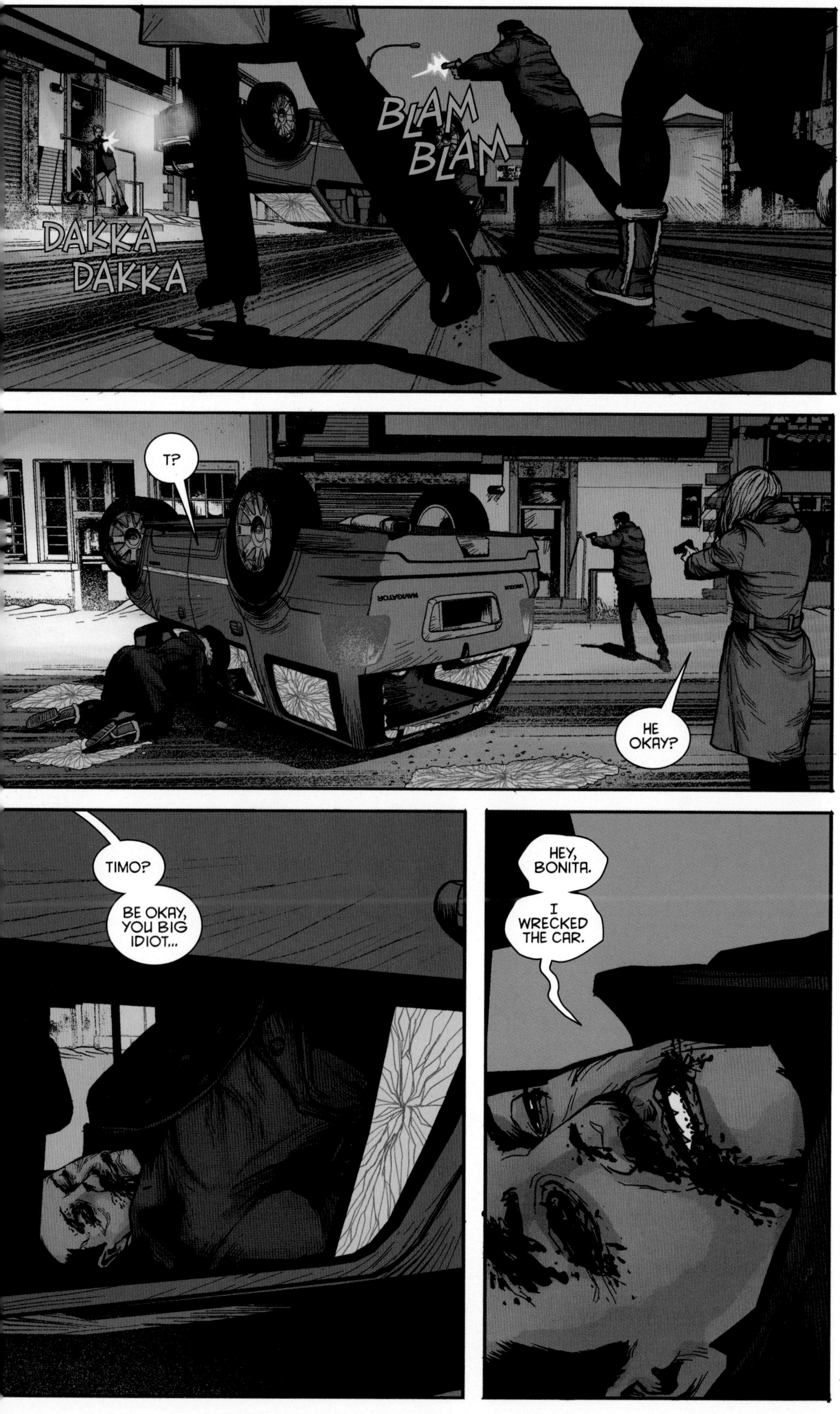
BLAM
BLAM
DAKKA
DAKKA
T?
HE OKAY?
TIMO?
BE OKAY, YOU BIG IDIOT...
HEY, BONITA.
I WRECKED THE CAR.

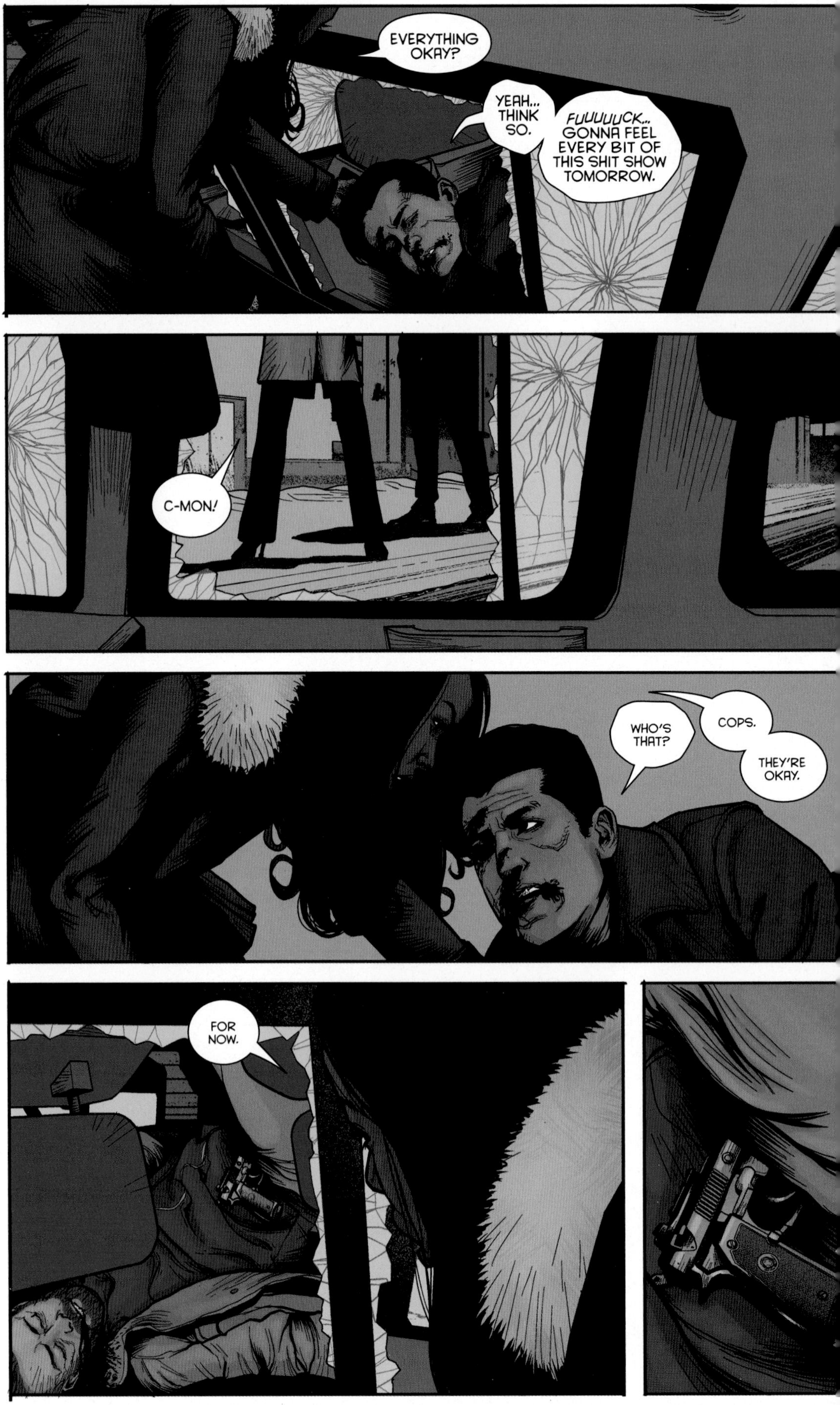
EVERYTHING OKAY?
YEAH... THINK SO.
FUUUUUCK... GONNA FEEL EVERY BIT OF THIS SHIT SHOW TOMORROW.
C-MON!
WHO'S THAT?
COPS.
THEY'RE OKAY.
FOR NOW.

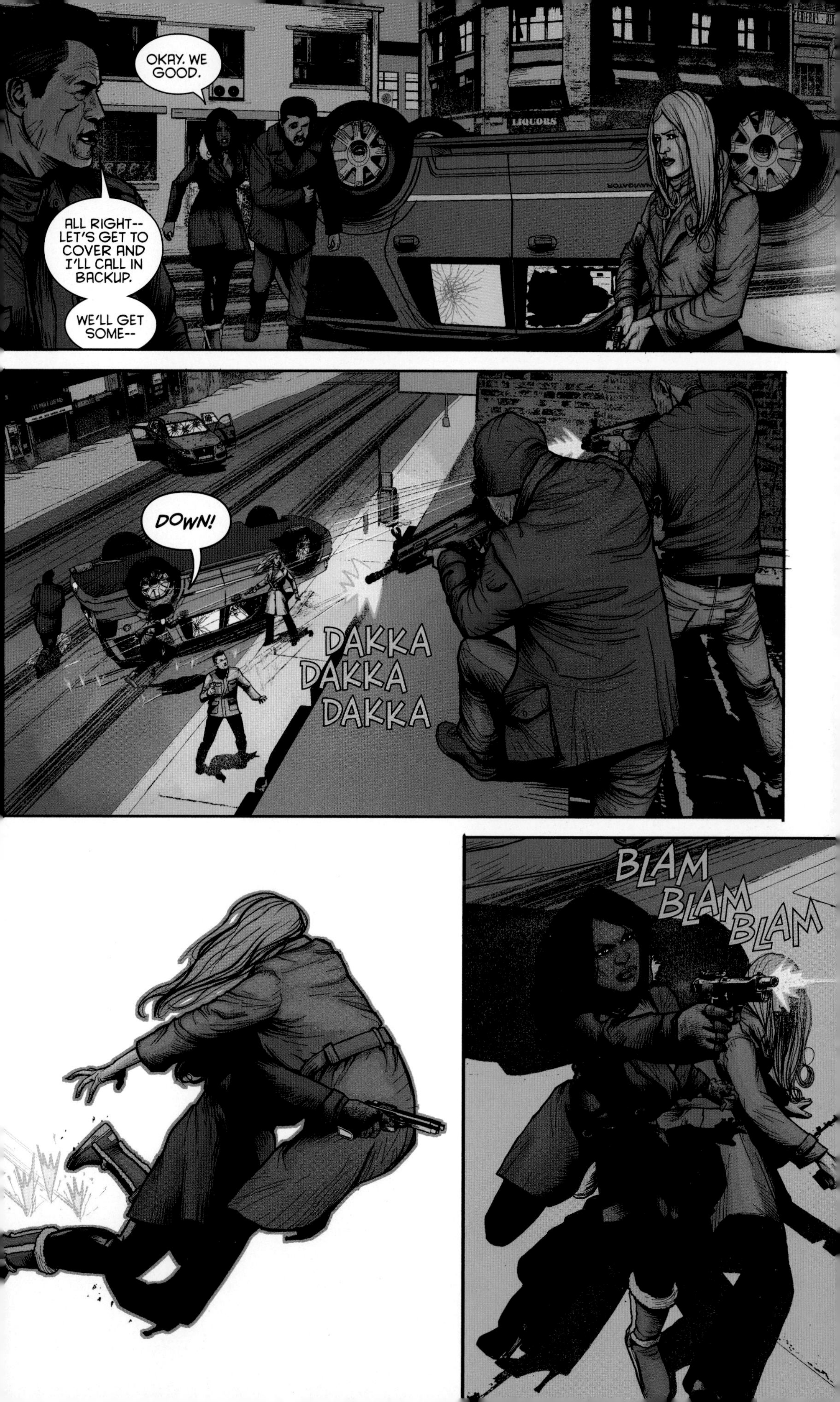
OKAY. WE GOOD.
ALL RIGHT-- LET'S GET TO COVER AND I'LL CALL IN BACKUP.
WE'LL GET SOME--
LIQUORS
DOWN!
DAKKA DAKKA DAKKA
BLAM BLAM BLAM

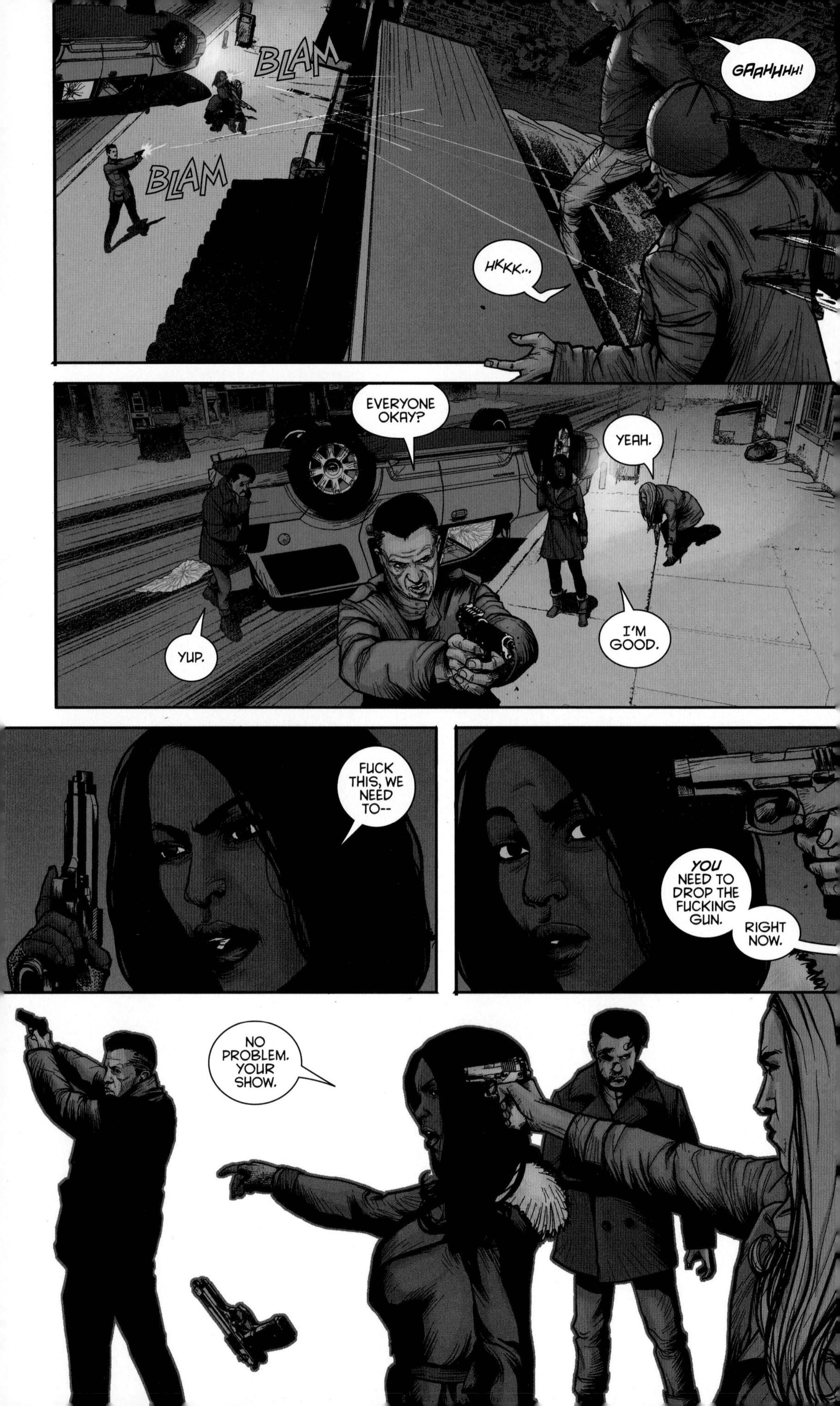

BLAM
BLAM
GAAHHHH!
HKKK...
EVERYONE OKAY?
YEAH.
YUP.
I'M GOOD.
FUCK THIS, WE NEED TO--
YOU NEED TO DROP THE FUCKING GUN.
RIGHT NOW.
NO PROBLEM. YOUR SHOW.

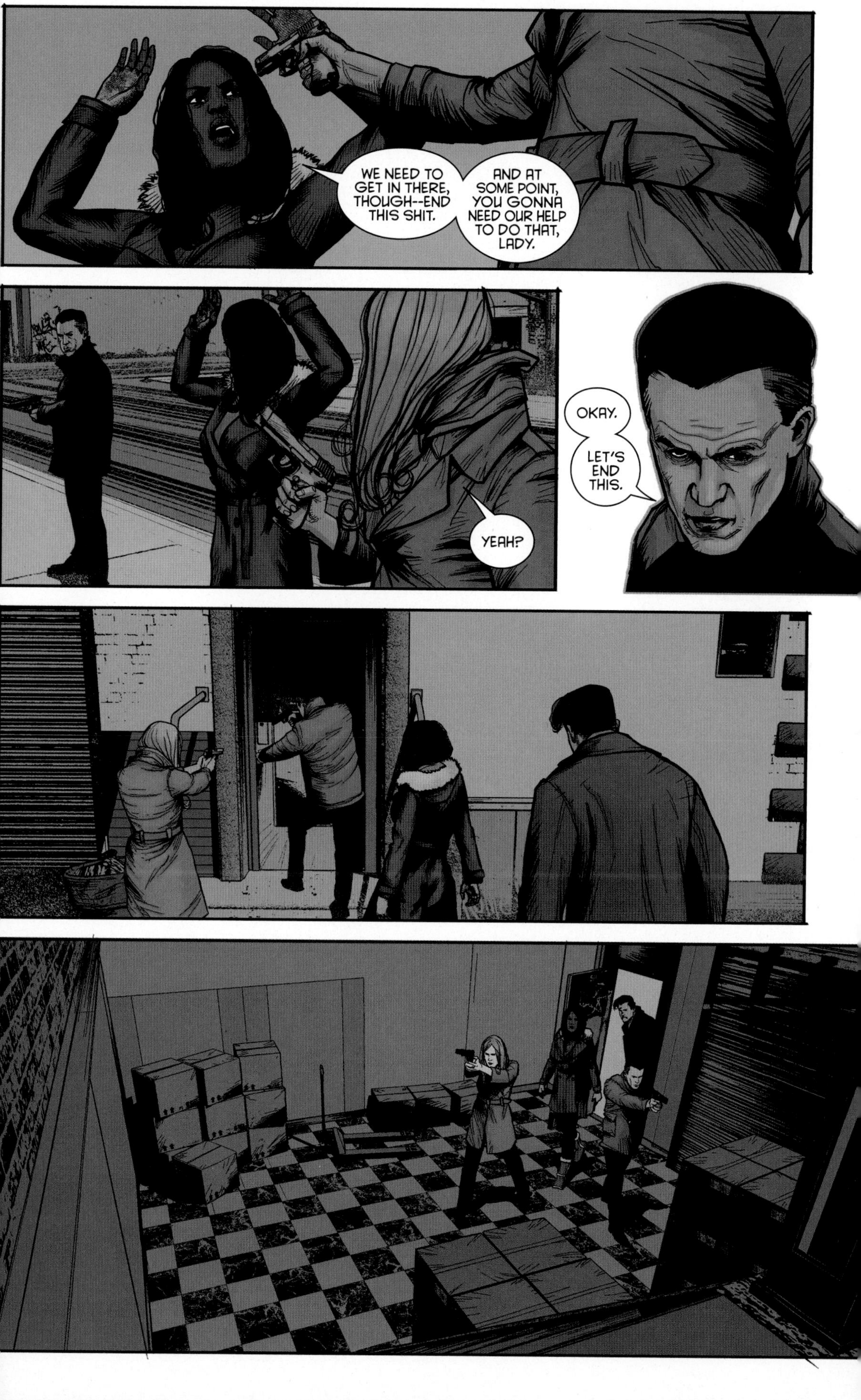
WE NEED TO GET IN THERE, THOUGH--END THIS SHIT.
AND AT SOME POINT, YOU GONNA NEED OUR HELP TO DO THAT, LADY.
YEAH?
OKAY.
LET'S END THIS.

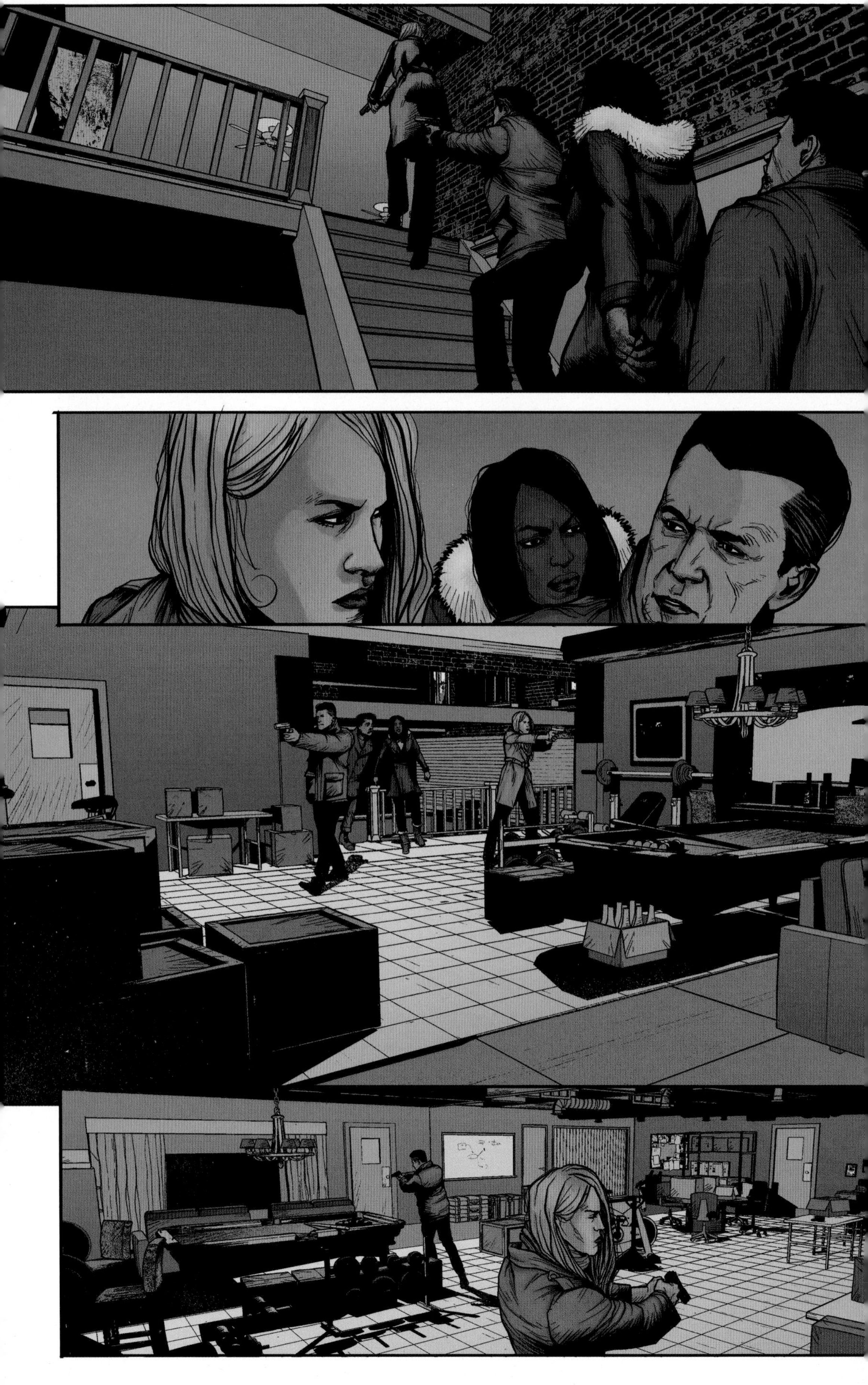

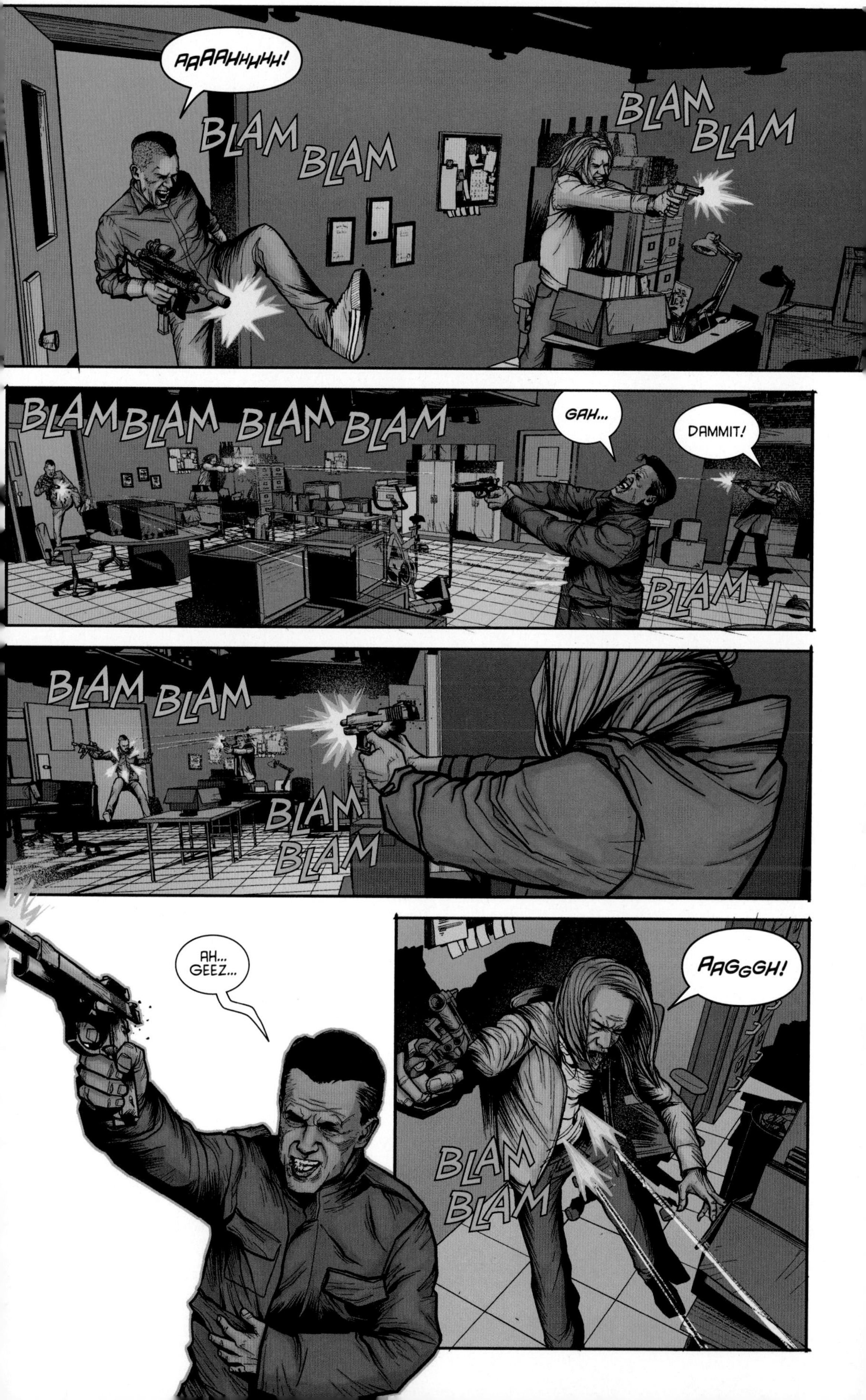
AAAAHHHHH!
BLAM BLAM
BLAM BLAM
BLAM BLAM BLAM BLAM
GAH...
DAMMIT!
BLAM
BLAM BLAM
BLAM BLAM
AH... GEEZ...
AAGGGH!
BLAM BLAM

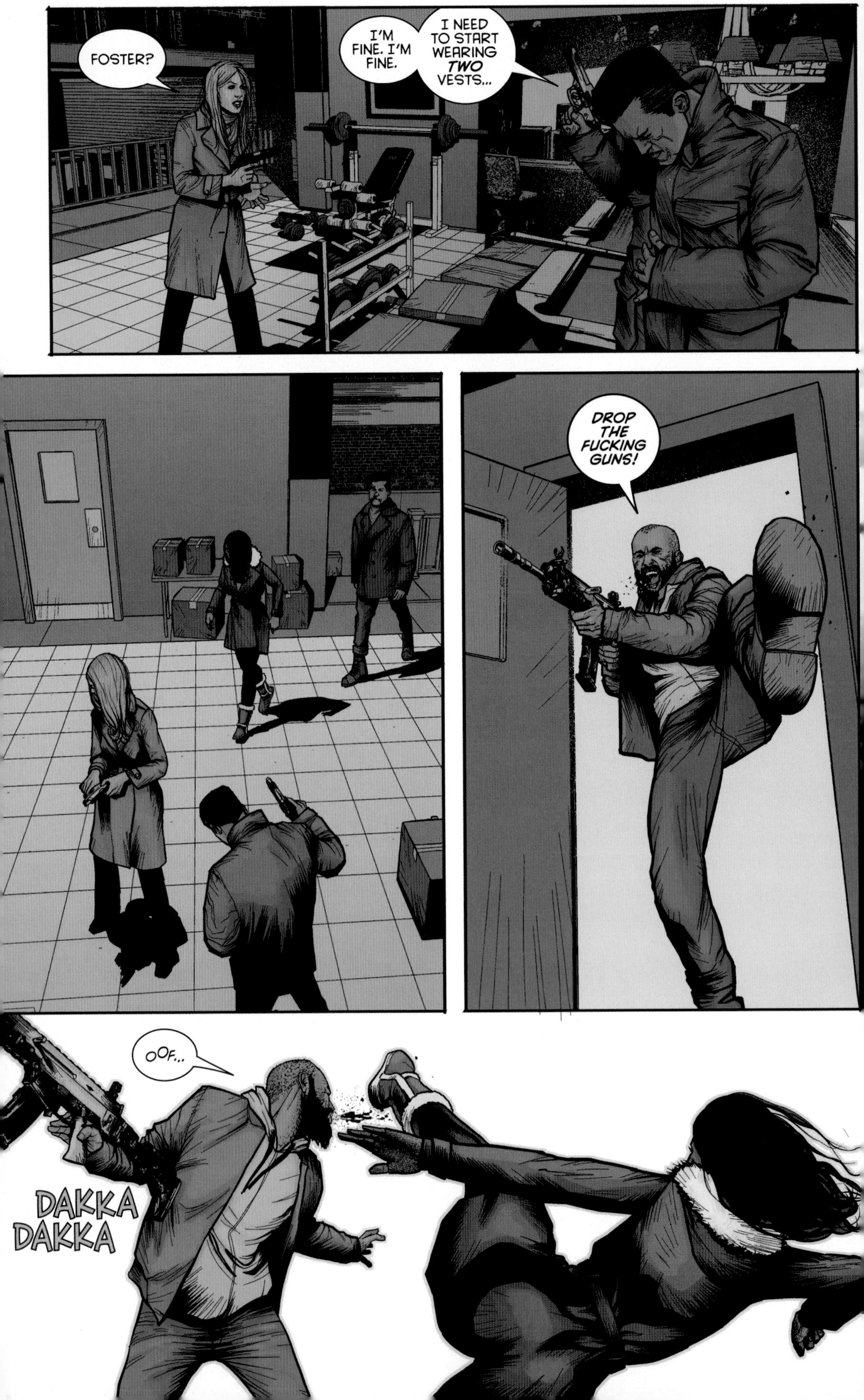

FOSTER?
I'M FINE. I'M FINE.
I NEED TO START WEARING TWO VESTS...
DROP THE FUCKING GUNS!
OOF...
DAKKA DAKKA

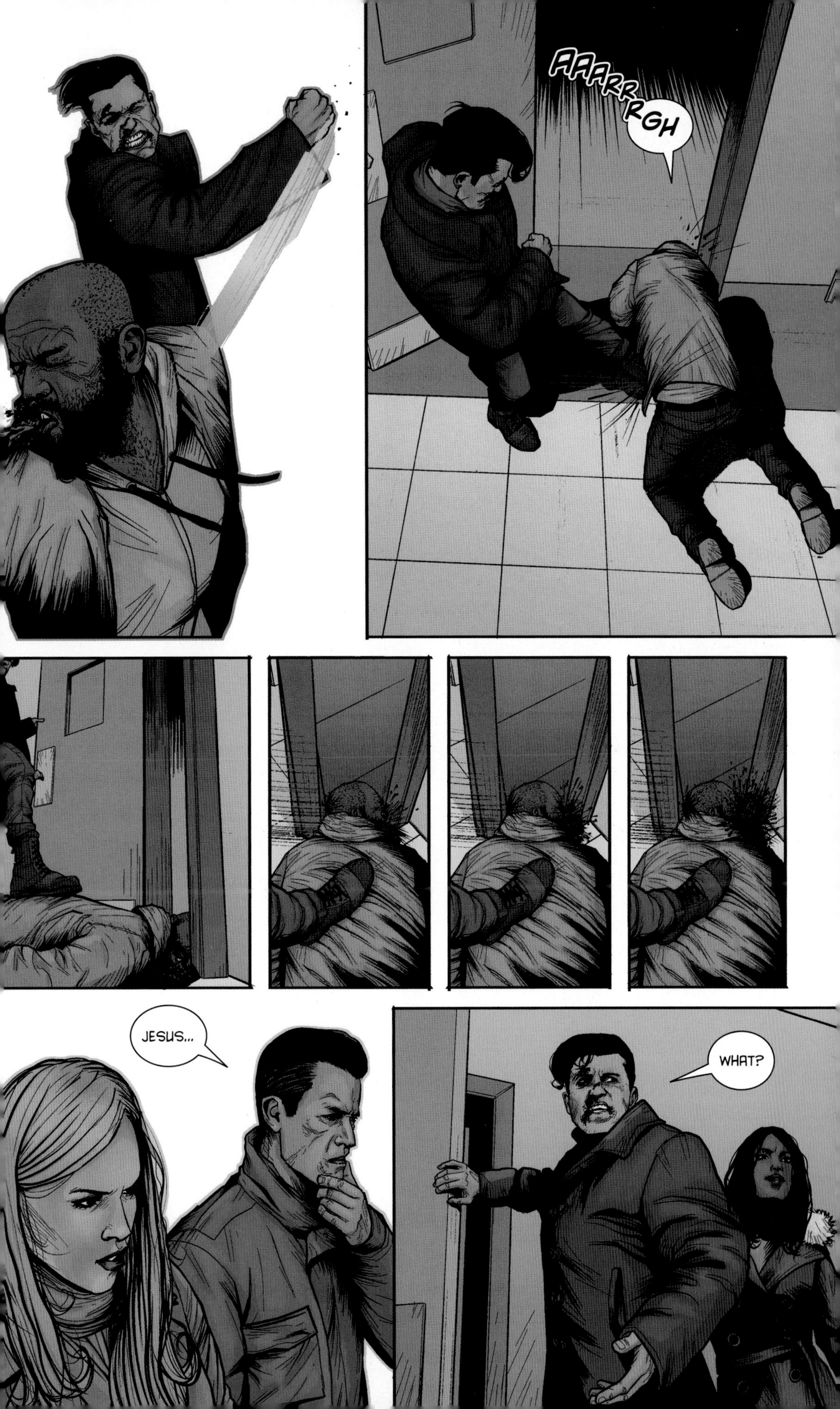

AAAARRRGH
JESUS...
WHAT?

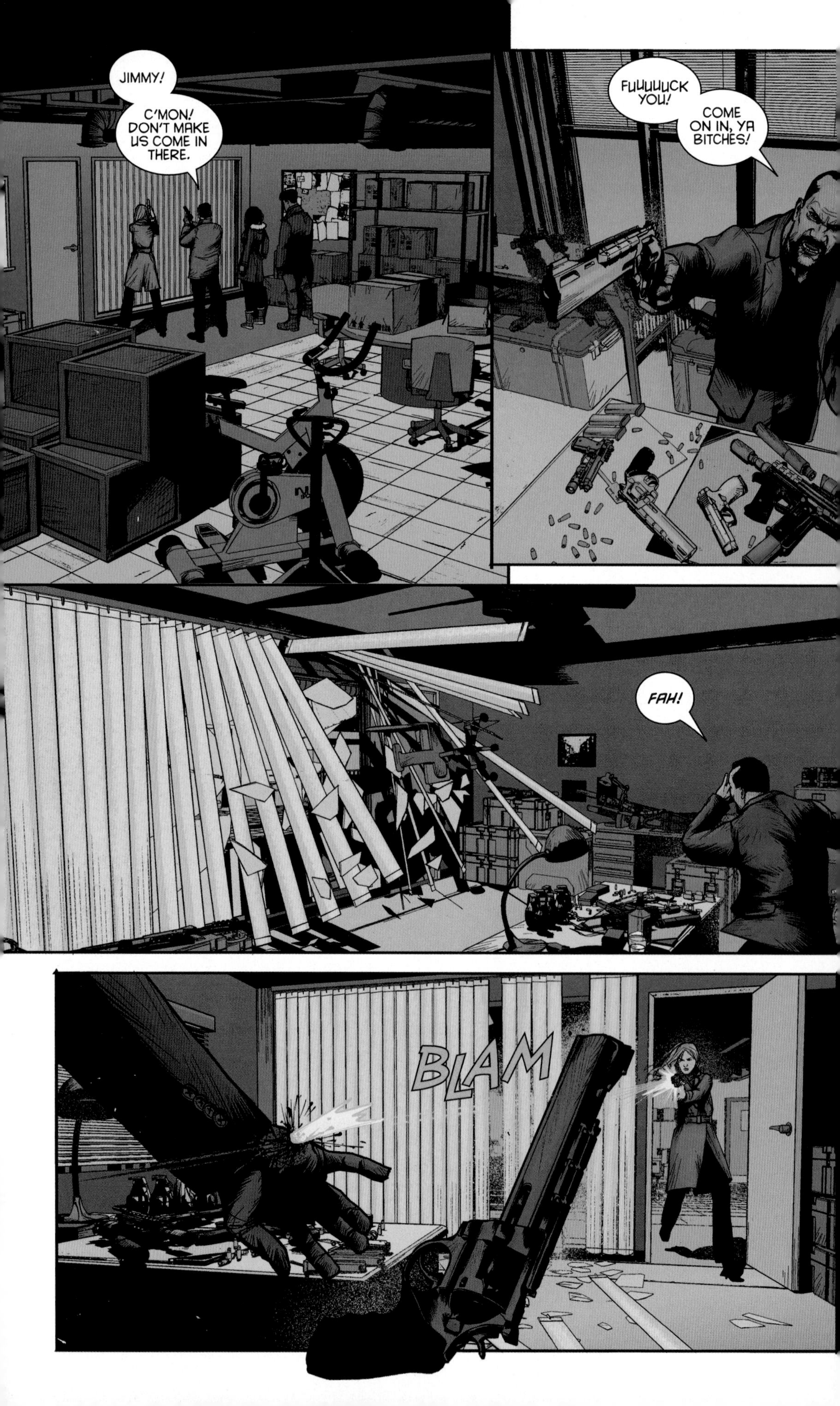

JIMMY!
C'MON! DON'T MAKE US COME IN THERE.
FUUUUUCK YOU!
COME ON IN, YA BITCHES!
FAH!
BLAM

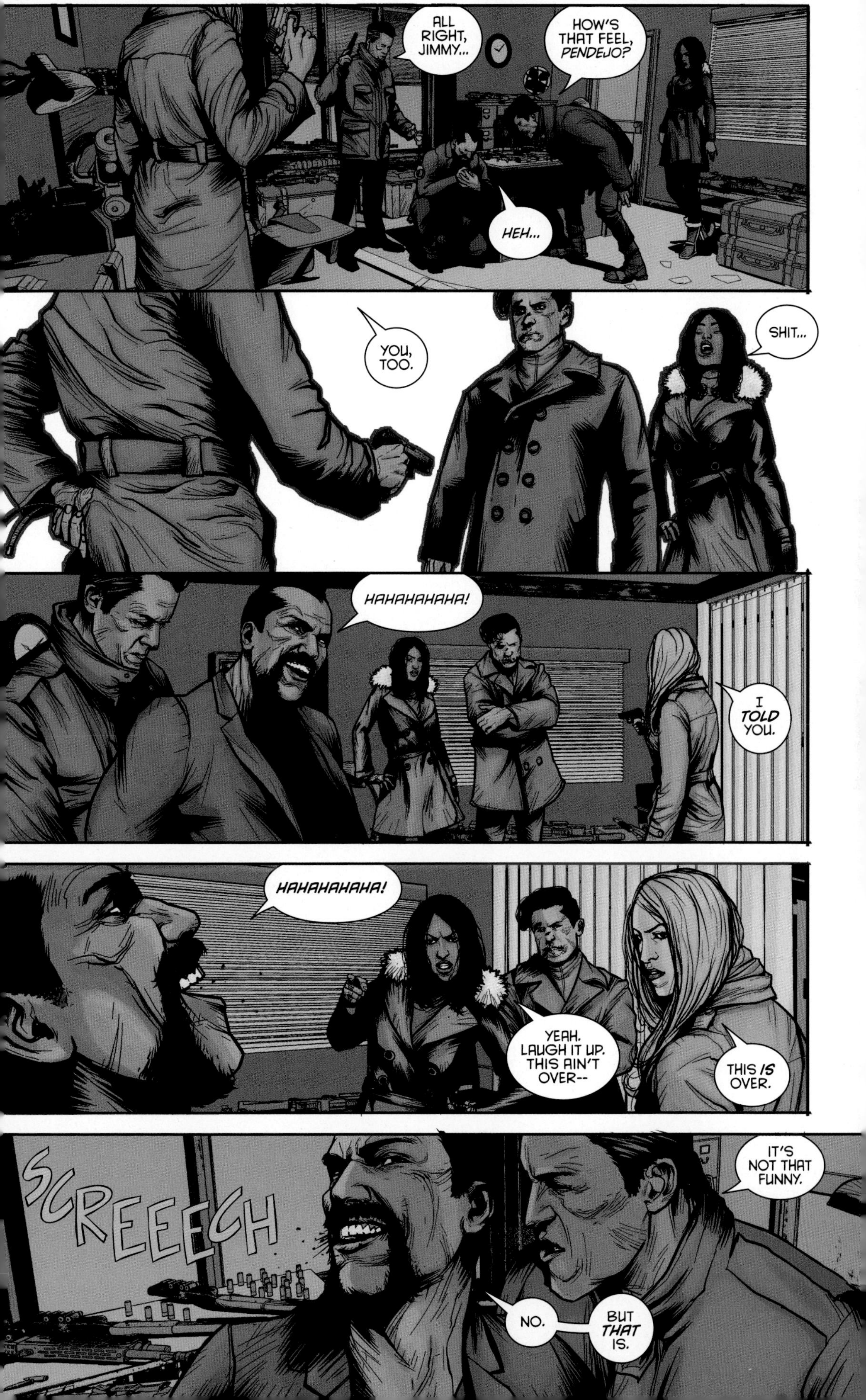
ALL RIGHT, JIMMY...
HOW'S THAT FEEL, *PENDEJO?*
HEH...
YOU, TOO.
SHIT...
HAHAHAHAHA!
I *TOLD* YOU.
HAHAHAHAHA!
YEAH. LAUGH IT UP. THIS AIN'T OVER--
THIS *IS* OVER.
SCREEECH
IT'S NOT THAT FUNNY.
NO.
BUT *THAT* IS.

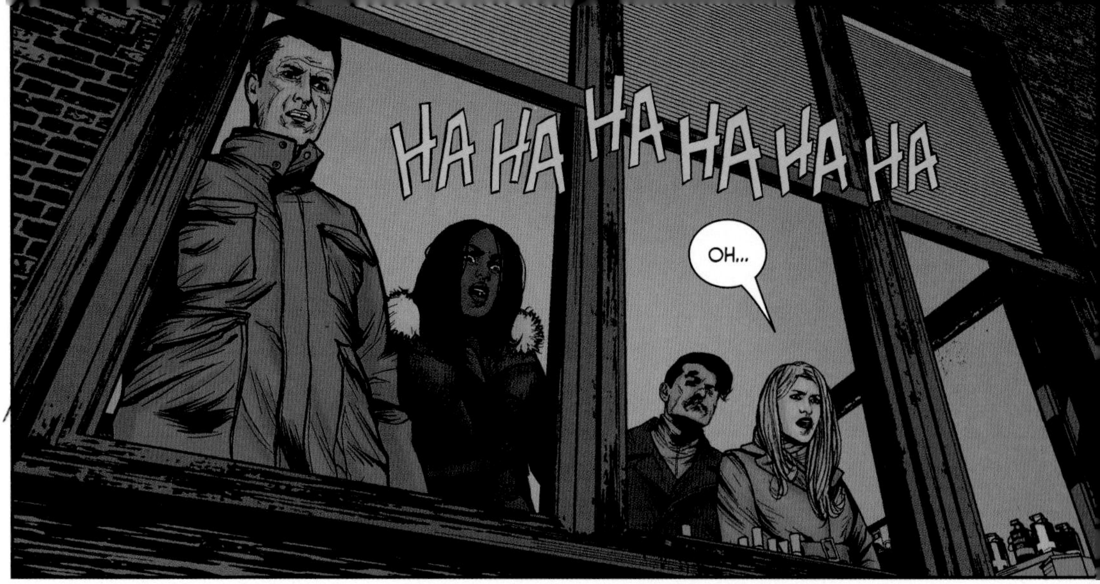
HA HA HA HA HA HA HA
OH...

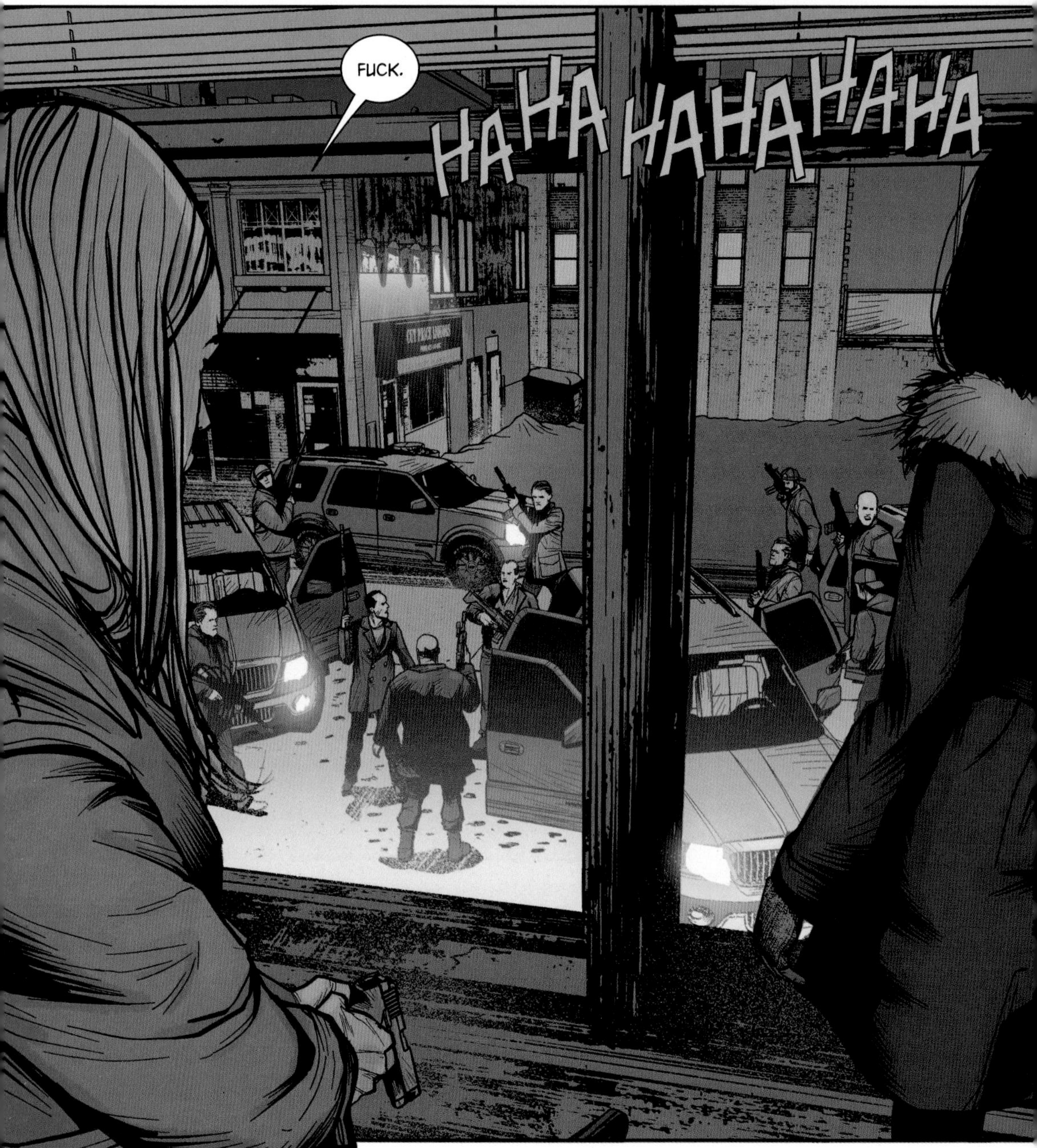
FUCK.
HAHAHAHAHAHAHA

CHAPTER 26

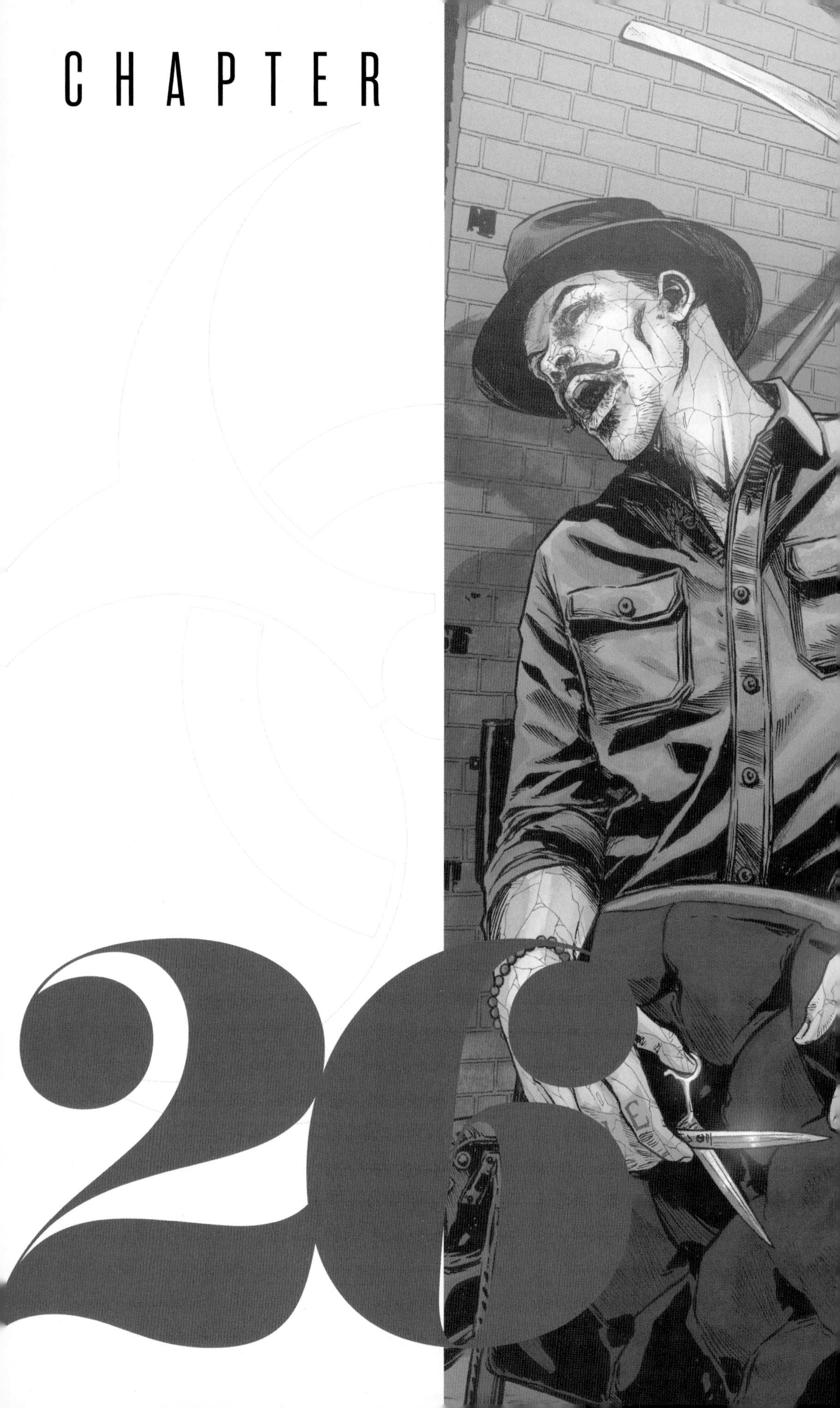

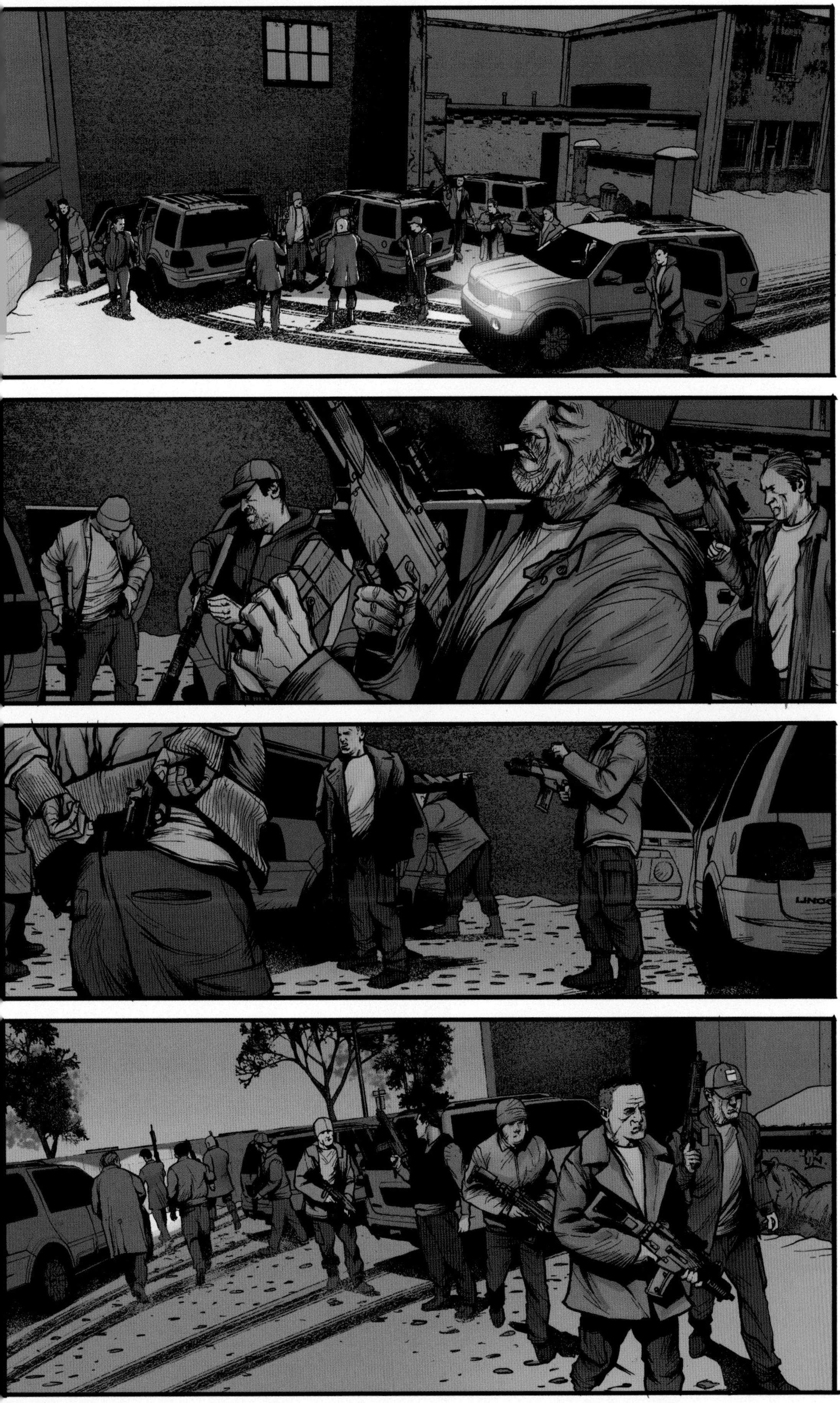

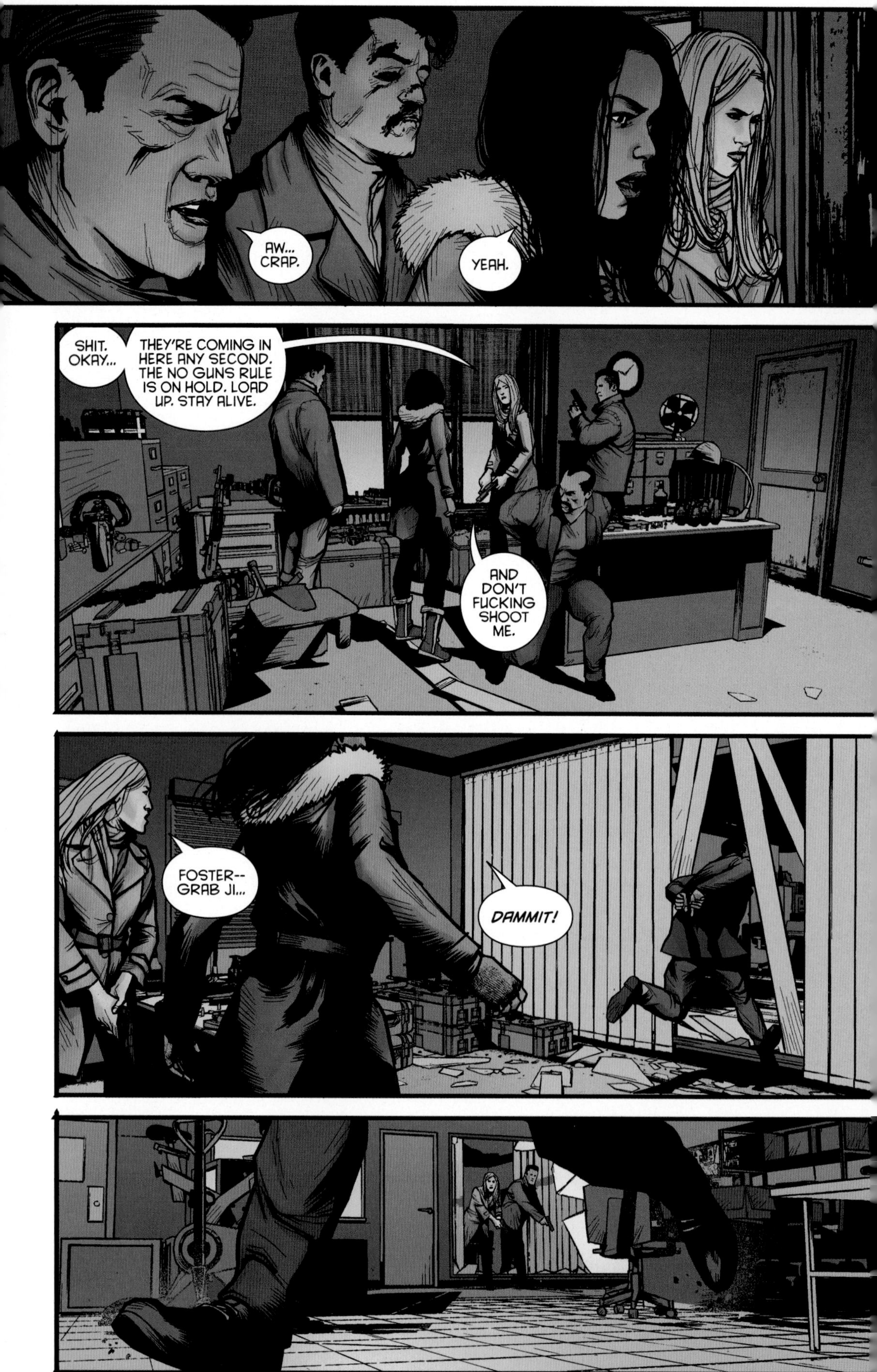
AW... CRAP.
YEAH.
SHIT. OKAY...
THEY'RE COMING IN HERE ANY SECOND. THE NO GUNS RULE IS ON HOLD. LOAD UP. STAY ALIVE.
AND DON'T FUCKING SHOOT ME.
FOSTER-- GRAB JI...
DAMMIT!

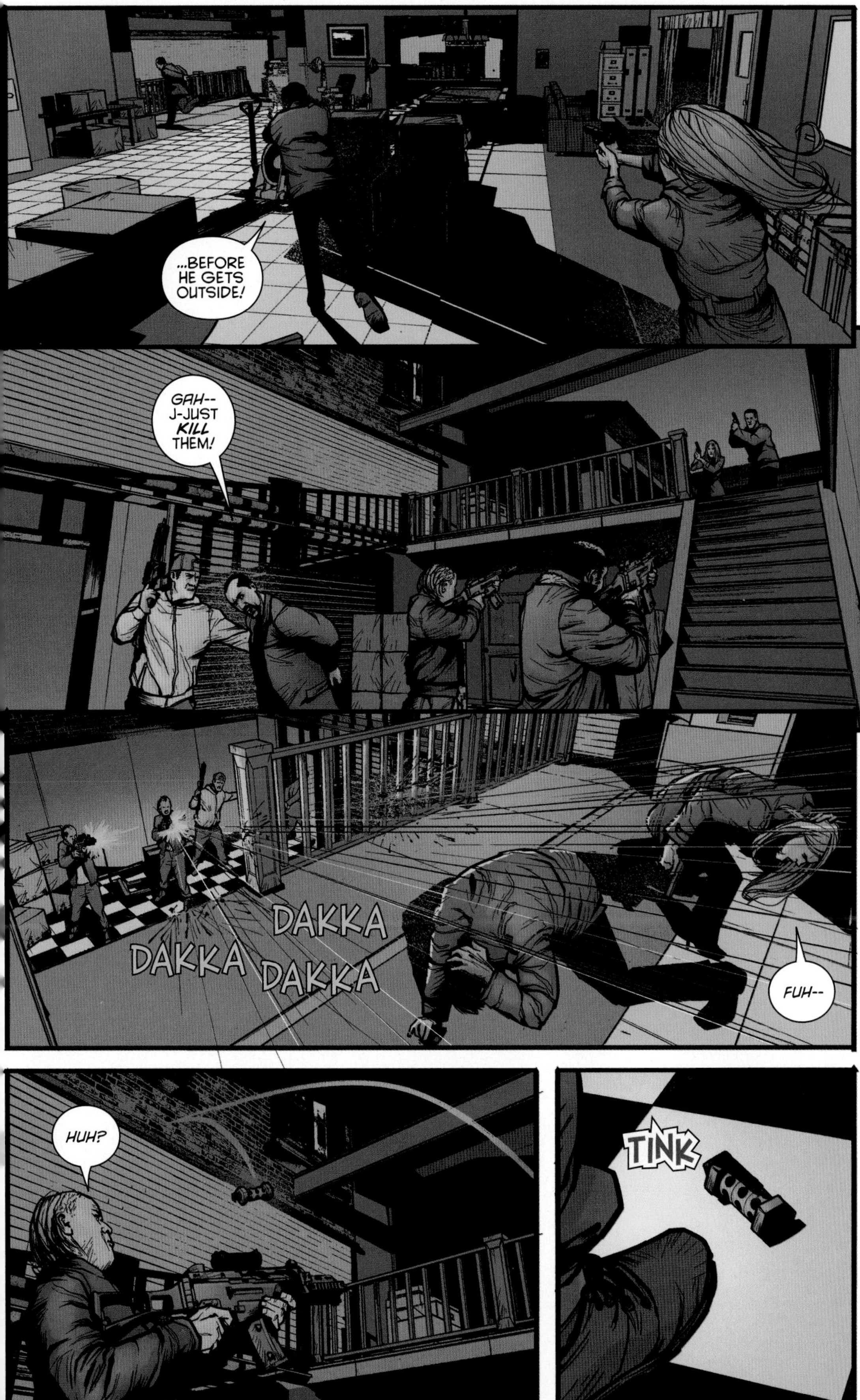
...BEFORE HE GETS OUTSIDE!
GAH-- J-JUST KILL THEM!
DAKKA
DAKKA
DAKKA
FUH--
HUH?
TINK

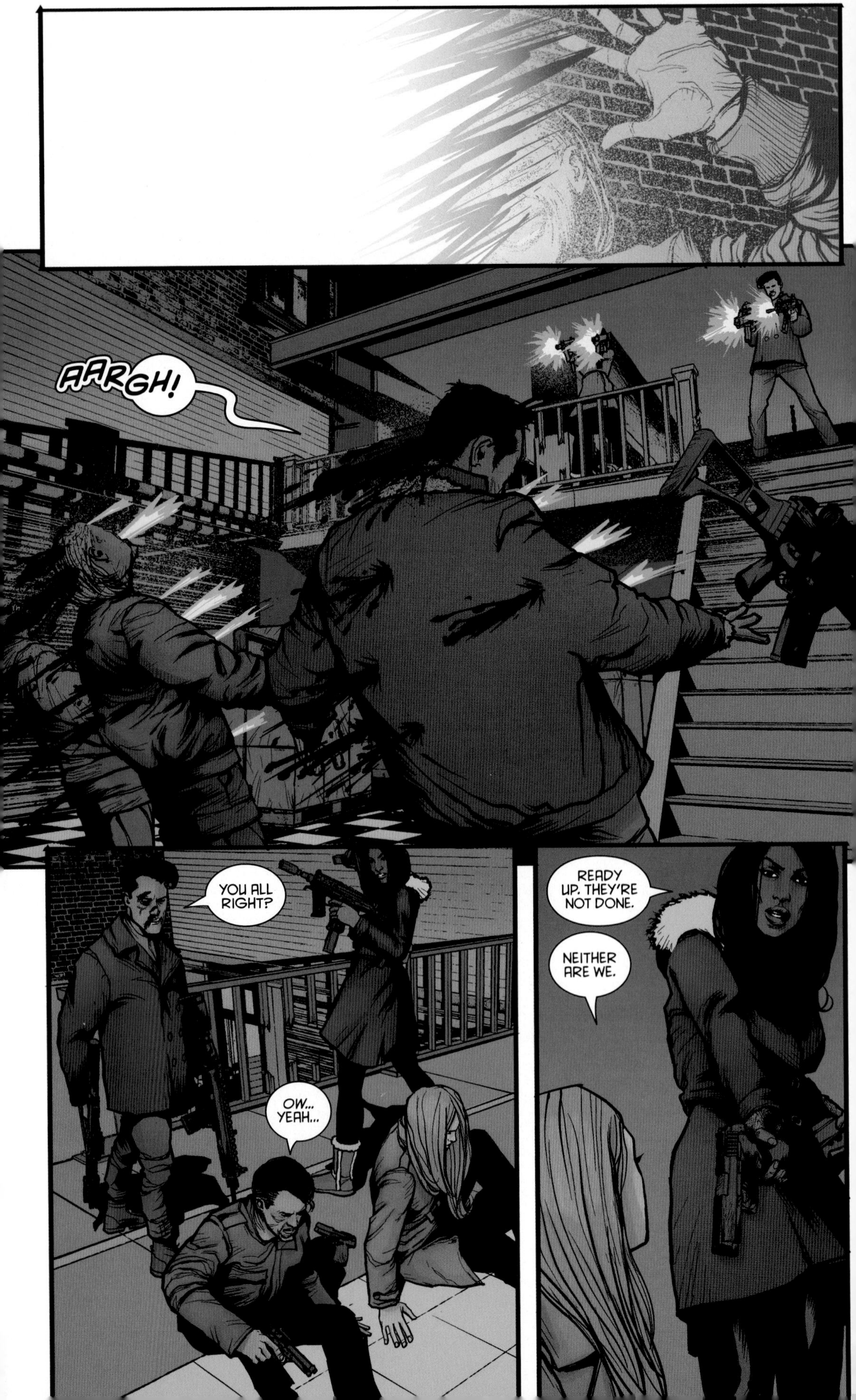

AARGH!
YOU ALL RIGHT?
OW... YEAH...
READY UP. THEY'RE NOT DONE.
NEITHER ARE WE.

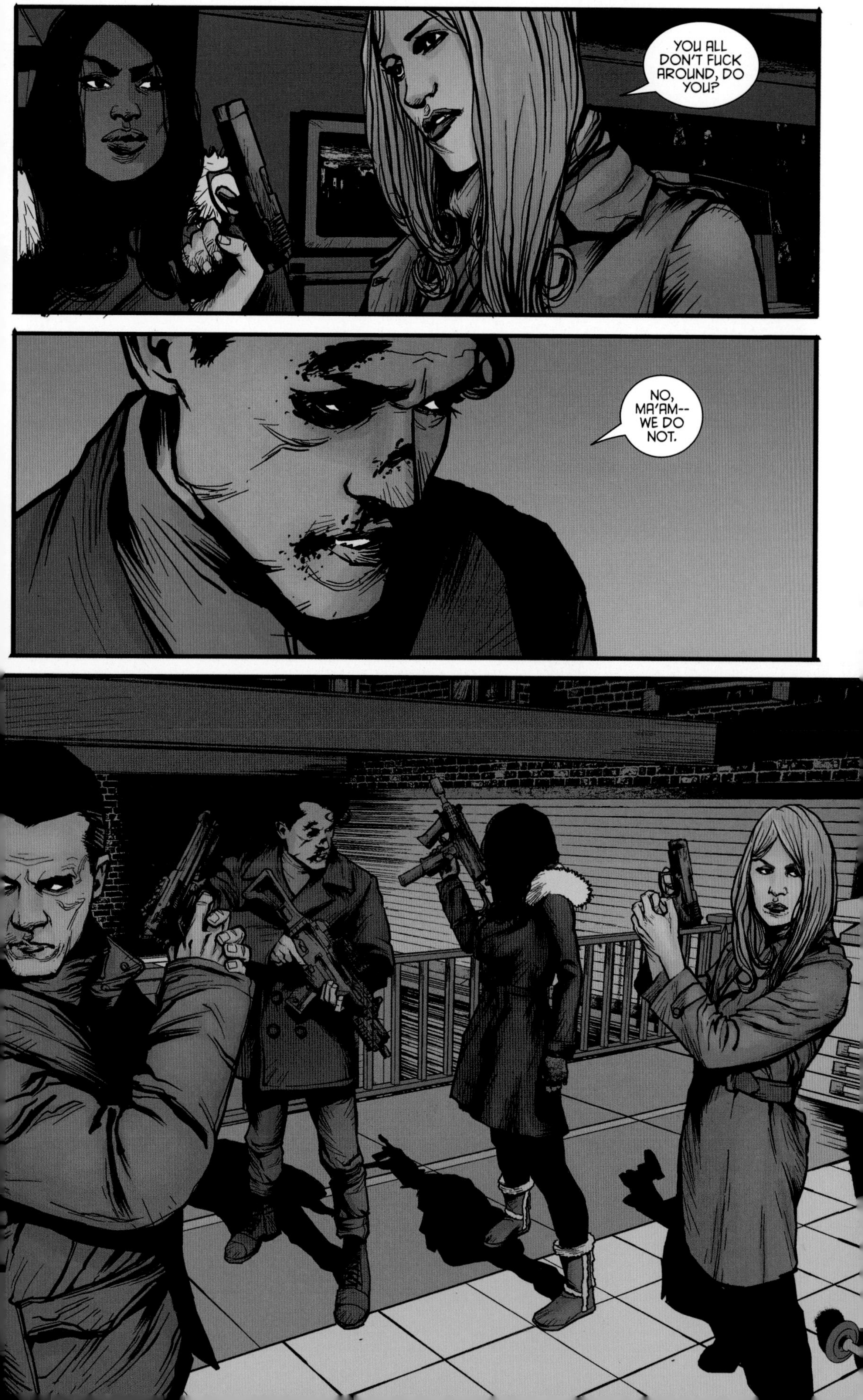
YOU ALL DON'T FUCK AROUND, DO YOU?
NO, MA'AM-- WE DO NOT.

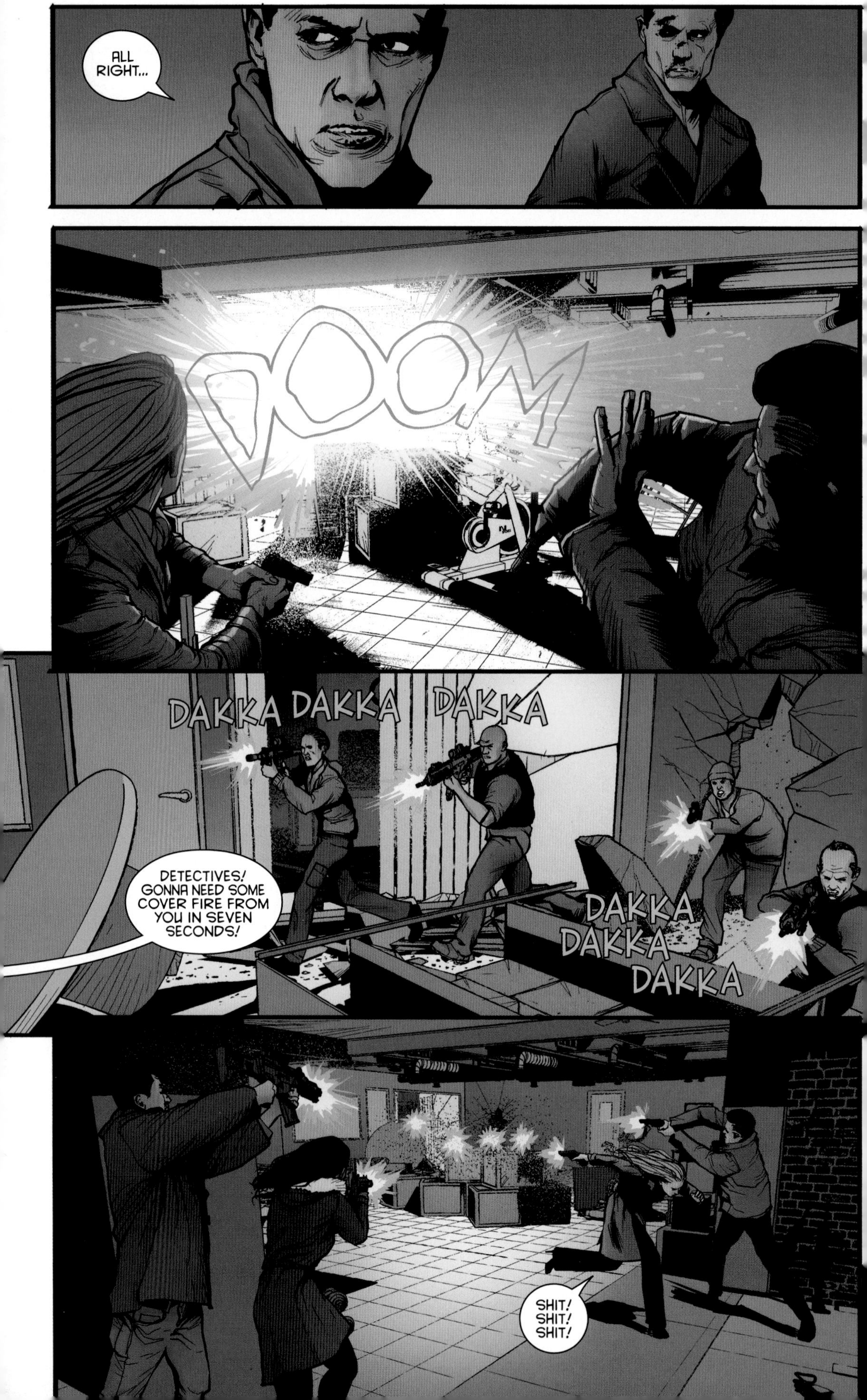
ALL RIGHT...
DOOM
DAKKA DAKKA DAKKA
DETECTIVES! GONNA NEED SOME COVER FIRE FROM YOU IN SEVEN SECONDS!
DAKKA DAKKA DAKKA
SHIT! SHIT! SHIT!

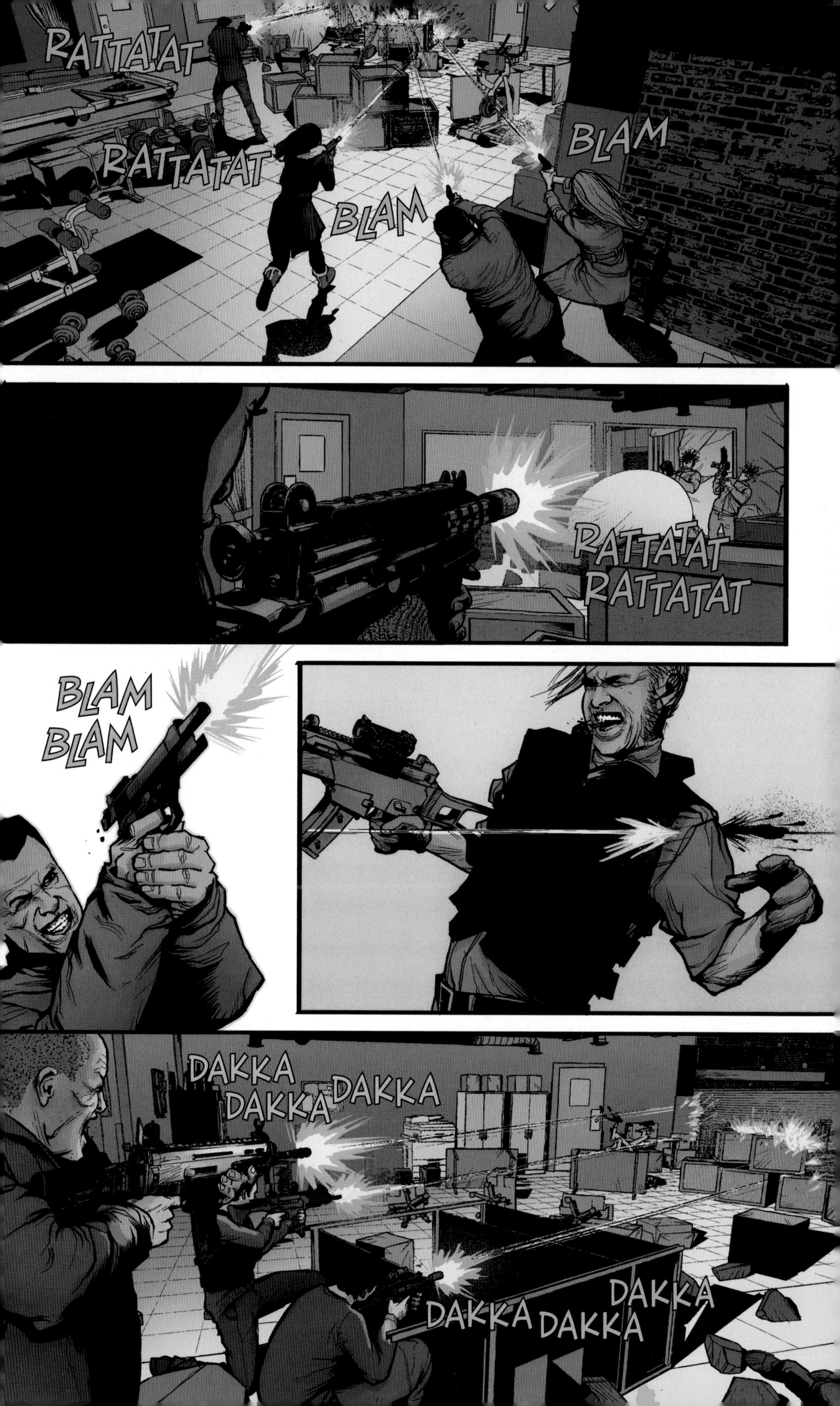
RATTATAT
RATTATAT
BLAM
BLAM
RATTATAT
RATTATAT
BLAM
BLAM
DAKKA
DAKKA
DAKKA
DAKKA
DAKKA
DAKKA

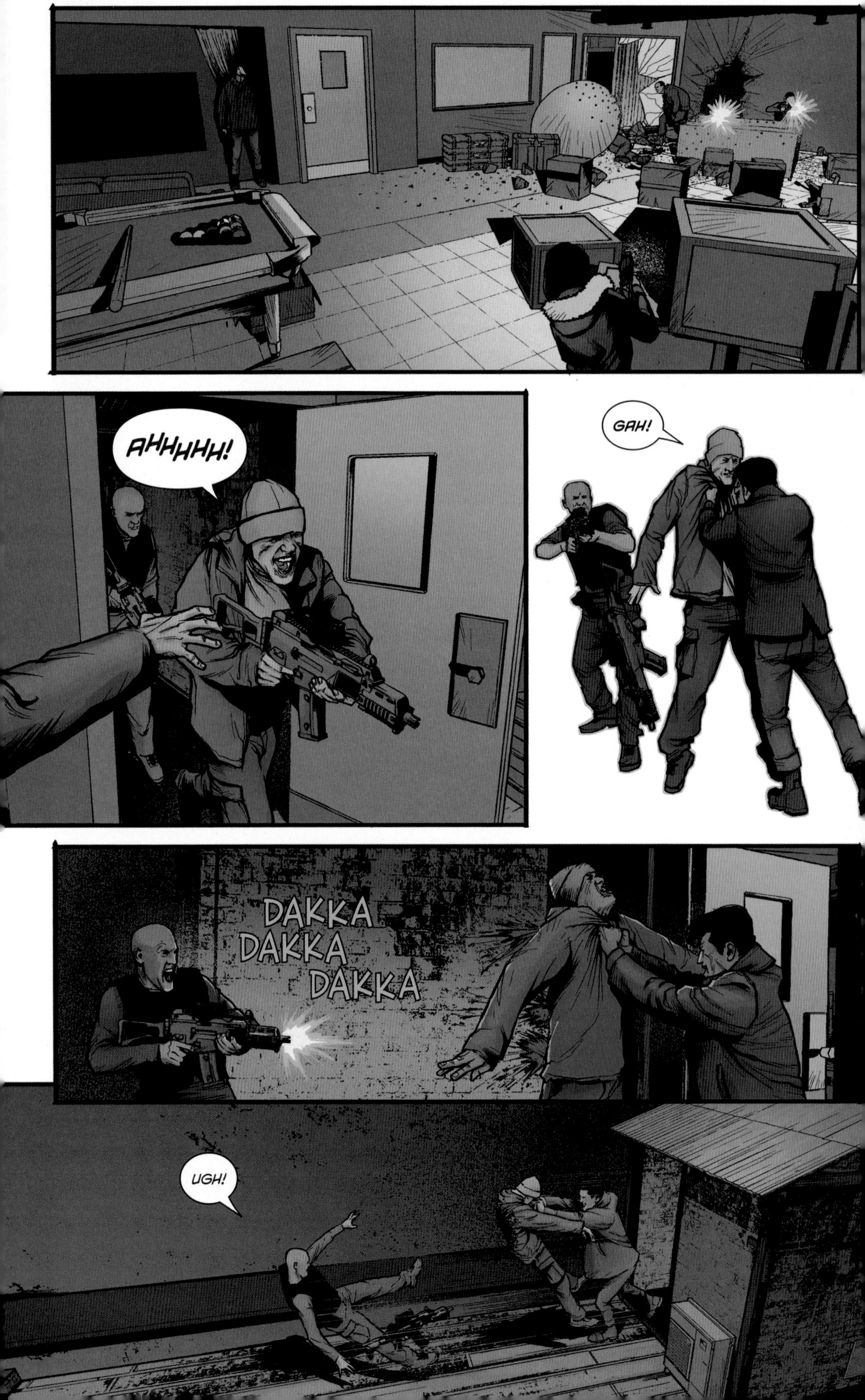
AHHHHH!
GAH!
DAKKA
DAKKA
DAKKA
UGH!

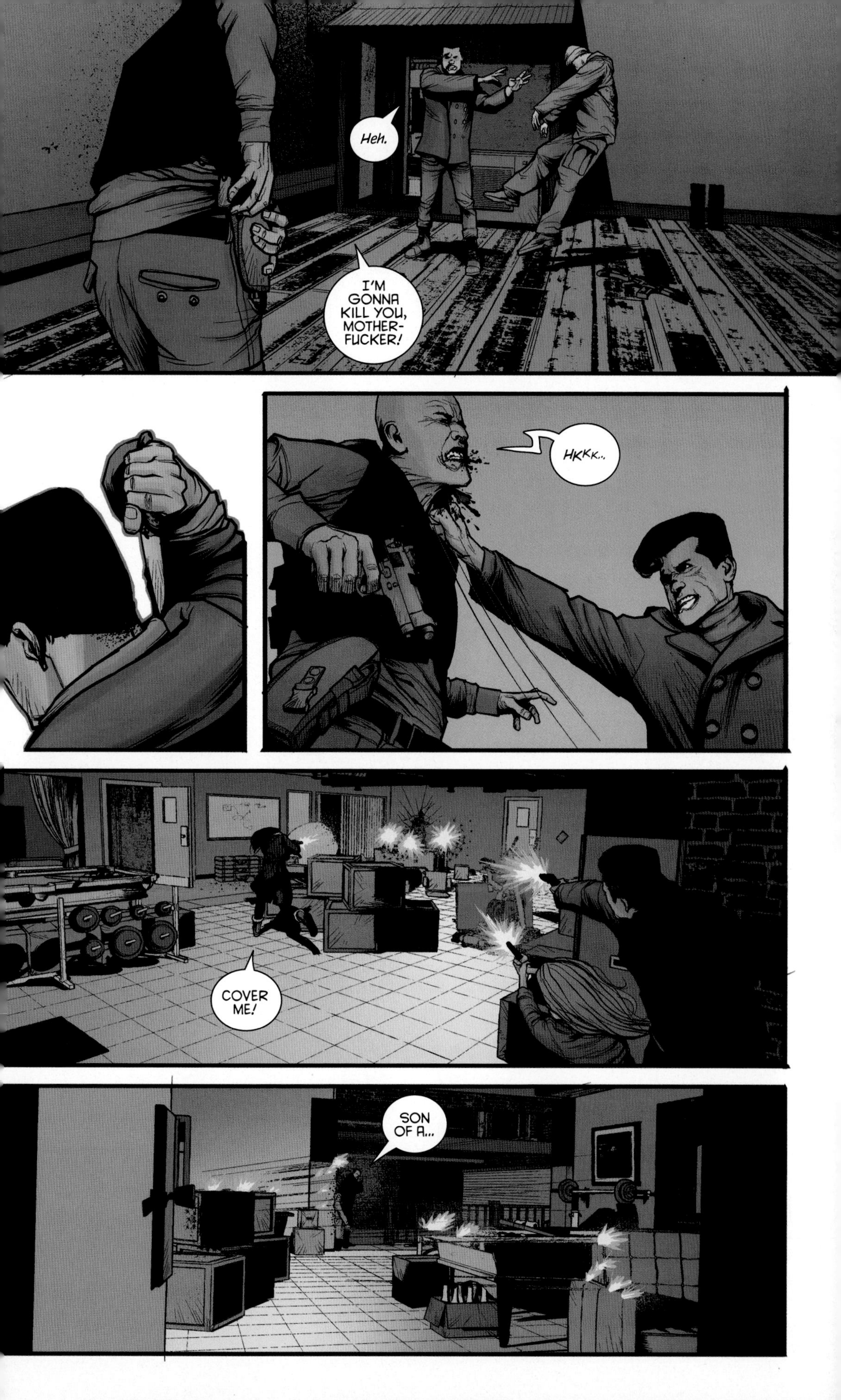

Heh.
I'M GONNA KILL YOU, MOTHER-FUCKER!
HKKK...
COVER ME!
SON OF A...

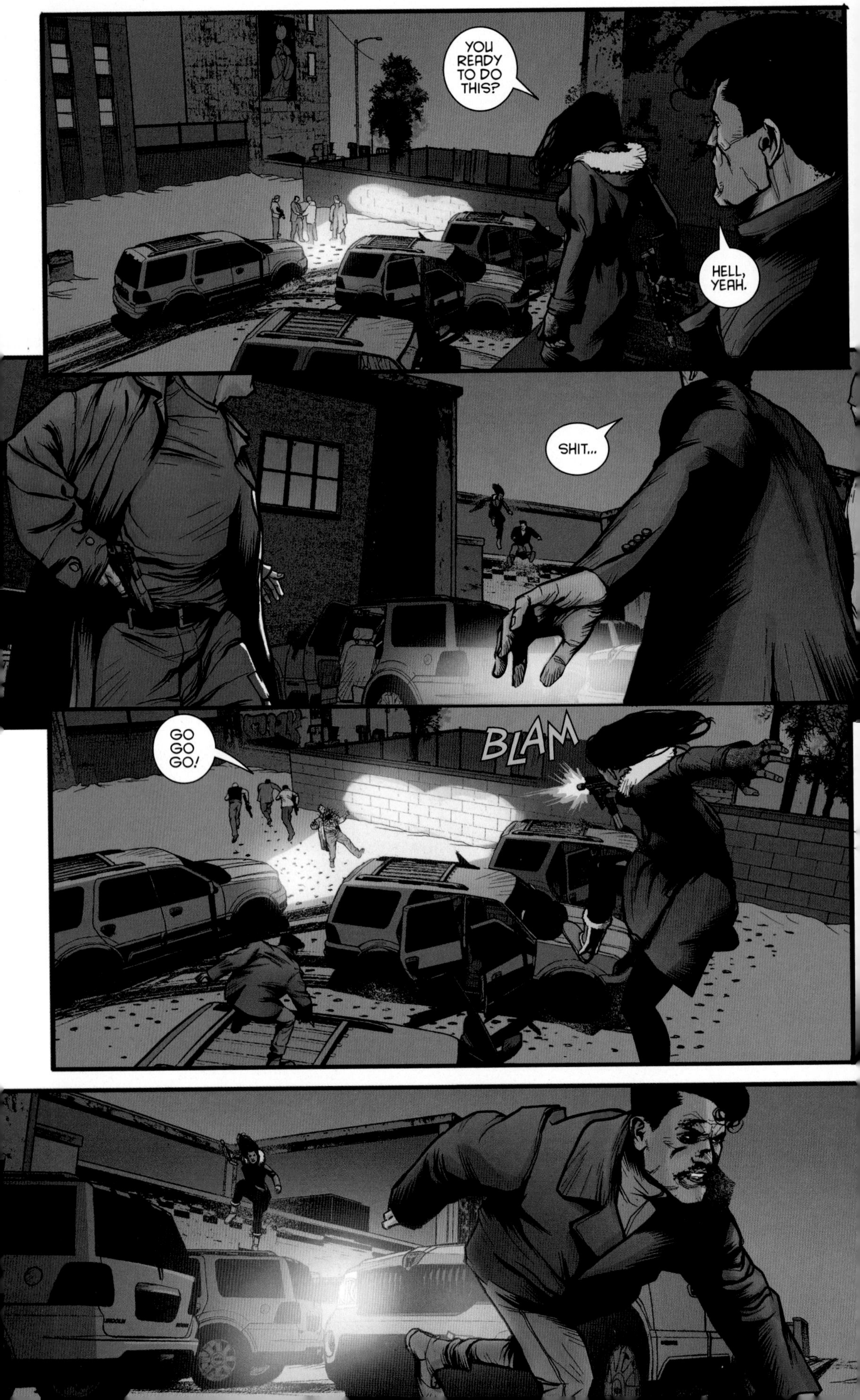
YOU READY TO DO THIS?
HELL, YEAH.
SHIT...
GO GO GO!
BLAM

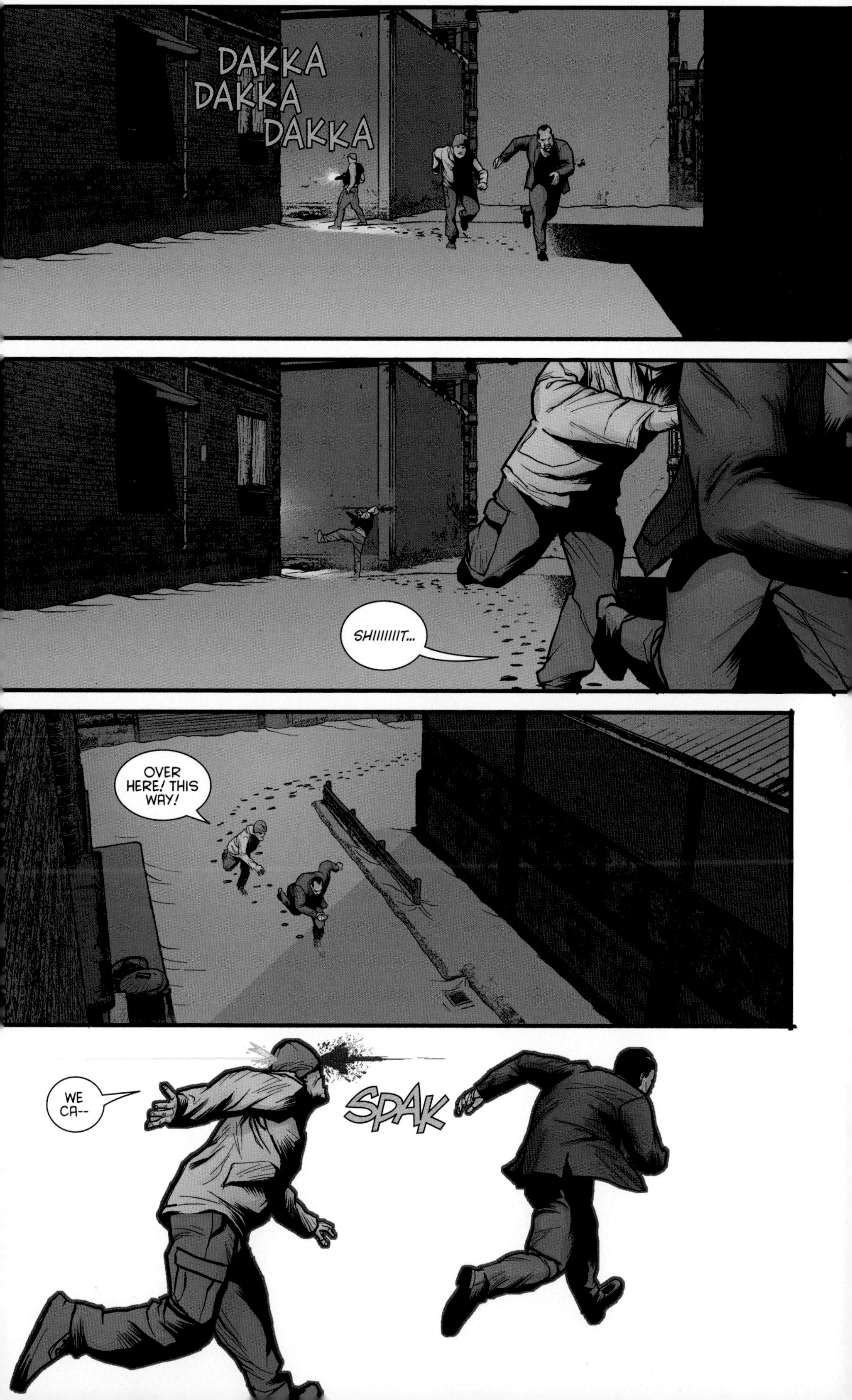
DAKKA
DAKKA
DAKKA
SHIIIIIIT...
OVER HERE! THIS WAY!
WE CA--
SPAK

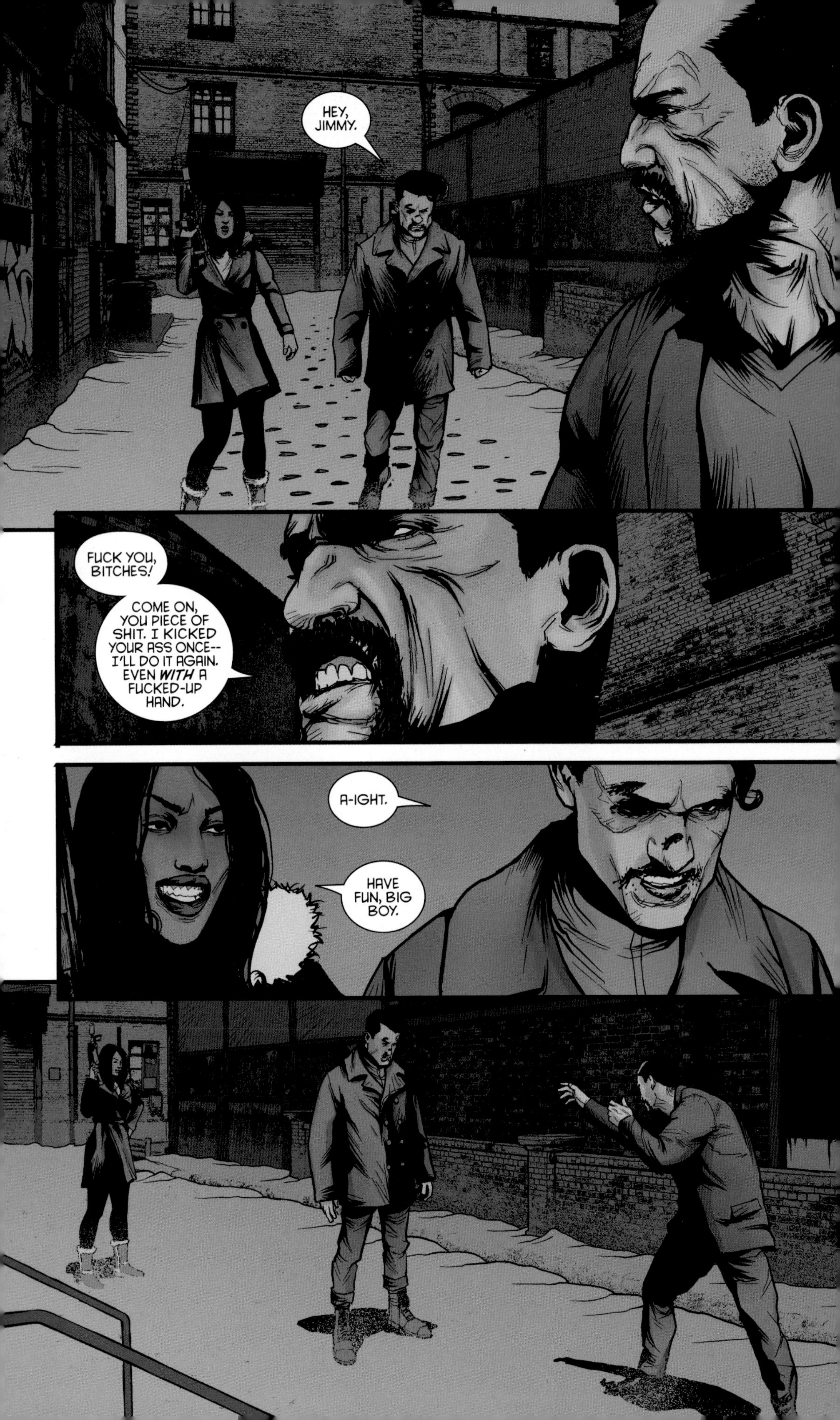
HEY, JIMMY.
FUCK YOU, BITCHES!
COME ON, YOU PIECE OF SHIT. I KICKED YOUR ASS ONCE-- I'LL DO IT AGAIN. EVEN *WITH* A FUCKED-UP HAND.
A-IGHT.
HAVE FUN, BIG BOY.

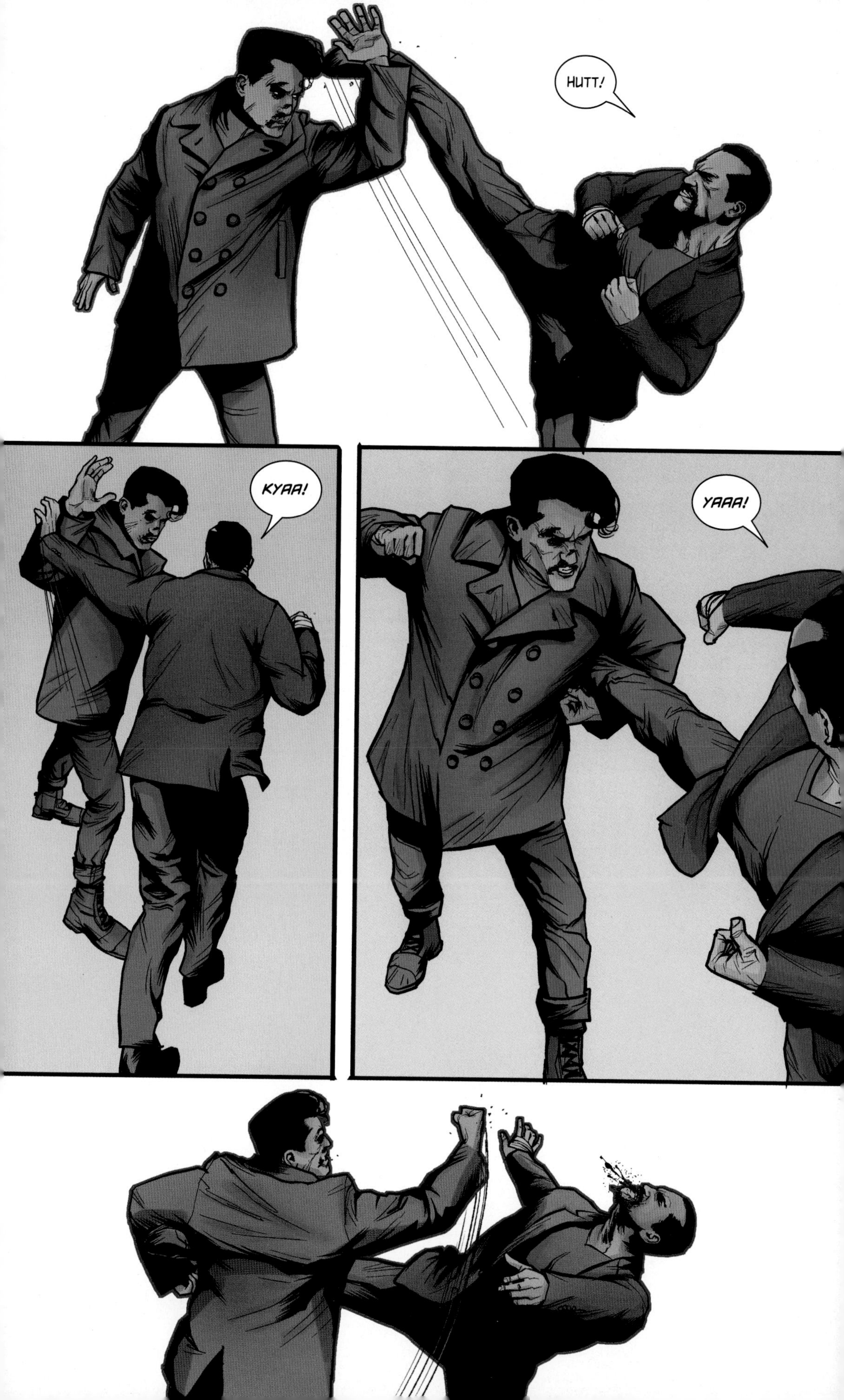
HUTT!
KYAA!
YAAA!

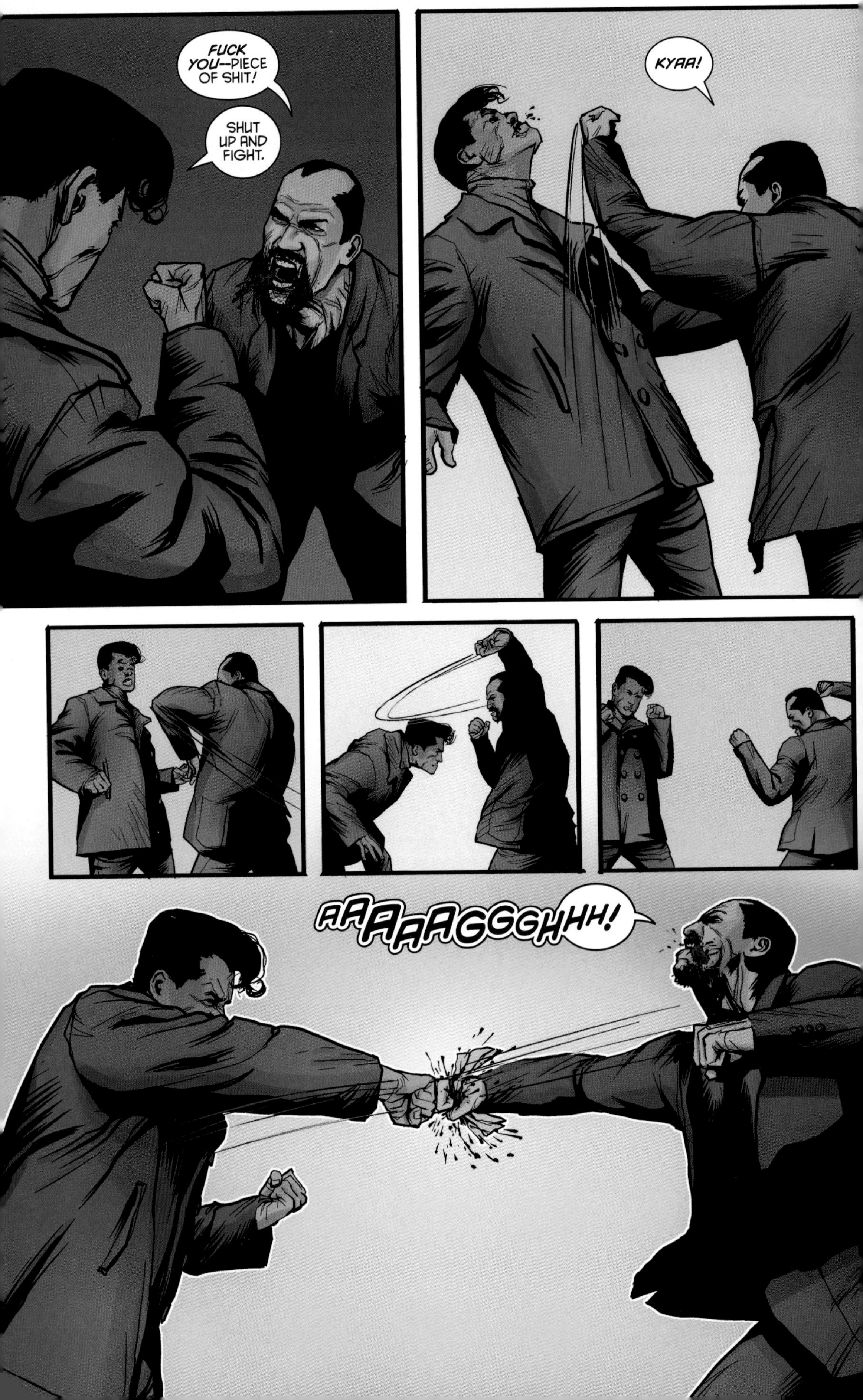
FUCK YOU--PIECE OF SHIT!
SHUT UP AND FIGHT.
KYAA!
AAAAAAGGGHHH!

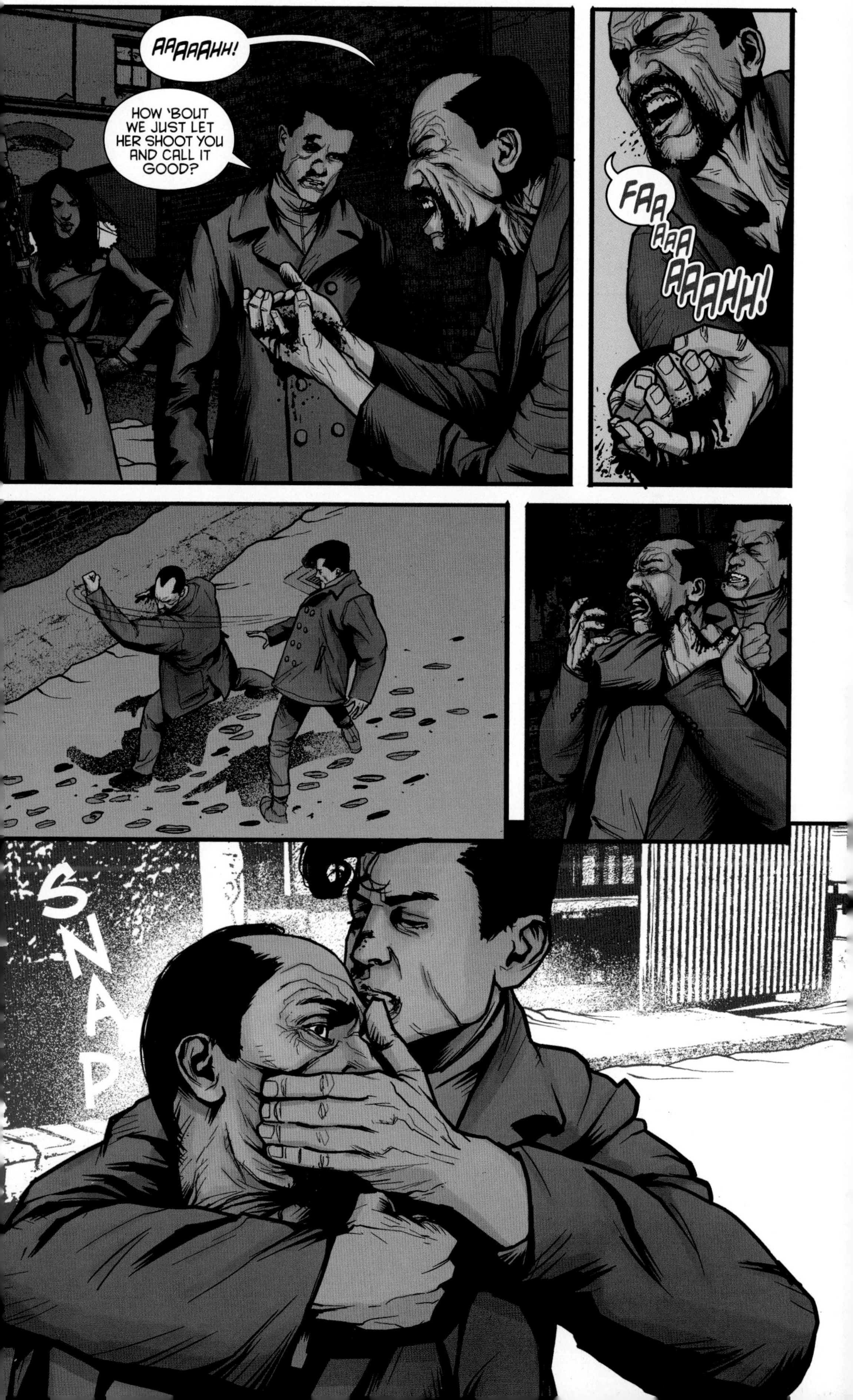
AAAAAHH!
HOW 'BOUT WE JUST LET HER SHOOT YOU AND CALL IT GOOD?
FAAAAAAAAHH!
SNAP

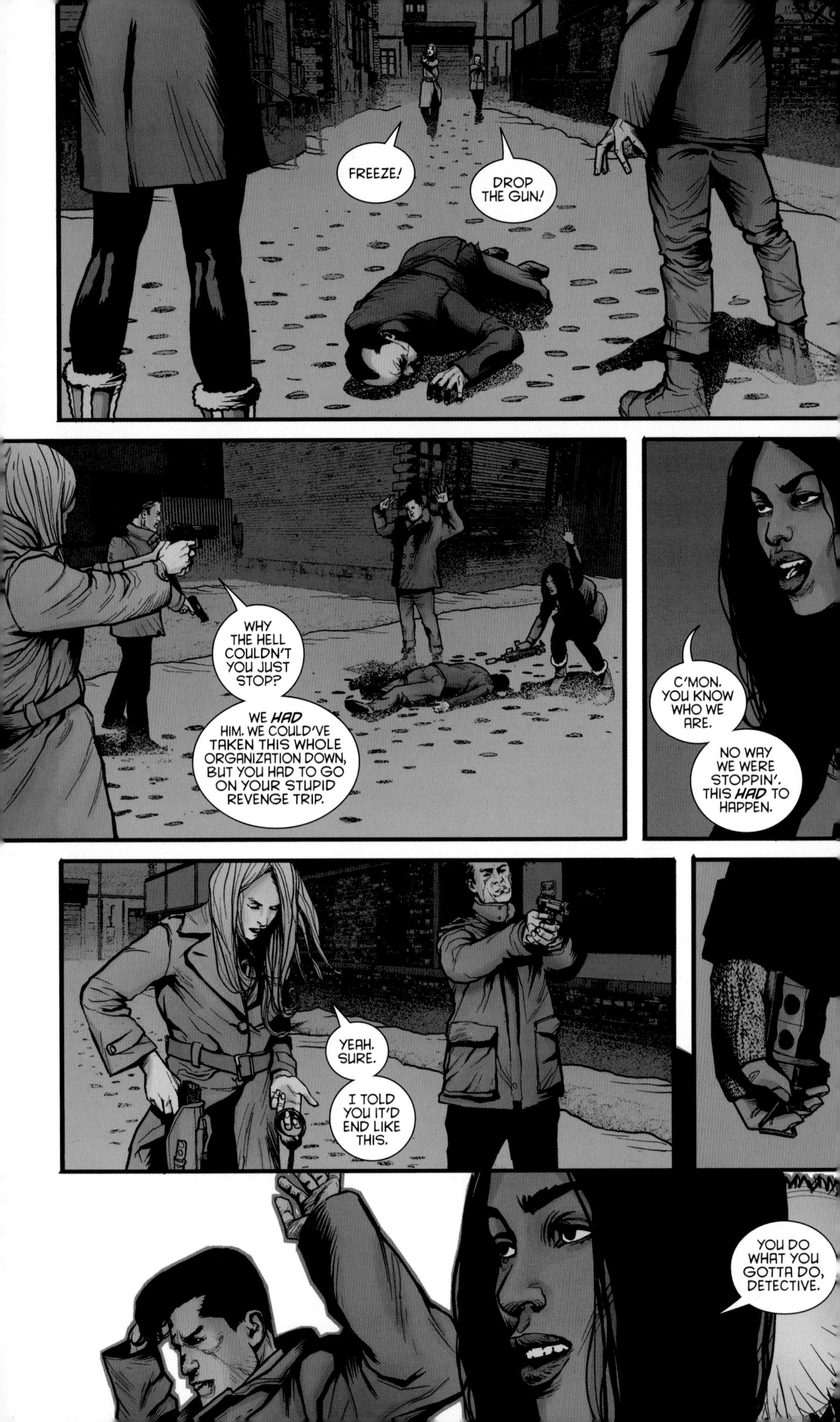
FREEZE!
DROP THE GUN!
WHY THE HELL COULDN'T YOU JUST STOP?
WE HAD HIM. WE COULD'VE TAKEN THIS WHOLE ORGANIZATION DOWN, BUT YOU HAD TO GO ON YOUR STUPID REVENGE TRIP.
C'MON. YOU KNOW WHO WE ARE.
NO WAY WE WERE STOPPIN'. THIS HAD TO HAPPEN.
YEAH. SURE.
I TOLD YOU IT'D END LIKE THIS.
YOU DO WHAT YOU GOTTA DO, DETECTIVE.

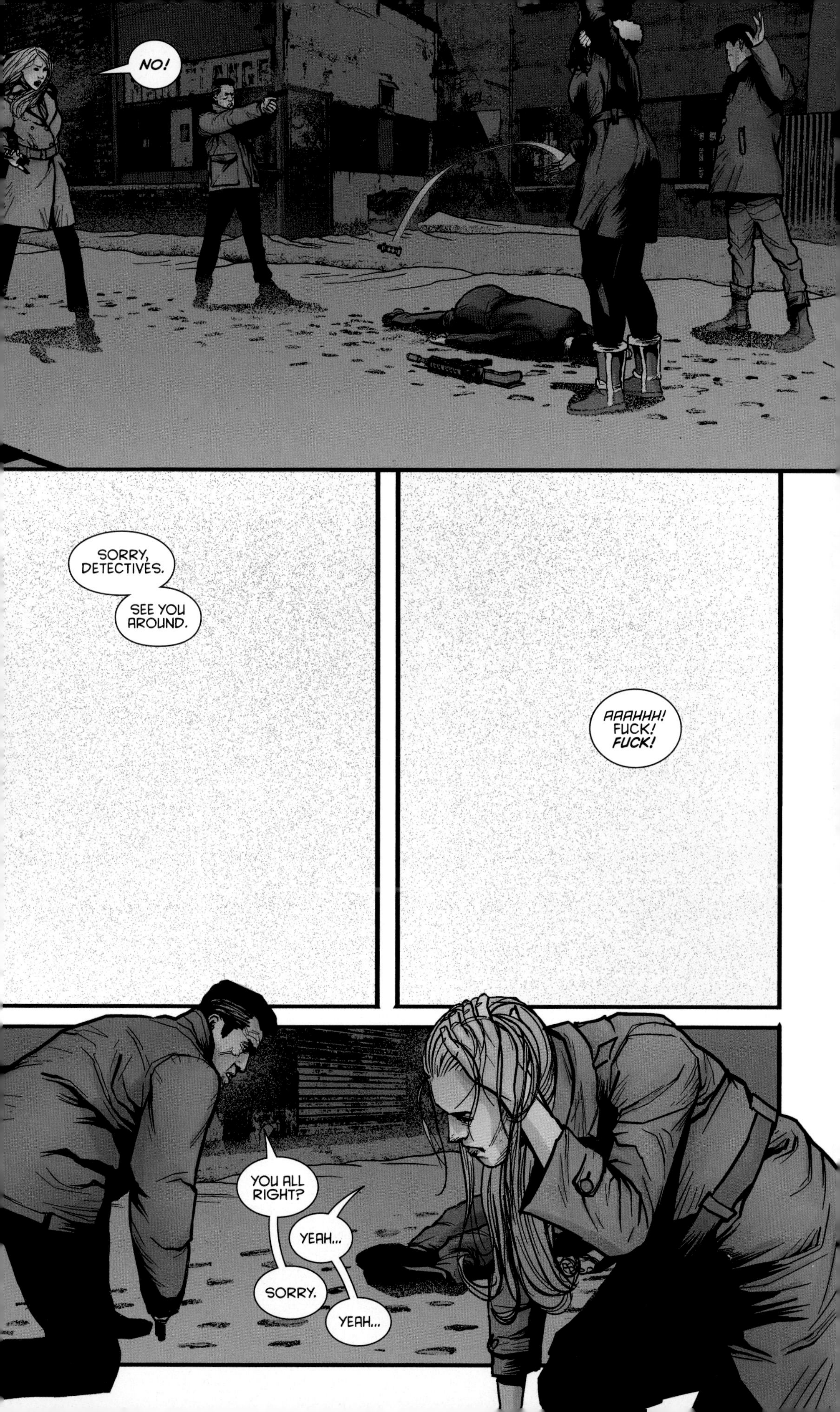
NO!
SORRY, DETECTIVES.
SEE YOU AROUND.
AAAHHH! FUCK! FUCK!
YOU ALL RIGHT?
YEAH...
SORRY.
YEAH...

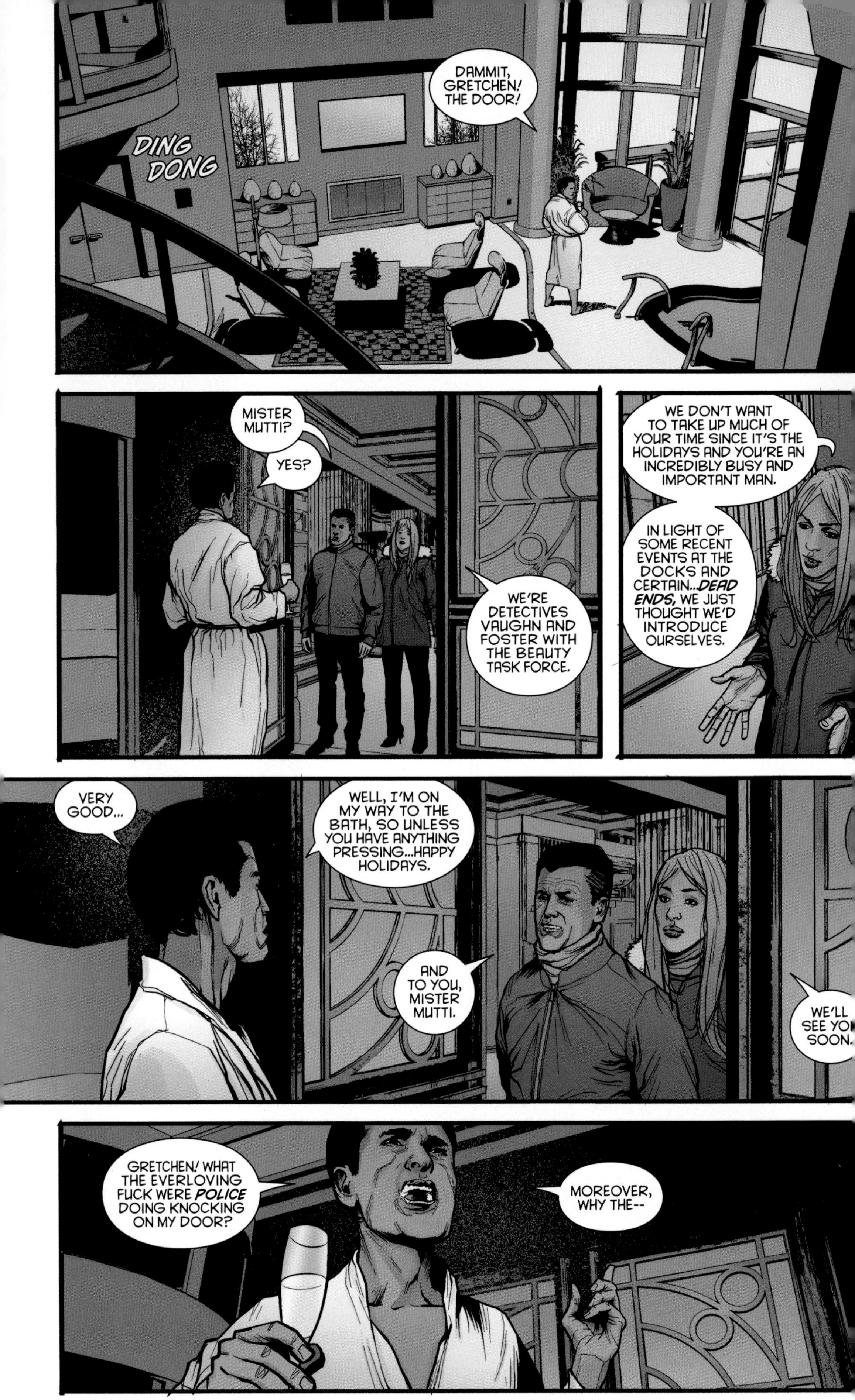
DAMMIT, GRETCHEN! THE DOOR!
DING DONG
MISTER MUTTI?
YES?
WE'RE DETECTIVES VAUGHN AND FOSTER WITH THE BEAUTY TASK FORCE.
WE DON'T WANT TO TAKE UP MUCH OF YOUR TIME SINCE IT'S THE HOLIDAYS AND YOU'RE AN INCREDIBLY BUSY AND IMPORTANT MAN.
IN LIGHT OF SOME RECENT EVENTS AT THE DOCKS AND CERTAIN...*DEAD ENDS,* WE JUST THOUGHT WE'D INTRODUCE OURSELVES.
VERY GOOD...
WELL, I'M ON MY WAY TO THE BATH, SO UNLESS YOU HAVE ANYTHING PRESSING...HAPPY HOLIDAYS.
AND TO YOU, MISTER MUTTI.
WE'LL SEE YO SOON.
GRETCHEN! WHAT THE EVERLOVING FUCK WERE *POLICE* DOING KNOCKING ON MY DOOR?
MOREOVER, WHY THE--

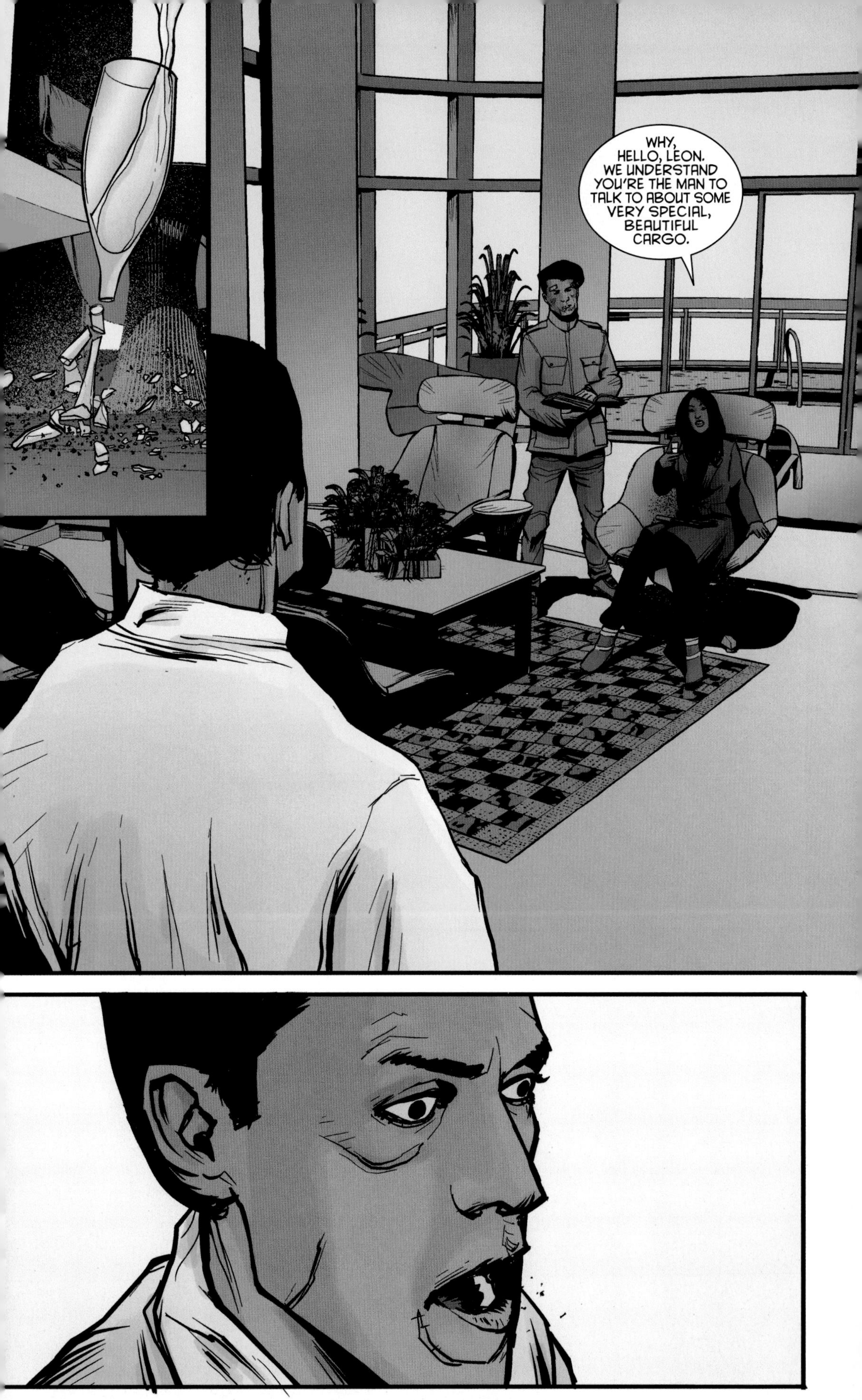
WHY, HELLO, LEON. WE UNDERSTAND YOU'RE THE MAN TO TALK TO ABOUT SOME VERY SPECIAL, BEAUTIFUL CARGO.

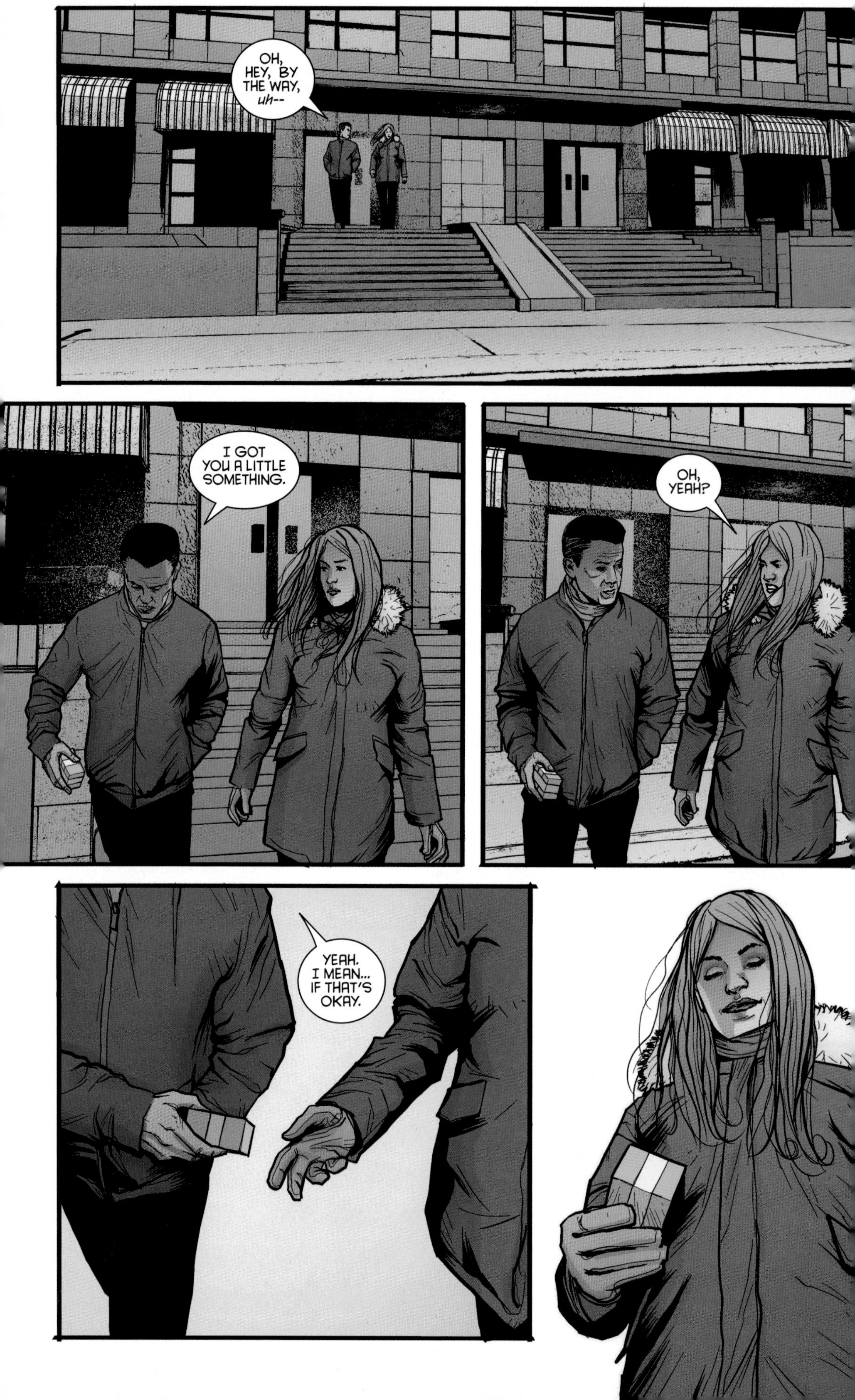
OH, HEY, BY THE WAY, *uh*--
I GOT YOU A LITTLE SOMETHING.
OH, YEAH?
YEAH. I MEAN... IF THAT'S OKAY.

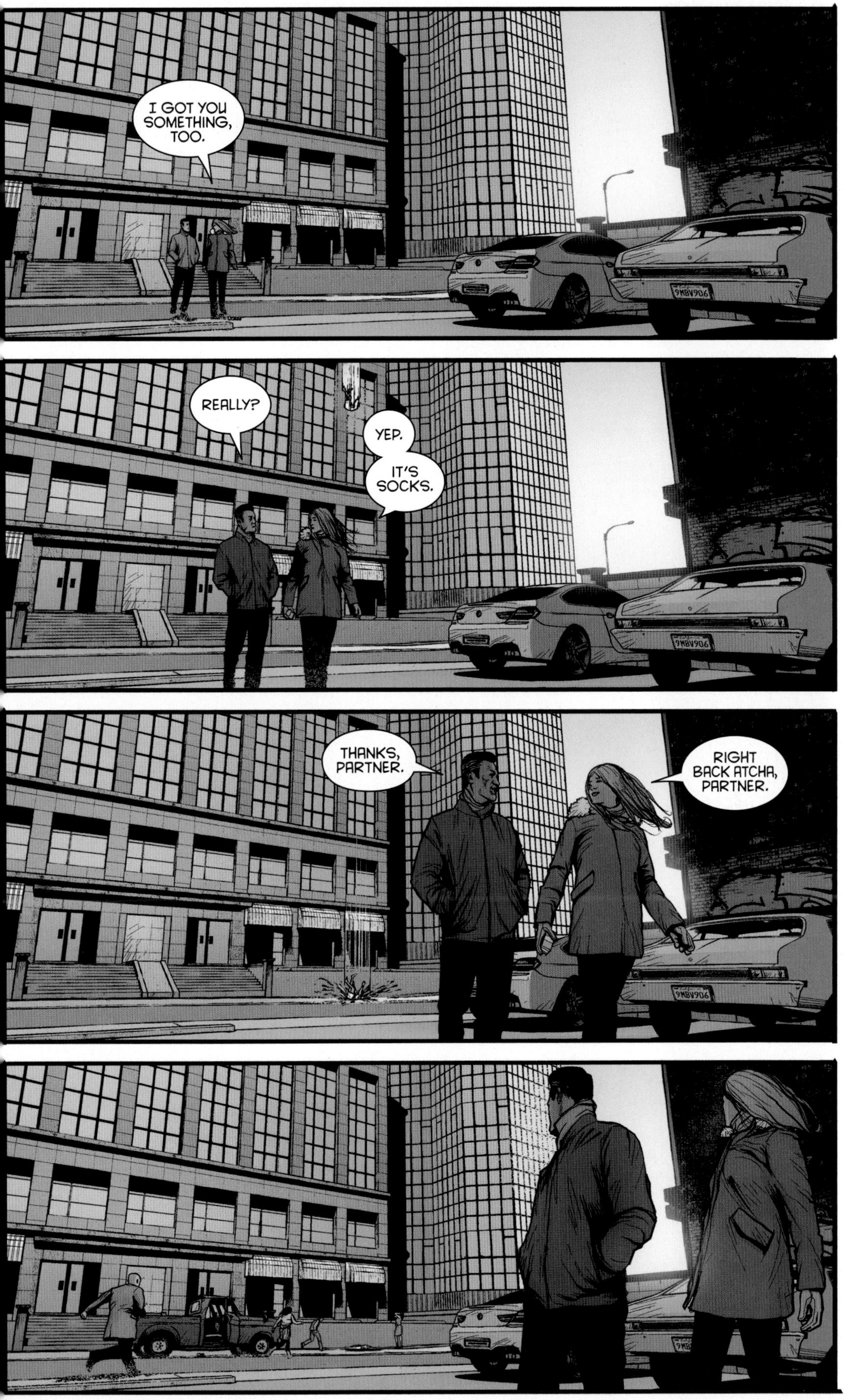
I GOT YOU SOMETHING, TOO.
REALLY?
YEP.
IT'S SOCKS.
THANKS, PARTNER.
RIGHT BACK ATCHA, PARTNER.

COVERS

ISSUE #22
Cover B
Evan Waldinger

ISSUE #22
Cover A
Jeremy Haun
& Nick Filardi

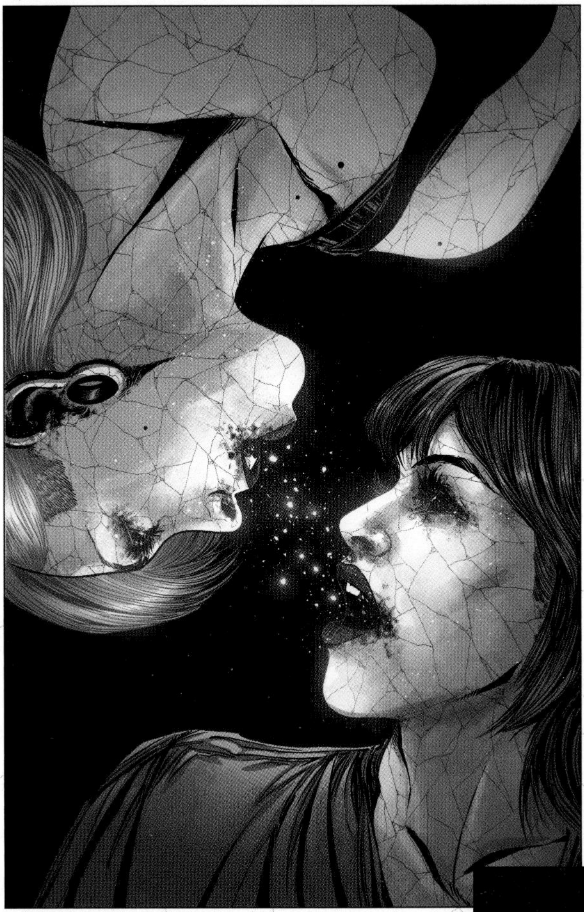

ISSUE #23

Cover A

Jeremy Haun
& Nick Filardi

ISSUE #23

Cover B

Kevin Mellon

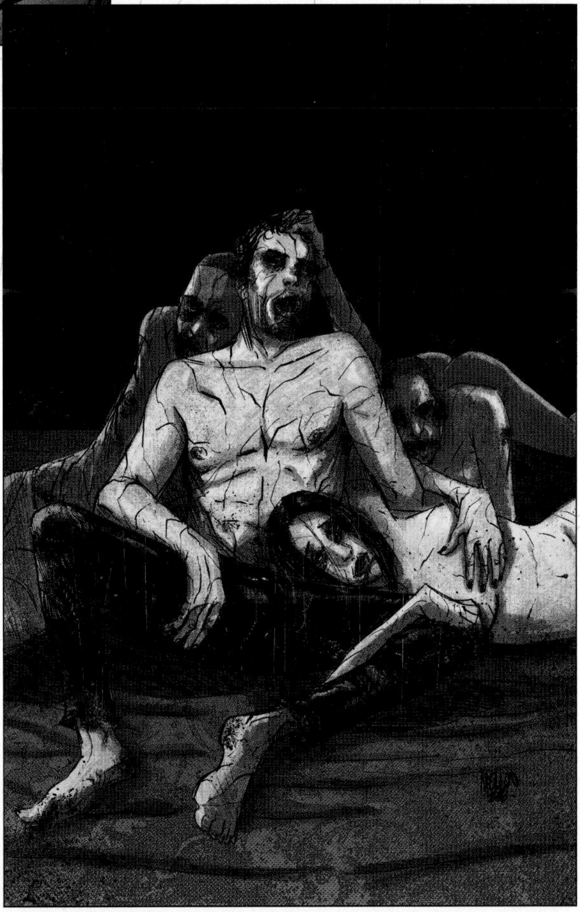

ISSUE #24
Cover A
Jeremy Haun
& Nick Filardi

ISSUE #24
Cover B
Thomas Nachlik
& Nick Filardi

ISSUE #25
Cover B
Andy MacDonald
& Nick Filardi

ISSUE #25
Cover A
Jeremy Haun
& Nick Filardi

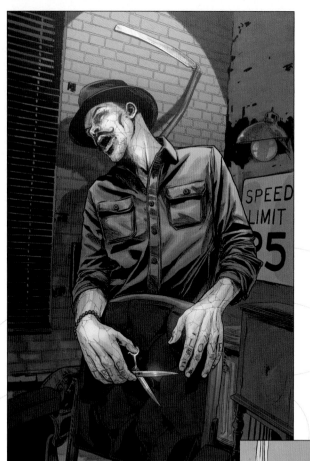

ISSUE #26

Cover B

Danielle Otrakji

ISSUE #26

Cover A

Jeremy Haun
& Nick Filardi

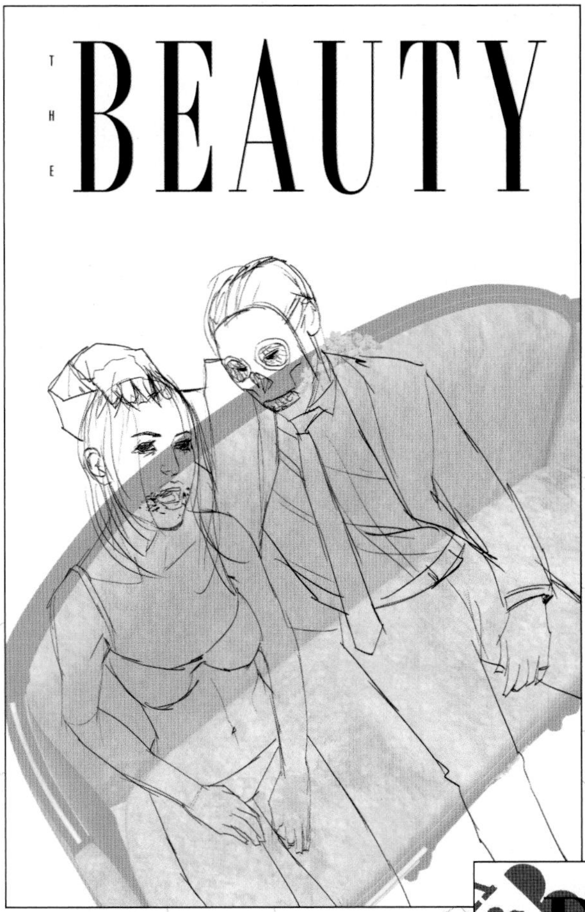
THE
BEAUTY

ISSUE #24

Unused Cover Layout

Thomas Nachlik

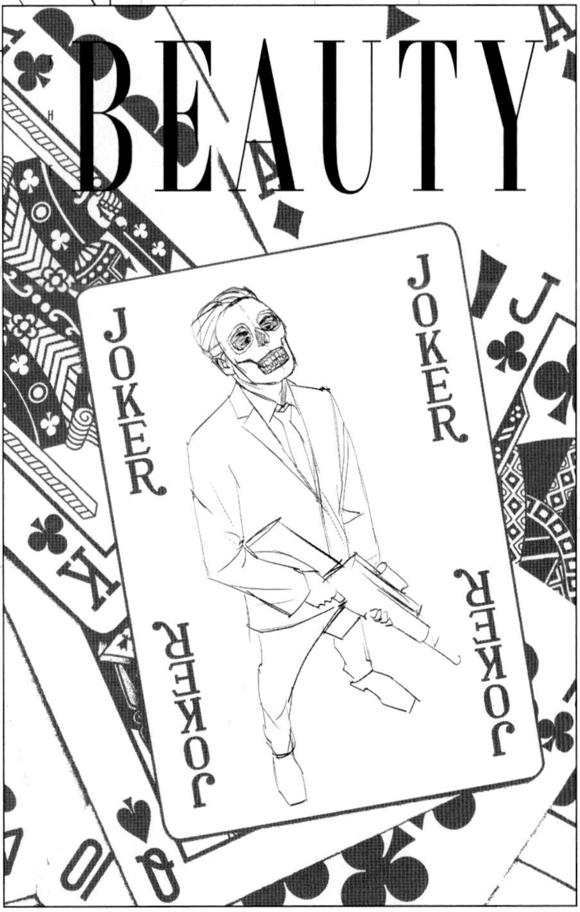
BEAUTY
JOKER
JOKER

ISSUE #24

Unused Cover Layout

Thomas Nachlik

BOOK THE BEAUTY
Issue # 22
Pg # 8

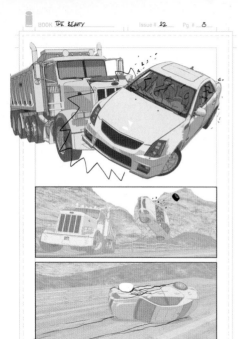

BEHIND THE SCENES

An interesting aspect of series artist Thomas Nachlik's art process is his use of 3D modeling software. He stages elaborate sets into which he can place the characters and let the action play out from whichever perspective he desires. Altering panel compositions can range from subtle to extreme. Doing this before he starts to ink helps Thomas design detailed places that immerse the reader in the world of The Beauty.

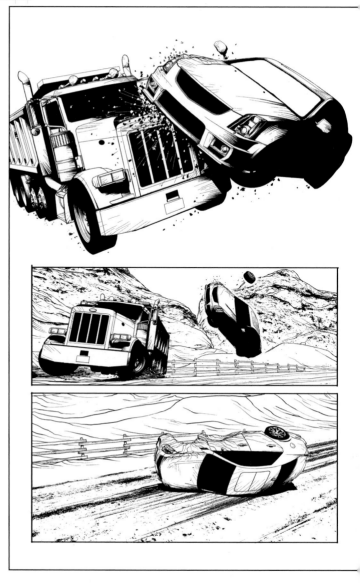

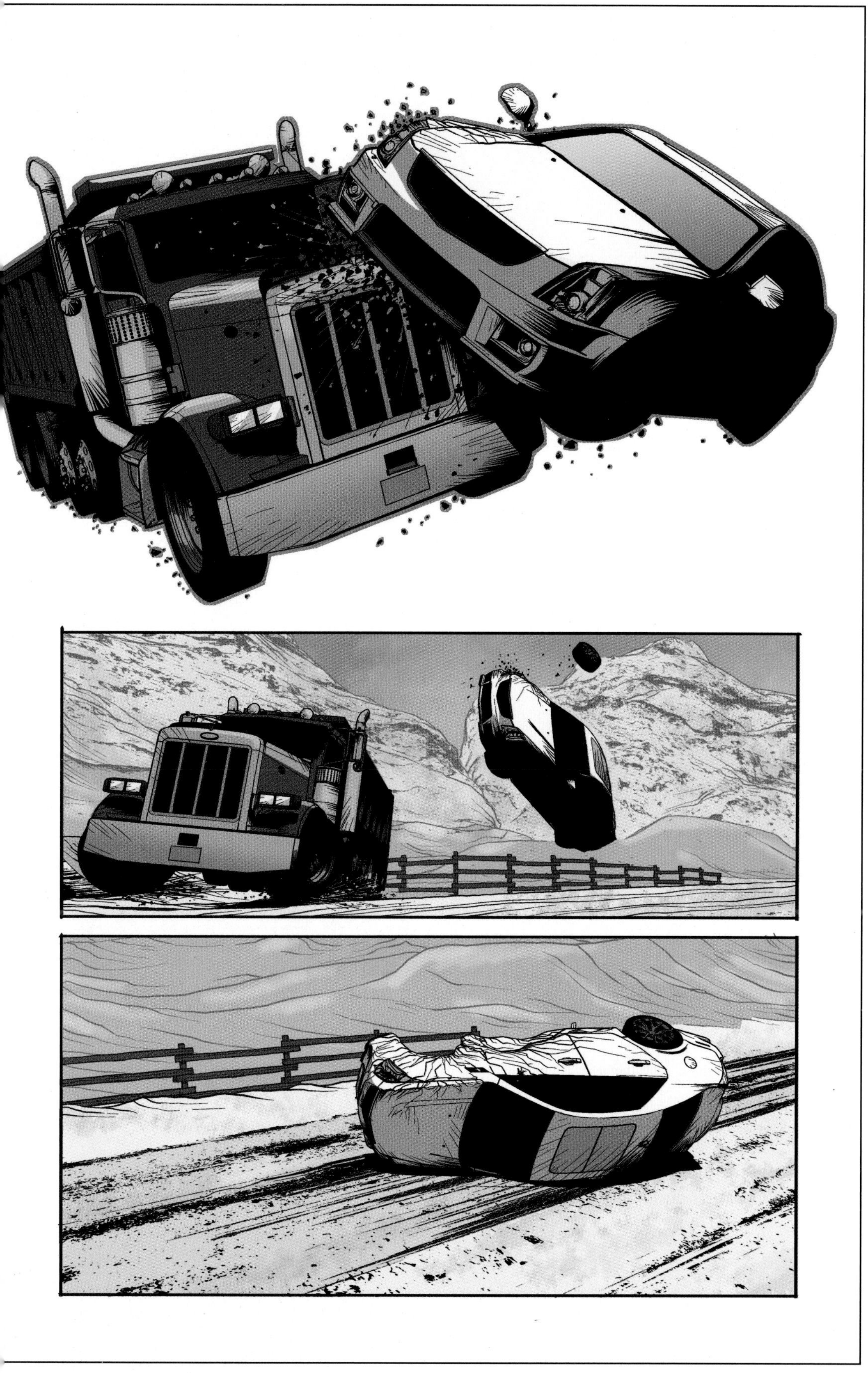

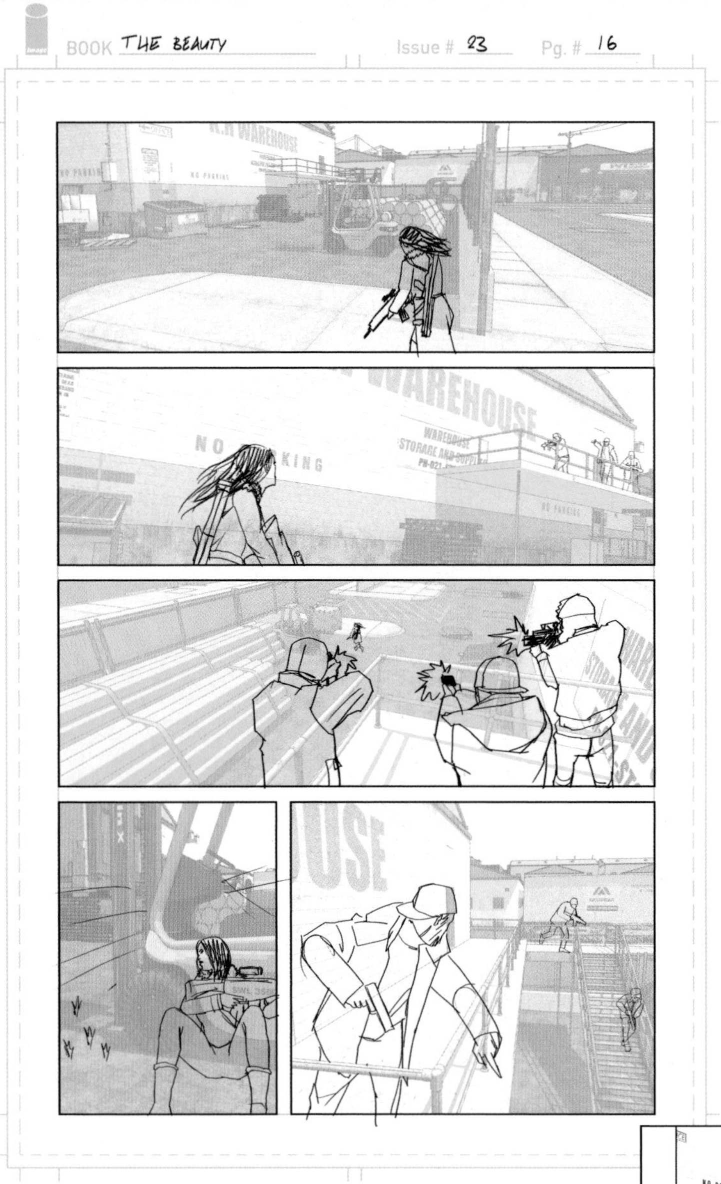
BOOK THE BEAUTY
Issue # 23
Pg. # 16
WAREHOUSE
NO PARKING
WAREHOUSE
NO PARKING

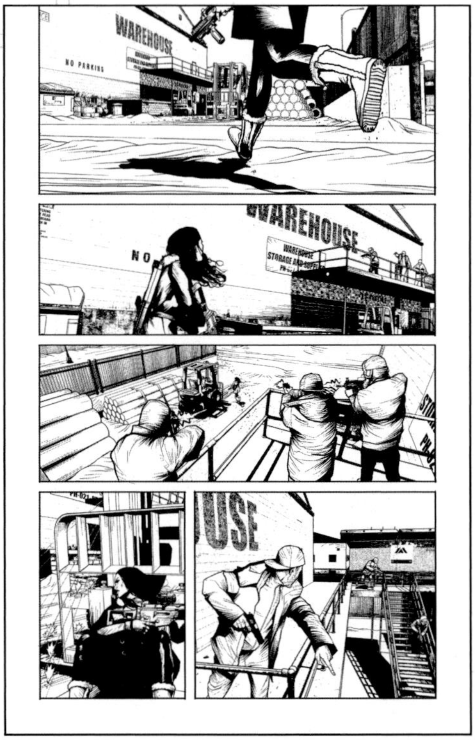
WAREHOUSE
NO PARKING
WAREHOUSE

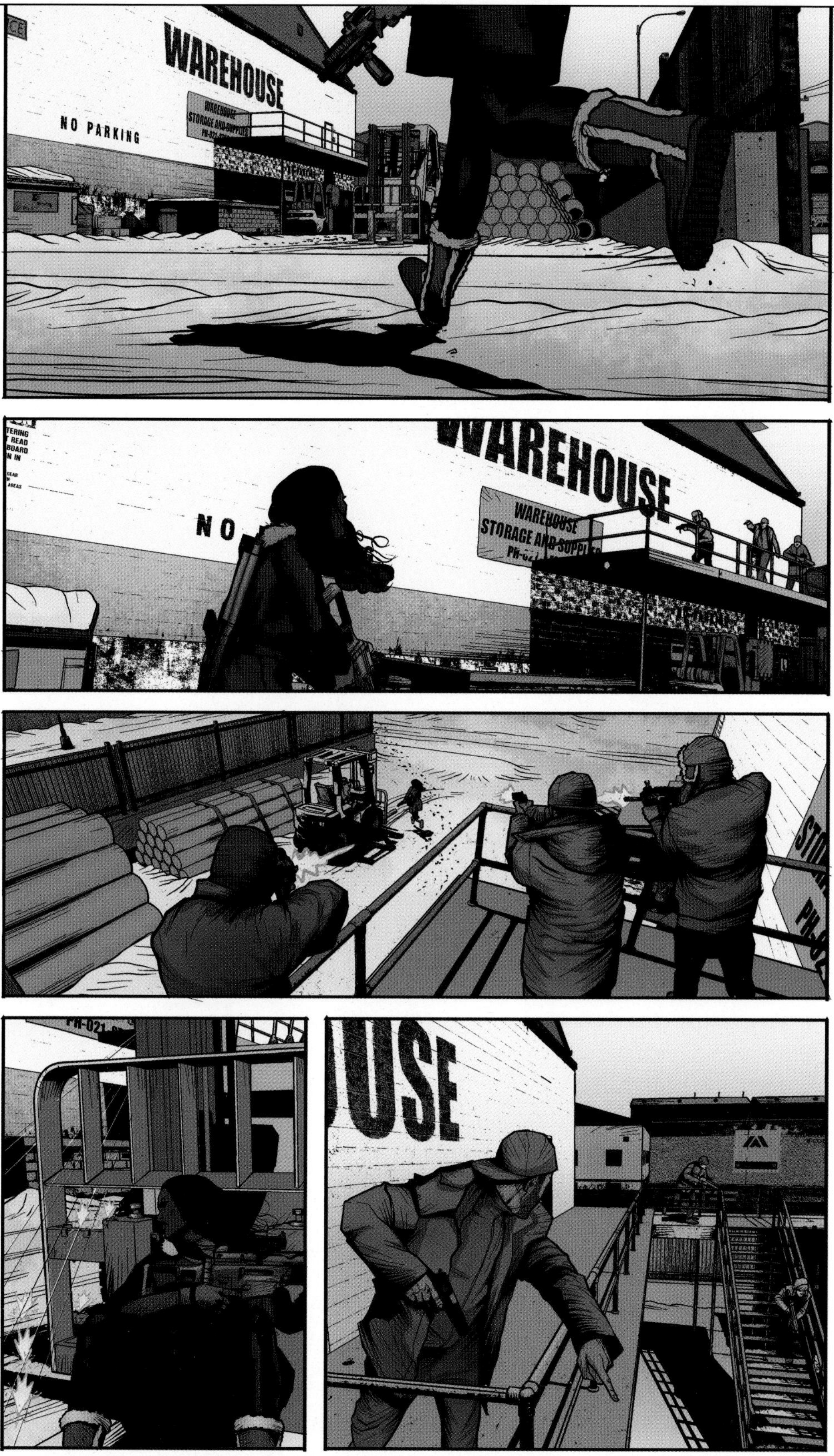
WAREHOUSE
WAREHOUSE
STORAGE AND SUPPLIES
NO PARKING
WAREHOUSE
NO
WAREHOUSE
USE

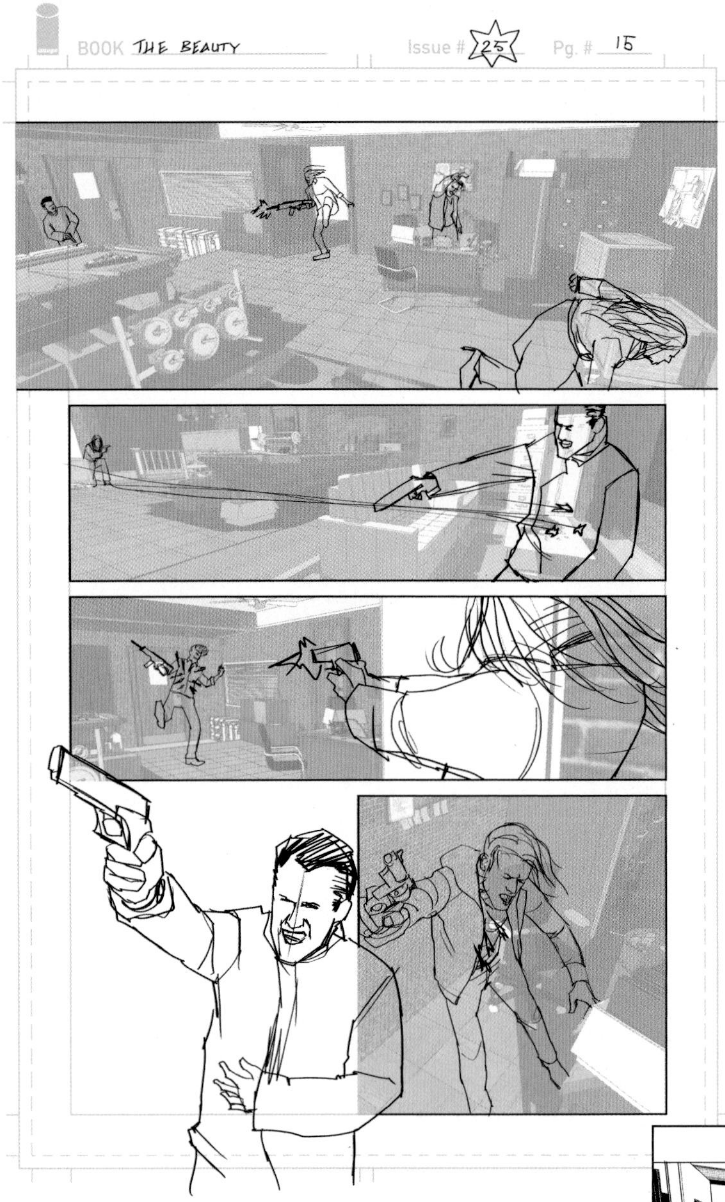
BOOK THE BEAUTY
Issue # 25
Pg. # 15
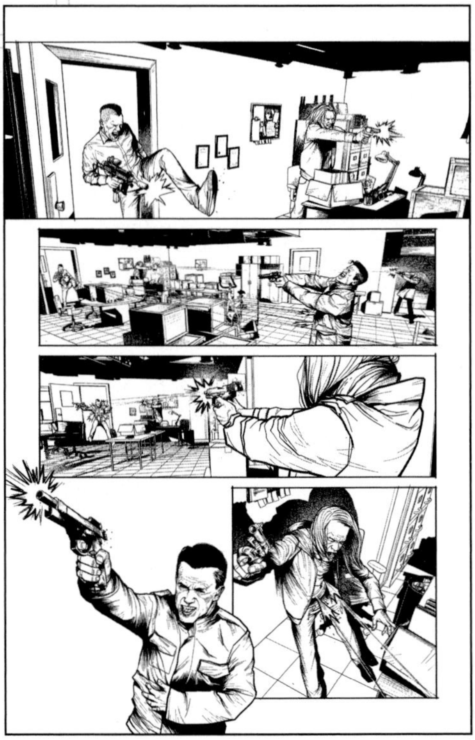

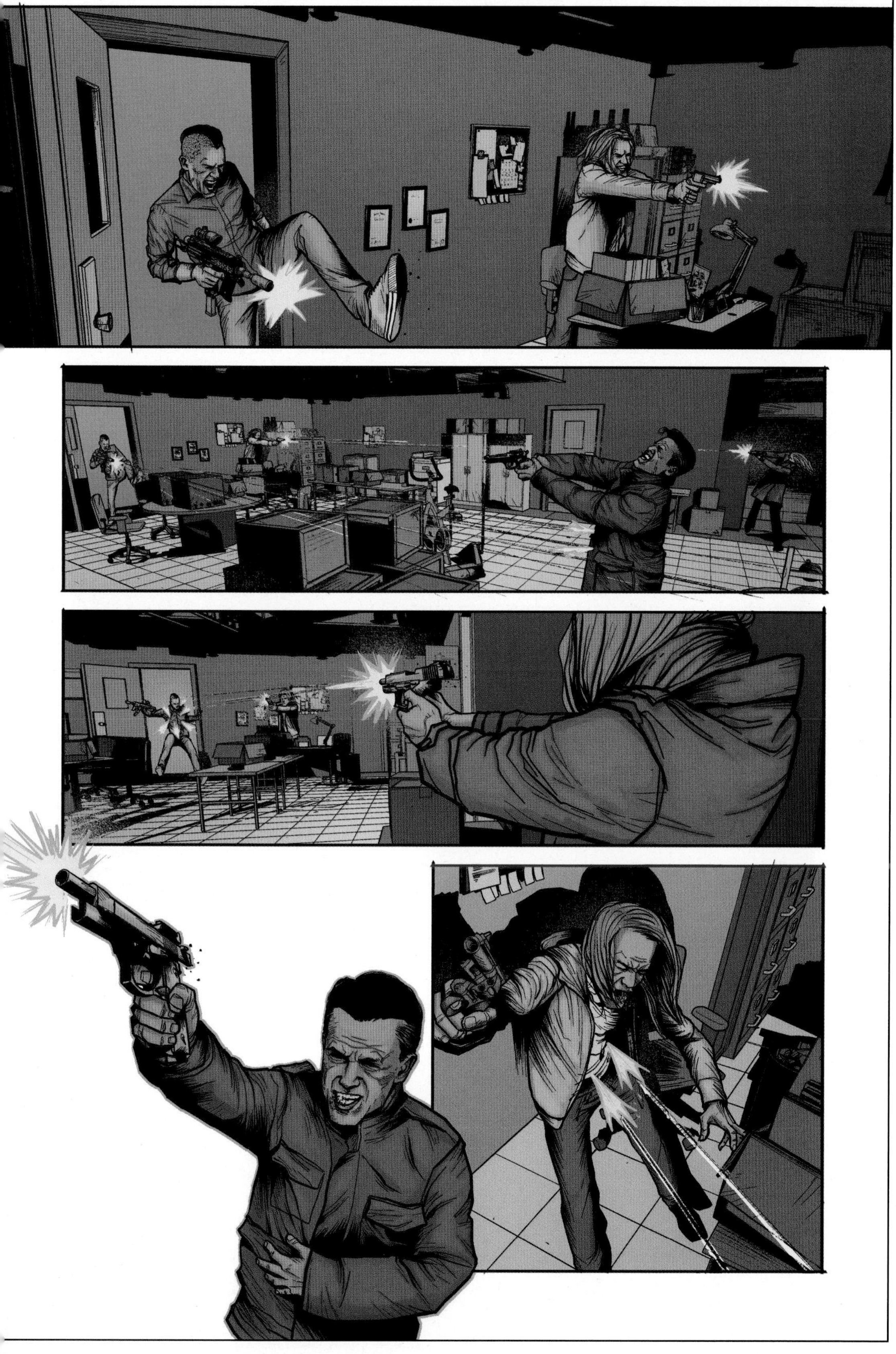

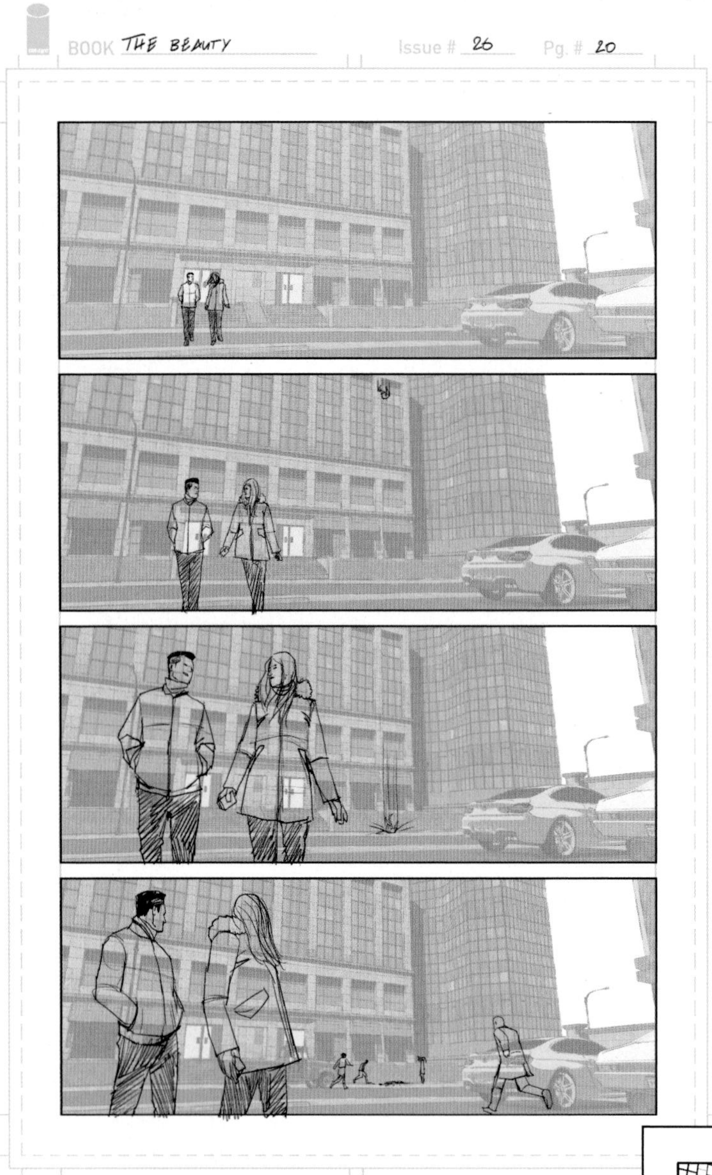
BOOK THE BEAUTY
Issue # 26
Pg. # 20

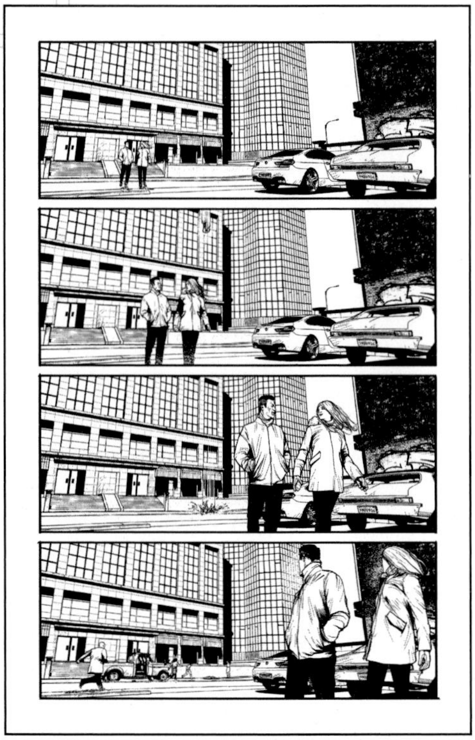

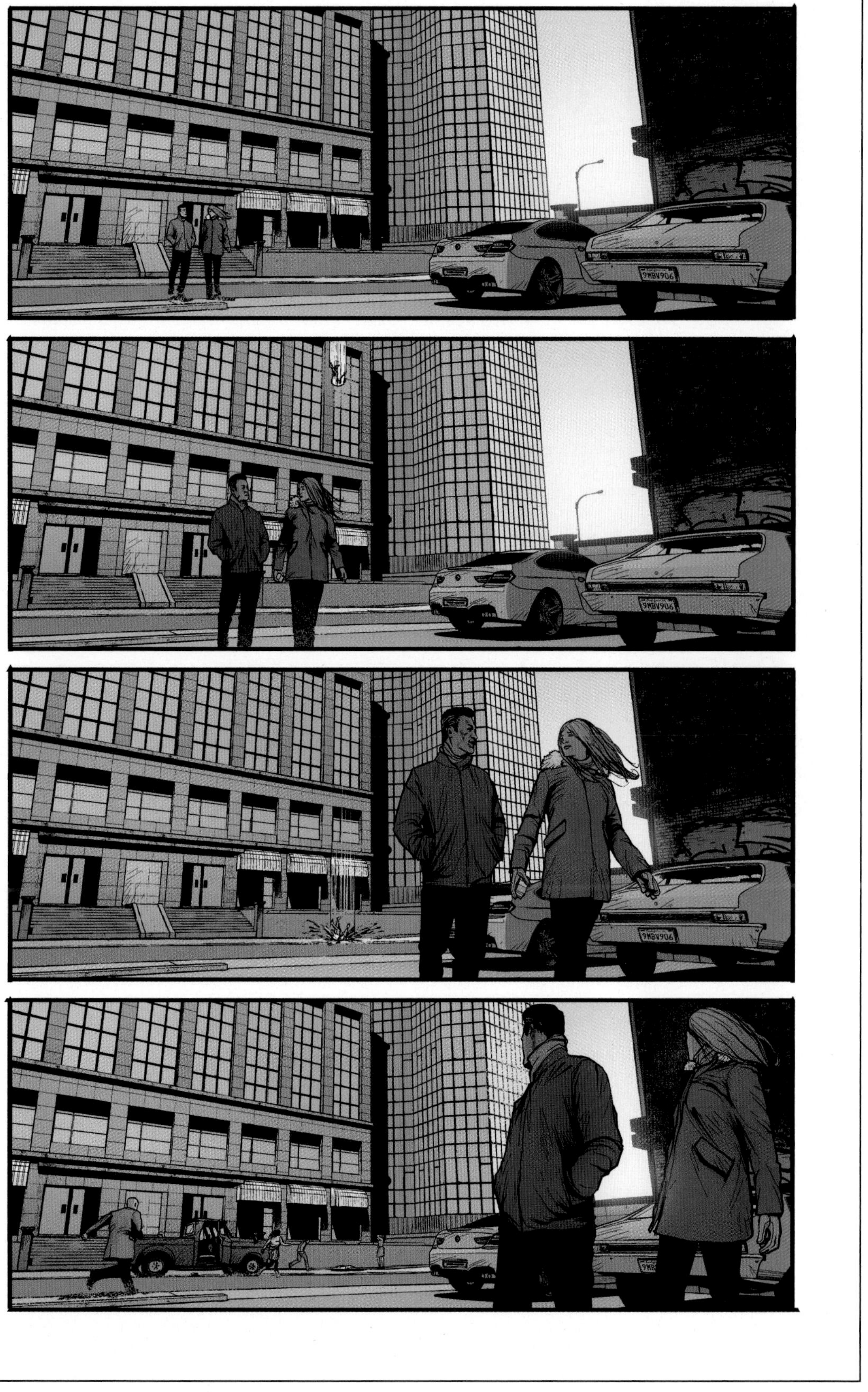
9MBV906

BIOGRAPHIES

Jeremy Haun, co-writer, co-creator and often artist for THE BEAUTY, has also worked on *Wolf Moon* from Vertigo, *Constantine* and *Batwoman* from DC. Over the past decade plus, along with wearing calluses on his fingers doing work for DC, Marvel, Image, and others, he has created and written several projects. Some you might know are graphic novel *Narcoleptic Sunday, Leading Man, Dino Day*, and most recently THE REALM. He is a part of the Bad Karma Creative group, whose *Bad Karma Volume One* debuted at NYCC 2013, thanks to Kickstarter funding.

Jeremy resides in a crumbling mansion in Joplin, Missouri, with his wife and two superheroes-in-training.

Jason A. Hurley has been in the comic book game for over fifteen years. However, none of you have ever heard of him because, until recently, he's been almost completely exclusive to the retail sector. In addition to comic books, he loves pro wrestling, bad horror movies, Freddie Mercury, hummingbirds, his parents, and pizza. While he's never actually tried it, he also thinks curling looks like a hell of a lot of fun. Hurley claims his personal heroes are Earl Bassett and Valentine McKee, because they live a life of adventure on their own terms. He also claims that he would brain anyone who showed even the most remote signs of becoming a cannibalistic undead bastard, including his own brother, without a second thought. He's lived in Joplin, Missouri, for most of his life, and never plans to leave.

Thomas Nachlik is a Polish-born illustrator, living in Germany with his wife and two cats. His client list includes Top Cow, Boom, Amazon Studios, and DC Comics.

Nayoung Kim got sucked into the world of comics by her husband from a graphic design caree They live outside Atlanta with two dogs and two cats- constantly fighting the urge to move west into the dese

Nick Filardi has colored for just about every major comic book publisher including DC, Marvel, Oni Press and Dark Horse. He's currently also coloring covers for THE BEAUTY. When he isn't buried in pages, you can find his digital likeness pulling up other colorists with tips and tricks at twitch.tv/nickfil, making dad jokes at twitter.com/nickfil, and just spreading dope art at instagram.com/nick_filardi.

Thomas Mauer has lent his lettering and design talent to award-winning books and obscure gems alike. Among his recent work are Aftershock Comics' *Dead Kings*, Image Comics' ELSEWHERE, COPPERHEAD, CRUDE, HARDCORE, and THE REALM.

Joel Enos is a writer and editor of comics and stories. His short stories have been published in *Flapperhouse, Bloodbond*, and *Year's Best Speculative YA Fiction*. He's currently the editor of THE BEAUTY, THE REALM, and REGRESSION, all published by Image Comics.